FOX HOLLOW

FOX HOLLOW
Olivia Hardy Ray

This book is a work of fiction. Names, characters, places and incidents are products of the author's imagination or are used fictitiously. Any resemblance to actual events, locales or persons, living or dead, is entirely coincidental.

ISBN: 978-1-64456-574-2 [paperback]
ISBN: 978-1-64456-575-9 [Mobi]
ISBN: 978-1-64456-576-6 [ePub]

Library of Congress Control Number: 2022951367

Copyright © 2022 by Vera Jane Cook
Published January 2023
by Indies United Publishing House, LLC

SECOND EDITION

INDIES UNITED PUBLISHING HOUSE, LLC
P.O. BOX 3071
QUINCY, IL 62305-3071
indiesunited.net

God not only plays dice, he also sometimes throws the dice where they cannot be seen.

Steven Hawkin

FOX HOLLOW

Fox Hollow Road Abduction Series

BOOK ONE

Olivia Hardy Ray

INDIES UNITED PUBLISHING HOUSE, LLC

Chapter One

It was a beautiful night in early August. The moon was so full it appeared fat — as if it had swallowed every star in heaven and glowed purely from the pleasure of consumption. Nick Dowling gazed up at the sky through the windshield of his new Jeep Cherokee. His wife, Jenna, had just sent him out for a quart of milk and he was pleased to go, happy to be driving out under the stars on the back roads of New Kingston. Except on this particular night, there were no stars — just the moon, contently serene as it trailed his car like a wayward balloon.

Nick tapped his hands on the steering wheel and started singing along with the radio. It was an old song that came through, something about leaving a Chevy at the levy. The music filled the evening stillness and mingled with the cricket's song, and the hooting of the owls.

Nick was pleased, the lack of static was not expected. Clear reception was not always a reliable luxury in the Catskill Mountains of Upstate New York.

The road ahead was empty. His beams were high and his speed, slow. The last thing he needed was a startled deer to show up in his headlights. He was lost in his thoughts, thinking about the time off he'd finally been able to take. This was the first of several long weekends that he and Jenna had been able to steal since they'd bought their second home in the mountains. Finally, his saved vacation days provided a perfect opportunity to hit the highway and leave Manhattan's sweltering concrete behind.

The music changed abruptly and the scratchy sound it made reminded him of an old phonograph needle that had skipped over a record. A song from the early eighties came through the speakers, with only a slight static sound, like cackle. It was Billy Joel's *She's Got a Way About Her*, the first song Nick had heard after finding himself waking up in a nasty looking hotel room so many years ago, dead broke. All he realized he owned back then was a pair of jeans and a rusty Gillette.

I don't know what it is, he sang out, just as his headlights illuminated a road on his left, a barely visible road — almost entirely hidden by trees.

"Looks familiar," he said aloud, smiling, as if someone sat beside him that might have agreed.

"I know that road," he whispered aloud. He hunched over the steering wheel. He slowed down for a better look. Something about the road was mysteriously beautiful, framed as it was by Pine trees that swayed ever so gently in the summer evening air. The impulse hit him like a spray of cold water, and he braked.

"Oh, what the hell," he said as he backed the jeep up. This impulsive action was not a predictable character trait of Nick Dowling's. But on this particular evening, before he could even think about having a second thought, he took a sharp left onto the road. Perhaps there was something about the moon that night, close enough to touch, a flirtation he could not refuse.

"Have I lost my mind?" He laughed, looking around, seeing nothing much of anything that warranted the fascination.

The road was narrow and dark, but he had just enough light from the moonlit sky to read the barely visible road sign: *Fox Hollow*.

Nick switched off the radio; he'd lost the clear station right after he'd made the turn, and the static was irritating. Slowly, he drove up the bumpy road. The night seemed wrapped in mesh, opaque and colorless. He accelerated his speed just a bit, attempting to see beyond his headlights, but there was nothing before him but the adumbration of trees; it seemed like hundreds of them standing tall against the sky, bending, and tipping their branches into the quiet swirl of the evening wind like visions between this world and the next.

The moon hovered at the end of his sightline like a big mysterious white ball, descending into the earth, as if being swallowed. But the edges of night were dull. Everything around him looked like a poorly developed print. Nick rubbed his eyes and watched as night's illusionary mist played havoc with his imagination and shadow monsters came out of the darkness, as tall as giants.

Something flashed through Nick's mind with voracious intensity. Was there magic on this road? All of a sudden, he had a memory, a childhood memory. It came out of nowhere: A boy fearing dragons in the night and dreaming of mythical sword fights in mystic forests with a moon as elusive as this one. Was he that boy? His memories of childhood didn't exist; his early life was a void. Yet there it was: a vision of sword fighting with a friend so small and light— Sir Lancelot in dungarees with his mother's pot for a shield.

Nick felt a sudden chill. Leaning in to switch off the air conditioning, a flash of light appeared on his hand, swiftly expanding, trapping his body in its glow, a blaze of cold and paralyzing illumination. His body froze and he held his breath. In moments, the light was everywhere, consuming the darkness as if from a hundred headlights.

"What the hell is going on?" Nick came out of his stupor and looked around frantically. It was getting increasingly colder, as cold as the dead of winter in Upstate New York can get. He started to shiver. But this was August and the night air had been warm. What the hell was happening? He could feel his heart pounding; it felt as if he were sitting inside a freezer.

Apprehensively, Nick looked through one eye. The light was still there, ubiquitous, the brightness; blinding.

Fear settled on his chest as if he were in the line of unexpected gunfire. He closed his eyes again.

"I am victim to my own vivid imagination," he said, staring once again into the opaque night.

The lights suddenly disappeared, as if they'd been chewed and discarded by the darkness.

"Kids with flashlights, must be … what else?" *But the cold? Strange weather condition? Well, maybe...in the mountains.*

Nick sat quietly, even patiently, until his fear passed, until it flowed out of his body, until his heart beat normally once again. When he felt calm enough, he stared back into the shadows and nervously surveyed the space around him.

He lowered his window halfway and made sure the lights were really gone. He was relieved to see that everything appeared normal in the evening's shadow and the air was warm on his skin. Once again, the moon bounced naturally in the sky, throwing a path of light before him, like a megalithic corridor inviting entry.

He accelerated slowly and drove forward. The moonlight faded back behind the trees, and the night became as dark as black ink. He nervously listened to the rocks and branches crunching beneath the wheels of his jeep and wondered if he'd lost the road and was driving further into the woods.

Nick couldn't see anything but his headlights, not even the trees. But then, sudden as lightning's flash, as if he'd willed it, the night was lit by a welcomed and sudden reappearance of moonlight.

"Where you been hiding?" he whispered.

He stopped the jeep. He needed a sense of direction. The moon was fuller than he had ever seen it, but there were no stars out to guide him, just some shadowy image in the sky that he couldn't quite make out.

What the hell am I doing in the middle of nowhere, playing tag with the goddamn moon? There was a threatening hush, a silence too barren to trust. The owls had ceased to hoot, and the crickets were far too silent.

Without warning, the stillness shattered into a million pieces by a sound that shook his body from inside out.

"Shit!" Nick cried, nearly leaping out of his skin. "What the hell was that?"

Like a drill in concrete, the sound was deafening. The darkness had been jarred by it, so intensely shrill it might have torn the sky in two, a sound so abruptly acuminous that it might have caused the moon to crack.

The intense lights vanished, disappeared as contiguously as a passing thought, back into the night. *Had he imagined all of it?* Nick brought his hands up to his face. They were shaking badly. *No, this was not imagination.* The suddenness of that awful sound had jostled him so badly that his heart beats were on overtime, and his favorite t-shirt was soaked in sweat.

He'd been on this road before. Of course he had; he'd seen the road in his nightmares. He dreamed he was here. And his dream had been a nightmare.

Right after Nick and his wife, Jenna, closed on their weekend getaway in New Kingston, their retreat from Manhattan's urgent and colossal perplexities, Nick's nightmares had accelerated. It was absurd to have them — monster nightmares belonged to children, not to men in their late forties. "I feel foolish to have so many of my dreams invaded by macabre caricatures," he told Jenna.

But he'd always had disturbing dreams, dreams he'd kept to himself until he had no choice but to explain them to his wife. He did so, after a careful edit.

"An odd thing for a grown man to have — nightmares," he'd said reluctantly.

"Not altogether unusual," Jenna had responded as she listened to his tentative explanations. "Maybe something is triggering some old and unresolved issues you have with your mother ... or father."

Nick scowled at that, wondering how he'd ever get out of seeing a shrink. It was absurd to think he needed one. Jenna insisted on blaming everything on his parents. But how could he blame anyone he didn't remember?

He accelerated over the stones and the broken branches of trees, hoping all the crap on the road wasn't scratching the paint off the jeep's body, or putting any frigging dents on his car. But he felt too uneasy to slow down and check out the damage. He just wanted to feel sane once more. This introduction to Fox Hollow had antagonized his sense of reality and had left him surprisingly disentangled from his perspective on who the hell he was or believed himself to be.

He looked up toward the sky. He felt as if he'd just driven in a circle, the shadowy cloud was still above him and it appeared to cover the entire sky.

He drove forward, afraid that if he didn't he'd wind up in a ditch — lost forever in the goddamn woods. His heart was getting a workout and his mouth felt like an old hot towel. He wanted nothing more at that moment than to reach civilization and grab a shot of whiskey.

"I've had enough of this amusing adventure," he said, his eyes riveted ahead.

Suddenly he noticed lights, as if coming from a house. Thinking he might finally be off Fox Hollow and onto a road that would take him into town, he breathed a sigh of relief.

"Shit," he said, as he got closer to the house. "Looks like a frigging dead-end."

He slapped his hand on the steering wheel. He was frustrated and anxious. He decided to knock on the door and ask for directions. He stopped the jeep near the driveway. It was quiet, desolate. He took a deep breath and confronted his fear. "Get hold of yourself, man," he said.

Nick stared back at the farmhouse. *It was familiar, which was not unusual, at every turn in upstate New York, there was a farmhouse.*

"A compelling sight," he said.

The house was stately and white. Lace curtains

moved with the wind, like the porch swing. He could hear the creak. The house stood against the night in shades of grey, like an old postcard photograph picked up at a flea market. Nick could see bicycles lying on the grass. A dog lifted his head from the porch and stared at him. Nick felt strangely nostalgic.

He'd assumed years ago that he'd been raised in Phoenicia, New York, because that's what it said on the hotel register when he checked out of the room he'd awoken in, with no memory at all of how he had gotten there. Phoenicia, New York, another small town not far from New Kingston, certainly in biking distance. Well, then, he must have been on a lot of country roads in his childhood, staring at houses just like this one. He never went to Phoenicia, though, it was too frightening to confront a past he couldn't recall, but he'd insisted on buying a second house in New Kingston after finding the town on a Google search for vacation homes. Had he subliminally chosen to be near Phoenicia?

He didn't have any answers, perhaps he never would. Perhaps he didn't want them. As he stared at the house, it drew him in, it engulfed him in some kind of black and white fantasy, like an old film he'd seen once, but there couldn't be a connection to this farmhouse, it hadn't been the town of New Kingston that was written on the hotel register, it had been the town of Phoenicia.

He stared at the house for several more minutes before the image faded, simply drifted off into the night, leaving behind a phantasmal mist. Nick drifted into the ebbing image, falling into a mindless stupor, as if inebriated, as if he'd just finished off a fifth of scotch.

"God," he cried out. "What the hell is happening to me?"

He struggled to escape the blank plateau into which

he had fallen, but he couldn't. It was as if his thoughts were being gripped by a distant hand. He suddenly had an image of the shadowy shape in the sky and felt as if he'd floated right up to it.

"Leave me alone!" he shouted.

His head fell sharply to his shoulder, an action that seemed to come from somewhere else, another person — another body.

"Stress can cause people to blank out," Jena once told him.

"Yes, of course, that's it — stress," Nick whispered. He looked back at the house again. The noise returned, overbearingly loud — the drill into concrete ... deafening.

Quickly switching the radio back on to fight the noise, he thought about screaming out for help. The sound hovered above him, precariously close.

He turned the radio up louder. *Nothing but static — Damn.*

The noise continued ... threatening to use its power ... devour him. It was directly over his head, so very close. He was almost lifted by it, lifted up to someplace far, as far as space.

"This is madness," he whispered. "This is impossible."

He had spent his entire adulthood distracted by the ordinary pressures of survival. He had never considered himself particularly introspective, not much caring to delve into the remnants of feelings hidden beneath the debris of inconsequential information — feelings his wife insisted were vital links to his mental well-being. Nick never questioned his life after waking up in a Chelsea hotel with no past. He walked out into the city and survived. Surviving took up all his time, owned his thoughts. He didn't need to know the rest, the forgotten past. The only choices he needed to make were the ones that he faced in his profession as a circulation vice president for a major New York newspaper. It took twenty years, but he finally had an executive's salary. Clearly, he was a survivor.

He didn't want to know his inner life at all. The dreams he'd had over the years had been too disturbing to probe — images of violent anger, blood everywhere he looked, murders he could not explain.

"My inner life is uneventful and average," he'd told Jenna when they first met. "I can't devote much time thinking about it."

And then, years later, new torment, new dreams ... monsters haunted his sleep, metaphors for himself, he surmised.

No, Nick did not want to find his past or obsess on any uncomfortable emotions, especially not with his dreams, blood on his hands, a dead child at his feet ... a battered woman.

"Am I insane?" He looked out into the night and shook his head. "Am I?"

He wiped his eyes with the back of his hand. He switched the radio back off and listened for the quiet stillness of night to return, soft and melodic. He listened until all he heard was the wind.

He stared back at the old Farmhouse and tears came to his eyes. He suddenly wanted to leap from the car and run to the front door, as if he belonged there, behind the majesty of its silent repose.

I'm home. Mom! I'm home, he wanted to shout.

His eyes blinked as the lights in the farmhouse flickered. He switched the radio back on. He needed the music to ground him, but the static had returned with an irritating repetition. He tried to find a clear station. He was agitated. He wanted to get the hell out of there. He knew that by now the only general store in town would be closed and he'd have to deal with the supermarket for a lousy quart of milk. He hated the supermarket, big, cold place ... *so why then can't I get the hell off this damn road and make it to the God damn general store?*

"Shit," he said, switching off the radio altogether.

The lights from the house flickered again, as if an electrical storm was passing over, but the night was clear. Nick backed the jeep up, deciding he would leave the way he had come in ... no need to ask for directions. As his breathing returned to normal, he was grateful for its steady rhythm. He was thinking like his old self, making rational decisions. It had all been imagination, just imagination.

As Nick backed up the jeep, he noticed a man at the window of the old house peering through a torn shade.

"What the hell happened to the lace?" he whispered as he stared in awe at the tattered blind. He quickly thought of his wife, how the hell he'd ever explain any of this to her, the look in her large dark eyes as she gave him that half parted smile and suggested therapy.

He sat quietly. His eyes drifted back to the house. He looked quickly for the dog. All he saw was a tired old porch — empty.....no porch swing and no dog.

"Shadows playing tricks," he said.

The oblique shape in the sky expanded and lowered itself closer to the earth.

Chapter Two

Could he have had an accident? He'd been gone for over two hours.

"God, Nick, it was only a quart of milk," Jenna said exasperatingly. "You should have been back by now."

She brought her thumb nail to her mouth and bit it. *So many changes in Nick. Ever since buying this house: sullen moods, an uncharacteristically quick temper, monster nightmares.*

It wasn't like Nick to be afraid, or to feel that he didn't have control.

Must be repressed emotions. She had mentioned that to him, and he'd laughed. Nick did not believe in repressed emotions.

"Were you ever molested as a child?" she had asked him that cautiously, trying to pinpoint what in God's name would bring on nightmares about monsters.

"No!"

He had been so adamant, his large eyes unusually small as he tightened his mouth and grimaced.

"Disturbing childhood experiences are often easily triggered by familiarity."

She had tried to be informative, not accusatory. "It's normal for people to become preoccupied by their earlier experiences, however subconsciously ... and then, act out. Perhaps, have nightmares."

"Maybe," Nick had shrugged his shoulders. He had clearly not been impressed.

Jenna remembered how frustrated she'd felt. She was too close to him to be of any use, and she knew it. She needed to get a little crafty, make her point without getting him defensive.

"Grotesque images." He had not looked at her when he spoke about his recent dreams for the first time. "Probing me with something. Strange, huh?"

She'd put her arms around him. "Well, would you agree that you're frightened by something?" she'd asked. "Was your father abusive?"

"Therapy is not the answer for everything, Jenna." He'd said, boring his vivid blue eyes into hers.

God, why couldn't she have been a gymnast or a dental hygienist, why a shrink? he must have been thinking.

She attempted again. "No, not everything" she said, "but man's psyche is a mystery that needs exploration, needs understanding, just as much as the universe needs to be understood ... wouldn't you agree?"

Jenna frowned and looked up toward the stars. Nick was unresolved. Maybe she'd always known it. She would have preferred to believe that he was not haunted by any emotional demons, but obviously, he was.

She walked out onto the side deck and took a chair. The night air was still, the stars, abundant. She thought back. Her husband's past was a murky tale, told in indifferent asides, avoided as passionately as Castor Oil. Jenna recalled, only at the beginning, there was doubt, only a moment in which she had wanted to run, to flee the attraction, to find sameness, less opposite attraction, and more common ground.

They had met in a loud, raucous singles bar in downtown Manhattan in the late 1980s.

"My past is over and done with," he'd told her, bragging that he'd never needed to have his head shrunk. She'd wound up next to him by chance, slinking in beside him at the crowded bar, taking in his good looks in profile. He'd just asked her what she did for a living, and she'd responded, wishing he'd been more unique. *Will he ask me what my sign is next?* She had laughed to herself.

"I'm obsessed on the future, not on days gone by." He seemed proud, as solid as a city skyscraper.

"Don't you think the past is important?" She'd smiled into his expressive eyes, noting to herself that his emotional baggage was so disturbing that he had repressed it into invisibility.

"No," he said, winking.

"Everyone has baggage, even me."

She remembered turning to face him then and how he had searched her face, intensely sincere, and then, diving into her gaze quite unexpectedly.

"Your mother." He leaned in close. "It's always about someone's mother, isn't it?"

She silently admired the cleft in his chin, his determined features.

"Your eyes are so blue," she'd said, "like cobalt."

"Ha, you're changing the subject." He laughed openly; his blond straight hair was slicked back. He was unnervingly handsome, not usually her type. Her sister, Laurie, always said that Jenna's type could be found behind a corduroy jacket, tassel loafers, a pipe and facial hair. Nick was all faded jeans, old Nikes and cashmere over a T-shirt, a smooth shaven and obvious contradiction.

"I believe that everyone needs therapy," she'd said, trying not to be too serious. "It takes courage to face one's demons."

She quickly surmised that she had turned him off. He clenched his jaw.

"I think every shrink in New York needs therapy. I'd agree with you there. As for me, all I need is a country walk, a good workout and a steak dinner."

Jenna sensed an emotional dead-end. "Were you ever married?" she'd asked him.

He gave her a brief nod. The question clearly disturbed him. "I'll never marry again," he said and laughed, as if it were a joke.

"That's not what I asked you," she responded.

He'd looked away, frowning off into someone else's glance, avoiding any further response.

Jenna Rubin came from a strong Jewish family whose values did not sanction falling in love with a man she was not planning to marry, or more appropriately, not planning to marry her. *Perhaps I should walk away now and not let the attraction continue. He would be too much of a challenge.* She would always remember the disappointment she'd felt, yet another man with commitment issues.

She'd downed the wine in her glass and reached for

her purse.

He turned his face back toward hers. "Will you join me for dinner?" he asked, putting his hand on her arm.

There is just something about him, she thought as she accepted. *Something compelling. What's one date?*

And almost from the beginning, she wanted to know him, intimately and completely, as he knew her. She'd held nothing back, her exasperation with her mother, the jealousy between she and her sister, Laurie, the guilt over being "Daddy's girl."

He never spoke about anything important, so how could he be so attractive, and yet, he was like a motherless boy. There seemed to be a sadness about him, a terribly lonely quality that drew her to him.

"Where did you meet your first wife?" she asked.

"I don't remember," he said and left it at that. He never showed her a photograph, never openly resented his ex-wife for the divorce, or for not bearing him children, or whatever.

"What was your childhood like?" Jenna needed to know, needed to know something.

"I was raised in Phoenicia, small town in upstate New York, small town parents. I rode a bike, went to school, lost my virginity with a perky, blond cheerleader, boring."

"Can I meet your parents?"

"Dead," he'd told her. "No siblings, no aunts, no uncles. That's why my 'baggage' as you call it, is no bigger than your wallet."

Jenna was disappointed; she'd never get to meet anyone that had ever been important to him.

He was obviously a rubric cube, not the kind of man she would have ever imagined herself with. He kept secrets. She should probably have confronted him with more conviction about his mysterious life. Here she was, a psychotherapist, getting through people's emotional blocks was a skill she was supposed to have.

The odd dichotomy was, that they were deliriously happy together and well suited. Their daughter, Ronnie, was born one year into their marriage and they decided not to have any more children. So, right after Ronnie's birth, Nick got a vasectomy, and three years after that, they got a dog. This was family enough, they'd said.

By the time they bought their vacation home in the Catskills, Ronnie was about to enter her second year in college. Their financial successes allowed them to pay cash for the house ... nothing to worry about but repairs and taxes.

"I want a beautiful old Colonial with shuttered windows and a wrap-around porch shaded by oak trees," she told him.

"We want an old house," Nick told every broker they worked with. "Don't show us anything built after 1930. We'll hate it."

But they wound up buying a large log home, newly built, with striking views and airy open rooms. A very good broker had convinced them to "just take a drive by" and the surrounding mountains compelled them into taking "just a quick look."

They joyously warmed to the conveniences of large and abundant closets — a master suite with a Jacuzzi tub — a kitchen with an island and stainless-steel appliances. They ecstatically paid the asking price, deliriously happy to make the three hour drive every weekend just to gaze at country cows, count the trees on their property, and admire their view.

Then, about three weeks after the closing, Nick had awoken in a cold sweat and said he'd been swallowed up by a gravitational force and given over to people who looked

like they'd stepped out of a Munch painting.

"The house is too new to be haunted." He stared at her helplessly. "What do you think is going on?"

Jenna didn't have any answers. Throughout their marriage, Nick had often awoken in the night saying his dreams had been unsettling. But he wouldn't discuss them when she asked. "No big deal," he'd say. And she would brush it aside; dreams happen, not all of them sunny.

Now the demons in his dreams had turned into monsters?

Well, I guess he must have run into someone. She walked back in through the sliding glass doors and threw herself on the couch.

She was always complaining about his lateness, how many demerits he must have accumulated in grade school.

But it was only a quart of milk. Not more than a fifteen-minute drive into town.

Jenna kicked off her shoes and lay back. "My husband, she whispered, "the enigma, sweet, sweet enigma."

Chapter Three

Nick opened his eyes and brought up his wrist to check the time. He must have fallen asleep. He'd been in Fox Hollow for over three hours. It had only seemed like minutes.

"Strange," he said. "It looks so different now."

He could make out the meadow at the end of his headlights. When he turned to his right, he saw the road he'd come in on. Finally, the way out. He backed up and turned around. But it was as if he'd never driven forward.

"Tricks of the dark, demons of the night." He laughed out loud.

The moon had risen in the sky, giving him a soft path of light, illuminating the way onto Mountain Road.

He let himself do sixty-five into Margaretville and managed to get the milk just before the A&P closed.

Jenna was on the couch when he returned. The little worry lines up over her nose looked deep, and he felt guilty. He wondered what the hell had ever possessed him to go off like that on some dusty, old back road for no apparent reason.

"I was worried, Nick. Are you all right?" she asked, with an agitation in her voice she tried to hide but couldn't.

Nick went directly to the kitchen and put the milk away. "You won't believe it," he called over his shoulder. "I got lost on some back road."

"How did you wind up on a back road?" Jenna asked, following behind him.

"I was feeling daring," he said, avoiding a direct answer to her question.

"Daring?"

"Well, the road was mesmerizing." He looked at her tentatively. "I felt compelled to turn onto it."

"At night?"

"Something just came over me."

"What road was it?"

"Fox Hollow Road, I guess."

She took the stool opposite him. "Fox Hollow Road?" she asked. "I don't know that road. Where is it exactly?"

"Well, I'm not really sure. It was dark. It's off Mountain Road though; the road that goes into Margaretville."

"Whatever possessed you?"

"I don't have any idea ... I was feeling adventurous, I guess."

Jenna remained silent and watched as he ate an Oreo cookie from the inside out. "Well, had you ever been there before?" she finally asked.

"That's just it, maybe. It felt familiar."

"Familiar?"

"I had a strange experience on that road, Jenna. Really strange."

Jenna leaned forward and cupped her chin in her hand. "What do you mean 'strange'?"

He could tell she turned anxious by his use of the word 'strange.' He'd soften the story as best he could.

"Well, the moon was going in and out."

Nick made a conscious choice not to mention the cold glow of lights, or the hallucinations — seeing lace instead of torn shades — dogs and porch swings that didn't really exist ... the sound of something abnormally loud, so close it might have cracked him in two.

"You were gone over three hours," Jenna told him, clearly disturbed.

"I know." He felt oddly out of place all of a sudden, the way he had on the road. "I had no sense of time. I'm sorry."

Jenna reached over and touched his face. "Ah, the magic road." She laughed lightly.

"It scared the shit out of me."

"Well, the moon was probably just fading, covered by a cloud I would assume."

"Well, yes ..."

"The dark frightens most people, Nick. It also distorts reality if you let it."

"I had a very strange experience out there," he repeated. *There's that word again: strange.*

"Well, I imagine being on a dark road alone at night would be scary," she said.

"Actually, I hallucinated," he said slowly. He hadn't planned to mention it ... but, perhaps, he needed a rational explanation for everything he thought he saw.

"What did you hallucinate?"

Nick took a deep breath. "Lights, loud noises and the moon was there and then it wasn't. It wasn't just a fading moon. It was as if I were caught between two different nights. I don't know, maybe I'm just reacting to stress."

"What are you so stressed out about, Nick?"

"I'm not sure; my job, probably."

She cocked her head at him and raised a brow. "Well, consider this: maybe you turned onto that road in order to confront something, or someone from your past … something or someone dangerous, or seemingly so to you."

"That doesn't make much sense to me … that I wouldn't be aware of what I was doing … that I wouldn't make a conscious choice like 'Now I'm going to confront my past.'"

"You may be ready to get in touch with something that's been repressed for a long time, Nick." She reached out and took his hand. "Perhaps you subconsciously chose to confront it now. Maybe it's got something to do with being in the mountains... Listen, I want you to talk with a therapist, honey. Sally would be a good choice, to start."

Jenna and Sally went back a long way. Sally Harnick had been Jenna's dissertation advisor in college, and they had remained friends. Nick had never warmed to her, finding her longwinded and about as much fun as calculus.

Jenna appeared determined and he knew, just by her posture, that she wasn't going to back down.

"I'm going to insist on it this time," she said firmly. "Something may have happened in your childhood that you're not dealing with, something you've never dealt with … and the memory of it is triggered by something up here in the mountains. The monsters in your dream signify someone; it's time to find out who."

Nick got up from the kitchen stool and walked over to a wall of glass windows. The stars filled the sky as he looked outside. The moon was no longer visible, and he searched for it, tried to figure out where in the sky it might be. It certainly seemed as if he'd been transported into a different night, one that had definitely been starless and moonlit.

"Where did all the stars come from?" he asked. Maybe they'd just appeared.

She looked at him with a surprised grin. "Nick, we talked about the stars earlier, how beautiful the sky looked with so many stars."

"The minute I hit Mountain Road, the stars vanished, and the sky was black, lit only by the moon, when it decided to appear, that is." He looked at her curiously.

"Maybe it got cloudy suddenly."

"Maybe."

"I want you to talk to Sally."

"I'm only a few years from fifty, Jenna. Don't you think I'm about as good as I'm ever going to get?"

"There's always room for improvement."

"Besides," Nick continued. "I think my nightmares have nothing to do with not having the perfect childhood."

"What then?" she asked. "Something specific that might have happened to you when you were little?"

"Something on that road was … otherworldly … like the dreams I've been having up here."

"I think you perceived that something was 'otherworldly,' Nick, but there's an explanation for whatever it was you may have seen on that road or thought you may have seen."

"Perception is alterable. That's the way I felt tonight,

like someone was altering my reality, making it theirs, confusing and contorting it and then giving it back to me as something else."

"Nick, what are you talking about?"

He put his hands to his head and rubbed his temples. "I'm tired. I don't know what the hell I'm talking about. I feel strange ... discombobulated. I had an unusual experience out on that road, and I can't make sense of it. I can't do that Jenna. It doesn't make sense."

She got up and put her arms around his waist.

"Nick," she whispered. "Everything makes sense once you dissect it. Now, I insist you speak with Sally. I'm going to call her for you. And that's the end of it."

Chapter Four

His body was covered by a net of some kind. Someone took a syringe from their pocket and punctured his arm. It made him wince. He'd been fished out of a dark river, not entirely dead, but nearly.

"Dream," someone whispered."

His eyes fluttered. His consciousness drifted. His body shifted. "Sit tight, Harrison," someone said. "Just a while longer." He was placed back in a shallow grave.

The dream filtered through his sleep like swirls of black smoke, choking him and closing off his breath. Repeated images burned through with violent strikes, vibrant shots of pain, jarring him awake.

Nick could feel his rapid heartbeats. Sunlight landed

on the wall. He swallowed. He could feel Jenna beside him, breathing in and out, precious small breaths that landed on his neck. He closed his eyes. The images faded. Gratefully, he turned to kiss her.

This dream was always edited. He'd had it for years, ever since he found himself without a past. He couldn't see the faces clearly, just the blood: on the walls, his hands, on the body of the child at his feet.

"You up, honey?" she asked. "Sleep well?"

He nodded, remembering more about the dream than he wanted to. The woman was always blond, beautifully, typically lovely. Her gown was wet, stained in a deep, dark liquid, like thick, red syrup. He knew it was her blood that stuck to his hands like a fist full of paste.

Jenna reached for him, her fingers trailed across his chest, circling his nipples.

Nick reached out to touch her. He felt the sweat on his mouth. The images returned: the board in his hand was split, the blood hard and caked. The child at his feet was a boy. Curls on his head were brown, like perfect toast.

"Hey, sleepyhead, you're awfully quiet." Jenna caressed his chin.

Nick was screaming, but no one heard. The blond woman was so still. Sunlight fell on her, made patterns on the wall. The child's body was weirdly bent, like a tossed doll, broken and still. Nick brushed away a tear that fell from his eye.

"Want eggs this morning?" Jenna asked.

Nick shook his head. His stomach turned as the stench of blood and death crept up his nostrils. He could see the woman, almost clear. He bent to close her eyes, blue and large, expressionless ... finally.

"I can heat some muffins, how's that?" Jenna snuggled close, her scent, country clean.

"No muffins," he said.

"Meet you in the kitchen." Jenna kissed his chest, his arm, his lips.

"Yeah, yeah," he said.

"Are you all right, Nick?" she asked from the doorway.

Closing his eyes, he nodded his head. The visions were blurry and surreal, the board in his hand, weightless, the blood made him sick.

He threw on an old pair of Khaki shorts. He wanted a shower, but he wanted coffee more. He could smell it, the fresh ground beans seductively leading him forward, giving him an aromatic path to clarity that he willingly followed.

Jenna stared at him as he entered the kitchen. Her smile fell into a pout, her eyebrows, into peaks.

"Nick?" she said, "Did you have another dream? You look terrible."

He nodded slightly. He couldn't lie to her, but he'd be damned if he'd tell her about this one, about over twenty years of 'this one.' *What would she think?*

"Want to talk about it?"

"The same," he said quietly.

She handed him his cup. Pensively, she sat on the stool. "More of the same, you mean?"

Nick took a hearty swallow. "It's unimaginable," he managed to say.

"Tell me about it," she said. "Can you?"

"Just more God damn monsters, Jenna, that's all."

"The same monsters, different monsters, what kind of monsters, Nick? Talk to me."

Her frustration was unsettling to him. He took another swallow of coffee.

"I'm not certain," he said.

Jenna got up and crossed the room. She put her hands

across her chest and stared out through the window. "Are you editing your dreams for my sake, Nick?"

Nick went to her. "What does it mean to dream about death?" he asked.

"Whose death?" She turned to him.

"Strangers," he said quickly. "People I don't know."

"A metaphor for something, wouldn't you say?" She attempted a smile.

He stared at her blankly.

"Let's have some more coffee, okay?" she said, as if coffee would loosen his lips.

But he didn't answer her.

"You need to speak with Sally about this. You might feel more comfortable talking to her."

He knew she was trying to be helpful, even if it felt like she was pawning him off on Sally.

"You're the one who's uncomfortable now, aren't you? You don't really want the details," he said, not accusingly, but sadly. "Men shouldn't have violent dreams. Right?"

"Violent? You didn't say they were violent."

Nick looked away; it had just spilled out. Well, maybe the spill was felicitous. Maybe it was time to get her perspective. He turned and stared at her. He spoke softly, unsure of his decision to reveal such gruesome images.

"In my dream, I killed someone," he began, with a hesitant pause. "I think," he added quickly. Nick looked at her. He really could use an interpretation. "I've been having the dream for years, Jenna. I never really wanted to tell you about it, but I guess I should. It's different than the latest monster dreams I've been having." He stared at her, as if searching for something.

"You never mentioned this dream until now?"

"I just didn't want to be psychoanalyzed."

"Dreams aren't meant to be taken literally, Nick. It's

clear you don't want to discuss your inner life with me so Sally can help you, if not Sally, then someone else."

Nick turned to the wall. *One thing about Jenna, when his hour was up, it was up*. She really *was* pawning him off on Sally, or maybe she really didn't want to hear what his inner life was revealing.

"Will you agree to it, Nick?" she asked.

It wasn't just his childhood that was missing; it was a multitude of things he couldn't remember. He'd never told Jenna that there was such a void in his life; she might force him into discovering that he was the only monster to fear.

" Nick. I'm concerned about you."

Jenna had broken through his thoughts. For a moment, he was confused again. He didn't know what she was talking about.

"What?" he asked.

She opened her eyes wide. "Sally? It will be an informal talk, that's all. She's not charging us, Nick. You're not a patient. Sally is a friend. She may recommend someone though. Will you be open to that?"

"I don't need a shrink, Jenna. I really don't think I need a shrink."

He was surprised he was going to challenge her on this, but he couldn't get the experience of Fox Hollow out of his mind, any more than he could get the violent images out of his mind: blood on the wall, on his hands, a dead woman, a murdered child, he'd been having that dream for over twenty years, but this experience in Fox Hollow, that was new. Was there a connection between everything that was happening? His dreams? Fox Hollow Road? He sensed there was.

"What else could you possibly need but therapy at this point?" Jenna said.

He knew she was frustrated by his refusal to admit that what he needed was a rational explanation for what was causing his nightmares, and a rational explanation for the hallucinations he'd had the night before. But to Nick, therapy was not rational, it was indulgent.

"I think I need a hypnotherapist. I need to remember things."

"What things?"

"The farmhouse that I saw in the dark last night looked like someplace I'd been before." Nick turned away. *Maybe it's time to talk about it, tell her I have no frigging past.*

"I see … a familiar farmhouse. Monsters? Sounds like a repressed memory, Nick. You need to let it surface."

"A repressed memory? Perhaps." He laughed softly. "But the violence, the dream I had last night … I think I killed someone in that dream, Jenna, and it keeps recurring, over and over and over again, for years." He said it carefully, afraid of her reaction. "I've dreamed it before … about killing someone. God knows, I wouldn't want to uncover any truth in that." He'd finally admitted it. He felt strangely lightheaded.

"Well, perhaps you're projecting your anger onto the fictional characters in your dreams." She smiled faintly, having given this smile several times a week to her patients, he was sure: the coaxing, gentle facial nudge.

"Do you know the person you kill in your dream, Nick?"

"No, I don't think so."

"You need to find out who you're so angry at."

"I'm not angry at anyone."

Jenna seemed ready to pull out her hair. "You obviously don't want to talk to me about it. Anyway, I'm your wife, not your doctor. It's best for you to speak to someone else."

She came to his side and put her arms around him.

"Okay." He sighed.

"Sally will help you discover what lies at the bottom of this." She kissed him. "Don't be afraid of violent dreams, people have them, especially men. It doesn't make you a monster, Nick."

"Yes, you're probably right," he said wearily.

"I'm going to put more coffee on."

She took on an uncharacteristic perkiness and he knew his hour with Jenna was up. She had reached her saturation point with his inner turmoil and his refusal to connect it to his dysfunctional childhood. For all he knew his parents could have everything to do with his dreams, or nothing at all.

Nick showered and came out on the deck through the sliding glass doors of their bedroom. He was wearing khaki shorts, an open white shirt and a brand new pair of Converse sneakers.

Jenna unplugged her headphones and wrapped them around her ipod.

"More coffee?" she asked.

Nick stretched himself out on a deck chair. "No," he said.

Jenna carefully segued into their usual country morning chatter and did not mention his dreams or his experience on Fox Hollow Road.

Nick smiled at his wife but kept the joke to himself, the recognition of her inner clock and his hour being up.

"We need more color in the den," she was saying.

Nick's thoughts returned to the road. *What the hell had happened to him out there?*

He listened haphazardly as Jenna transitioned from the subject of white birch trees, and how many to plant on their property, to what did he think of the color yellow for the guest room?

"Perhaps we should find Fox Hollow Road, confront it by day," he interrupted.

"Nick, have you heard a word I've said?"

Nick looked over and admired his wife's beautifully shaped legs all curled up in front of her; the skin on her thighs touching and sweating from the morning sun, slightly arousing him — her dark eyes hidden under the hat she always wore to shield her from burning, and he tried to smile.

"Do I like the color yellow? No, I don't, but I would consider yellow for the guest room. I don't sleep in the guest room."

"What about white birch trees?"

"Over there." Nick pointed with his chin. "Somewhere over there."

He leaned his head back and felt the sun on his face. He'd briefly noticed that his wife was grinning at him, but her dimples held another dialogue that still questioned his sanity. He could tell she thought he was understandably sullen, and about to become withdrawn, even potentially boring as hell. He wished he could think of something funny to say.

"You can put white birches anywhere. They look good anywhere," he told her as he removed his dark glasses and tried to smile again — tried to force himself toward giving a damn where the hell they put their Birch trees.

Jenna peered at him and sipped her coffee. It was a bright, blue day and her husband's eyes popped out at her, complimenting the blush of the sky, cerulean in color and large, like that of an eagle. Then he shielded them again behind dark glasses like precious gems too vulnerable to expose. She didn't want to leave the house. She never did. She just wanted to be there. She loved it. All she ever really wanted to do was put up curtains, rearrange furniture, read her garden catalogues, and explain to Nick why using some Pottery Barn pieces might work just splendidly for their decor if they were mixed in with some interesting touches of "old country stuff."

She watched Nick pick up a day-old newspaper and open it. It wasn't his paper, Nick never read *The New York Times* on the weekends. He always felt that reading *The Times* was too much like being on the job.

"You want to go find that road, sweetheart?" she asked softly, despite herself. She knew that's what he wanted. She could feel his restlessness.

He lowered his sunglasses and grinned. "Is this therapy?" he asked sheepishly.

Chapter Five

They'd been driving around in circles for what seemed like forever, and they still couldn't find the road or the sign for Fox Hollow.

"It's like it was never there," Nick said.

Jenna looked out the window. Mountain Road was narrow, too small for two cars at once, and the drop from the ravine was steep.

"This road gives me vertigo," she said, averting her eyes.

"Don't look over the edge."

"Doesn't look like there are any little roads to turn off on at all, just driveways."

Nick agreed and drove back toward Margaretville, wondering if he'd hallucinated his entire experience. It appeared as if Fox Hollow Road didn't exist.

"How about lunch?" he asked. "We might as well."

They took a little table in the back of The Flower Patch, a small and tastefully decorated café nestled between an old dirt lane and a supermarket parking lot. As they settled into comfortable white wicker chairs and ordered sandwiches and iced tea, Nick glanced nervously at his wife. He felt the tension in his neck and wondered if he shouldn't just leave well enough alone, but he had to keep going, he had to pursue it.

"I'm trying to find a road," Nick said to the waitress who brought their lunch in wicker baskets, brimming over with chips. She set the baskets down in front of them.

"Fox Hollow Road," he said.

The waitress closed her eyes for a bit, as if searching for knowledge of the road's whereabouts. She appeared in a swoon, but the spell was broken by her high-pitched response. It made Nick jump.

"Oh, I think it's in Roxbury," she said. "I think Andes has a Fox Hollow Road, too. Which one you looking for?"

Nick felt his stomach fall. If there was no Fox Hollow Road in Margaretville, he was a madman.

"The one right up Walnut Street," he said slowly. "It's somewhere off Mountain Road. I took it last night. I was coming in from New Kingston."

The waitress looked over her shoulder. She was short and round, and her words seemed to bounce off the wall. "Hey, Margie, you know where Fox Hollow Road is around here?" she called out.

Nick turned and looked at the woman she was addressing. She too had too much energy for his mood, like a wound-up puppy.

"No Fox Hollow Road around here. You must have been on the other side, near Andes," the other waitress hollered back.

Nick would not accept insanity. He was on Fox Hollow Road in Margaretville, damn it: he knew where the hell he was. He almost stood to his feet. It took all his control to remain seated, to speak without raising his voice.

"No, I remember being on Mountain Road. I was nowhere near Andes. It's got to be close by," he insisted.

Oh yeah," a voice offered.

Nick turned his head sharply. A man at the counter had spoken out. Nick felt a disturbing familiarity as he took the man in, no reason he would know him, but he felt he did.

"You must be talking about Satan's Path," the man said.

"What?" Nick asked.

The stranger wiped his face with a napkin. "I know where Fox Hollow Road used to be, but it's not called that anymore, hasn't been called that in years. It isn't really called Satan's Path either, just in jest. He had mustard on his lips, but as he turned he managed to wipe it away with his tongue.

One of the bubbly waitresses turned toward Nick. "Oh yeah, Satan's Path is up Mountain Road," she said.

Nick looked at her. She had pink ribbons in her hair, as pink as her sneakers. Otherwise, she was colorless, and her eyes matched her hair, lackluster and pale.

The man who had called to Nick was about Nick's age and wore a baseball cap. His face was ruddy, and his stature was large, his orange hair was the color of the orange donut awning across the road.

"Satan's Path was once called Fox Hollow Road, about forty years ago." He swiveled around on the counter stool.

"Now, the real name of the road is Robert Nichols Road. It's hard to see the road sign in the dark, all those Pine trees."

Nick put his coffee mug down. His uneasy feeling intensified. "Why do they call it Satan's Path?" he asked.

"Weird things happen up there."

Nick forced a smile. "Oh?"

"Um," he grunted. He seemed distracted, as if conversation was too heavy a burden, especially after the Quarter Pounder Burger Special he'd just eaten.

"It has to be a different road then; I had enough light to a road sign when I turned in. The road dead ends at a farmhouse, I think. It's got some cut-offs, but they don't go anywhere. It was dark though, the moon kept going in and out so I couldn't be sure of anything."

Nick felt desperate for agreement. He didn't care what the road was called, he just needed to know it existed.

He watched as the man got up and walked to the register. He burped pleasantly with each step. Normally, that would have made Nick smile, but not today.

"Sounds like Satan's Path to me. That's strange about the sign," he added. "Must have been an old one you saw."

Nick looked at his wife; she was following the conversation as if there wasn't anything absurd about it. He heard the man offer to show him the road. "If it's that important to you," he was saying.

Then he started going on and on about the damn road sign, how he never noticed any old signs up before. Nick felt perplexed "I know what I saw," Nick said and glanced at Jenna, who gave him a reassuring wink.

The man dropped a few quarters into the tip cup at the register. Margie was clearing his lunch. Her bouncing voice gave Nick a headache. She was asking the man about the old road. Nick was beginning to feel he should have never brought it up.

The man drummed his fingers on the counter. "It was called Fox Hollow Road back in the '60s, before the disappearances," he was saying.

"What disappearances?" Nick asked.

"Oh, a couple of kids," he said, and continued to tap his fingers. "Two boys, Rob and Nicky."

Nick felt as if someone had slammed the back of his head with a board.

"Before your time, girls," the man said. "You wouldn't remember, probably weren't even born yet."

"Oh, I think I remember hearing something about a kidnapping." Patty came out from the kitchen, her pink high tops clutching her tiny legs like clips. "Two kids disappeared on Satan's Path, right?"

Nick put it together fast, the devil did something bad on Satan's Path. He remembered the farmhouse, how the peaceful serenity had turned sour so quickly. What had been the truth, he wondered? What he saw or what he wanted to see?

"It was because of those disappearances that the road got named after Satan," Nick heard the man explain. He was speaking to the floor, as if troubled by his tale.

"Both those boys are said to be buried up there but neither one of them has ever been found," he said and stared intensely at Nick. "Rob and Nicky," he added. "I think about them every now and then."

"Nicky?" Nick quickly glanced at his wife, who didn't seem to pick up on the coincidence.

"Yeah, he was some weird kid."

"You knew the boys?" Nick asked.

"Yeah, I knew them," he said.

Jenna suddenly jumped in and asked. "Who did it,

who killed them?"

Nick wondered if she'd finally made the connection. One kid had his name.

"They never found the killer, suspected some old man that lived on the property, but he was never held responsible. But they never found the bodies either, so who knows if there ever really was a murder." The man put his hands deep in his pockets and stared at Nick. He suddenly became lighter, as if the memory had lost its weight.

"I was there that night, too. I was sleeping on the porch with Carl Nichols." He looked at the waitresses and smiled. "I was lucky, I guess."

"Carl Nichols?" Nick took another sip of his coffee.

"Robbie's younger brother," he said.

"Oh." Nick looked into his cup and didn't raise his eyes.

This was getting too bizarre. *There was a murder out there? And one of the kids was named Nicky?* He quickly looked at Jenna, but she was too engrossed in the story to notice he was about to hyperventilate.

"Carl and I didn't hear anything. We didn't wake up until the sheriff came and got us. We were both on a screened in porch on the side of the house."

"So that's what happened to Fox Hollow Road, they named it after Rob Nichols?" Nick leaned on his elbows and questioned him, trying to appear nonchalant despite the knot his stomach was in.

"Yeah, no one calls it that though. It's just known as Satan's Path." The man looked back and forth between Nick and Jenna. "Hard to find."

"Well, how can we find it?" Jenna asked, "the one that *used* to be called Fox Hollow?"

"Well, like I told you, I'm going over that way. I can

show you," he said as he stood up straight. "Pete Shelby." He extended his hand. "I do some work for the owner up on Satan's Path — general carpentry, landscaping, things like that. No one up there but him; you going for a visit?"

"No, just looking around," Nick said.

Pete shrugged. "Oh, no harm in that, I guess. You have a name?"

"Oh, sorry. Nick Dowling." Nick got up and took his wallet out of his back pocket. "My wife, Jenna."

"Nick Dowling?" Pete stepped back into a chair and caught it just before it fell over. "You shitting me?" He laughed nervously and stared at Nick. "This is weird, man," he said.

"Is something wrong?" Nick asked. He noticed that Pete's expression seemed deformed. Something about his name had thrown this guy into shock.

Pete pushed the chair back under the table. Nick noticed his face had turned a non-color, beyond white.

"Is this some kind of a bad joke? Carl put you up to this?" Pete seemed to be struggling to find humor in the situation.

"What are you talking about?" Nick asked slowly. "Who's Carl?"

"Carl was Robbie's brother. I mentioned that before, remember?"

"Oh, yeah." Nick couldn't take his eyes from Pete, the poor guy looked sick.

Pete stared at Nick intensely, as if he was going to say something, but then he changed his mind. "Weird coincidence, not worth mentioning, I guess. Well, want to see the road?" he asked.

Nick tossed his half-eaten sandwich back into the wicker basket. Jenna downed her glass of tea and took the sandwich with her. They followed Pete out of the restaurant and watched him get into to a brand-new Explorer, so covered in mud it was hard to see the color.

"Wait for me. I'll pull behind you." Nick said to Pete. "I'm in the lot."

Nick knew that Jenna was trying to assimilate the information. It was strange and getting stranger, one of the two boys having a name she could identify with her husband? His unusual sojourn on Fox Hollow Road the night before?

"There was a murder on that road, Jenna. Don't you find that interesting?" Nick said softly as he reached for her hand. "I've got the name of one of the murdered kids. Strange, huh?"

"I do find it an unusual coincidence, but I doubt if that murder has anything to do with you, Nick," Jenna said. "You're very much alive."

He was disappointed. Of course it had to do with him, why couldn't she see that?

He got inside the jeep and took the wheel. "Local boy must do well up here, he's driving a brand new Ford Explorer." He smiled at his wife.

"Do you know that guy Pete from anywhere, Nick? He seemed surprised by your name," Jenna asked.

"Nope. I don't think so."

"You sure?"

Nick followed slowly behind Pete's truck. "Well, there's some familiarity but I can't place him," he said.

"My God, Nick. He almost had a coronary when you introduced yourself. Are you sure you don't know him?"

Nick didn't answer his wife. He couldn't remember a damn thing about his youth so how could anyone from it be familiar? His shoulders felt tenser than stretched rubber bands. He forced his thoughts onto the present scenario and his body relaxed somewhat. Maybe the road held the answers.

"Satan's Path." He shuddered.

"How gruesome," she said.

Nick followed Pete's Explorer as it turned onto Walnut Street, which soon became Mountain Road, and that led them in the direction of New Kingston, and out toward a little town called Bovina. They passed swiftly by a number of back roads with names like Pine Lane, Rose's Bush, and Cherry Hill. But Fox Hollow Road was not among them.

Chapter Six

They weren't on Mountain Road long before Pete's car made a slow right turn. Fox Hollow Road, or as it was now known, Robert Nichols Road was a difficult road to see, hidden as it was by Pine trees.

"We must have passed it by five or six times." Nick laughed. "You really have to know where it is."

He noticed a private property sign on an open gate as they drove in, sagging and water weary, it hung with a tired tilt.

"I didn't see any private property sign last night," Nick said.

The stones under the jeep's wheels crunched and the branches of the trees hit the side doors as they drove forward. The same open meadow Nick remembered seeing through the moonlight eventually appeared before them.

"The road sign said Robert Nichols Road, not Fox Hollow Road." Jenna eyed him peculiarly as she said it. "Are you sure this is right?"

Nick nodded his head and looked up toward the sky. "There's probably a sign around we didn't notice." Nick watched Pete pull his car up to the side of the meadow and stop. "That old sign is around here somewhere."

"Then this is the road you were on?" Jenna asked.

"Looks different in daylight but this is it."

Nick realized his shirt was sticking to him, though it wasn't really that hot. The silent road seemed antagonistically quiet, and the surrounding trees appeared to sway defensively, shielding their secrets.

Pete removed his baseball cap. Nick noticed how short to the scalp his hair was cut as he and Jenna joined him at the meadow.

"Have we met before?" Pete gave him a perplexed smile, almost like an accusation.

"No, I don't think so," Nick said quickly, though he didn't entirely believe that. There was a familiarity that he couldn't place.

"Well, your name ... Nick Dowling ... but you couldn't be *him*. Look, it's been bothering me the whole ride over here, should have said something back at the café."

"What's that?" Nick felt edgy. *Did he know this guy or not?*

Pete laughed as he continued to stare at Nick "Never mind, you might think I'm crazy. I assume you're city people?"

"Yeah," Nick said and nodded his head like he was watching a ball bounce. He was aware of Pete's intense interest in him, aware he'd just changed the subject, that he'd wanted to bring something up and didn't.

"Is this the road you were on last night?" Pete asked.

"Yeah," Nick said.

"That's the old Nichols place," Pete said pointing toward the farmhouse. "We're in the hollow, Fox Hollow."

Nick could hear Pete's footsteps in the dirt as he walked up toward the house.

"Andrew Quinn owns it now," Pete said, turning back to them.

The name hit Nick hard. "Quinn?" he said.

"Yeah," Pete looked surprised. "You know him?"

Nick had a quick image, but it faded fast. He had a sense that pieces of his memory were about to surface, and he couldn't tell if he was going to welcome it.

"What a fabulous old porch," Jenna said, as she looked toward the farmhouse.

Her voice had startled Nick. For a moment he had forgotten she was there.

"The house needs work, doesn't it?" Jenna turned back to Nick and forced a grin. "It's big and friendly looking though, a perfect old place."

"This used to be the Nichols' farm," Pete said. "The land extended all the way back to Route Twenty-Eight. The Nichols sold off more and more land as they got older. Quinn's got about fifty or sixty acres left, though."

"He lives there alone?" Jenna asked. "The house seems so big for just one man."

"Yep, just him. He bought it off the Nichols right before they moved away. Florida, I think. They retired about seven or eight years ago."

"I guess we're trespassing," Nick said.

"Well, yeah, but I wouldn't worry. He won't shoot you long as you're with me," Pete seemed to snort. "Like I told you, I work for Andrew Quinn but I'm really the boss. He listens to me, not the other way around."

"Does he live here all the time?" Nick asked. He wondered if the old man had seen him out there in the dark, sitting in his car, staring back, seeing lace and dogs and bikes on the lawn, as if he were on some sort of hallucinatory drug.

Pete creased his forehead. He was pondering something; he looked like he'd been asked a profound question, one he couldn't answer. "Yeah," he finally said.

"I saw some guy staring at me from the windows last night," Nick said with an attempt at lightheartedness.

"Well, he might have shot you then. He's trigger-happy. No one likes to see a stranger on their land at night, especially Andrew Quinn."

"What's the house like inside?" Jenna asked. "I'd love to see it."

Nick could always count on Jenna's curiosity when it came to old houses. He wanted to see it as well, but probably for different reasons.

"Well, it's not as beautiful as it used to be when the Nichols' had it. Really want to see it?" Pete seemed eager to please Jenna. "I can probably get you inside. Quinn won't care. He never gets any company."

"No, that's all right, I'd feel intrusive," Jenna said.

Nick felt disappointed and wondered how he might change her mind.

"I wouldn't worry about it. Well, want to see it?" Pete asked again.

"No, I don't think so." Jenna suddenly turned to Nick. "So how do you feel about the road in the daytime?" she asked.

"Not much," he said.

"Are you sure, Nick?" She stared directly at him, like a police detective might have. "Are you uncomfortable? You're perspiring pretty badly."

"It's hot," he said firmly.

She pulled him aside, slipped her arm through his and walked him away from Pete's hearing.

"It's a pretty road, but I'm not sure why you're so fascinated with it. It was probably a lot more threatening under the light of a full moon," she whispered.

"I think I'd like to see the house before we go," Nick said. "I bet it's a great old house. Looks so familiar to me. I might even recall something."

"What? Recall what?"

"Memories."

"Memories? What memories?"

"I don't know."

Jenna stood in front of him and met his eyes with an intensity that unnerved him.

"What is it about the house that's familiar, Nick? You grew up at least ten miles away."

"Yes, I know but it just looks familiar," he said.

"I really don't want to go barging in on an old man," Jenna insisted.

"What's so special about this road? Did you know the Nichols?" Pete asked, as he put his baseball cap back on his head and stared at them curiously.

"No," Nick said. "I didn't know them."

"Quinn would probably welcome the company." Pete laughed.

"I'll wait for you in the car, Nick," Jenna suddenly announced and walked toward their jeep.

"I thought you liked the house and wanted to see it inside." Nick caught up to her. "Come on. It'll be fun." He attempted a grin in Pete's direction.

"I'll wait until the owner of the house invites me in," Jenna said.

After Jenna walked toward the car, Nick turned his

attention back to Pete. "I guess I'd better go."

"Where are you from?" Pete asked quickly, clearly stalling his exit.

Nick had always tried to stay off the subject of Phoenicia, even though Jenna kept insisting she wanted to see his hometown. But how could he talk about a town he couldn't remember? Find his school? Show her his childhood home? He kept getting out of it, making excuses. Luckily, Jenna didn't like leaving her own backyard.

"Phoenicia," Nick mumbled.

"Where?" Pete looked startled.

Nick instinctively knew he'd said the wrong thing. "Phoenicia," he repeated, more clearly this time.

"That's amazing." Pete was looking at Nick's face like he was reading a road map. He lapsed into a running monologue, all about his family moving to Phoenicia right after the kidnapping. He was saying he went to school in Phoenicia, just moved back to New Kingston, maybe ten, fifteen years ago.

"No kidding?" Nick looked back at the house. The last thing he needed was getting into reminiscing about Phoenicia with Pete. After all, he and Pete would have known each other; they appeared to be around the same age.

"We moved away in the early '70s, not long after Robbie and Nicky disappeared. I was very young."

Pete was talking quickly, as if he were trying to get somewhere. It seemed to Nick like he would never shut up.

Nick mumbled something. He was making conversation, trying not to appear rude but he knew Jenna wanted to go home.

"My wife got a job teaching school around here, so we

48

moved back right after we married. I married a hometown girl." Pete broke out into a wide grin. He seemed out of breath.

Nick had a sinking feeling. If he really was from Phoenicia then why didn't Pete recall him?" His memories were blocked, but Pete's weren't.

"I don't remember you," Nick said quickly, looking away.

"You look a bit like Harrison Hinckley." Pete studied him closely. "But other than that, I don't know you either."

"Harrison? That name doesn't ring a bell."

"Ah, he's dead. I meant, you looked like him when we were teenagers."

"Oh?"

"So you weren't born in Phoenicia, then?" Pete asked him.

"Yes, I was," Nick said, as he looked back at Jenna. She was giving him lethal looks from the car, and he knew it was only a matter of moments before she starting honking the horn.

"How old are you?" Pete asked.

Nick really felt like he was getting the third degree, or about to get it. He didn't know how old he was, but he estimated his age as close as possible.

"Forty-eight."

"I'm forty-six; that's probably why we don't remember each other. I was trailing you in school by two years."

"Yeah, I guess so."

Pete stalled for a bit, as if he were weighing his words. "Well, you want to see the house?" he finally said.

"I do, but we have to go," Nick said, looking toward his wife again. He knew this whole experience was difficult for Jenna. It didn't compute and Jenna did not like when things didn't make sense.

"Look, thanks for bringing me here. I appreciate it, but my wife clearly wants to go home. I'll have to come back another time to see the house."

"So you think you know this road, huh? Maybe you were here before and that's why you remembered it as Fox Hollow?" Pete stared at him. "It hasn't been called Fox Hollow in nearly forty years," he said.

"Right."

"There's a name for that … when you think you've been someplace before."

"Déjà vu."

"Yeah, that's it." Pete said.

Nick nodded. Would he ever get rid of this guy, he wondered?

All of a sudden, Pete took a deep breath. "Look, I've been wanting to say this…."

"*What now*, Nick wondered. Would this be it, the third degree?

"I used to play with a kid called Nicky. I didn't want to mention it in front of your wife, it's kind of weird. But right here in New Kingston. Right where we're standing, as a matter of fact. Me and Robbie and Carl Nichols used to play with Nicky. He disappeared with Robbie, like I told you. The weird thing is, his last name was Dowling, like yours."

Nick couldn't believe what he'd just heard. The kidnapped boy not only had his first name, but he also had his last name.

He heard Jenna start the car.

"You could be him … except…"

"Except what?"

"Were you born here?"

"No, I told you, I'm from Phoenicia. I know it's weird

about my name but it sure wasn't me you played with. I never set foot in New Kingston, not until my wife and I discovered it. At least, I don't remember ever being here. I certainly wasn't born here. Sure is a hell of a coincidence, though."

"That kid, Nicky, was strange," Pete said. "There was something wrong with him. They said he was a savant. You know what that is?"

Nick nodded slowly.

"You a savant?" Pete asked.

"No," Nick said.

"Nicky didn't speak to anyone else but Robbie. Quite a coincidence you having his name and feeling like you were here before. But you're not a savant, so I guess you can't be Nicky Dowling, right? Not the Nicky Dowling I knew."

"Yeah, right," Nick said.

"Weird, huh? Life is weird sometimes, huh?"

"Yeah, yeah, it is."

Pete turned abruptly and walked away. "I'm going up to the farmhouse now. I'm working on Quinn's roof." Pete spoke over his shoulder. He had dismissed Nick, finally. "Got to mow his damn lawn first, though."

Nick watched him walk away.

"I'd stay off these roads at night; easy to lose your way." Pete called back and waved.

Chapter Seven

Pete drove up the road, increasingly disturbed by this confused stranger calling himself Nick Dowling.

"Hey, old man," Pete called as he walked in the front door.

Quinn was in the kitchen, which is where Pete usually found him this time of day. The usual UFO crap Quinn read was piled up on the kitchen table — books, newspapers, pamphlets on 'aliens among us' and all that shit. The guy was a real whacko.

"So, any aliens land this morning?" Pete asked, quite seriously.

Quinn looked up as Pete pulled out a kitchen chair and sat.

"I don't pay you to ask questions." Quinn went back to his paper.

Pete pulled a toothpick out of his shirt pocket and started picking his teeth.

"Did you hear what I said, Pete?" Quinn said, putting down his paper and leaning in towards him. "I hope you're not waiting for an answer."

"You really believe in that shit?" Pete asked, swooping the toothpick into his mouth and then out again with his tongue.

"Well, that took real talent." Quinn scowled.

Pete chuckled and pushed his chair back on two legs. "I've got interesting news."

"Your wife fart out another baby?"

Pete's chair came down with a thud. "You see me down in the field with a couple of people just now, asshole?"

Quinn nodded. "Anymore trick questions?"

"You want to know who the man says he is?"

"Not really."

"So you don't care that I'm on your property with two complete strangers?"

"As long as they don't pick my fucking roses. Hey, do I get a prize for answering your dumb ass questions correctly?" Quinn glared at Pete.

"Listen here, you perverted old bastard. I was just making chit chat with some guy from the city who says his name is Nick Dowling."

Quinn looked like he'd seen a ghost. He leaned in. "What the hell are you talking about?"

"Maybe your little boy toy has come back from the dead?"

Quinn stood up and crossed the room. He stood over Pete's chair.

"What the fuck are you talking about?" he repeated.

"He says his name is Nick Dowling, but he's not

53

spastic so I guess it's just a weird coincidence."

Quinn went back and sat down. "Yeah, fucking weird."

Pete threw his toothpick in the trash and walked out the kitchen door, leaving Quinn to stare into space, most likely wondering if ole Pete was pulling his leg.

He went back to the barn and pulled out Quinn's John Deere. He figured he'd cover the side lawn and finish the back later on after the sun left. He was distracted by this guy who called himself Nick Dowling, couldn't think of anything else but how strange it was.

Memories stirred up in Pete's mind while he rode the mower up and down and watched the grass spit out, and the weeds flatten under the blade. These were memories he didn't like having, even though they were serving him well. Quinn had a pension, family money and a guilty conscience. Lucky for Pete, he at least had that.

Pete didn't like thinking about Robbie. He didn't much care about Nicky. That kid had been a real fruitcake, always talking about spacecraft and space people. Pete still remembered that. He even had Robbie believing his tall tales. Even that old fool Quinn thought the sky was full of aliens.

"They took 'em," Quinn told everyone after Robbie and Nicky disappeared. "Space creatures took 'em off."

The next thing Pete knew, Quinn was off the force and in some loony bin in Kingston. He didn't see Quinn again until he and Darla moved back to the area. By that time, Quinn was old, couldn't chase any more boys into the woods.

Pete didn't have to say a word to Quinn when he came up the road looking for work. He just named his price. He needed a job, and Quinn needed to forget what a fucking perv he'd been. Shit, Pete thought, Quinn probably killed both Robbie and Nicky. Who else could have done it? It certainly wasn't space aliens. Neither he nor Carl said anything though. No, never said a word about Quinn. They'd been ashamed to admit they'd been molested. Now of course, Quinn was paying for Pete's silence. Who would have believed it anyway? That nice Sheriff Quinn likes to sit little boys on his lap? No way. Until Quinn went nuts, he was an upstanding citizen.

Pete looked over toward the house. He thought he saw Quinn getting some shovels out of the shed.

Pete turned off the mower. "Hey," he called. "You want me to dig any holes for you, Quinn? I'll give you a nice discount."

"I can dig my own goddamn holes," Quinn shouted back, tossing a shovel on the ground. "Finish up my lawn and my roof and get the hell out of here, jackass."

"Whatever you say, boss," Pete turned the mower back on and drove it down toward the front lawn, killing a few roses from Quinn's prize bushes along the way.

Chapter Eight

Through the large picture window in their bedroom, with all the lights off at night, Jenna could see nothing but stars.

"Remember?" she whispered.

"Humm?" he asked sleepily.

"East Hampton?"

She heard him laugh softly. Making love under their Catskill Mountain country window was surely better than all the young and foolish summer nights they had spent screwing on the beach in East Hampton, just to screw in sand with the waves teasing their toes. They had to hope they wouldn't get stepped on or caught in the glow of someone's flashlight. It was sexy, but risky.

"Something nice about making love in your own bed." Jenna smiled and cuddled in his arms. He touched her nose with his finger, and then, trailed down to her breasts, gently rubbing his face against her skin.

"I'm cold," she said.

Nick pulled the happy flowered sheet over her and lay back. He looked out into the night.

They had often lay like that for hours, watching the stars smile and twinkle like

friendly, coquettish invitations. It was almost as if they were watching the unfolding of the universe, and some intelligence in the mesmerizing sky over them was winking out a code, a map to infinity.

"Are you sure we were on the right road, Nick?" Jenna asked.

"I'm positive."

She wanted to believe him, but it was just too surreal. The sign clearly read: Robert Nichols, not Fox Hollow. Perhaps the old sign had been knocked down by the wind, they never did find it.

"Do you think that God is evolving as we are?" he asked. "Or is there an end to arrive at, a final evolution that looks nothing at all like God, as we think of God?"

Jenna did not like to talk about God with Nick. He was too indecisive in his beliefs. She decided to ignore his sudden need to philosophize.

"I felt uncomfortable just barging in, you know?"

She had felt badly about not wanting to see the house. It had seemed so important to Nick.

"Why don't you go back to the road with Pete tomorrow? He did mention that he could get you inside Quinn's house, and if you think it will help you resolve something, then I say do it," she said.

Nick kissed the top of her head. "Good idea," he said quietly. "There has to be a reason why that house is so damn familiar."

"Are you having memory issues?"

"Don't we all have memory issues?"

"Don't you think you probably know that guy, Pete?"

She wondered what he was keeping from her. He obviously had to be keeping something from her.

"Well, Pete actually started to look familiar to me, particularly when he took his cap off," Nick said. "And then, telling me that I've got the same name as that murdered kid ... I don't know, Jenna. Something strange is going on. That coincidence about my name is just too incredible."

Jenna turned to him and put her arm on his chest. "Dowling is a common name, honey."

Nick opened his mouth wide; clearly, to him, it was so obvious. "Oh, come on, don't you think the coincidence is unbelievable?"

She did think it was strange for Nick to have one of the murdered boy's names. But she really wanted to dismiss the whole thing. It was too unsettling.

"There's an explanation for everything, Nick," she said.

Nick looked at her. "Exactly."

Jenna cuddled closer in his arms. Her husband was in such distress over this sojourn on Fox Hollow Road. She wondered why he couldn't remember anything about his connection to New Kingston if he had one. After all, he was from Phoenicia, and he said he'd never been to New Kingston before in his life. But he clearly must have been. Why would the farmhouse be familiar to him if he'd never seen it before?

"Pete and I should know each other, shouldn't we?" he asked.

Of course Nick was confused. She was confused, as well. If he really was from Phoenicia why hadn't Pete recognized him? Phoenicia was a very small town.

"Pete is probably someone I never paid any attention to."

Nick was obviously going to answer his own question.

"But it's sort of like the road and the goddamn house. How about the name Quinn? You know, Jenna, I remember the name Quinn from somewhere, too. My memory has holes in it. My frigging brain is like Swiss cheese." He laughed, as if trying to downplay the strangeness of it.

"Why are you having memory issues, Nick?"

"Early Alzheimer's?" he joked again.

Jenna stroked his arm. "Do you think that the Quinn you knew is the same man who lives in the farmhouse now?" she asked, propping herself up a bit to stare at him. *Why is he having such a hard time remembering all this*?

Nick let out a long, slow breath. "I'm connected to the name Quinn somehow, like that farmhouse, I'm connected to that too. I know it. I'm going back to the road tomorrow, Jenna, Maybe it'll come to me. I must have been subconsciously led to that house the other night."

Jenna moved close to his ear and kissed the lobe. "Do you want me to come?" she whispered.

"Didn't you?" he asked sheepishly.

She noticed his eyes were teasing as he turned toward her and gave her his sexy grin.

"Oh, yes," she said softly.

"I think I'd like to go alone," he whispered, breaking the spell between them. "If you don't mind."

"No, but you're not going to call the redneck?"

He shook his head. "No. Pete will distract me. I need to be alone out there on Fox Hollow. I think that whatever it is that's out there needs me to be alone when I confront it."

"Out there? Nick, what are you talking about?" She shot straight up and put her hands across her chest. "It's within you. There's nothing out there but what's inside your head. There is no *it* that needs you to be alone."

"I meant to say. Confront the memory," he said, "that's my *it*".

"Did you feel isolated on that road? Is that how you felt as a child — isolated?" She slipped down again into his arms and held him.

"This is not about my feelings of isolation. It's bigger than that. I know it doesn't make any sense. But I'm going to follow my instincts on this because I don't have a choice. I am connected to that road somehow, and somehow that road is connected to my nightmares ... to my past."

"But your past isn't missing Nick. You should remember any connection to that road."

Nick lay there silently and didn't speak.

"You're looking for answers in the wrong places."

He reached over to kiss her lightly. Then he leaned back and spoke softly.

"It's just too coincidental. Something compelled me to pull off onto that very road. And I've got the murdered boy's name. I mean, don't you find this whole thing extraordinary?"

"I think you're trying to connect yourself to Fox Hollow, for whatever reasons, maybe a longing to have roots somewhere — normal parents and a normal childhood in some wonderful old American Colonial farmhouse. Perfect."

"Before I can accept your analysis, Jenna, I have to find out what's going on for myself." He looked deeply into her eyes. "Finding out about a murder up on Fox Hollow ... it's all starting to unravel. It's got to involve me somehow, but I don't know how, or don't remember how. Maybe I was too young to remember that something about that kidnapping is connected directly to me."

"There is no Fox Hollow Road anymore, Nick." She dismissed him and closed her eyes.

"Exactly." He nodded his head. "But I remembered the road as Fox Hollow Road."

"You saw a road sign, Nick," Jenna said, her eyes still closed.

"I have a connection to Fox Hollow Road ... or whatever it's called."

"See, you're suppressing your emotions, not expressing them. You're making excuses for the truth." She turned on her side. She was tired. If he continued talking she'd never be able to fall asleep. He'd pass his nightmares on to her.

"You're wrong," he said softly.

"Oh, God, Nick. Go to sleep," she snapped. "You're starting to sound psychotic. All this nonsense about a mysterious road sign ... it's just a subliminal way of trying to heal, trying to heal old wounds. Missing information could simply mean insignificant information— and that is all it means."

Chapter Nine

Nick had eight uninterrupted hours of sleep and felt exhilarated. He looked out over the mountains as he drove down the long dirt drive. He loved mornings in the country, the slow fog lifting over the valley and beautiful herons flying low over the meadows, looking for a watery place to land.

He felt guilty when he thought about Jenna and all his unanswered questions, his omissions. He knew she was having a hard time trying to decipher his dreams, but so was he. He wished he had concrete answers to give her, but he didn't. And when those answers came, he wondered, would she accept them?

Nick found the road quickly this time. It was easy to spot the towering Pine Trees coming up the hill when you knew where to look for them. They were slightly bent toward each other and lost in a graceful sway by the wind's embrace.

He drove forward and pulled the jeep over in front of the meadow. He stopped between two maple trees. They seemed like introductions. He stared out over the dandelions and purple wildflowers, *...and if I stare long enough, perhaps, my life will unravel ... every damn moment of it ... right from the beginning.*

He leaned against the door of the jeep. He was distracted by his thoughts; he could almost hear someone calling to him.

Robbie?

He quickly glanced over the large open meadow. It was covered in a ghostly vapor, thicker than he'd ever seen the morning mist, more like a web. Clouds floated above his head, deliriously content. Way out where the trees graced the entrance to the woods, their branches swaying in the morning music of the wind, Nick thought he caught a glimpse of someone. He squinted his eyes and stared as hard as he could; a boy was there. He was absolutely there.

"Hey!" Nick called. His voice echoed and reverberated back.

The meadow was quiet. Off in a distance, some deer grazed on the grass and Nick realized how early it was. The sun was not yet warm enough for an August day. The deer stared back at him, then turned and ran past the arms of the dancing trees.

Nick pulled his sweatshirt over his head and walked toward the farmhouse. The boy had disappeared, vanished like lightning. Nick felt strange, as if he'd landed in some obscure place and nothing was where it should be. He didn't know what he was going to say if Quinn approached him, angry that he was trespassing. Perhaps, "just bird watching," he'd utter, or "great place for Tai Chi." Of course, he would apologize profusely for invading Quinn's privacy.

Private property? Sorry, didn't realize it. Please don't shoot me."

Memories were slowly surfacing for Nick, images that had always seemed alien and far were now clear, a medium-built broad-shouldered man with a lot of thick black hair. The vision of a man he thought might be Quinn. The man wore a uniform, and it was unsettling to think of him, the gun around his waist, the sound of his boots as he walked on the grass, the creak of leather.

Nick stopped and turned sharply behind him. He'd felt a presence. Sure enough, the boy had reappeared.

"Hey, kid." Nick walked to him. He had blond hair like Nick's own, and he was around ten years old. He was just standing there, smiling; his hands in the pockets of his jeans. His feet barely touched the ground. He was beautiful and light.

"I won't bite you." Nick said softly.

He heard a voice. *Robbie? Robbie? You were late, Robbie, you were late.*

Nick blinked only once, and the boy vanished.

"Robbie? Shit," he said. "Shit. Where the hell did you go?"

Come with me, Robbie. Please hurry! I waited so long, I waited forever. You were late, Robbie ... late.

"What?" Nick stood very still and listened. He looked over the immediate area, but the boy was too fast and must have run back toward the house, using some secret road that Nick couldn't see.

Nick closed his eyes.

Robbie?

Nick opened his eyes. There it was again; he was

being summoned. The boy stood before him. He was grinning and his straw like hair fell into his eyes.

"Good God," Nick said. "Are you real? Are you really mistaking me for Robbie? Shit, I'm seeing spirits, aren't I?"

Nick panicked and stumbled back over his own feet. He fell to the ground. When he got to his feet and looked around. The boy was gone.

"Hey you!" A voice called out.

The sound had come from the farmhouse. Nick saw Quinn on the porch as he turned. Quinn was staring back at him, peering with his hands on his forehead to block the glare from the morning sun. Nick was suddenly afraid. His heart began to race. Quinn got off the porch and started towards him, taking large, intimidating steps. Suddenly, pictures flashed across Nick's mind, flowing effortlessly, following each other in quick succession, like a slide show. People appeared – a woman, a man, children.

"What the hell?" he whispered. The more he looked at the house, the stronger the visions became ... a blue room with white curtains, white as hospital sheets. There were wooden planes on the shelves. *Daddy, he wanted to cry. I'm home! He wanted to shout.* He wanted to scream at the top of his lungs, *Daddy, I'm home! I'm home!*

Nick shook his head, as if trying to stop the visions, to slow them down so he could search them, hold onto them. He watched as Quinn got closer, the house in the background, remained a virtual photo album.

Nick stared at the old farmhouse. He dropped to his knees. "Mom?" he called out toward the kitchen, beyond the dining room — where a woman sat near the window, her light hair pushed back from her face and pinned behind her ears.

"What are you doing?" Quinn asked tentatively, as if he had stumbled upon a madman. "You talking to yourself?"

Nick stiffened. He stood up straight. The images left him. He breathed deeply. There were tears in his eyes. He tried to find more images of the house, but Quinn stood there like a solid piece of steel barring him from seeing anything but the expanse of his chest.

"Are you all right?" Quinn asked. "You look sick."

Nick held out his hand. Quinn did not take it.

"Who were you calling? Are you alone?"

"Nick Dowling," he said quickly. "I know Pete Shelby."

Quinn stared at Nick "Oh, yeah, that's right. He told me about you. Tells me you knew the Nichols?"

"No. No, I don't know them. I know the old road."

Quinn appeared to be looking at him through a microscope. "Oh."

"Nick studied Quinn's features as well. His hair was thick and almost completely gray. He was handsome in an irregular sort of way; a bit overweight. He had a very pronounced nose, like some prehistoric bird, and large dark eyes, like a bull.

"Andrew Quinn," Quinn said, as he extended his hand. "Were you born here, Mr. Dowling? There was a kid years ago, disappeared from here…."

"With my name…yes, I know. But no, I wasn't born here."

"Where are you from?" Quinn asked.

"Phoenicia," Nick said. He seemed to be quite a curiosity for Quinn, the way he was being stared at.

"Phoenicia?"

"Yes," Nick answered.

"Hmm, that's interesting. You're not from around here?"

"Well, Phoenicia isn't far." Nick looked more closely at Andrew Quinn. "Did you ever wear a uniform? You do look kind of familiar."

The question took Quinn by surprise; he looked as if he'd bitten into something foul. "What kind of uniform?"

"I'm not sure."

"So you think you've been on this road before, huh?" Quinn put his hands across his chest.

Nick stared at his arms and noticed how hairy they were. Briefly, he remembered a man with a lot of hair on his body carrying him somewhere he didn't want to go. He remembered scratching the man's arms and staring at the hair, so dark and thick he couldn't see any skin.

"It's familiar to me, but maybe it reminds me of someplace else, some place in Phoenicia." Nick laughed nervously. The sun had gotten warmer, and he felt like jogging. He felt like taking as much distance from Quinn as possible.

"Déjà vu?" Quinn laughed.

Nick forced a smile; it made his jaw hurt. "I hope you don't mind my coming up here?"

"You could be a ghost, you know?" He stared at Nick so hard it made Nick look away.

"Come any time you want. I don't believe in ghosts."

"Thank you," Nick said politely.

"I've got a good fishing stream up behind the house. You like to fish?"

"Thanks, I'll remember that. But I'm not much of a fisherman."

Quinn looked out toward the field, before turning back to stare at Nick. He stared at him for a long time before he spoke.

"Why come to Upstate New York if you don't like to fish?" Quinn asked suddenly and gruffly.

"It's a city thing."

Quinn stared at him blankly.

"To want to be in the country," Nick said slowly.

"Don't bring any dogs on my land. I don't like dogs. Their urine kills my grass. You don't have to leave, though. You can stay. Hell, have a picnic, if that's what you want. I don't give a damn. Land is land."

"Thanks."

"Well, bye now." Quinn said as he started to walk off, his steps heavy on the ground. "I've got things to do."

"Do you have a son, Mr. Quinn?" Nick asked suddenly. He wanted answers, answers that would prove him sane.

Quinn stopped in his tracks and turned.

"What's that?"

"Do you have a son, maybe a grandson?" he asked nervously. Yes, of course, the little blond boy must be related to Quinn, even though they seemed so unusually and disparately different.

Quinn put his tongue up under his lip and shook his head. "Nope. Why?"

"Oh, there was a little kid around here. I'm not sure of his age, ten, maybe."

"Lots of little kids around here," Quinn called over his shoulder as he turned and continued back to the house.

Nick heard the door to Quinn's porch slam shut. He walked back to his jeep and drove away from the farmhouse, but very slowly, as if he wasn't sure he really wanted to leave. He read the road sign as he drove out. Robert Nichols Road it read.

"How would I have known that nearly forty years ago, this road was called Fox Hollow?" he whispered. He would have been around ten years old then. But he couldn't remember ever being there. Yet why did he see so many visions of the farmhouse right before Quinn approached him? He knew exactly what it looked like inside the house, how the furniture was arranged, the color of the walls.

He'd never told Jenna the truth, never revealed that one morning he woke up in a hotel room in Chelsea, with one hundred dollars in his pocket and no name, no past and no memory of who the hell he was.

"Who checked me in?" he had asked the desk clerk.

The poor man had stuttered. "Why, you checked yourself in, Mr. Dowling."

Nick grabbed the register book. There beside his name were the words: Nick Dowling, words with no meaning or connection. Beside the column for hometown, he had written: Phoenicia, New York.

When Nick walked out into the snow on a cold morning in 1977, that's all the memory he had.

Quinn grabbed his shovel.

"You fucking creeps are playing games? You think you're going to frighten me, you fucking creeps."

The door slammed loudly behind him as he walked briskly behind the house and up into the woods with his wheelbarrow.

"I'm going to piss on your fucking graves," he said.

Way off in the distance he heard a car on the road.

"Who's that creep you sent here, huh?"

Quinn shoved the shovel into the ground and pulled up dirt.

"You playing games with me? I'll turn your fucking little ugly body of bones over to science, you hear?"

He dug deep, one shovel full of dirt and weeds and rocks. He didn't stop until he hit it.

"Shit," he said and fell to the ground. "I got it," he

called out toward the sky, sweating profusely, breathing too hard for a man his age.

The plastic bag wasn't heavy anymore though. At least he wouldn't have to strain himself. He hauled it out and threw it on the wheelbarrow: Bones, nothing but bones.

He'd find a better grave, a newer hole in the ground. Maybe he'd put it near that old stone marker up toward the end of the meadow, like a true grave.

"Why'd you bring him back?" Quinn cried. "Why'd you bring him back you little bastards?"

Chapter Ten

Jenna was anxious to call Sally that evening. Nick had to talk with her as soon as possible, especially after the crazy story he came home with, telling her that a ghost showed up in the field?

She'd fill Sally in on the details and ask if she could see Nick on Monday night. Nick was driving back to the city on Sunday, leaving Jenna the new truck to get around in. He had to work until Wednesday, but he'd taken the rest of the week off. He was using some accumulated sick time and saved up vacation days that would give him three more weeks of four-day weekends.

After Nick relayed his experience in the field with Quinn, and the image of the boy he'd seen, but possibly "hadn't really seen" — Jenna was concerned, perhaps more now than ever.

"It was incredible, Jenna," he'd said.

"Did you see the boy or not, Nick?"

"I can't be sure."

Jenna listened politely, but she silently interpreted his unbelievable story as some unresolved need for attention.

Childhood traumas, she thought as Nick described the inside of the farmhouse, believing his images to be telepathic communications from a dead boy.

She said very little, but she knew that the deep crevices above her nose were probably pronounced, and her lips were turned down, the way they always were before she started to weep.

"You don't believe me?" Nick said as he caught her expression. "You think I'm delusional?"

Jenna shook her head and put her arms around him very gently, as if he might resist.

"I don't believe in spirits." She laughed softly.

He broke away from her quickly. "But that's just it. I don't either. You know I don't believe in that crap. When you're dead, you're dead. I've always said that, Jenna. But this kid ... I don't know, he was like a shadow. But I knew what he looked like. I knew the color of his hair; I even knew the color of his eyes. That must be what a medium experiences, don't you think?"

"I haven't the foggiest," Jenna said, trying not to show apprehension.

"I tell you I saw him."

"Nick, I think you're experiencing hallucinations — a memory that's begun to resurface and it's so disturbing that you shield yourself from it with imaginary occurrences. The memory is quite traumatic, I'm sure."

Nick looked bewildered, as if he might say more but decided against it.

"I agree, I must have experienced something in my childhood that was probably very traumatic, and it could be connected to that boy's kidnapping. Maybe I saw him, and his friend murdered, and I've blocked it out."

"But you didn't live in New Kingston as a child, did you, Nick? You were raised in Phoenicia. That's what you told me."

Jenna was agitated, and she wanted to go into another room and slam a door, sit in a chair all alone and read a good book, escape into fiction. She watched as her husband seemed to struggle with some inner voice.

"Were you raised in Phoenicia, Nick?" she asked.

"Yes, yes, of course, I was raised in Phoenicia, but the farmhouse in New Kingston is still familiar. Maybe I just don't remember going to that field as a kid; maybe I was very young. Maybe someone took me there. How the hell would I know what that road used to be called nearly forty years ago, Jenna? I mean, the two towns are a bike ride apart. It's conceivable that I was there."

"Well, maybe you did see the house when you were young, and you developed a fantasy about it. Maybe the house signified something you desperately wanted and didn't have … a normal happy home life."

Nick collapsed down on the couch. "I know exactly what it looks like inside that house. Explain that."

"You don't have any proof that you're correct about what the house looks like inside, Nick."

He clenched his teeth and walked away. She wondered why it was at all important for him to remember a house. He was putting far too much onus on something that didn't really matter.

"Well, do you remember hearing anything about the kidnapping? It must have been really big news around here," Jenna said as she walked to him and took his hand.

"Maybe photographs of the inside of the house were published and you retained the images."

"I'm getting a communication from that boy."

"The ghost?"

"Yes, maybe."

Nick watched as Jenna threw herself back into the cushions. He decided not to be intimidated by her rigidity. He began to wonder if he'd found a clue to his past. Maybe Phoenicia had been a mistake. Could it be possible that his memories were resurfacing? Was he Nicky Dowling? But the boy called him Robbie, and Pete said that Nicky was a savant; he wasn't a savant.

"I need to get inside the house," he said. "It will trigger something. I'm sure of it. That boy somehow communicated to me what the house looked like on the inside." *Either that or it's my own memory rising to the surface. God, maybe I lived there.*

Jenna stared at him. "Okay, let's make it our business to get inside the house, then."

He reached out for her hand.

"Quinn said I could come up any time. Let's go up this weekend, find an excuse to use his bathroom or something."

"I have never accepted psychic phenomena as anything to take seriously. I believe people are intuitive and I believe in coincidence, but the buck stops there. You seem to be giving everything a metaphysical explanation. I never thought you had any interest in that kind of nonsense. I'm sorry, but that's how I feel. I don't believe in ghosts. You either saw that boy or you didn't."

He put his head in his hands for a while before he spoke. Finally, he looked up at her.

"I saw him," he said.

"I'm sorry. I don't mean to sound haughty about it."

"Didn't you invite Laurie up for the week-end?" he asked.

He watched as Jenna looked as if she might burst into tears. "What has Laurie got to do with any of this?"

Nick ran his hands through his hair. He knew the relationship between them had always been strained. Jenna constantly admitted that she had always felt shut out of her sister's relationship with their mother — both Laurie and Doris had been so overly emotional, according to Jenna. They were both obsessed with the occult — reading their astrology forecasts together like little witches over a cauldron. Nick had listened patiently over the years as Jenna relayed how her sister and their mother would sit cross-legged on the den floor every Saturday night with a Ouija board between them, pretending to conjure up dead spirits. "Isn't that just the stupidest thing?" she'd ask him.

Jenna had always had a low tolerance level for Doris and Laurie's interest in what Jenna termed "paranormal babble." As a result, Nick was constantly on his guard around Laurie, going out of his way not to take her side over Jenna's, always reacting just as Jenna reacted to her sister, with an exasperated, "Oh, Laurie, really!" But, now, he was curious to talk to someone who had even a basic knowledge of psychic phenomena.

"I just wanted to get her take on things," he said defensively.

He watched as Jenna went to the phone.

"Can you see Sally on Monday night if she's available? I'm going to call her right now. I should have called her a lot sooner."

Nick looked out of the large glass window. The sky

was covered in a misty gray light. One lone star twinkled back at him. He might as well talk to Sally. Hopefully, that would appease Jenna for a while.

"Therapy is the answer, not my outrageous sister and not some little ghost playing hide and seek in your imagination. We'll go out to the house this weekend and see if we can get the redneck to show it to us, and you'll see Sally, deal?"

Chapter Eleven

Nick had never seen Sally's office before. He was impressed, but not surprised that it would look like something out of *Architectural Digest*. He stood back and admired the art, a lot of Byzantine type cherubs hanging over plush beige upholstered couches and wonderful old thick wooden tables that looked authentically scarred, and historically correct. When he heard Sally enter the room he turned abruptly toward her.

She had aged very little since he'd last seen her. She looked as if she swam a mile each day. He knew she was well over sixty, but she still had one of those long, lean swimmer's bodies and an open, unlined face.

"Nick? Good to see you again," Sally said as she extended her hand.

Nick noticed that she wore high heels, and her stature

was most impressive.

"Sally." He smiled politely as he grasped her hand firmly and shook it.

She led him into her office, as comfortably decorated as her waiting room, and much larger, a rather elegant square room. Nick noticed a buttercup-colored leather chair and sat.

"People sure do spend money on their psyches, don't they?" he said.

"Would you prefer to lie down?" she asked, ignoring his comment.

Nick shook his head. He did not want to be treated like a patient and resented the implication. He was distracted and he wanted to get his fifty minutes of Sally Harnick over with. He needed time alone so he could probe his mind for any memories that connected him to Fox Hollow. He was convinced that he'd found clues to his past. If only he could figure out what it all meant, nothing of which he was going to discover lying on Sally Harnick's couch.

"Your good taste doesn't surprise me," he said with a smile, looking beyond her to a beautiful wooden statue of a nude woman.

"I hope the décor relaxes my patients. That's my intention."

"I'm not one of your patients, Sally."

"No, not formally, but isn't that why you're here, Nick, to talk to me?"

"Yes, at Jenna's insistence."

Sally leaned back and brushed the hair from her face. He watched as she looked at him with resolved patience, waiting for him to speak. He felt anxious as he crossed his legs and remained silent.

"So? What's going on, Nick?" she finally asked.

"Actually, nothing's going on. I've had some disturbing dreams. I suspect Jenna's told you about them?"

"Why don't you tell me about them?"

Nick blew some air out of his mouth and uncrossed his legs. "Which ones?" he asked.

She looked surprised.

"Well, there are the 'since we bought the house dreams,' and then, there are the 'before we bought the house' dreams."

Sally smiled slightly. "Let's begin with your most recent dreams, Nick ... I assume those would be the 'since we bought the house dreams?'"

"Okay." He sat up straight in his chair. "I'm on a dark road and a gravitational force comes out of the sky and sucks me up."

"Those dreams started right after you bought the house?" Sally asked.

"Yes."

"Gravitational force?"

"Yes."

"What ... like a vacuum cleaner?"

"Sort of."

"Go on."

"That's it."

"What happens to you?"

"I'm never returned."

Sally leaned forward in her chair. She wasn't smiling, but she wasn't frowning either.

"Does this gravitational force ever materialize into a person?" she asked.

"In a sense," Nick said quietly.

"And?"

"It's frightening."

"How so?"

Nick thought back. Images came to mind.

"Well, the person is grotesque, actually. He has a big head and it's dented; it's a very strange head, too large for his body."

"What about his eyes, and his ears?"

"His eyes are very dark, like black holes."

"What about his ears?"

"He doesn't have any ears."

"I see. Is this thing a man?"

"In the dream, he seems to be. He's very powerful."

"What did your father look like?"

Nick wanted to laugh but didn't. How could he tell her that he had no father, not one he could remember anyway? He shook his right hand; it had become numb.

"Non-descript. Gray. What does this have to do with my father?"

"Gray hair?"

"No, he was bald," he lied. "But he always looked gray to me, like he was going to fade away." Nick couldn't help but smile to himself. That was a good one, a shrink should like that.

"What's wrong with your hand, Nick?"

"Fell asleep, I guess."

"How did you feel about your father?"

"Look. This isn't about my father," Nick said quickly and stood. He walked to the window and looked down on Central Park West.

Sally stared at his profile a while before she continued.

"Then what is it about, Nick?" she asked.

Nick slowly turned to her.

"I'm not clear on it yet, but I think it has something to do with a kidnapping upstate."

"Go on."

Nick walked back to the buttercup chair and sat. He leaned forward and looked into her eyes.

"I think I'm psychic — I know things about a crime that happened around 1967. There were these two children, boys. They were kidnapped up state."

"And what does that kidnapping have to do with your dream?"

Nick got up again and walked back to the window.

"I'm not sure yet."

"But you think they're connected?"

"Yes, I do. Look, these two boys were either kidnapped or murdered in their back yard and buried there. The crime was never solved, and the bodies were never recovered. Maybe the boy is trying to tell me who did it."

He looked at her. She appeared to be thoroughly absorbed. "I can't put the pieces together yet, but I feel like this kid is leading me toward something ... something I should know."

"And how does this kidnapping connect to the alien monsters you see in your nightmares?" she asked as she sat back.

"Aliens? Did I say anything at all about aliens?"

"That's what they sound like to me ... these grotesque creatures without ears."

Nick decided to play with her and avoid shocking her further.

"We don't really know what aliens look like, do we, Sally? In a child's mind, something or someone that hurts him is a monster, an alien of sorts. Well, maybe, I'm picking up this child's nightmares. Can you be open to something like that, Sally ... that I'm psychic?"

"I'd like to discuss those creatures you see in your dreams."

"Creatures? Is that what I called them?"

"Well, there's a perception," she began slowly, "wouldn't you agree, that aliens don't have ears?"

"There's a perception of what God looks like, too," he said. "Do you believe that as well? My God could look like a bug. Your God could look like a man." He chuckled.

"It's not important what I think God looks like, Nick."

"Bullshit!" he said suddenly.

Sally paused a moment. "Bullshit?"

"We all care too much about what God looks like. He's perfect, Sally, like Charlton Heston. But aliens? Ugly, weird little creatures. Well, if there are aliens among us, they'd better run for the hills. We'd kill them before we'd let them integrate on our planet and prove their existence. Socialize with buggy looking monsters? Ha! Can you see that? Caucasian, African American, Asian and *Other. N*ow, that's funny." He laughed loudly. "We'd need a new box, wouldn't we, like white, black, yellow, or *gray*? Gray Power!"

Nick sat back in his chair feeling like he'd just jogged a three- minute mile.

"Perhaps we should have a box that says arthropods?" she said, clearly humoring him.

"I never gave it much thought before, but I think we don't know shit about the universe ... or God for that matter."

"So you think a space ship landed and aliens got out, Nick?" she asked him softly. "In your dreams, I mean."

"I don't know." He put his head down and stared at the design on her expensive antique rug. It was like a Rorschach. "I just don't know."

Sally studied him, clearly concluding that he must be bonkers.

"I'm not crazy, Sally. I'm just repeating my

experiences because you asked, but since we bought the house upstate, I've changed. I've become attuned to something quite extraordinary, and I don't have any concrete explanation for it." He punctuated his words carefully.

"Let's get back to these two murdered little boys," Sally said as she took her glasses off and put the stem to her lip.

"Okay."

"Describe them for me."

"Well the one I see, he looks a little like me," Nick said casually.

Sally put her glasses back on. "Then it's important to retrieve all the knowledge we can about this particular boy. Would you agree?"

"Yes, I would agree."

"And does this boy have a name?"

"Nicky," he said softly. "He calls to his friend, Robbie." Nick stared into her eyes. "They say he had my name, Nicky, Nicky Dowling."

"Could you be talking to yourself, Nick?"

"I talked to a boy." He didn't say it at all angrily. He was feeling more despondent than angry.

Sally leaned back away from him. He knew what she was thinking. He was clearly on his way to a serious breakdown, and he would never trust the process of therapy enough to seek help. He also knew that that was what she'd relay to Jenna.

Chapter Twelve

Laurie Rubin pulled down a well-worn suitcase from the top shelf of her closet and started packing for a long weekend upstate with her sister and Nick. She folded a sweatshirt and jeans and placed them carefully on top of a pair of long-sleeved cotton pajamas. She remembered how cold nights in the Catskills could be and haphazardly wondered if she should pack flannel instead. But she seemed unable to reach a decision; her thoughts were too much on her last conversation with Jenna. All of a sudden, the perfect husband is talking to spirits, or as Jenna would have her believe — having a nervous breakdown. Laurie always thought there was more to Nick than his polite tolerance of her, no doubt inspired by the iron hand Jenna had around his affections. So, now the guy has some soul, and her straight-laced sister was doing what the rest of the world does to those with the gift — turns it to crap.

So be it. Something was now unraveling her sister's perfect world and exposing a vulnerability that Laurie had never seen before. For all the years her sister had been married, everything had been perfect. She and Nick never fought, and their daughter never got on her nerves. Her husband was disgustingly perfect, and sex was as constant and all-consuming as it had been when the gorgeous Nick Dowling had first swept her off her feet.

What bullshit! Laurie thought as she picked up two bottles of *Cloudy Bay*, a crisp and expensive Sauvignon Blanc from wine rich New Zealand. She had spent days searching for the popular vintage and had extravagantly splurged on it. She carefully packed the bottles between her sweatshirt and her cotton PJs. Jenna rarely drank wine, but Nick would appreciate it. He was the connoisseur. Jenna would probably seethe at what she would over sensitively interpret as an insult, but she'd seethe quietly, trying to appear as perfectly composed as a goddamn shrink confronting Jack The Ripper — pretending not to notice that Laurie had brought nothing for her but the perfunctory hug, the sisterly peck on the cheek, and her nonsensical acceptance of Nick's new psychic ability to lift the veil of the spirit world and confront lost souls.

Nick had offered to pick Laurie up at her apartment and drive her upstate. She was grateful not to have to rent a car and incur yet more expenses; not when she'd recently thrown several new pant suits on to her Macy's charge card and needed new headshots. She had just landed a fabulous part off- Broadway. But who ever knew how long a show would run? She tried not to be pessimistic, but she couldn't help it. She'd been in the theatre too many years not to be. Anyway, she was eager to speak with Nick alone, out of Jenna's earshot, and was surprised that her control-freak sister had allowed Adonis to park his chariot at her door and bend her ear about his musings with the dead for three long uninterrupted hours.

They'd been idling over the George Washington Bridge for twenty minutes, making small talk, before Laurie finally reached over and turned the volume down on the radio.

"Tell me what's going on, Nick," she said solemnly

She watched as a smile broke out across his face and she wondered just how honest he was going to be with her, Jenna's sister; knowing he would always protect Jenna from any embarrassment, especially where she was concerned.

"What do you mean?"

He was playing with her now, even though he knew he was with the expert, a believer — and someone to whom he could really talk "paranormal babble," as Jenna so graciously termed it.

"Are you psychic, Nick, or are you crazy?"

He laughed one of those big hearty laughs and Laurie could see the creases near his eyes — George Clooney creases — all-American-boy-ages beautifully creases — Nick Dowling creases. Grrrrrrrrr, Mr. Handsome, better now than ever, creases. Damn it, but Jenna always managed to get the guy, aside from the fact that it was Laurie who had always been termed "the pretty one," not as smart as her summa cum laude sister, but a real little dimpled, brunette dish, whom Jenna had always berated for spending more time on her eyebrows than her emotional growth.

"What do *you* think?" he finally asked and turned to grin at her as the car stood in a community of honking horns and he shifted into park.

"Being psychic is a gift, Nick. I don't take it lightly."

"I agree," he said, implying a more serious tone.

"Usually, people are born with an ability to commune with dead people. It's not something that just happens to you in middle age," she said, watching his expression closely. "But I suppose it could."

"I'm not aware of ever being sensitive to being some sort of a medium before," he said, as the traffic slowly advanced and he shifted back into drive.

"But you could be now, is that what you're saying?" Laurie asked.

Nick nodded.

"You saw the spirit of a boy?" She turned to look at him. She needed to see as much of his expressions as she could. After all, this could be one colossal joke her jack ass sister decided to play on her, and she'd catch the grin as it broke out across his face.

"Is that what Jenna told you?"

"Well, Jenna told me that you're having a breakdown and she insisted you talk to Sally Harnick, who probably reiterated that." She looked at him carefully, searching perhaps, for any possibility that he was teasing her. "She mentioned something about the ghost of a boy, though."

She watched him as he laughed. He was obviously trying to downplay his experiences, if in fact, they were real.

"I've had some nightmares," he said and shrugged.

"Jenna mentioned it," Laurie said. "What are the nightmares about?"

"Jenna didn't give you any details?"

"No. She just said you're having nightmares and you think you've seen a spirit, some boy who was kidnapped upstate and possibly murdered. Is he in your nightmares?"

"No. The nightmares are about something else."

"What else?"

"A force that sucks me up and takes me away, odd looking beings too."

Laurie looked beyond Nick and out over the Hudson River.

"Do your nightmares ever feel like you're being taken … lifted?" she asked him thoughtfully and slowly.

"Lifted?"

"Yes," she said quickly.

"You could say that." He turned to glance at her profile. "You want to hear this from the beginning?"

"Yes, I would."

Nick brought his attention back to the traffic and spoke low, as if he might be overheard. He relayed his experiences in Fox Hollow, detailing everything — how compelled he was to turn on to it, to follow a road that no longer existed, one that hadn't been called Fox Hollow for nearly forty years.

Laurie continued to stare, no longer at him, but out toward the skyline of the city. Neither of them spoke for several seconds.

"Jenna mentioned something about your sense of time," she said, breaking the silence.

"My sense of time was off that night, yes."

"Missing time? You can't account for hours, maybe even days?"

Nick looked at her and raised his brow.

"No, nothing that elaborate. But I was on the road for over three hours. It felt like minutes. It was a very strange sensation, to say the least."

"That's happened to me," Laurie said.

"Really? And so, what was it? What caused it?" he asked.

"I thought I was sleeping, but who sleeps for thirty-two hours? I'll never forget it; I must have been abducted. I have no memory of waking up and going back to sleep at all."

Nick turned and stared at her. "You are so strange, Laurie. And here I am, becoming just like you."

"Why aren't you taking me seriously, lover boy? I'm on your side."

"I'm sorry," he said. "I've had a lot of old programming not to take you seriously."

"You're forgiven." She studied him intently. "Look, many people say they've been abducted."

"Yes, I know," he said as the car finally turned onto the Palisades Parkway, and they picked up speed. "I've heard that."

Laurie continued to stare at him a while before she spoke again. She never would have believed this of Nick. He was clearly telling the truth.

"I think you've had an abduction experience, Nick. That's what your dream sounds like to me."

"What about the spirit I saw? That was no alien. That was a boy — a boy who was probably murdered in Fox Hollow nearly forty years ago."

"I don't know how it all relates, but I do think you've experienced something that is other worldly. Maybe being abducted gives us some kind of psychic ability to see the dead. You should contact my friend Sam; he might have some answers."

"Sam?" he asked with an edge of anxiety in his tone.

"Yes. He investigates strange phenomena," she told

him."

"Like people who talk to little dead boys?"

"Yes. He also investigates alien sightings. He interviews people who have had abduction experiences, or anything supernatural. He has photographs, actual sightings on record of aliens, ghosts, stuff like that. He can hypnotize people to find out if they've actually experienced legitimate abductions."

"Legitimate abductions?" He tried to laugh. "Is that an oxymoron?

"Look, Nick, there are people who swear they've been abducted, swear they've seen beings from another planet. Sam has written books on it. You should read one of his books."

"Well, I have had these thoughts that seem to come out of nowhere," he said slowly.

"What thoughts?"

"Well, about aliens, actually. Sometimes, when I close my eyes I see fleeting images of shadowy people. You could say they look like aliens. They're the monsters in my nightmares, but what is most frightening about them is their resemblance to us."

"Some say they are us, what we become."

"I can't explain it ... but I don't think the boy is real. I saw him but he isn't real. Maybe he's an alien?"

Laurie remained silent for a while before she spoke again. She was being thoughtful, making a concerted effort not to be impulsive. "But he looks like you or I?"

"He does. He certainly doesn't look like a monster."

"I dated Sam Hollander last year. Do you want me to call him? He lives in Manhattan. He's actually a doctor. He's got a PhD in psychology. It didn't work out between us, but I wouldn't feel funny calling him."

He turned to her. "Will you come with me to the

road?" he asked. "I think you might be able to help me. Maybe your sensitivity to psychic phenomena will bring that little kid out of the woods, and you'll see him too, and we can question him."

"Jenna won't approve," she said, "about you and I going off together to that mysterious road to conjure up spirits."

She noticed that he picked up some speed and passed the car in front of them.

"I need your help," he said adamantly. "I have to understand what's happening to me. Jenna sees my experience as a psychological problem. You know as well as I do that it has nothing to do with some neurotic sense-memory."

"You tell her you're going off alone with me and I don't want to be around to hear the explosion. She'll think we're bonding — sharing something she finds distasteful, like Mom and me and our interest in the theatre and other 'airy fairy nonsense' as Jenna so tactfully puts it."

"I'll deal with Jenna," he said. "You deal with the 'airy fairy nonsense.'"

"And what about Sam, should I contact him?"

"I'll think about it," he said.

Chapter Thirteen

One could cut the tension with a knife that evening. Jenna was so distracted by Nick's obsession with Fox Hollow that she barely took any notice of the wine he put on ice and raved about for hours. The sisterly peck on the cheek was even returned with a brief hug. Jenna even drank the damn wine and grinned admiringly at her sister when she told them she had just landed a role in an off-Broadway show.

"So, you're finally getting the work you deserve." Jenna said.

Laurie looked up. Jenna's support was surprising. "Wouldn't you know it," Laurie said. "Everyone is calling me now that I've developed character lines. I'm even reading for a television pilot on Tuesday, and we start rehearsals on the play in a few weeks."

Jenna threw her leg over Nick's, appearing more manic than Laurie had seen her in recent years.

"So what's the play about?" Jenna asked.

Laurie wondered what had brought on this sudden interest in her career. She was certain it was insincere, as usual. Laurie's pursuit of acting work had always been a sore spot; something Jenna always said she was wasting her time with. Jenna had always seemed only mildly interested in whether or not her sister was making any progress in her chosen profession, preferring instead to berate her for her hapless love life, her destructive choices and her completely irresponsible outlook on protecting her assets for a long and lonely old age.

"It's about a dysfunctional family. The husband goes mad and fantasizes that his wife is having an affair."

Laurie noticed that Nick had suddenly jumped to his feet and walked toward the kitchen.

"How sweet," Jenna said.

Laurie gave her sister a confused stare. "Well, actually not. He winds up killing her."

"How gruesome." Jenna pinched her eyebrows together and scowled.

"God, how is it that we can make entertainment out of murder?" Nick called from the kitchen.

Laurie felt disappointed; she expected a bit more enthusiasm.

"Actually, the play is very poetic," Laurie called back.

"What the hell is poetic about killing your wife?" Nick yelled.

Laurie was surprised at the anger in Nick's tone. "It's a play, Nick, just a play," she said. "There is poetry in violence, you know, think Shakespeare."

"Does he really kill her?" Nick poured himself a full glass of wine as he took a seat beside his wife.

"Yes, he kills her," Laurie said.

"Ah." Nick sipped his wine and looked off.

"Why didn't he just divorce her?" Jenna asked.

"Where would the drama be in that?" Laurie gave her a smile.

"Who do you play, the wife?" Jenna leaned forward on her elbows, possessively resting one of them on Nick's leg.

Laurie shook her head and reached her glass out to Nick for more wine.

"No, I have the lead. The shrink." She gave her sister a broad grin.

"The shrink? Oh, really." Jenna found that hysterical and fell back into the cushions; her laughter rose manically.

"So, does the bastard get caught?" Nick asked.

"Well, yes. The play is in flashback, sort of like *Equus.* Remember *Equus*? I know it doesn't sound terribly original, but it's a great play." Laurie smiled, hating herself for feeling she had to defend it.

"It sounds a bit stupid. What makes murdering your wife at all interesting?" Nick shrugged his shoulders and raised his eyes.

"Does murder upset you, Nick?" Laurie asked suddenly. His reaction had pissed her off. "Because it's not the evening news, it's just a Broadway play."

Nick turned white, the color of chalk. He stared at her with a lost expression. Then he seemed to snap to. "Don't mean to be rude," he said.

"This is the first lead I've had in seven years."

Much to her surprise, Jenna reached over Nick to grab her hand.

"You'll be great. I know it. You'll knock em' dead. Won't she, Nick?"

"Dead? Well, I hope not literally." He managed a weak laugh as he raised his wine in an elaborate toast, and they clinked the tip of their glasses together, several times. Then, before Laurie could taste the wine on her tongue, Nick brought up the road and the farmhouse in what appeared to Laurie as a dismissal of her recent stroke of good luck. It was almost as if something about the play had disturbed him.

"About tomorrow....." he said.

Laurie was surprised at Nick's indifference to her; it was her sister who usually brushed her off, revealing her typical polite interest in her career. So it would seem, her life was worth less than five minutes to Jenna or her husband. Neither one of them asked the obvious, who's directing the play? Where's it being performed? When does it open? Anyone I know in the cast? Or whatever. That was usual for Jenna, but not for Nick. But then again, she assumed, he had a lot on his mind.

"Yes, we're all going out to Fox Hollow tomorrow to search for the ghost, right Nick?" Jenna blurted out.

Laurie was surprised that Jenna would be so glib about it and wondered just what form of therapy she was using on Nick. She watched as Nick walked over to their wall of windows and slowly turned to his wife. The backdrop behind him was a show of stars, laughing flirtatiously, blinking like a hundred children in the sky with pocket lights.

"No," he said unwaveringly. "*Laurie* and I are going out to the farmhouse tomorrow. I need to get at the truth, and you, my dear wife, will be a distraction."

Jenna sat forward, nearly knocking her wine to the floor. "Oh, really? A distraction to whom — you, Laurie, or the little ghost?"

"I'm just trying to get at the bottom of this, Jenna,"

Nick said.

"You don't think I need to get to the bottom of this? And besides, we made a deal."

"But you don't believe in other possibilities," Nick said. "We're coming at this from two different angles. I need Laurie's sensitivity right now."

"Sensitivity to what? To the occult? C'mon."

Jenna's temper was clearly rising, and then, maybe it was too much white wine because she got up very suddenly and stumbled.

"Easy does it," Nick said as he ran to hold her up.

Jenna looked into his eyes. Laurie could see that Jenna didn't seem to be able to focus on him.

"You don't really believe there's any validity to this crap?" Jenna asked.

Nick turned to look at Laurie. "This is just my point, just what I'm talking about."

Jenna turned sharply and started up the stairs. "You're being as stupid as Laurie can be when she talks about all that voodoo nonsense," she yelled back over her shoulder, her slippers pounding against the wooden stairs.

"Jenna," Nick hollered, as he followed behind her, carefully reaching for her arm so she wouldn't trip again, "I need to go alone. You know that!"

"Bringing Laurie is not going out there alone!" Jenna screamed, right before she disappeared behind the door to their bedroom with Nick at her heels.

Laurie stared out over her coffee the next morning. She had never been aware of any tension between Nick and Jenna before, but now, she could see that this was no joke. Nick was experiencing something that was deeply disturbing for Jenna.

"Did you make enough for two?" Nick asked as he came down the stairs and walked into the kitchen, giving Laurie a tentative smile.

Laurie nodded. As she poured the coffee into a mug, she spoke to him over her shoulder.

"How is she this morning?" she asked.

"She's not used to drinking. She didn't mean to be unpleasant."

Laurie slid the mug over the counter toward him. "I'm used to it," she said as she got back on the stool and stared at him. "Is she coming down?"

"She's getting dressed." he said.

Laurie looked at him for a moment before it registered. "She's dressing? Not because she's joining us, I hope?"

Nick sipped his coffee and avoided answering her.

"Nick, do you want to get to the bottom of this or what?"

"She's promised to behave herself."

"Jenna doesn't keep promises."

"You're being unfair, Laurie. I've got to live with the woman. How can I include you and not my own wife in this craziness?"

"Is it craziness, Nick?"

Laurie watched as Nick cupped the mug in his hands and put it gently back on the counter.

"No, it is not craziness. It's real to me, and perhaps to you, but to Jenna my experiences are something she can explain away psychologically. I've got to let her watch me have a mid-life crisis — or whatever it is she thinks I'm going through. I've got to let her think she's helping me get through it. I just can't shut her out."

Laurie heard Jenna's footsteps on the stairs and went

for another cup of coffee. When she turned back around to sit at the counter she caught the end of Jenna's kiss across Nick's cheek.

"Did you sleep well, Laurie?" Jenna asked, as she slid onto the stool next to her husband and looked at her sister impishly.

Nick got up and slid open the glass doors to the deck. Laurie felt the cool morning air on her arms.

"I'm going out to lie in the sun," he said as he turned to them. "Let me know when you two are ready to leave. We're going to have a picnic."

"You think that Quinn guy will let us use his meadow to picnic?" Laurie asked.

"I think so. He seemed accommodating — told me to fish in his stream. We just have to figure out how to get inside his house. I'm going to sketch it exactly the way I saw it in the vision I had … then we'll see if my sketch matches my vision … and if it does…" He grinned at Laurie. "I'm going to throw up!"

Laurie laughed with him and turned back to Jenna. Jenna avoided her eyes and watched Nick slide the doors shut behind him.

"I'm not used to drinking wine," Jenna said.

"Not exactly an apology," Laurie said. "I don't appreciate your calling my beliefs nonsense, Jenna."

"I'm sorry, Laurie. But don't shut me out of this. This isn't going to turn out to be two against one, the way it was with you, Mom and me."

"You think anything paranormal is a bunch of shit, that's why Mom and I excluded you."

"Yes, but Nick's experiences are not a bunch of shit. He needs help. Sally said he might be having a break down, and that it could be serious."

"I told you what I thought about that pompous ass's

opinion."

Jenna glared at Laurie and went for the pot of coffee on the counter.

"This is not really your concern, Laurie," Jenna said sharply. "Nick just thought you'd have some insight, that's all."

"Well, that must have been why I was invited here. Certainly, it wasn't to spend time with my sister. I haven't spent time with you since we were forced into it by the confines of childhood."

"I invited you out. Nick didn't. I always invite you out, don't I?"

"What do you mean *always*, Jenna, you've only owned the house less than six months," Laurie said, as she stood and leaned in toward her sister. "This is my second visit, and I'm only here because it's an emergency."

"Precisely," Jenna smiled. "But still, on my invitation."

"Tell me this, Miss Shrink, don't you think that subconsciously you knew that I'm the only one who can make some sense of your husband's behavior, and that's why you want me here for this *second* visit?"

"Oh, please!" Jenna screeched and Laurie noticed that it had startled Nick, who sat upright in his chair and peered back in through the glass.

Laurie knew she was pushing it, but she slowly reached out for Jenna's arm.

"You need to let me have this time with Nick. He knows I'm sensitive to psychic phenomena and you're not."

"What?"

"I don't ask you for much but trust me for once in your life. Nick's problems are not going to be solved with a little therapy. This is very complex. I think I can help him understand what's going on because I've had experiences similar to his."

"You're serious, aren't you?"

Jenna looked at Laurie for a long time before she walked to the large glass doors and opened them.

"Nick, honey," she called. "Perhaps we should leave Laurie behind … let her enjoy this beautiful sunny day on the deck? You and I can handle Mr. Quinn by ourselves."

Laurie watched as Jenna turned back to her and slid the glass doors closed.

"Paranormal babble. I can't take it seriously, Laurie. If I leave him alone with you God knows what outrageous tales he'll come home with."

"Your beliefs are a deterrent to what we're trying to accomplish."

"Be that as it may, I'm coming with you."

Chapter Fourteen

Andrew Quinn was on the porch of the old Colonial farmhouse. As they drove up the drive, they could see him, appearing small, then at once, overbearingly large. Quinn put his newspaper down and squinted in their direction.

Nick felt a gulp in his throat as he stopped the car in front of the house and waved at Quinn. The old man eyed him oddly and did not wave back.

"That guy gives me the creeps," Nick said through his teeth. He wondered if he'd ever get Quinn to invite him inside the house. Maybe they'd have to stage an emergency. He watched as Quinn begrudgingly walked toward the car.

"You forget something the other day?" Quinn asked as he put one hand on the door and leaned down toward

Nick.

Nick put on his friendliest smile as he stuck his head out the window. He introduced Quinn to his wife and heard Jenna say she'd been admiring his house.

"That's my sister-in-law, Laurie, in the back." Nick said quickly. His grin was so wide he was sure that only his gums showed.

Quinn looked inside the car and craned his neck. He acknowledged Laurie with a grunt.

"Well, what can I do for you?" he asked, turning back to Nick. "Pete Shelby's not here yet. I expect him soon, though. You looking for him?"

"Well, actually," Nick said. "We wondered if we might picnic in your meadow?" He paused and stared at Quinn, who did not respond. "We brought some sandwiches and soda, no alcohol. We'll clean up after ourselves. Promise."

"Huh?" Quinn straightened up and stepped away from the car.

"Remember? You said I could come back and use the field, fish or whatever? Look, it's okay. We don't want to intrude. It's just that it's such a great meadow for a picnic." Nick laughed uncomfortably. "Our land isn't flat enough, right Jenna? Mostly we use the deck," he said, smiling back at Quinn. "It's not the same."

"Your house is quite wonderful, Mr. Quinn. What year was it built?" Jenna called out.

Quinn leaned into the window and frowned at her. "Don't know. Late 1800s, maybe."

"So, you knew the Nichol's?" Nick asked nonchalantly and turned off the engine.

Quinn nodded. "Well, sure. I bought the house from them, didn't I?"

"Yeah, Pete told me that. He said they owned a lot of land," Nick said.

"All of Fox Hollow. Sixty or so acres left; that's all I have."

"Terrible thing about their son, wasn't it?" Nick shook his head and gave Quinn a solemn frown.

Quinn's eyebrows came together, and he pulled his lips over to the left side of his face."Yeah," he said.

"They say he's buried around here, huh?" Nick asked, as an aside, staring at Quinn's rosebushes, as if he had little interest in the answer.

"Nothing buried around here," Quinn said.

"Well, that's true. They never did find any bodies, did they?" Nick tapped his fingers on the steering wheel and looked off. He didn't want it to appear as if his idle conversation mattered at all.

"I don't keep up on old news." Quinn looked bored.

Nick took off his sunglasses and met Quinn's eyes. "Can we picnic in your meadow, sir?"

"Sure," he said, after a pause. "What the hell, I don't believe in ghosts, but don't let me find no litter out there, you here? And don't disturb my land. You can't pick my flowers, not even my wildflowers, you hear?"

"I give you my word, sir. We'll treat your meadow like our own," Nick said, feeling foolish, as he held his hand out to shake Quinn's, who ignored the gesture and walked away.

Laurie looked out over the mountains, they appeared peacefully non- threatening. The sun was warm, and the summer breeze moved quietly through the trees. She closed her eyes and listened to the branches welcome the wind and sway in soft acceptance.

"It's odd what he said, isn't it?" she asked.

"Said about what?" Nick turned to her.

"He said, 'I don't believe in ghosts.' Odd thing to say, wasn't it?"

"Yeah, but he's a weird old man and I've got the dead kid's name."

Nick stared back at the house as he sketched. Jenna lay on a blue blanket, her head on Nick's jacket.

"I don't feel the presence of any spirits, Nick," Laurie said.

"Why don't you go into a trance state, meditate, levitate, or something like that?" Jenna said, without opening her eyes.

Laurie and Nick exchanged an amused smile.

"Here," he said as he handed his drawing pad to Laurie. "That's what I think the house looks like inside. Quinn has probably furnished it differently, but the layout should be the same. It's amazing, the way I can see it. It's like a memory."

"You think the boy is sending you the images telepathically?" Laurie asked.

Nick nodded; despite the fact he was thinking otherwise. He couldn't help but wonder if knowing what the inside of the house looked like was actually his own memory returning, and it had nothing to do with the boy's spirit. *Maybe, he'd been one of those kidnapped children?*

"We have to get inside then," Laurie said.

"I hate to be a spoil sport," Jenna interrupted, with her eyes still closed, "but all these old houses look alike."

Nick ignored Jenna's comment. "Well, isn't this just perfect," he said.

"What?" Laurie asked, following his eyes.

"That may be our ticket in." Nick quickly stood up and waved as Pete's Explorer came to a stop at the edge of the meadow. Pete stared out at them through the open window.

"What are you doing here?" he called out to Nick.

"Oh, hi," Nick said as he jogged over to Pete's jeep, trying his best to appear like an old friend.

"Quinn told me I could picnic out here in his field," Nick said, a little too excitedly.

Pete looked confused. "Why?"

"Well, I don't know. It's a pretty field, sort of like Central Park. We're homesick, I guess." Nick knew he sounded absurd.

"Well, whatever turns you on."

"Remember when you volunteered to show us Quinn's farmhouse?"

"Yeah?"

"My wife, Jenna, she's really dying to see it today. You know, she didn't feel well the last time we were here. She loves old houses. Do you think you could show us inside the house? She'd appreciate it."

"I thought she needed an invitation from the old man?"

"Well, can you get us one?"

"Look, his house is not for sale."

"No, no, no. I don't want to buy it. My wife just wants to see it, that's all. You know how women are about houses." Nick grinned and winked at the same time.

Pete shrugged. "Well, sure, sure. Meet me up on the porch. Like I said, Quinn won't mind. He does what I tell him to do."

Nick hit the side of the car as if he were slapping it on the back.

"Thanks, Pete. We'll drive right on up."

Nick felt his heart race again as they drove toward the

house. It reminded him of a bomb, how many ticks to go before it explodes? The house as it used to be appeared in his head with all the clarity of clear glass. On his sketch he had penciled in the colors of the furniture and the walls, even though he didn't expect anything to look the way it used to ... the sunny, yellow room, the red and white checked kitchen.

"Quinn has probably painted the walls a different color," he said to Laurie, who was studying his sketch in the back seat.

"Are these airplanes on the shelf?" Laurie asked.

"Yes, toy models."

"There are so many," she commented.

Nick turned off the engine and took the sketch from Laurie. He pointed to a place on the pad, briefly taking notice of his wife's obvious avoidance of his artwork. "This is Robbie Nichol's bedroom."

Laurie leaned in and studied the sketch more closely.

"He and his father loved toy model planes, and they built them together from scratch."

"How do you know all this?" Laurie asked.

Nick had a conflicting and lingering sensation that he'd found his memory, at least some of it. "I guess I'm picking it up from the boy telepathically," he said quickly. He had to keep playing it that way. He was psychic, not an amnesia victim getting his memory back, and he had to stay conscious of that. He glanced at his wife. How would he ever be able to admit that his real identity was too disturbing to uncover, that he couldn't face the truth, and that twenty years of his life was missing, and it may all have begun at this farmhouse?

"I think you've spent your whole life longing for male bonds, Nick." Jenna spoke with a comforting reassurance, the same comforting reassurance, he was certain, she gave to her patients.

"The pictures on the wall are of birds," he said as he turned back to Laurie.

"Oh, God, Nick," Jenna said with an abrupt laugh. "Every redneck out here has pictures of birds on their walls. What did you expect? Picasso? How do you feel about what I just said, that you've been longing for male bonds all your life?"

Nick glared at his wife. "Are you willing to take this at all seriously, Jenna?"

"I'm sorry, Nick, it's just that everyone up here loves birds and little boys fly toy planes. That's what little boys do with their fathers, Nick."

"I know everything there is to know about this house," Nick said as he got out of the jeep. "For instance, I know that the attic is finished, the third stair creeks when you step on it, and the kitchen window sticks. There's got to be an explanation for how I would know these things, Jenna."

"I guess you really do speak to spirits then," Jenna said.

Nick was becoming increasingly irritated with Jenna and wished he'd insisted that she remain at home.

"I wish you'd take this more seriously," he said.

Nick looked over at Pete. He had carried over some lumber from his truck and was resting it against the porch column. Everything appeared natural and pleasant, like a Rockwell illustration. Nick felt at any moment he would slip back in time and embrace the normalcy of his childhood. Normal until what ... what had happened that had made his normal life so strange?

"Hey, Pete," Nick called, taking his mind off the sadness he felt. "Is it all right with Quinn if we take a look at his house?"

"Yeah, he's in the back. He told me I could take you through, even though he thinks you folks are weird. Well, c'mon in."

Jenna and Laurie quickly walked inside but Nick felt that he couldn't move; he felt as if his feet were stuck to the ground. Pete stood at the door and watched him carefully.

"You coming, Nick?" Pete asked as he held the screen door open.

Nick couldn't do it, not yet. He felt unprepared to step into the house. Sadness enveloped him again ... grief, longing.

"Give me a minute," he said, and his voice shook; he hoped Pete hadn't noticed he was about to cry, to bawl like a boy with a bloody knee. The old screen door slammed shut behind Pete.

The door had creaked loudly, it reminded Nick of something, that creak. Yes, nights his father would come in late and wake him up with the creak of the porch door because his bedroom window had been directly over the porch. He looked up.

His heart was still beating like a time clock. He faced embarrassment if his sketch backfired, turned out to be proof of his insanity rather than proof of his ability to converse with little dead boys. He really couldn't win either way though.

"You're not going to believe this, Nick. So far, the rooms looks exactly like your sketch." Laurie appeared on the porch with a mile wide smile. "You coming in?"

"Be right there," he said.

"The third stair creaks!" she told him as she hurried back inside.

Yes, the whole house creaked, a sound he loved ... like the lemon shine on the tables, the softness of cowboy sheets and the green grass stains on his jeans. He took a look around him. The mountains sloped in the distance, familiarly silent. He had a brief sensation of vertigo but dismissed it and turned toward the screen door. He had to do this. He was relieved that his sketch had matched up to reality.

Something like a bark stopped him just as his hand turned on the doorknob. He looked over the side of the porch. A happy old mutt looked back at him; his hair was so thick you could lose your hand in his chocolate-colored fur.

"Hey, boy. Where did you come from?"

The dog's tail raced wildly back and forth. He appeared ready to pounce forward as he looked at Nick through a happy glow of recognition.

"Come here, boy." Nick laughed and jumped off the porch. The happy mutt turned in friendly circles.

"Nick!" Jenna called, with apparent irritation.

By the time Nick jumped back on the porch the happy mutt was gone.

Chapter Fifteen

The first thing Nick saw when he stepped inside the parlor was the sunlight; it poured in, so bright it put everything else in a haze. Streams of lemonade streaks of sun came through. The white curtains billowed, pushed lightly by the breeze heard rustling through the trees beyond.

"Jenna?" he said softly. "Is that you, Jenna?"

Through the haze he saw a women turn. Her dress was long, with a pattern of white and lavender checks. It wasn't Jenna at all. Jenna was small and dark.

"Robbie?" he thought he heard her say.

"No, I'm Nick," he said and stepped toward her. The image sharpened. He could see her smile. Her hair was the color of honey and pulled back off her face. She was a pretty woman with dimples in both of her cheeks.

"Mom?" he whispered.

"Nick?" Laurie said suddenly, as she came up behind him and took his arm. "This is quite a house."

"Do you see her?" he asked. He was shocked, quite sure he'd seen a ghost.

"Who?" Laurie quickly looked around.

Nick noticed they stood in the parlor alone.

"She called me, Robbie," he said to her.

"Who called you Robbie?" Laurie asked.

"I'll tell you later," he whispered as Jenna came up beside them.

"This place has great potential," Jenna said. She put her arm around his waist.

Laurie went back to Nick's sketch pad. "Library to the left," she said. "Yes, there you are, just the way you drew it, Nick."

"Really?" He glanced at the pad.

"Yes, the stairs are straight ahead." Laurie turned and looked over her shoulder. "The living room is to the right. God, Nick, everything matches your sketch!"

"What are you folks doing?" Pete asked as he walked into the room. "I told you, Quinn's not selling."

Nick ignored him and walked into the living room. He looked around. It was cluttered with too many tables and chairs. The lazy boy was so old it swooped, and the couch was the color of a faded piece of steel. It made him sad.

Nick sat on the tired old couch. "This isn't at all right," he said. "This room was beautiful once; I know it was. I can actually see it the way it used to be."

He got up and peered down the hall to see if Quinn was anywhere close by. "It's an awful mess now though, isn't it? There were always flowers in the sun right over there on that table. And the couch was soft and yellow."

"Do you actually see it the way it once was?" Laurie

asked.

"I'm seeing the boy's images," he added quickly. "I must be." But it was all too close, all too familiar to belong to anyone else but him.

Pete stared suspiciously at Nick. "You psychic or something?"

"Yes. I believe I am." He knew Pete thought he was out of his mind, but he didn't care what Pete thought. He decided to keep pretending he was psychic; he had no other choice for the moment.

"Robbie's room was blue," Nick said.

"You've been here before, haven't you? But you can't be Nicky. Nicky was kind of spastic." Pete laughed. "He's also dead."

"Let's continue our tour," Nick said, avoiding Pete.

Pete grabbed his arm. "Hey, you can't be that little kid, Nicky, we used to play with. I mean, that kid was really weird. He talked so fast you could barely follow what he was saying. Did you not die or something...? Maybe there was a cure for what you had?"

"I'm not Nicky," Nick said briskly. *But am I Robbie? Well, that remains to be seen.*

"Now right through this arch is a dining room," Laurie said, like a teacher at a blackboard with a ruler in her hand. *Right past Alaska is Russia, children.* She noticed that Jenna was glaring at her.

"What are you doing?" Jenna asked.

"If we turn left, we hit a large kitchen," Laurie continued, trying to ignore her sister. Laurie pointed her pencil forward as she walked out ahead of the others.

"This is amazing, isn't it Jenna?" Laurie, who was not the type to giggle, did so.

"I've seen enough," Jenna announced.

Nick stood firm. "I'd like to see more of the house. We haven't been upstairs."

"Nick, this is absurd. Laurie seems to think she's Sylvia Brown, that arrogant old psychic who's made a fortune bullshitting people."

"Quite the contrary," he said. "No, quite the contrary. This house is exactly as I've sketched it. That accounts for something, doesn't it?"

"I'm going to wait in the car," Jenna said. "I'm starting to feel a little stupid barging in on an old man and acting like some asinine psychic detective."

"I think I just saw the murdered boy's mother. I'm having visions of things that no longer exist, like the road sign," he said as he followed her back into the foyer.

Jenna stopped at the front door and turned to him. "Nick, I've reached my limit. I've had it with this nonsense. You're not even trying to uncover what's really going on with you."

"But that's exactly what I'm doing, Jenna."

"I'm bored with all this hocus pocus, Nick." Jenna exclaimed loudly, as she turned away. "Don't be long, will you?"

"Well, well, what's the rush, little lady?" Quinn asked, nearly thrown off his feet by Jenna's exit as he walked through the door.

Nick was undecided, should he follow his wife or not? Would it be unkind not to? God knows, she must be feeling tremendous anxiety about his sudden plunge into the Twilight Zone.

Quinn stared at him, clearly finding himself in a family drama. Nick noticed that he looked awful, like he'd just finished some pretty strenuous work. His face was red and sweaty, and his clothes were sticking to his body.

Laurie was breathless as she ran into the room and relayed to Nick that the kitchen window sticks.

"The kitchen is kind of messy. I haven't had a chance to clean things up," Quinn said. He was out of breath and Nick could see how rapidly his chest was moving.

"Oh, that's okay, sir, we appreciate the tour." Nick held Quinn's eyes. "Thank you for letting us have a look. Old houses are … I don't know … special, aren't they?"

"I think my wife is driving up." Pete said as he glanced through the front door screen. "Darla brings me my lunch when she's not teaching. I trained her well, huh?"

Nick suddenly felt as if the small rug he was standing on had been slipped away and he was going to fall, but much deeper than the floor, much, much deeper.

"Darla?" Nick said and went quickly to the door. "Did you say, Darla *What's so familiar about that name?* He held fast to the wall for support. Memories surfaced like a blast of cold weather. He put his hands to his head and rubbed his forehead. *Darla, Darla Paine.*

Suddenly, he remembered a young girl's sweet innocent kisses all over his naked body and the memory swept across his mind like a wave being chased onto shore by a storm.

Pete stared at him and brought his eyebrows close together. "Ah, yeah, Darla's my wife. You know her?"

"Nick, what is it?" Laurie tugged at his arm.

"I remember Darla from Phoenicia. Was her maiden name, Paine?"

Nick walked toward the front door and stared out over the driveway. Shit, Darla Paine had been someone he'd dated, he was sure of it. He couldn't see her features clearly, but he remembered the name … the sex. Nick was suddenly aware that he and Darla had been one hot item. He felt as if his whole life were going to come over him in one fell swoop and burst his memory wide open.

"Well, yeah, yeah. Paine was her name. Why?" Pete stammered, coming up behind him.

Nick felt embarrassed. When the hell could Darla have gone out with Pete? Why the hell hadn't he recognized Pete if he had dated his wife back in high school? But he dismissed the thought. He was getting his memory back. God, he was actually going to remember his youth. Yes, of course, the night of the prom ... Darla had let him do the deed. He saw it vividly in his mind's eye, though her face was still shadowy, unclear. But the elation of it made him giddy all the same. Yes, he remembered now, he had promised to stop if it hurt, and he hadn't pumped her twice before she started hollering that he was killing her. Didn't matter though, they'd found another way, and he'd spent that whole summer in a euphoric frenzy with Darla sucking on his cock like she'd just discovered licorice. "Let's leave all that fornicating to the rabbits, Nicky," she'd wept in his arms.

"Wow!" he said aloud.

Nick stared at Pete and wondered how Darla would react. Hell, they were so mad for one another. She had broken his heart when she left town to get her degree in education. He never thought he'd get over it.

God, I really did have a life in Phoenicia. My God, it's so clear. Finally, it's all coming back. But then, why is this house so familiar to me?

"You know my wife?" Pete interrupted his thoughts.

Nick nodded slowly and walked quickly through the door with Pete at his heels.

Chapter Sixteen

Cecile Nichols reached up with a lazy stretch. The sunlight made her feel deliciously cozy, streaming in through the windows the way it was, with a cheery brightness. She held her face toward the warmth and yawned for a good thirty seconds.

Griffin Nichols looked up from his paper and smiled over at his wife. She'd dozed off in that chair for over two hours and she hadn't even quipped at him for being so noisy when he turned the pages of the *Miami Herald*, as though he was crinkling it on purpose, just to keep her up talking to him.

"You must be reading something good. You're being quieter about it than usual," she said.

Griffin looked up over his glasses.

"There's nothing good in this damn newspaper worth

reading today." He folded the paper and put it on his lap. "You went into some trance-like sleep, dumpling. Anyway, you snored like hell, and it kept me from concentrating on anything."

Cecile reached down and stretched her arms around her ankles, letting out a long, deep breath. She wondered if she should mention that she'd just had a dream about Robbie;

fell into some deep sleep in the middle of the afternoon and dreamed about their son. But she couldn't bear to see his disappointment. He'd always get so damn upset with her if she mentioned Robbie. Well, why shouldn't she mention him? She didn't believe that Robbie was dead, and Griff did. Cecile had never believed it, not without a body — not without seeing for herself that some monster had stilled his breath. But Griffin had been insisting for years that she had to let go of all her illusions about Robbie being alive and accept the fact that he was gone. "We have to move on Ceil," Griff would say. "We have to accept God's will." But for Cecile, grief was a wound, open and raw, refusing to heal just because it came from God's will.

This particular dream had been different than all the others. In this dream, her son had become a man, not even a young man, but the age he would be now, nearly fifty.

"Griff?" she began, as she put her chin out and let the sun fall on her features like an embrace. "I dreamed of Robbie just now. I must have fallen into a deep sleep."

Griffin picked up his newspaper and opened it with a loud snap forward so the pages would lie as flat as possible.

"He was a man, full-grown. He was the age he would be today, and he was standing in the parlor of our old house. I called to him, and he said, "*Mom*?" He said it like it was a question and he needed the answer from me ... I was young in the dream, just the way I was the last time he ever saw me. I was wearing the same dress, the lavender one with the white lace on the collar, and that old mutt we used to have was out on the porch barking for Robbie to come out. Remember how old Crocket loved our boy? Remember, Griff?"

She heard him clear his throat and pick up the paper again. He turned a page, snapping it just as loudly as he had snapped the other ones.

"He was so handsome and so tall. Oh, it was our Robbie. I am sure of that. He looked about to cry when he saw me. I wanted to reach out, and yet, I couldn't touch him. I wanted to touch him so badly, but I couldn't. Oh, Griff, it was so real, so very real."

Griffin turned another page and coughed softly.

"You want some water, honey?" she asked.

Griffin nodded. As she passed by his chair he reached out to hold her hand. She felt him squeeze it briefly before letting it go.

Cecile ran the faucet until the water felt cold on her fingers. She stared out at the neat little townhouse across the road and thought about the last time she had held her eldest son in her arms. She went to the refrigerator for ice cubes and remembered the last words he had ever said to her.

"Got to protect Nicky from the space people tonight, Mom," he had said, right before going out to sleep under the stars.

"Space people, son?"

"Don't worry, Mom. There's a full moon tonight."

"All right, Robbie, all right. Just be careful, okay?"

"They want Nicky, Mom. They think it's special that

Nicky is a savant," he'd said.

"Well, it is special, isn't it, son?"

"You want to bring me some of that leftover chicken, Hon?" Griffin called out from the living room.

"Yes, dear," she said as she gazed through the kitchen window until she didn't even see the neat little townhouse across the road anymore. No, she just saw the dream and the grown-up man she recognized as her son, Robbie. His eyes were filled with memory, so much pain followed. But she felt joyous, not how she usually felt when she thought about Robbie. Usually, it felt like she was dying — like despair was caressing her heart and pulling her inward.

"Robbie," she whispered as she touched the gold cross around her neck. "Robbie?" she repeated as she looked toward the sky and remembered how shockingly blue his eyes had been.

"Griffin?" she said, as she walked back to her husband and handed him the water. "I'd like to see the leaves turn this year. Can we go up north? We can stay with Carlton. I've missed seeing the leaves turn. We've been here so long now. Seven years, isn't it? Why, we haven't left the state of Florida for seven years." She covered his hand with her own and sat on the arm of his chair.

Griffin smiled up at her. "You forget my chicken?"

"I'll get it for you."

"You know how I feel about being around Carl and ... his ... partner," Griff said slowly.

"Oh, Griff," she said and slapped his arm. "Please, dear. We'll have a lot of fun and Carlton will just love having us. The world is changing Griff ... and he's our son."

She watched him put the paper back in his lap.

"Oh, well, why not? Why don't you give Carlton a call

and see if it's all right? We'll take the van and drive up. I'd like that."

"Thank you, Griff," she said as she leaned over to kiss his cheek.

He took her hand and held it tightly while she stroked his hair and thought about her dream, and her missing son, Robbie, and how sad the man in the dream had looked. He was a full-grown adult man, and yet, he seemed to need her; seemed to need her so badly that it had left her with a blissful feeling, the way she had felt on the morning he was born. The dream had been so unquestionably real, like something that had actually happened. It had been a calling of some kind. She was sure of it; a message from Robbie. Yes, she was sure of it.

Chapter Seventeen

Nick watched intently as a sharp looking black Mustang pulled behind his Cherokee and came to a stop. He wondered what he'd say to Darla after all these years. His memory was still muddy, but images were emerging. He was recalling vague outlines of people he must have known. *Yes, of course, Darla*. He wished he could see her face more clearly, but he couldn't. He remembered making love to her, though, that old barn, the hay sticking to her back in the heat of the sun. But her face was still lost behind a fog.

He could see Jenna in the passenger seat as she tilted her head and looked into the rear-view mirror. Laurie stood at his side and followed his gaze, trying to see what he seemed so interested in. Nick was breathing quickly and every muscle in his body was strained toward the black car.

Pete walked over to his wife. Nick heard him say, "Hey, sweetie."

"What's going on, Nick?" Laurie asked.

"Well, I'll be damned," Nick uttered, as he watched Darla step from the car. Pete quickly kissed his wife's cheek. Then he leaned in and whispered something into her ear. Darla's glance shot up to the porch where Nick was standing.

Nick slowly started walking toward Darla. He could see that Jenna was watching him.

When he got up close, he took a good look at Darla Paine's face. He was confused; nothing attracted him to her ... but maybe ... back then...

Something flashed across his brain. He suddenly had a clear image, clearer than any of the others ... eyes that were sensual and light, hair like flame. This woman's hair was stringy and a dull shade of brown, not full, and fiery at all.

Nick shook his head, as if to rattle his thoughts. He felt nauseous. The Darla Paine that had just emerged in his memory had been a knockout. She had been so tall that she met his eyes when they stood to embrace. No, this woman was definitely not Darla. This woman was not even as tall as Jenna.

"Hi," Nick said cautiously, as he held out his hand. "I'm Nick Dowling."

"Hi," she said, apprehensively, as she shook his hand and stared at him.

"Remember, Darla, I mentioned him?" Pete said.

"I'm from Phoenicia," Nick said to her and shifted his weight; he was surprised he wasn't stuttering. "I dated a girl in high school named Darla Paine."

"You don't say?" Pete said and eyed his wife

suspiciously.

"Forgive me, if I don't remember you," Darla said.

"You look different, too. Darla Paine is not a common name, though. Well, I'm sure the years have changed us both," Nick said, trying to convince himself.

"When did you graduate?" she asked.

Nick was glad he had an answer. Jenna had asked him when he'd graduated high school right after they'd met. So, he did the approximate math, that's all he could do.

"1975," he said."

He knew he could be wrong. He surmised that he must have been at least twenty years old when he woke up in Chelsea in 1977. He had studied the only things hanging in his closet: a pair of bell bottom jeans, an old pea coat and a Grateful Dead sweatshirt. Then he stared at his image in the glass. Twenty, he'd decided.

"From Phoenicia Central?"

"Yes," he said. "Phoenicia Central, class of 75'."

Darla made a giddy sound, like a yelp. "This is weird, but I graduated Phoenicia Central, class of 75', too."

"Really?" Nick stared at her.

"But I don't remember you. The only boy in my life in my junior year was Harrison Hinckley. He was a senior, but it was just a crush, never went anywhere. Pete and I were together by twelfth grade."

"Didn't we go to the prom together?" Nick asked.

Darla shook her head. "No, I went with Pete."

"I saved her from Harrison." Pete laughed, returning his gaze to Nick.

"I guess I'm really confused," Nick said quietly, studying her features.

"You look familiar, though, you look a lot like Harrison. Everyone wanted to go out with him." She paused for a moment. "But you don't seem like Harrison.

He was very hyper."

Nick turned away from her as he heard the door to the jeep open and shut. The three of them watched as Jenna came toward them. Nick felt Jenna take his hand.

"My wife, Jenna," he said to Darla.

Darla acknowledged Jenna with a brief smile.

"I have a cousin by the name of *Darlene* Paine," she said, turning back to Nick. "I think she dated someone named Nick in high school, but I'm not sure. His name was something like Nick, maybe Dick … or Rick. I only met him once. Do you remember, Pete?" she asked and turned to her husband.

"No," Pete said.

"Maybe I'm mistaken," Nick said. "Good to meet you," he called over his shoulder as he turned.

Nick's eyes met Laurie's as he walked toward the house. She sat on the porch steps and watched him carefully. Jenna hadn't said anything, but she appeared distressed as she walked by his side, he could feel it.

"What was that all about?" Laurie asked, as Nick sat on the steps beside her.

"What's going on, Nick," Jenna asked as she sat next to him and took his hand.

"I don't remember dating anyone named *Darlene* Paine in High School. I am sure I dated a girl named *Darla* Paine. I was really into her at the time. I would have remembered her name."

"She doesn't remember you?" Jenna asked, as she looked back at the woman sitting in the Mustang with Pete Shelby. "Why are you having memory issues, Nick?"

"That woman is not Darla Paine," Nick said simply, ignoring his wife's question.

Jenna studied Nick a moment before she spoke. "Honey, high school was a long time ago. Don't you think you might have confused the name? They are similar. I'm sure that woman is who she says she is."

"But they don't even look alike." He glanced at Jenna. Maybe it was finally time to admit that he didn't have a clue as to where he came from; he didn't even exist prior to 1977. The only thing he did have were bad dreams, dreams that might be a mirror into his own history and reveal truths that he'd desperately cast away so he'd never know what unspeakable acts of violence he might have been capable of.

Maybe Jenna had been right all along, and he really was having some sort of breakdown, especially now that bits and pieces of his memory were surfacing and not adding up. Nick was terrified of hurting his entire family with this void that hid his life behind walls of what? Resistance? Maybe, that's all his visions were about; they shielded him from a devastating self-discovery. Maybe that's all he had wanted from Laurie, someone to support his delusions.

Nick sat between the two sisters and brought his hand to his mouth.

"I don't understand," he whispered.

Jenna put her hand on his knee. "I've always wanted to see your hometown. Let's go to Phoenicia," she said. "Maybe being in Phoenicia will clear things up."

Nick looked at his wife and cocked his head. "Is this therapy?" he asked softly.

How the hell would he get out of this? His hometown was a word on a register book in a hotel in Chelsea. He wouldn't even know how to find Main Street.

"Did you date anyone else in high school, Nick?" Jenna asked.

"Betty Logan." The name fell out of his mouth. He closed his eyes. *Shit, another girl*, a pretty blond, built like a pin up model.

"What did she look like, Nick? Do you remember? Are you confusing the two women?" Jenna reached out to touch his hair.

"No way. Betty didn't look anything at all like Darla," Nick said.

"Well, what did she look like, Nick?" Jenna asked.

"Betty was blond, blue eyes. She was curvaceous. I believe I lost my virginity with her," Nick said apologetically, suddenly remembering how she'd made him promise to wear a condom. He must have run down to the drugstore for a year's supply. All of a sudden, the images were there.

"She was pretty, then? Jenna asked. "No wonder you've never mentioned the women in your life. I would have felt terribly intimidated."

Betty's face came into view. It was a very lovely face; her lips were full and enticing and her nose turned up. "She was a knockout," he said. "I don't remember her all that well though. I dated her before I dated Darla.." He smiled halfheartedly. "The guys never shut up about how well she was built."

Nick had images of himself standing beside a locker talking to a boy with red hair. Could that boy have been Pete Shelby? Two other boys stood near. They were all laughing, book bags flung over their shoulders. "Watermelon bra," one of the guys said. "Betty with the boobs," said another.

Jenna raised her eyes at Laurie and attempted a bit of humor. "Leave it to a man to remember how well she was built, but nothing else."

"This is the strangest thing," Nick said. "Doesn't make

sense."

"Let's go find Betty Logan, Nick." Jenna took his hand. "I'm sure she'll be happy to see you. She might even remember if you went out with a *Darla* or a *Darlene* before you dumped her."

"Betty Logan had a lot of guys in her life. She was one of those super stars in high school, everybody was after her." He remembered holding her hand. He remembered her kiss. "Darla was pretty too, though, but in a different way."

"Well, let's try and find them, Nick. You have to be mistaken about Darla's name, that's all," Jenna stood up. "Obviously you didn't date anyone named Darla from Phoenicia," she said softly, glancing at the Mustang.

From the corner of his eye Nick could see Andrew Quinn at the side of the house. He wished he could remember Quinn as clearly as he was beginning to recall his teenage sex life.

"We'll be leaving now, Mr. Quinn," Nick called as he got to his feet.

Quinn muttered something back and waved his hand in the air.

Nick noticed that Quinn had cleaned himself up a bit. He'd changed his shirt and his hair was wet, as if he'd just washed it.

"Thanks for letting us see your house," Nick said.

"Just a house, isn't it?" Quinn grinned.

"It's a terrific house," Jenna said nervously.

"Terrific?" Quinn chuckled. "Well, I guess I should say thank-you?"

Laurie forced a polite nod at Quinn and followed after Nick and Jenna. As she slid into the back seat of the

Cherokee Laurie noticed that Jenna had taken the wheel. Laurie hadn't said a word about Nick's confusion over Darla Paine. She was trying to decide whether or not she believed Nick anymore. Maybe, Mr. Perfect, was an imposter and he was going to come up with some bizarre story about having had amnesia. He might even produce a whole other family from some distant past. Maybe, the charming Nick Dowling had some devious plan up his sleeve, and he was a crafty fugitive whose real identity was buried as deep as a keepsake off the Titanic.

Laurie put her knuckles up to her teeth as she stared out the window. *No*, she thought, *no, not Nick. I can't believe that about Nick. It must be something else. It must be! There must be something to his identity confusion that coincides with an abduction experience.*

She decided right then and there that she'd have to call Sam. That was the answer, the only answer. She knew Sam would know what to do, might even be familiar with the connection between memory confusion and alien abductions. He would certainly know if Nick's experiences had anything at all to do with anything paranormal.

Sam had been a real bastard to her, breaking off their relationship so abruptly she didn't know what had hit her — another woman, she had surmised, but he never said, never offered her any explanation. Well, so be it, Sam Hollander was still an expert on all things paranormal. She'd break down and call him, strictly professional, she'd tell him, "strictly professional."

"Everything is going to be all right, Jenna," Laurie said, as she reached around to touch her sister's shoulder. "We'll get to the bottom of this."

But it was Nick who reached back to take her hand.

"Got any theories?" he asked.

Laurie shook her head. She caught her sister's eyes in the rear-view mirror and noticed that the glance Jenna gave her was vulnerable. It was easy to read the fear in her eyes. Laurie knew what she was thinking now: *Nick must surely be losing his mind.*

"Let's look up *Darlene* Paine when we get to Phoenicia," Jenna said, "just for the hell of it. You have obviously confused the names. We'll look up both Betty and Darlene. No need to take this so seriously."

I've lied to you all these years, Jenna. I've never existed prior to 1977. My past may be your worst nightmare.

Jenna was speaking but he barely heard her.

"Who remembers names anyway?" she was saying. "It was thirty years ago, after all."

Chapter Eighteen

Nick stared at the two-block town. It hit him like he was at the end of a giant magnet, and he was covered in steel; he'd never been here before in his life. For Nick, everything looked like something painted in obtuse brushstrokes, not meant to be taken literally.

How am I going to explain this to Jenna? He'd have to tell her about his memory loss; it would soon be clear that he didn't know where the hell he was, or who the hell he was. She'd force him to remember the unthinkable ... murders so deeply hidden he'd rather fall into madness than face them.

Jenna pulled the car over on Main Street. He knew she was upset. He felt like he was wearing a mask, shielding the man his wife had known all these years. He must appear to her now like a sudden stranger.

Laurie leaned in from the back. "How does it feel to be back home?" she asked.

Nick noticed that Laurie's eyes were as round in diameter as a soup pot. She must think he's crazy too. He should try to make light of it.

"I don't remember this town at all," he said, feeling the truth, at this point, was best. "It's changed in thirty years."

"Couldn't have changed that much. What's going on with your memory, Nick?" Jenna reached out tentatively and stroked the side of his face.

"Nothing is the way it should be," Nick said as visions sprang up in his mind: street signs — winding roads — trees that sprouted some sort of orange fruit, small, like a nectarine. The sky rippled like waves in water.

"You haven't been here in years, Nick," Laurie said, obviously trying to make him feel more comfortable about the improbability of not recognizing his own hometown.

"Yes, Nick. It's been a long time. You're right, towns change," Jenna assured him.

Nick sat forward and stared through the glass window.

Laurie watched nervously as Jenna reached into the glove compartment for a scrap of paper. She took her cell phone from her purse and dialed information. She asked for a listing for Darlene Paine.

"She must have married and moved on," she said. "No listing."

"See if you can find a number for Betty Logan," Laurie said.

There had to be an explanation. Why were the wrong

names on the wrong faces for Nick? Laurie wondered if even Sam could explain it.

Nick stared blankly ahead while Jenna called back information. Laurie knew before she asked that there wouldn't be a listing for Betty either. But after a moment she heard her sister say, "Oh? Yes, yes, please, give me that number."

"You got it?" Laurie asked. She watched as Jenna quickly scribbled something down on a piece of paper.

"Well, not for Betty, but there is a listing for a Walter Logan. Maybe that's her father."

"Maybe," Nick said, as he stared at his wife.

"How many Logans could there be in a town this small?" Jenna handed her cell phone to Laurie. "You're on, sister actress. Find out if she's Walter Logan's daughter. If she's married, see if you can find out where she's living. Tell Walter that you knew Betty in High School and you're trying to look her up while you're in town. Whatever information you can get will be helpful."

Laurie took the cell phone from Jenna and dialed. "It's ringing." She smiled in Nick's direction and noticed that his expression was unfamiliar.

"Mr. Logan?" Laurie said as someone on the other end picked up.

Jenna and Nick listened as Laurie amicably told Walter Logan that she had known Betty in high school and wanted to get back in touch. They watched as she nodded her head and repeated, "O*h, really*? Could I speak with her then?"

"She's there?" Nick asked in amazement.

Laurie nodded. "He went to get her."

"Everything is going to be fine, Nick," Jenna said quickly. "You'll feel better after you speak with Betty. I'm also convinced that you dated Darlene in High School, not

Darla. You're just a bit confused, sweetheart, nothing to worry about."

Nick took the small phone that Laurie handed him and held it to his ear.

"Betty?" he asked nervously. "It's Nick, Nick Dowling from school."

Laurie assumed there was a pause on the other end. Nick repeated himself and waited.

He held the phone away and put his hand over the mouthpiece.

"She doesn't remember me," he whispered. He picked the phone up again and continued. "We dated," he said.

Laurie watched as Nick put his head back. "What is she saying?" she whispered.

"That I'm mistaken. She went out with Harrison in High School, but no one named Nick."

Nick wet his lips and tried again. He brought the phone back up to his mouth. "I bought you a charm ... it was the drama masks."

Nick listened to the voice on the other end. He made a couple of grunts in response but after a bit he held the phone in the air. "She asked me how I knew about the charm."

"That's enough, Nick," Jenna said softly. She took the phone from him and snapped it shut. "Did she tell you anything worthwhile?"

"She said no one but some guy named Harrison called her Betty. Her name is Elizabeth Tennyson now. She's just here visiting her cousin, Walt, but she lives in Bedford Hills, New York. She asked me if we might know each other from Bedford."

"This doesn't make any sense," Jenna whispered.

"She said Harrison gave her the charm. They were in drama club together." Nick put his head on the dash.

"Shit," he said loudly, "This is unbelievable!" He looked back onto Main Street. "That woman never heard of me."

"Nick, your name isn't really Harrison Hinckley, is it?" Jenna asked.

"What? No," he said.

"Maybe you have some sort of memory confusion. Is that possible, Jenna?" Laurie asked.

"In certain cases, it is," Jenna said.

"I don't exactly remember every guy I dated in high school. I can't even recall Mark Hecht's hair color, the big love of my life in those days. I remember just little things about him, like the smell of Clearasil on his cheeks." Laurie laughed.

Jenna turned around and peered into the back seat. Laurie noticed that her sister looked strung out, like she was close to screaming.

"I want to see where you grew up, Nick," Jenna said with a determined edge to her voice. "Do you remember how to get there from Main Street?"

"I don't have a clue," Nick said. "I'm not sure about anything anymore."

"Come on, Nick, humor me. I want to see the house you grew up in." Jenna gently coaxed him. "Try to remember."

Nick knew he was having an anxiety attack; his breath was irregular. "There's a road," he said.

"What road?" Jenna asked.

"I don't know … wait. Laurel, I think. Laurel Road." Nick opened his eyes and stared at her. "It's like snap shots in my brain, not memories. What's happening to me?"

Jenna put her hands on the steering wheel. "Don't

worry, we'll sort this out."

He remembered something ... a road and an old car. He'd parked the car on the road to kiss someone goodnight, hadn't he?

"If we follow the road we're on, we should hit a stop sign." Nick looked around. He had a sense of where to go, but he wasn't sure where the knowledge of that was coming from."

"Let's give it a shot, Nick," Jenna said. "Let's find the house you grew up in. That might jostle your memory."

"Up that way, I think." He pointed ahead. "Look for Laurel Road and turn onto it. Follow the road until we hit the first stop sign."

"Okay," Jenna said.

"I lived in a farmhouse," Nick said. He wondered if he'd find it at the end of Laurel Road, but he knew he wouldn't. He knew his wife was perplexed. She was doubting him. How the hell could he not be able to find the house he grew up in?

"Everything looks different," he tried to explain.

"Yes, of course, honey," Jenna said.

When they got to the first stop sign Nick got out of the car and surveyed the area.

"The road to the left is a dirt road that dead-ends," he called out. "We can only go straight ahead ... or turn right."

"Is it familiar?" Jenna asked as he got back into the jeep.

"Not really," he said. "Make the right turn. We should hit another stop sign soon. When we do, turn right again. I think the house should be the first driveway on the left, after we make the turn."

Jenna reached out and patted his arm. "It'll make sense soon; you'll see."

At the next stop sign Nick watched anxiously as Jenna made the turn.

Laurie came out of her cocoon and removed her glasses. She leaned all the way into to the front seat and peered ahead.

Jenna pulled off the road and stopped the car just before the drive. "You can't see any houses from the road," she said.

"It's up at the end of that drive," Nick said.

"What name is on the mailbox now?" Laurie asked as she rolled down the window and looked out.

Nick got out of the car and went over to take a look. He'd absolutely entered the Twilight Zone, now he was sure of it. He read the name on the box. It hit him the way lightning might have. *What the hell was going on? Had he really found his home?*

Jenna quickly got out of the car and ran up to him. "What is it, Nick?" she asked as she took his arm.

"Look," he said softly, his face an ashen color, as he stared at the red mailbox.

"Good God, it says, *Dowling!* Nick, your parents are dead. Did they leave the house to relatives?"

"I don't have any relatives."

Laurie got out of the car. "Let's pay the Dowling's' a visit," she said. Jenna looked into her eyes and nodded agreement.

"Yes, come on, Nick. Let's drive up there. This is just too much of a coincidence. Maybe you had family you didn't know about? I mean, that is possible."

Nick had never been to Phoenicia in his life. He was absolutely positive of that. His past didn't exist here. If he had relatives, they'd never looked for him. If he'd murdered anyone, it didn't happen in Phoenicia. Phoenicia was just a name on a register. Whoever these

Dowling's' were, they had no relationship to him at all, and he knew it, but he'd have to pretend. He realized that he could be Robbie Nichols, the other kidnapped boy from Fox Hollow. The farmhouse in New Kingston was familiar, and even Quinn was familiar, but not this, not any of it. But why then, did he wake up in a Chelsea hotel as Nick Dowling and not Robert Nichols? Nothing made sense.

"Nick," Jenna said softly, "We have to understand what's happening to you. We have to follow this through to the very end. We have to arrive at an explanation for all this confusion you're having about your life."

Nick slowly nodded his head and let Jenna lead him back to the Jeep. His body felt light, as if he might fall, or simply float away.

They drove up the drive. Nick sat forward. He felt a vague familiarity about his surroundings but nothing concrete. He couldn't understand why the familiarity came and went.

"Is that the house you grew up in, Nick?" Laurie asked, as they stared at a small Dutch Colonial.

"It's different," he said and his voice broke; he was thinking of the farmhouse in Fox Hollow. "I have a photograph in my head ... like a still ... it doesn't match this."

"But you led us here," Jenna said. "Did you grow up here, Nick?"

Nick looked at her and didn't answer. *I grew up in a farmhouse in Fox Hollow.*

Jenna anxiously stopped the car at the entrance to a small white garage.

"Well, what do you think?" She turned to him. He could tell she was trying to keep it together.

"No one appears to be home," he said. "Let's go."

But, just at that moment, an attractive elderly woman came out of the house and stared at them from her porch. She had on a red and white apron and her long, gray hair was piled on top of her head in a neat braid.

"Can I help you?" she called.

Nick saw that she watched them closely as they got out of the car.

"Are you looking for someone?" she asked and leaned further off the porch.

Nick slowly walked up to the woman. He stopped in front of the porch steps and attempted to smile.

"My name is Nick Dowling," he said uncomfortably.

The woman gasped, and the skin on her hand turned red from the strength of her grasp on the railing. "What did you say?" she asked, almost inaudibly.

"My name is Nick Dowling," he repeated. "I think I used to live here." He realized how strange that sounded and looked away.

Why did I lead Jenna here?

"Tom?" the woman called loudly, not taking her eyes from Nick's.

"It seems like such a coincidence that you have my last name." Nick tried to laugh, to make light of it.

"What is it, Nan?" Tom Dowling asked, as he came through the door and stared at Nick. He was thin and walked with the help of a cane. His hair was quite thick for a man his age and had remained mostly brown.

Nick extended his hand. "Nick Dowling, Sir," he said, and watched Tom Dowling's face redden. Nick noticed that his expression appeared pained.

"Who did you say you were?"

"Nick Dowling."

"You're not my son Nick," the man said as he narrowed his eyes and tightened his lips.

"Your son was named Nick?" Nick stepped back and stared at him. "The kid in the field, you're his father?"

"Get off my land before I call the police," Tom yelled out as he descended the stairs. Glaring into Nick's eyes, he stopped short and raised a fist in the air.

"I'm sorry, Sir. I didn't mean to upset you," Nick said, stepping back.

Tom Dowling clenched his fists tighter together. "What the hell are you up to?" he asked.

"You're not related to my husband?" Jenna said. "We thought you might be."

Tom Dowling seemed about to put his hands around Nick's throat.

"Is this some kind of cruel joke? You one of those little bastards that used to bother us all the time?" he said and narrowed his eyes.

"No, Sir," Nick said.

"Get the hell out of here!" Tom Dowling said angrily. "You son of a bitch."

"Tom, wait!" Nancy Dowling quickly interjected as she stepped off the porch and walked right up to Nick. Nick looked back into her eyes as she stared into his.

"Nicholas Dowling was kidnapped and murdered in 1967," she said softly.

"Yes, I know about that ... the kid in Fox Hollow. My name is Nick Dowling also, but I'm not the kid who was kidnapped, obviously."

"He was our son." The man said sternly.

"Oh," Nick said.

"He was our son," the man repeated.

"I'm sorry," Jenna said.

"What do you want?" Nancy Dowling asked.

Jenna carefully walked toward Nancy and tried to explain as best she could.

"My husband says he grew up in Phoenicia, isn't that right, Nick? It's clearly an odd coincidence that he has your son's name. I'm terribly sorry to disturb you like this but it's all so unusual."

Nancy Dowling looked back at Jenna but said nothing.

"We moved here from New Kingston thirteen years after Nicky's abduction, and we've been here ever since. No other family in town with our name," Tom said. "Far as I know, there never was."

Nancy Dowling reached for her husband's hand. "We bought this house from the Miller's. They owned it nearly fifty years. The Millers had a son, Andy. They had a daughter too. It was a sad thing what happened to her … she was murdered … horrible crime … husband killed the child too. The Miller's moved away after that. You can find them in Arizona … Sedona, I think. Maybe they can help you."

Nick felt dazed and reached out for the banister to keep himself from falling. *A woman was murdered, a child.* He wanted answers; he wanted to scream out questions.

"We thought we'd be able to escape the publicity after thirteen years, but the kids still bothered us. They'd come all the way over here to Phoenicia and tell us Nicky's ghost was haunting the old Nichols place. The ghost tale never ended, just passed down from one town to the next," Tom said with obvious resentment.

"I'm sorry," Nick said tentatively. "Really, I'm terribly sorry."

"Your name may be Nick Dowling but you're not our Nicky, and you certainly never lived in this house. There's some confusion, Mister. Our boy was blond, like you, but you're not our son," Tom Dowling said, his face showing lines deep around his eyes and mouth.

"But my husband grew up here." Jenna said. "Didn't

you, Nick?"

"That's impossible," Tom Dowling said.

"I don't understand what's going on, Jenna," Nick said and turned back to the Dowling's. "Could I be your son? Maybe...."

"Our son was autistic." Nancy said, cutting him off.

Nick stared at her. "I know that," he said. "I guess that answers my question."

"I'm sorry that you're confused, but you're clearly not related to us," Nancy said.

"Why the hell doesn't anyone know who I am?" Nick fell to his knees as if dragged to the ground by a heavy weight.

"Nick." Jenna came to his side and attempted to soothe him.

He put his head in his hands and rocked his body back and forth. Jenna took him by the shoulders and looked into his eyes. "It will be all right Nick," she said.

Nick looked up and searched her face. He saw the fear in her expression though she still appeared to be in control. Her husband's mind was blowing up right before her very eyes. Maybe when an amnesia victim's memory returns, it's inconsistent ... jumbled. He quickly tried to justify the improbability of what was happening to him. He looked back at Laurie. Her expression was dazed and bewildered.

"I'm not crazy," he whispered. "But I can't explain this. I can't explain any of this."

Chapter Nineteen

Carl Nichols watched Pete Shelby's truck as it came up the road. He rarely saw Pete Shelby anymore and he was grateful that he spent less time in town these days and didn't have to. He had just gotten an advance for a new mystery novel, and he had a deadline to meet. Most people knew better than to show up at Carl Nichols's house unannounced, especially when he'd just started work on a new novel, but Pete Shelby was never one for protocol.

Carl saved his work and went outside. "Hey, Pete," he said. "Haven't seen you in ages."

Pete walked up on the porch steps and stared at Carl without saying anything. Carl knew that Pete would rather meet a black bear on the road than have to give him ten minutes. So then, what the hell was he doing here?

"Hey, Carl. How's it going?" Pete finally said.

"Well, I'm right in the middle of a new chapter." Carl leaned against the rail, hoping that he'd take the hint.

"Well, I guess you're saying that you don't have time anymore for your old friend, Pete; is that it?"

Carl sat down on one of the welcoming wicker chairs that lined the porch.

"Not at all, Pete. Good to see you. Have a seat."

Pete stared out over the mountains. Darla was always talking about how beautiful Carl Nichols's old Victorian farmhouse was. Of course, a woman would love it. No real man would. It certainly made Pete uneasy to be seen sitting on such a prissy porch, with everything so blue and white, flowers all over the place. Pete was almost too big for the seat of the chair, and he wondered if the dirt on his pants would stain the yellow cushions on Carl's wicker chairs.

"How've you been Carl?" he finally said.

"Now, I know you didn't drive all the way out here to ask me how I am."

Pete tapped his nails on the arm of the chair and continued to stare across the road. He watched the Wainwright's cows graze and then brought his eyes up to the red barn across the way.

"Nice piece of property you have here, Carl."

"You want a beer, Pete?"

"Sure would."

"You promise to tell me what's on your mind if I get you one?"

"Sure will."

Carl went back toward the kitchen as Pete moved

down to the porch steps and sat. He thought about this strange coincidence and tried to figure out what it all meant — some stranger turning up, claiming to be Nicky Dowling. He wondered what Quinn was thinking. Quinn's obsession with little Nicky had been so frigging perverted. He used to whack him across the head, call him *stupid boy*, and then try and touch him all over the place. Pete would sure like to forget those days. Hell, he never would have dredged up the memories, not until this guy showed up with Nicky Dowling's name, not even having to see that asshole Quinn every day of his life made him think of being a kid on the old bastard's lap.

"So, what's up, Pete?" Carl asked as he sat back in the chair.

Pete turned. He noticed that Carl had placed his beer in a glass on the table between the two wicker chairs. He got up from the steps and sat back down in the chair he had vacated.

"There's a guy from the city, bought a house over in New Kingston. He says his name is Nick Dowling."

Carl took a swig of his beer and put his foot up on the little fancy ottoman in front of him. He sat perfectly still. Pete eyes traveled to Carl's designer sneakers and noticed that his socks were red and white stripped, like the flag.

"Yeah, so?" Carl finally said.

"Jesus, Carl. Don't you remember Nicky Dowling, the kid that disappeared with your brother?"

Carl put his beer down. "I was only seven years old, Pete. So, no, I don't actually remember the kid."

"Don't you think it's strange that this guy appears out of nowhere and says his name is Nick Dowling?"

"They were murdered, Pete. Coincidence, that's all."

"But they never found bodies. I always wondered why they never did."

"My brother is dead, the other kid, too. End of story."

"Look Carl, this guy says everything looks familiar to him. He made me bring him inside your old house. He got lost on the road 'cause he said he was drawn to it. He kept referring to the road as Fox Hollow. I don't know, Carl. It's really strange."

"Pete, my mother told me that Nicky Dowling was a savant. Is this guy a savant?"

"Well, that's just it. He's not, but he's blond and..." Pete's voice trailed off and he put his hands around his glass of beer and stared at the foam. "Look, do you still have those old newspaper articles?"

"Why?"

"Do you have them?"

"I'm sorry, Pete. I don't have time for this nonsense," Carl said, as he got up abruptly and put his hand on the screen door.

Pete jumped up and grabbed his arm. Carl looked back at him with a slow smile.

"I do believe you're serious, Pete, otherwise I wouldn't be feeling your hand anywhere near mine."

"I am serious, Carl. For Christ's sake, something really weird is going on."

Carl looked as if he were just about to throw Pete off the porch, but instead he said, "All right. If it'll make you happy. C'mon in. I'll get the newspapers, but I don't know where you're going with this."

"Thank you, Carl."

Pete followed Carl into the house, after wiping his feet several times on the large welcome mat at the door.

"Wait here," Carl said. "I'll go to my room. I've got the newspapers up there in a trunk; Mom always insisted we keep them."

Pete walked into the living room after watching Carl

climb the stairs. He felt badly having to dredge up his brother's disappearance, but he had to tell someone. It was just too strange the way this guy, Nick Dowling, was acting.

Pete sat in an old comfortable chair that reminded him of something he'd seen in his grandmother's house. The tall pane windows were swaged with soft blue cotton curtains and were letting in the sun. Pete stared at the old couch, covered with fringed throws, and draped as if adorning a woman's shoulder. Toile pillows were haphazardly tossed about on chairs with high backs and short, curvy, oak legs. The table before him was piled high with country catalogues and paperback books. *Darla would love the room*, he thought to himself as the tall orange flowers beyond the windows seemed to be flirting in his direction, and the dark shine on the old plank floors gleamed so high he looked for his reflection in the wood.

Carl returned with the newspapers in his hand. He sat on the couch. "Come over here," he said to Pete.

Pete got up reluctantly and took a seat beside Carl on the old couch. If he grew up to be homophobic he had good reason. Hell, how many times had Quinn come after them both, getting him and Carl in the back of the Nichols's old barn, scaring the shit out of them. It was "their secret," he told them. Hell, Pete hated the son of a bitch. He got his revenge though. He was getting three times as much for odd jobs than he'd get anywhere else. He was going to get the house too when the old man died. He assumed it was guilt, or fear that kept Quinn throwing money Pete's way. But it was payback for Pete. The old man probably thought he was buying his silence, but he was really paying for the sense of power Pete felt now, years later. Maybe Quinn thought he didn't remember that far back but every time he overcharged the old bastard Quinn knew, deep down inside, that Pete remembered every sick perverted moment. Might have turned Carl into a fruitcake, but not old Pete, nope, it made him smart.

Carl had the paper spread out on top of all the catalogues and paperback books. On the front page of the local Catskill Mountain News, was an old headline: *Local Boys Missing Over Three Days*. Below the headline were two family photographs, two smiling children, appearing as if they could have been brothers, similar in appearance, both of them, shyly smiling.

"There you are," Carl said, "Nicky Dowling. Is it the same person?"

Pete took the old newspaper close to his eyes and stared at both photographs. After a while, he shook his head.

"I can't tell. This guy could be either kid. I mean, he could be Robbie, too. They both had such blond hair. They looked alike."

"What do you mean; you said his name was Nick?"

"Yeah, but he's not retarded."

"Autistic, Pete. From what Mom told me, Nicky was autistic."

"Do you have a clearer old photograph of Robbie?"

"In my office, yeah."

"Well, can I see it?" Pete asked.

"Why?"

"Just a hunch."

"All right, knock yourself out."

"Quinn's been acting strange. Ever since this guy showed up he's been weird," Pete said as Carl led him into a spanking clean office with dramatic views of the mountains beyond the white lace.

"Quinn has always been weird. He must pay you a fortune to fix things for him, afraid you're going to tell everyone he's a perverted old fuck, uh? Hey, he buy you that Explorer, Pete?"

"Fuck you, asshole."

"Easy, Pete."

Pete might have taken a swing at Carl but where the hell would that get him?

"Look, there's been something different about Quinn since Dowling showed up. I found him digging something up in the woods the other day, heard him screaming out there like a madman. Whatever it was, he reburied it further out in the woods. He told me it was an old dead dog he needed to move, but I don't know, the old bastard doesn't like dogs. He's never had a dog in his life, far as I know. And he hangs on to that shovel like it's a bag of gold."

"That's a picture of Robbie on the bookcase," Carl said as he leaned against the door and watched Pete study the photograph.

"I don't know ... could be," Pete said.

"Just what are you saying, Pete, that this guy is my brother, Robbie, or that Quinn's got a body in the yard?"

"Shit, man. Look, Carl, he could be, I mean, this guy could be Robbie."

"My parents are coming to stay with me in a few weeks. I don't want them hearing about this. You understand? Don't spread this around. You'll just start a hurtful rumor."

"I think you need to meet this guy, Dowling." Pete said earnestly and watched the sun glare into the room and reveal the striking blue of Carl's eyes. "You really need to meet this guy, Dowling," he repeated.

"Sure, Pete," Carl said slowly. "Sure, I'll meet him, but I

just think it's a strange coincidence, that's all."

Chapter Twenty

Jenna Dowling sat in a booth at the back of the old Irish Ale House on West Seventy-Ninth Street and ordered a coke and a hamburger. She was anxiously waiting for Sally, who'd just called on her cell phone to say she'd be late, and to go on and order without her.

Jenna had insisted on returning to the city with Nick, even though he wanted her to remain in the country. "Don't cut your vacation short on my account, I'm fine," he'd said. But for Jenna, that was not an option, even though he had assured her he needed the distraction of work — the circulation numbers —the bullshit from his boss — the manic, depressive energy at the paper.

"I'm not leaving you alone, Nick," she insisted.

Nick's bizarre experiences were keeping both of them up past dawn thinking up explanations for the inconsistencies that had surfaced in his history. Of course, Nick kept repeating that he didn't understand what was happening to him, but Jenna had come to other conclusions.

She had to talk to Sally. Sally would tell her what to do, how to handle Nick's apparent amnesia. Her mother and daughter were due back from Europe in just a few days and the last thing Jenna wanted Ronnie to hear was that her father may be losing his mind, or that his whole life had been false, and no one knew who the hell he was.

Jenna couldn't find a logical explanation for her husband's memory issues. Perhaps, he'd developed some sort of psychotic disorder, or perhaps, he was lying, feigning confusion, but for what purpose?

The few hours they'd wound up spending with the Dowling's, in Phoenicia, had turned out to be even more disturbing than it had been to meet them initially. The older couple had taken pity on them because Nick was so apparently distraught, and they had invited them all inside their house. Nancy Dowling was even kind enough to serve coffee. It had been an interesting couple of hours.

"Just what is autism?" Nick asked, as he looked over at Tom Dowling. Jenna could tell he was struggling to regain his composure.

"Well, the symptoms of autism vary from child to child," Tom told him.

"I've heard that they sometimes have special gifts," Nick said.

Tom Dowling nodded. "Yes, some of them do. Nicky was a savant. He had unusual abilities for a boy his age, but he couldn't really concentrate for very long on his studies. He couldn't sit still for more than five minutes.

One of the only people he ever spoke to directly was his friend, Robbie. Nicky was always a very nervous child, very hyperactive. He bonded with Robbie Nichols, which can be an unusual attachment for autistic children. But Robbie was a good kid, always paid Nicky a lot of attention."

Jenna made a conscious attempt to smile at Nancy Dowling. She felt sorry for the woman, and more than a bit guilty for dredging up painful memories.

Tom Dowling lit a cigarette and sat back. "Nicky told us that he had solved the mysteries of the world, even the mystery of time, space and God." Tom blew the smoke out into the room with an exaggerated sweep of his hand, proudly remembering his son. "And death, too," he added.

"Mysteries of God? Death? Pretty heavy stuff for a child." Nick reached for his coffee and looked into Tom Dowling's eyes over the rim of his cup.

Nancy Dowling leaned in and offered Nick a refill.

"A fancy vanilla brew I picked up in Woodstock this morning," she said.

"Very good brew." Nick extended his cup for more of it.

"He was just a kid, but the effects of autism probably gave him a different perception on things," Tom continued. "It happens, sometimes. Nicky knew all about formulas and equations and he'd spew this stuff out like he was a professor. Of course, I don't know how accurate he was, but he'd get this glazed look in his eyes and start talking about space and time. He told us that God was a logical entity."

"Yes, because God contained all opposites, such as life and death," Nancy added.

"And those opposites had to be contained somewhere," Tom said. "Nicky told us that the universe is an ongoing spontaneous occurrence of opposites."

Tom seemed lost in the recollection for a moment, but then, he seemed to shrug the memory off. "Oh, he said so many things of that nature."

"How did he explain the mysteries of death?" Laurie eagerly asked.

Jenna wanted to laugh, *as if the child really had those answers*, she thought.

"Well, he defined death as an alternate reality, one that exists in an alternate world. Nicky insisted that there were many alternate realities. He explained it as illogical to believe that anything that had ever lived could cease to be. He said that when you die, you also contain life All of us are an imprint in time. It has something to do with life containing death and death containing life. It wasn't either – or, it was the same. He tried to explain what he was talking about by using the analogy of turning a light off and on ... how the effect of the light remains. He used to tell us that what you see with illumination doesn't alter what you've witnessed when the light is switched off; it's just hidden from your view, momentarily. He said that *is* and *isn't* couldn't exist without the other. They both contain the same amount of truth."

"So then, an alternate reality is something we can't see but that makes it no less real, is that what he meant?" Nick asked.

"I suppose so. Nicky told us that any one of us could alter what we experience as being real. He said that people's perceptions change according to revelations." Tom Dowling put a teaspoon of sugar into his cup and stirred it. "Nicky said that there were space people behind Robbie's house that came from a future time. Their spaceship was inhabited by people who were from an alternate reality. They could manipulate perception."

"Really?" Nick said and reached for Jenna's hand. She wanted to squeeze his hand but didn't. She could tell that he was actually taking the ramblings of an autistic child as seriously as Einstein's theory of relativity, and it angered her.

"According to our son, the people from this spaceship wanted to take him away with them because he had an ability to understand the perception of time. He could perceive things that were not yet known," Tom said.

"Well, I guess that makes sense." Nick looked at Tom earnestly.

"Oh, really, Nick," Jenna quipped and dropped his hand.

"Nicky told us that he could alter a person's experience of what they perceive as fact. He said that even death was another form of perception. When a person dies, the body simply sheds itself of some outer layer, and continues on in another form. This form can be seen by others … like the light bulb … existing but hidden behind the concept of death. He explained God's time as eternally present. For Nicky, anything that is, or once was, is imprinted and captured forever. He said it was illogical to think that the light from a bulb isn't hidden behind darkness. He compared death to the invention of electricity, how it was always there, just waiting to be discovered. Nicky said that the definition of death is also waiting to be defined and altered. Even God will be understood one day … as a spontaneous occurrence, created in a moment of all things past and present. Nicky said that God contains the power of a timeless perception" Tom slowly shook his head. "It's amazing that I still remember all that stuff he'd come up with."

"Autistic children can be very unusual," Nancy said, trying to explain away her son's gibberish as she glanced at her husband. "There's still so much we don't understand about children with special abilities."

Tom looked at her. His expression was sad. "Nicky said that death, in our time, is perceived as what's missing. In a future time, death will be illuminated as what's found. Ha! I wish I could believe that, but pretty advanced for a ten-year-old, wouldn't you say? But, if our Nicky still exists, why won't he come back to us? Why won't he tell us he's okay?"

"We see things we expect to see, according to Nicky? Is that what he meant?" Laurie quickly asked, sitting forward in her chair until she was almost falling out of it. "We assume truth as we experience it? It's like an agreement, until it's altered?"

Tom Dowling nodded, "I guess so. Nicky repeated things very quickly. It used to make it sound like everything he said was factual. He told us that the aliens are puzzled by us because we exist in madness. He said there is a cure, but we haven't arrived at it yet."

"The cure?" Jenna asked.

"Agreement," Tom said. "The only way to cure madness, Nicky told us, is to create an action to alter its course, and then agree to it."

Jenna could tell that remembering Nicky was still painful for the Dowling's. She stood up abruptly and walked to the window.

"Are autistic children usually so imaginative?" she asked, tossing the words over her shoulder.

"Well, yes, sometimes they can be," Nancy Dowling said as she looked carefully at Nick. "Our son told us that he would be abducted by space people who would take him to live in their reality. And then, right after he said that, he disappeared."

"Then it's possible that the boys weren't murdered, they were abducted?" Nick asked, feeling a hollowness in the pit of his stomach like he was getting at something too bizarre for anyone to accept.

"Oh, Nick, really." Jenna shook her head in exasperation.

Nick avoided looking at her and sat back down. He slowly reached out for another sip of his coffee.

"The other boy … Robbie … did Nicky say they would take him as well?" Nick asked.

Tom Dowling leaned back in his chair. "No, he wasn't a savant," he said. "They only wanted Nicky."

Nick looked at him with mounting anxiety. "But they still took Robbie?"

"Took? We don't know that," Tom answered. "Nicky told us that the aliens abducted people all the time and brought them back to their spaceship. They took people who were thought to have disappeared. Children, men, women, it didn't matter."

"They must have had some purpose," Nick said. "The aliens, assuming they were aliens."

"Well, we certainly don't know what they are, do we?" Tom suddenly put his face in his hands. "Our Nicky had a very adventurous streak. If there really were aliens that night our son would have probably gone with them willingly."

"What about the other boy, was he adventurous?" Nick asked.

"You're not taking Nicky's ramblings seriously, are you?" Tom asked, you look as if you're buying it.

"I find his ramblings interesting." Nick said quietly.

"Nicky said we could all manipulate reality, create

156

alternate ones just by shifting agreements between people. He defined it as eradicating what we think of as truth through a shifting belief system. In other words, by convincing enough people that Jesus turned water into wine, we actually make it so. A flat world is suddenly believed to be round. A universe is believed to be void of life except on earth. One day, perhaps, that won't be so," Tom said.

"Then it's possible that we're capable of being manipulated, especially if other beings may be responsible for our evolution," Nick said.

"Some people do say they've seen spaceships," Laurie interjected.

"Well." Tom sighed. "Nicky would say it's because they agreed to see them."

Nick looked at Tom and wanted to comfort him. "That's why your son can't come to you; he's not accessible to you in your reality. But he does exist ... I mean to say, he *could* possibly exist."

The last thing he wanted to admit to this sweet couple was that he'd spoken to their son at the old Nichol's place in New Kingston. He was glad he had caught himself in time. These poor people didn't need the burden of his delusions.

"What did the police say about Nicky's story?" Jenna asked as she walked back to the couch and sat. "Did you tell them anything about space people?"

"We didn't find it relevant. The police believe both children were abducted by a child offender and murdered. We concur." Tom sounded certain.

"You didn't believe your son?" Laurie asked as she looked from Nancy to Tom Dowling and studied their faces.

"We don't believe in space creatures," Tom Dowling

said with the same certainty in his expression. "Nicky had an active imagination. We believe our son was murdered, though we'd rather believe he went to live on Mars, safe and sound."

Nick got up from his chair and sat near Tom. "How can I explain what's happening to me?" he asked. "I have just discovered that nothing about my memories coincide with reality. I'm not at all sure of who I am. How does that happen unless my perception of who I am has been altered in some way, unless my memories have been invaded?"

"Perhaps, you have amnesia?" Tom stared at him.

Nick looked off. "Don't you think it's possible that your son and his friend were abducted by space beings?" he asked, slowly turning his attention back into the room.

"There aren't any space people," Tom said.

"Just because we can't see them doesn't mean they don't exist," Nick said quickly. "Were human beings logical to dinosaurs?"

"I wish I could agree with you," Tom Dowling said. "But until humans existed, they didn't."

Nick looked over at Laurie with a questioning silence, then turned his attention to Jenna.

Jenna stared at the floor. She looked angry, angry at having her world compromised by a lunatic husband with an ambivalent past, and a belief in aliens.

Nick found her eyes. "Are you all right?" he asked.

"Sure, Nick, sure. I'm fine," she said.

Chapter Twenty-One

Sally sat down quickly, grabbing her napkin, and fanning it out, nearly blowing a utensil to the floor.

"Whew, sorry, I'm late. My God, you look terrible."

"I haven't slept in days," Jenna said.

"That hamburger looks sumptuous, but you haven't touched it."

"I've been lost in thought."

"C'mon, tell me what's bothering you. It's going to take me twenty minutes to get a waiter over here, anyway." Sally turned her head around and waved an arm in the air. After a brief moment, she turned back to Jenna. "See, what did I tell you? They're ignoring me," she said. "It's my age. Invisible."

Jenna slid her plate closer to Sally so she could take some of her fries. "Nick has replaced his past with someone else's," she said.

Sally stopped popping the fries into her mouth and listened.

"He was not recognized by his high school girlfriend, he pretended to be Tom and Nancy Dowling's son, but he isn't. It seems that the real Nick Dowling was an autistic child who was kidnapped and murdered in 1967."

"So, he took this kid's name from a tombstone or an old newspaper article?"

"He must have. For the last twenty years I have believed that I was married to Nick Dowling. He told me his parents were dead and he was raised in Phoenicia, New York. Now, he could have been raised on the moon for all I know."

Jenna stopped talking as the waitress took Sally's order. She noticed the lines around Sally's eyes. Her expression was more intense than usual, and it made Jenna's stomach flip.

"I'm a little afraid of this, Jenna. I'm not going to lie to you," Sally said.

"What do you mean?"

"Why is he protecting his past?"

"Could he have amnesia?"

"Why isn't he aware that he has amnesia? Besides, amnesia is usually only temporary. Even a major trauma wouldn't cause a memory block for over twenty years. It's highly unlikely. He might repress a memory, several memories, but not his entire identity. If he's an amnesia victim, he'd know it and he would have told you."

"What is going on?" Jenna put her hands through her hair. She felt about to cry.

Sally reached over the table and placed her hand on Jenna's arm. "Look," she told her, "you're going to have to dredge it all up — birth certificate —hometown records —

whatever you can get your hands on. You've got to find out who he really is and why he's been lying about it."

"My sister thinks he's the victim of an alien abduction."

"What?" Sally threw back her head and laughed so hard that several people turned in their direction.

"Laurie had the nerve to tell me that she thinks Nick was kidnapped years ago by people from another planet," Jenna whispered.

"Laurie has never played with a full deck, has she?" Sally laughed even harder and took a sip of water. "Start in New Kingston, see if you can get birth records for babies born around the same year as the real Nick Dowling. See if Nick was on the periphery somewhere. Cover every small town in the area."

"What do you mean?"

"Well, maybe he knew those kidnapped children, or knew of them. If he really was raised out that way then he certainly must have heard about the murders. It must have been really big news back then; people are probably still talking about it. Maybe he took the identity of one of the boys, years later."

"Why would he do that unless he was running away from something, Sally?"

"Precisely. Jenna, your husband might be hiding some gruesome secret. You've got to find out what it is."

The waitress put a breadbasket on their table and poured them water from a cloudy plastic pitcher. The noise volume at the Old Irish Ale House had risen. Jenna took a long sip of her coke and wondered what, in God's name, her husband was running from.

"Sally, Nick believes he was abducted also."

"You mean, by aliens?"

"Yes, after our visit with the Dowling's, he's convinced

of it."

"It's a shield to keep you, or himself, from the truth," "Sally said, "I'm afraid it could also be a psychotic disorder of some kind. There are no such things as space aliens. Don't you dare let him think you're buying into that nonsense because he'll try to hold on to those illusions. Nick knows you're too bright to believe him. He should know better."

"At first, he said he was just psychic, now he wants me to believe he was abducted by a UFO?"

"I pretty much surmised when he came to talk to me that he was going to use some pretty bizarre shields to suppress the truth."

"He mentioned aliens?"

Sally peered at Jenna over her glasses. "Jenna, he needs something to hide behind. Unfortunately, he married you and not Laurie, and you're not buying little green men."

Chapter Twenty-Two

His breath came out slow and steady. It was like awakening from a disturbing dream he couldn't remember. It took a while before he realized he was sitting on the ground. It was dark and he could barely see in front of him. The river smelled like a locker room, pungent and sour. He tried to recall his dream, but his head was like a balloon, full of helium. He had been shivering in the dark night, but his clothes were dry. How could that be, he wondered? He'd jumped in the river but how did he get out? Probably swam, he surmised. His thoughts started making a bit more sense. He remembered the fall and he almost screamed out. God, how did he survive it? He stood to his feet. He was unsure and had to steady himself with his arms outstretched. It made him woozy. He collapsed back down on the ground.

He reached around into his pocket and found a wad of bills, at least twenty-one-hundred-dollar bills. Uncanny, he had emptied his pockets before jumping. Someone put the money there, but who? Where the hell was he? It didn't take long to figure it out, he heard the traffic. Tough fucking luck, he'd wanted to kill himself and had failed in his mission, so now he'd be charged with Natalie's murder. He wasn't meant to die then; he was meant to live. He crawled up the steep embankment. It was empty when he got to the top. Nothing there but a concrete walkway. He had to get to the other side, he had to get to Gregory's. He couldn't go home, he had to get upstate. He held out his hand and made it over another embankment. He crawled up yet another concrete hill until the sound of traffic enlivened him. The tooting horns reminding him that he was meant to be a part of it, this loud, energetic swirl of life. He felt good holding out his hand until a cab stopped before him. He held out the wad of bills and said, "take me to the Catskills, little town of Olive. I'll tell you how to get there."

Sam Hollander had a small office in an old Brownstone on MacDougal Street, in Greenwich Village but he lived in Gramercy, near the park. He passed a doorman every day and walked into a fancy elevator with brass doors. From his windows he could see the Empire State building. Never-the-less, he loved the village and spent a lot of time there, reading his morning paper in coffee houses and grabbing lunch in small little hole in the wall Mexican or Japanese restaurants.

He and Laurie had met for the first time in a coffee shop one afternoon. She had noticed that the book he was reading was on alien sightings. "Interesting material," she had said as she leaned in toward his table. "Do you believe in it?"

"I do this for a living," he said. He knew he appeared defensive. Being defensive was a learned behavior, having begun years ago when his brother Elijah called him a madman.

"You're a writer?" she'd asked.

"Well, I research, and I write about it." He handed her his card.

Laurie scanned it quickly. Sam Hollander, *Extraterrestrial Sightings and Unexplained Phenomena.* He thought she appeared curiously impressed.

Six months later, after great sex and so much in common that they never ran out of things to say to one another, Sam stopped calling. A few weeks after their last date, she'd passed him on the street and had approached him like an old friend. *Well, why not?* She noticed that he appeared uncomfortable, and his eyes darted toward the traffic light.

"Haven't seen you in a while, Sam," she'd said sweetly, "Are you all right?"

He'd reached out and touched her gently on the shoulder, but he spoke over her head, avoiding her eyes, "Busy schedule this month. I'll call you soon. Maybe we'll catch a movie?"

"Sure," she said as he led her to the other side of the street in his gentlemanly fashion. She assumed he'd stop, talk some more, but he briskly walked off in the other direction when they reached the corner. She watched as he raised his hand in the air, like an afterthought.

"I'll call you," he'd tossed the words over his shoulder without looking back.

She watched him disappear, his long, vintage dark coat, making him look like a quintessential eccentric. She'd noticed that he seemed to skip away, as if running, darting into the shadows with his ambiguities.

But now, she had the perfect excuse to see him again. There she was, in dire need of Sam Hollander's expertise on other worldly phenomena. Nick had given her the perfect opportunity to force her presence in Sam's life and twitter whatever remnants of affection were still hiding behind his suit of armor.

"Laurie?" Sam said, "What a surprise."

Laurie frowned, remembering how he had said he'd call and never did.

"My brother-in-law has been abducted," she said into the phone, not wanting to waste any time leading up to it.

"Really? And how do you know that?" he asked, with a humorous grin she was sure she'd see if he were standing in front of her.

She knew his thoughts; this crazy story she'd concocted was only a ploy to find herself back in his bed. But she relayed the strange circumstances anyway, how no one from Nick's past remembered him, the ghost in the field, and his bizarre experience in Fox Hollow. Laurie realized, after giving him a ten-minute monologue, that he was either listening so carefully one could hear a pin drop, or he had fallen asleep.

"Hey, are you there Sam?"

"Interesting story," Sam said.

"Well, yeah."

"Look, how well do you know this guy?" he asked her. "Could he be playing a joke on you?"

"Sam, I've known him over twenty years. He's

married to my holier than thou sister and he's been a relatively conservative person, on the outside anyway, from the time I met him. All of a sudden he's speaking to spirits, and he has missing memories from his past. It's out of character."

"You're brother-in-law? How totally bizarre."

"Yeah, totally bizarre."

"Hum, "Sam said, "Are you sure he isn't running from something? Most abductees have childhoods in Nebraska, or Oklahoma, or wherever. They don't just appear out of Manhattan."

Laurie went into another monologue about Nick's nightmares and his vision of alien looking people. Us but slightly different.

"That's interesting," Sam said.

"You've already said that." Laurie had an impulse to hang up.

"You know for a fact that no-one from this guy's past knows who he is?" Sam asked.

Laurie sensed that his interest level seemed to rise a notch.

"I was in Phoenicia with him, Sam. I was in New Kingston when he ran into his supposed ex-girlfriend. No-one knows him and he doesn't know them."

"Look, I'd be willing to talk to your brother-in-law."

"That would be great; he's feeling pretty desperate."

"Why don't you come to my office tomorrow? I've got some information on alternate realities that I can share with you prior to meeting Nick. It could shed some light on this."

"Alternate realities?" Laurie suddenly remembered what the older couple had told them about Nicky Dowling's ramblings.

"How about three o'clock?" Sam asked.

Laurie didn't really want to see Sam under these circumstances. He was supposed to call on his own, apologize for his bad behavior and beg for forgiveness.

"Sure, Sam, I'll be there," she said, already thinking about what she'd wear, the aloof composure she would project, hoping she was finally over him enough to appear disinterested.

Sam was sufficiently curious but suspect. Was Laurie's brother-in-law telling the truth? He didn't take what people told him at face value, but he knew about identity switches, all those experiments with memory. Many people under hypnosis had recalled lives other than their own. They would come out of their hypnosis sessions completely confused, often forgetting their names for a moment. He didn't know why the aliens would be so fascinated with memory, but they obviously were. Many of his patients had told him that their minds felt emptied during the abductions, like everything had been spilled out, and then filled again.

Chapter Twenty-Three

Laurie looked across the room and watched as Sam got out an old dusty book on space sightings. She loved the slight, studied movement of his body, the prominence of his nose as it narrowed to his lips, the dark intelligence of his noticeably large eyes. Yes, he was undoubtedly the most appealing man she'd ever known.

"It says here that some abductees put under hypnosis have spoken about a spaceship called Pharaoh's Star," he told her. "They describe their experiences of the ship as feeling like they've come upon an alternate reality, as if the experience of it could be real but they're not positive."

Laurie sat upright in her chair and looked at the book Sam was reading. She noticed he had on those terrific glasses, the thin burnt copper looking frames that seemed so meticulously chosen. She watched as the hands that had once stroked her so gently, tapped on the sides of the old walnut desk.

"It's your book? Your name is on it."

"Yes, I wrote it," he said.

"Pharaoh's Star?" she read the title off the front cover.

"Yes. Pharaoh's Star is a ship, actually, its many ships. According to the people who say they've been on these ships, they see substance cities, cities and towns exactly like our own mother earth."

"What's that have to do with alternate realities?" she asked.

"The Pharaoh's communicate from a non-physical place because they don't exist in our time frame."

"Nonphysical place?" Laurie shook her head. "I don't understand."

"It has something to do with time," Sam said as he put his hand on his chin. "When they enter our hemisphere they are actually entering a time sphere different than their own. For all practical purposes they shouldn't exist, but they do ... or can, I should say."

"Thanks for confusing me more." She laughed.

"Their present is our future. According to our concept of time, they shouldn't exist."

She cocked her head to one side and raised a brow. "I'm lost."

Sam sat back and put his feet up on his desk. "It seems that several of my patients have revealed, under hypnosis, that Pharaoh's Star is built by us ... as a savior ship."

"What do you mean?"

"Well, it seems that these aliens have come into our hemisphere from quite another dimension, as I said."

"Why?"

"When these ships are first built, and I'm not sure in

what century they were built, but the ships were filled with engineers, teachers, scientists — all of our finest and most gifted citizens were sent to live in these spaceships."

"Why?" Laurie asked again.

"To establish life and erect a home planet."

"I don't follow you."

"During the Black Century over eighty percent of Earth becomes uninhabitable." Sam looked into her eyes. "The ships are built by us before all of Earth becomes uninhabitable. We have nowhere to go except space."

Laurie felt anxious, remembering the television special she'd recently seen on global warming. "It sounds like Noah's Ark."

"Many say the Bible is a human premonition."

"What else?" Laurie asked.

"I've been told that these pioneers build their cities very much like our own. They are referred to as substance cities. Apparently, America is really wiped out during a period they call the "Black Century."

"You're kidding?"

"No."

"What happens then?"

"These brave pioneers build schools, banks, run businesses. They establish a world of pacifists and humanitarians that exist for centuries. I'm told it's a bit of a Utopia."

"You mean, these people exist in space?" Laurie said.

"Well, not as they were. Over time, something happens to them. You see, many of the people that were left on earth were already physically deformed by nuclear waste. Then, after several centuries, the humans on the spaceships evolved differently because their atmosphere was unnatural, generated by machines."

"What do you mean?"

"Their skin tone changed; it became almost transparent. Their offspring was eventually born without the gene for hair. Ears become obsolete because sound is carried differently, and ears were no longer needed in the same way. Most of the people on the ships communicate technologically, but also, I'm told, telepathically. They're clearly much more advanced than we are today."

"Yet they abduct people."

Sam shrugged, "For good reason, I'm sure, though we may not understand it."

"What do they do for fun?" she asked, half-jokingly.

"I don't know. I'm told that musical instruments become antiques. They have some sort of strange space art. Their theatre becomes all mime, but their architecture replicates ours, at least in the old sections where the substance cities are erected. They wanted to feel at home, replicate Mother Earth."

"What happens to them?"

"They come under attack by the Government of Interplanetary Alliances."

"Under attack?"

"Yes, for abducting female eggs from Earth women as early as the 1940s, but this is not detected and acknowledged for years, not until scientists in the Black Century discover the presence of alien DNA. The aliens don't purposely hurt us, of course, but they do try in earnest to produce babies that will look more human — like their own ancestors. It's called the Amos Project. Amos was the first pioneer on Pharaoh's Star. Unfortunately, the evolution is painfully slow."

"So, we eventually attack them?" Laurie asked, horrified by the prospect. "Because we discover they abducted female eggs?"

"No, that wasn't the reason. You see, they don't have

the gene for war — for aggression of any kind. Like ears, aggression was no longer needed, no longer a part of their make-up. They were unable to protect themselves from interplanetary wars. Wars became the norm back on the planet Earth. That's the destiny before us, I'm afraid. Apparently, this so-called Government Alliance found the Pharaoh's pacifism very threatening. Non-violence becomes an unacceptable way of life. The Earth we inhabit now becomes a feeding ground for evil after the Black Century."

"So these humans were becoming too human for the Government?" Laurie was perplexed, how could we regress to such a degree, she wondered.

"Precisely." Sam nodded. "It seems that even the Pharaoh children were in danger. No mercy shown. Some of the Pharaoh's escape by moving the ships. They are earth pioneers, the off-spring of heroes, actually, but they'll never get the credit for it."

"But this future hasn't happened yet." Laurie said.

"Well, in a sense, it has. Time, as they interpret it, has no linear pattern."

"So, they live on the ship, these people?"

"Yes. When the ships are clustered together they look like stars, thus the name Pharaoh's Star, the name of the lead ship. Pharaoh's Star will eventually lead the way to safety when the planet Earth melts."

"When Earth melts?"

"According to my patients, our planet becomes a hot shell with not a trace of life left on it. Eventually, our planet is doomed. Those who wish to live as a Pharaoh will be guided by the night sky, by the lights of Pharaoh's Star. Nothing that's going to happen anytime soon though."

Laurie put her face in her hands. "What happens to

the people once they get to Pharaoh's Star?"

"They live on their ships, searching for a habitable planet. Unfortunately, they have a deep mistrust of their ancestors, and they won't communicate in this time sphere, won't warn us of our devastating future."

"I can't say I blame them for not communicating with us," Laurie said softly. "But then, why come to earth at all, when there's no chance of connecting with us?"

"I would have to guess, but I think they want to help us understand our need for self-destruction. I think that's why they seem to be so fascinated with the way we think, what breeds evil and what breeds compassion. Maybe they're trying to eradicate violence, once they understand it, once they understand us. Since they evolved from us, from humans, they feel they can eventually merge into our existence unnoticed, and perhaps, alter the course we're on. Our world is not only on the path of extinction, but the people on Earth become more and more violent as the geography of our planet deteriorates. Perhaps, the Pharaoh's feel they can eventually save the human race from a destiny that can only be altered by people who can manipulate time. The aliens want to create a new future. I assume they find our present society frightening — perversion — murder —not to mention drugs, sex and rock and roll." He attempted to laugh but only managed a smile.

"Are any of them here?"

"They might be here. They might always have been here. Mostly they abduct us and probe our minds. They study aggression a great deal because aggression is what destroys us. The Pharaohs are not made up of as many opposites as we are. There is no day and night on Pharaoh's Star; their emotions do not rise and fall as ours do. They don't bring pain upon each other, and because they understand death, they don't fear it. You and I, and the rest of society, all of society, would be dinosaurs to them."

"What does any of this have to do with Nick and his vision of the boy?" Laurie asked.

"I'm not sure, but it is possible he was abducted, and his mind was screwed with." Sam walked over to the window and looked out.

"This is so like a grade B movie. His mind was screwed with?" Laurie said. "Why Nick?"

"Fiction and fact are not dissimilar."

"If what you're telling me is true, they're not."

"Look, maybe that's why Nick sees the boy; his sense of time has been altered by his connection to the Pharaohs. The boy's death does not mean that he isn't contained in time. I can't see him, nor you ... but Nick could."

"Do you actually believe this?"

"How can I really tell the difference between what may be real and what isn't? I listen to my patients, and I try to disprove it. Until I can prove it's false, I have to assume it's truth."

"So, we are their Neanderthal man?"

"Well, that's how they would see you and I, as primitive. Patients who don't even know each other are incredibly consistent about the creation of Pharaoh's Star."

"The Pharaoh's are saviors, in a sense, aren't they?"

"Yes, and there are saviors all over our world, Laurie. And what do we do to saviors? We crucify them. We are a society in which many rational truths are considered radical, and saints are considered absurd ... and weak. How could we expect these people to come forth? Would Jesus come forth today?"

Laurie looked away. "Are you saying that plant life, animals and children disappear from the earth because of our greed, because of our ignorance … and indifference? Please tell me you're kidding."

"If you're asking me if we're in the Black Century … Well, if we're not, I can tell you this, it isn't far off."

Laurie stood up, sitting was impossible at this point.

"Let's get back to Nick, Laurie, that's why you're here," Sam said softly.

She looked at him. Something in his eyes made her reach for the sides of a chair and hold tight.

"Why not hypnotize Nick?" she asked. "Would that help?"

"Well, yes, if he'll allow it."

"Can I be in the room when you hypnotize him?"

"If he agrees to it."

Sam was still staring at her, and she suddenly felt embarrassed. Her eyes traveled to the floor, and then, back again to his gaze.

"Good to see you again, Laurie," he said, a bit uncomfortably.

She wasn't sure how to respond. "I guess that's my cue to go," she smiled broadly. "Or is it my cue to stay?"

He didn't answer her and looked down at his fingers.

"I'll see when Nick's available. What's your schedule?" She asked quickly, feeling like she'd just made a royal ass of herself.

"I'll fit him in, just call me."

Chapter Twenty-Four

Nick drove up to Bedford Hills, New York, and checked his map for Clear View Drive. He'd looked Betty Logan up in the phone book under her married name and found a listing for a Douglas and Elizabeth Tennyson. He wasn't exactly sure what he was going to say, but he was determined to follow every lead. He had to get to the bottom of these bizarre experiences before he really did lose his mind. Perhaps, all Betty had to do was see him and she'd remember who the hell he was.

Nick tried to get it straight in his head. When was the first time his safety net fell apart? All those years of seeing himself with a bloody weapon and two bodies at his feet; all those years of having his dreams haunted by fear, fear that his amnesia was protecting him from some horrible truth. And still, he'd kept it together. But after buying the house in New Kingston it all began to return like broken glass, splintered memories, spoon fed visions of people he might have known, or might not have known.

By this point, Nick wasn't quite sure whether he was having a bona fide breakdown or not. If his memory was returning, why was it so disassociated? Had he been heralded off to some planet and raised in space? He was certainly beginning to feel like that could be the only possible explanation ...but how does that explain the splintered memories?

Nick was pushing himself to pull the answers out of his psyche, but his mind still remained flat. His memories didn't seem to move forward or backward; they appeared like frozen images. He remembered Betty Logan and Darla Paine, the names, but not the faces. He remembered the sex, but he had trouble recalling anything else. When he thought of Betty, their affair appeared in his head like a sudden high. Yet he was strangely detached, almost as if he were reading a textbook about sex instead of actually having had it. It was like a fantasy. One hell of a hot lay; that was Betty, wasn't it? He gave it to her good, all right — standing up — sitting down — in the barn — covered with hay and dirt — lying on dirty sheets in a hot, cramped room listening to Blood Sweat and Tears and old Patsy Cline records ... hadn't he?

"Can I help you?"

Nick looked up and blushed. He knew it immediately. There was no way in hell this handsome, middle- aged woman, with hair as brown as a chestnut, could be, or ever was Betty Logan. No way in hell this woman could have ever screwed him in the backseat of a Ford

Convertible or jerked him off surrounded by cow dung and chickens. His memory quickly faded back into its hiding place.

"Betty?" He smiled meekly. He felt nauseous. Instinctively he put his hands to his temples and rubbed his head.

She looked at him carefully.

"My name is Elizabeth. I haven't been called Betty for a long time." She eyed him as if she were looking for the meat cleaver he might be hiding behind his back.

Nick gazed into her blue- blooded good-looking face and took in the cheekbones. He didn't have to look any further. He knew by the size of her shoulders that she was flat-chested — no Betty Logan here, no "watermelon bra."

"I think I have you confused with someone else. Remember, I called you the other day?"

"Oh, yes." She stepped back. "You hung up on me too." She clearly felt threatened. "I've a contractor upstairs right now. He's got a crew of three."

"Look, I'm sorry to bother you and I'm sorry I hung up on you ... but you see, I dated a girl named Betty Logan in high school. Well, sort of dated her. Actually, I had an affair with her," Nick blurted out. He tried to smile but he felt tense. He wondered if she'd think he was a nut job and start screaming.

"Really?" Elizabeth laughed. "I hope you're not coming back to stir up any risqué memories. I'm happily married."

Well, at least she had a sense of humor. Nick took a deep breath. He felt relieved.

"Oh, no, no, I'm married, as well, but I'm trying to find out why no one I went to high school with remembers me. I know it sounds bizarre but I'm just trying to get to the bottom of it."

"Phoenicia Central? Was that the school?"

"Yes," Nick told her. *I would imagine, only high school in Phoenicia.*

"I remember you; I think. What's your name again?"

"Let's see if you remember," he said.

She nodded enthusiastically, and her hair fell onto her forehead, covering her eyes. "Don't tell me then. I'll think of it. Can't remember what name you mentioned when you called."

"Do I look familiar?" he asked.

She brushed the hair off her face. "A bit, maybe," she said.

"Did you know Rob Nichols?"

"I don't think so. Look, would you like to come in?"

"Sure," he said, realizing she wasn't afraid of him anymore.

"I really do have some construction workers upstairs renovating my bathroom, but we can sit out by the pool. It will be quiet there."

"Sure, sure, I'd like that," Nick said as he stepped inside and followed Elizabeth Tennyson down a long gracious hall and through the large paned French doors that took them out to the patio. Nick noticed beautifully framed photographs of Elizabeth and Douglas Tennyson, two good-looking people laughing back at him from their Technicolor world— two good-looking people in signature sports shirts with three smiling daughters and a Scottish Terrier, two handsome, wealthy people who had never known what it was like to screw each other in pig shit, of that he was certain. Yet, that was the memory he had of a woman named Betty Logan.

Nick took a seat facing the Olympic-sized black bottom pool and opened the first button on his polo shirt. He was glad the shirt was signed, and his shoes were clean; glad he'd made enough money to look like a rich man, just for occasions like this. It's probably what got him through the door.

"Have you taken a day off work?" she asked. "I've been off a week, to oversee the construction on my bathroom. You can never trust these contractors."

Nick gave her a nod of agreement.

"You're not Billy Boyd, are you?" she suddenly asked.

"No," he said softly.

"You want something to drink?" she stood up quickly.

"No, really, I don't want to put you to any trouble."

"It's no trouble."

Nick watched as she went to a phone and apparently dialed her kitchen. She very sweetly asked someone named Karen to bring a pitcher of iced tea out to the patio.

"Thank you," he said.

She turned to him and studied his face. "You look somewhat familiar ... but sorry ... It isn't coming to me."

Nick sighed deeply and blew out his breath.

"Oh, no!" she suddenly yelped and quickly came back to her chair. "My God, you're not Andy Miller, are you?"

Nick shook his head and watched the little pout that came to her lips. He tried hard to remember her face. She was pretty, but not the Betty Logan who appeared in his mind, not even close.

Nick pointed a finger toward her and grinned, "Girl most likely to succeed?" he asked the obvious.

"Yes! I was accepted to Columbia, you do remember. There were only a handful of us that went to college at all, but I went to the crème de la crème." She giggled.

All of a sudden, like a flash of memory, Nick had an image, something about the drama club. Yes, the murdered blond girl in his nightmare was in the drama club, too. He wasn't exactly sure how he knew that, but he felt certain.

"There was a girl in the drama club, a blond. I can't recall her name, but she was a looker."

Elizabeth scowled. "Oh, God, you mean poor Iris."

Nick sat forward in his seat, "Iris? Yes, and she was very popular, right?"

Elizabeth cocked her head at him, and then, she suddenly looked as if she'd bitten into a lemon. "Not really. She was kind of a nerd ... pretty but nerdy."

Nick felt his confusion mounting again as he took a glass of tea from Karen, a cute young woman who smiled at him so alluringly that it made him shift his weight in the chair and look away. But as she placed the tray on the table in front of him, he looked back and tried to appear pleasantly flattered by her attentive exploration of his good looks. He felt ambivalent, as if he wanted to wink at her, but didn't. God, that was out of character for him; he'd never been a flirt.

"Wait! There were a few guys; they used to drool over this other blond in the Drama Club. Pete Shelby, Ross Medina, Robert Brown, Harrison Hinckley, they were all making fools of themselves over her."

"What was her name?" Nick asked.

"My God, Harrison? What a dirty joke, Harrison? You've changed a bit, but yes, of course, Harrison?"

"I'm sorry?" Nick felt confused.

"We dated, you and I. Remember? Still the clown, the practical joker, aren't you?"

Nick wasn't sure what to say. "We did? We dated?"

"But you're not Harrison, you couldn't be."

"No, I'm not Harrison."

"You look like him. Well, not altogether, but the years do alter our youthful charms, don't they?"

"I thought Harrison was dead?" Nick said impulsively.

"Oh, yes, I believe he is," she said. "But no one knows for sure."

"What was the girl's name?" Nick asked.

"What girl?"

"The popular one that all the guys liked?"

"Natalie Miller."

"Natalie Miller?" Nick quickly thought back to what the Dowling's in Phoenicia had told him, that the Millers had owned their house … and he had gone right to it.

"Yes, Natalie Miller. She was Andy's sister," she said in a whisper, as if it still mattered. Harrison married her. Harrison always got the girl."

"What did she look like?"

"She was a blond, very stacked." Elizabeth looked uncomfortable for a moment and added, "As you guys like to say."

Nick put his glass back on the table and put his head up toward the sun.

"Yes, that's her," he said quietly. "I must have confused the names. I'm sorry."

"Oh, not to worry, I do that all the time."

"She's dead?" Nick asked slowly.

"Yes, she's dead," Elizabeth said and blushed slightly. "She took Harrison from me in high school. He was such a bastard with women. But I never would have taken him for a murderer. I'm sure he's innocent."

Nick wondered what his connection was to Harrison Hinckley, his dreams, Natalie Miller, his resemblance?

"This Harrison guy, he killed his wife?"

"Yeah, that's what they say. I guess I should consider myself lucky that he dumped me." Elizabeth looked toward the sky and sighed.

Chapter Twenty-Five

From his desk window he could see the top of the hill and Pete's muddy Explorer racing toward his house.

"Ah, shit, what the hell does he want now?"

Carl slammed his latest chapter on the desk. He swiveled around in his chair and stood up.

"Steve?" he called as he walked into the kitchen.

Steve was in his chef's hat and Williams Sonoma apron. The spoon was almost to his lips. He showed a broad smile as he looked over at Carl; his teeth strikingly white against his black mustache. "My best sauce ever," he said.

"If it tastes as good as it smells I'll have to agree with you." Carl went to the back door and peered out.

"What's up?"

"Pete Shelby is paying us a visit."

"Why?" Steve asked and took some sauce off his spoon, "Oh, my God. Yum."

"Don't invite him for dinner, okay?"

"You don't think he'd like my Beef Danube?" Steve raised his eyes. "Or could it be the company? An intimate little dinner party of queer men?"

Carl laughed loudly. "A bit of both," he said as he walked back into the parlor.

Pete's steps could be heard on the wooden steps. All of a sudden, he was staring through the screen.

"Let me in, Carl," Pete said.

Carl opened the door and stepped aside. He noticed a green book in Pete's hand.

"You're not going to believe this," Pete said as he walked past Carl and eyed Steve briefly.

"Hello, Mr. Shelby," Steve sang out.

Pete grunted out some form of greeting before following Carl into the living room.

"Take a look at this," Pete said as he shoved the green book into Carl's hands.

Carl looked up, "Our yearbook?"

"Yeah." Pete started circling the room.

"I don't get it."

"Phoenicia Central, class of 1975."

Pete stood in front of Carl and stared at him, as if he didn't have a brain in his head.

"You're losing me." Carl shrugged.

"Nick Dowling isn't in it."

"I'm not sure I follow you." Carl sat down on the sofa and began leafing through the book.

"Nick Dowling said he graduated from Phoenicia Central in 1975, then why isn't he in there?"

"He had the date wrong," Carl said. "Likes to lie about his age?"

Pete was clearly agitated. "He's not listed with the freshman or the sophomores or the juniors, why the hell not?"

"I don't know. Maybe he's lying about where he went to high school."

"Why, Carl?"

"Well, I don't know." Carl stood up. "What are you getting at?"

Pete walked over to the window and looked through; without turning he said, "I think he's your brother, Carl. I think he's Robbie."

"Then where's he been?" Carl asked slowly. "All this time ... where's he been?"

"I don't know." Pete turned around and looked at him. "Maybe he was kidnapped."

"My brother would be over forty years old. Christ, he'd be nearly fifty. Why would it take him so long to come home, Pete?"

"You think somebody is playing some sort of sick game?"

Carl felt angry. Some total stranger was out there dredging up an old crime? He didn't know why, but he sure as hell was going to find out.

"I'm going to have this guy investigated, Pete. Steve is a lawyer. I'm sure he knows someone who can do it for us."

"Steve? Oh, yeah, yeah, sure, I think that's a good idea, Carl, because someone is fucking with us."

Jenna had refrained from actually calling Nick a liar because she didn't think he was. For Nick, his delusions were real, and she had to pretend to accept them, at least to a certain degree.

Nick had relayed his meeting with Elizabeth Tennyson as if the whole thing made sense, even though, for Jenna, Nick was desperately trying to give reality to his illusions, that was clear. She listened patiently as he told her how the experience of finding yet another person who had no idea of who he was had increased his anxiety. Yet, this disturbing sojourn to a stranger's doorstep had escalated Jenna's concern over what appeared to be an ever-increasing psychological breakdown.

Chapter Twenty-Six

"My brother-in-law has invited us to the country. He wants to meet you before he agrees to a hypnosis session with you next week."

"Really?"

"He wants to get a sense of you, make sure he trusts you, I guess," Laurie said.

"It's not enough that you trust me?" Sam hadn't planned to say that. It just came out because he'd been distracted, lost in his own thoughts. But she didn't altogether trust him. He knew that.

"Who says I trust you?" she quipped.

He knew he'd startled her with that remark. Seeing her again he realized he'd missed her. He'd actually talked himself out of seeing her anymore, he felt too raw. He doubted he'd ever get over his divorce. Well, maybe it was time to come out from under his shell and give their relationship a chance.

"Busy for dinner?" Sam asked.

"How's eight?" She said quickly, obviously feeling the same.

"Eights fine. Ponte Vecchio's?"

"Sure," she said softly.

He felt incredibly excited, remembering nights of back tables, red wine, and her laughter landing on his ears like the music of a harp. He'd been foolish to break it off but at the time, he felt as if it were the right thing to do.

They met up at a little Italian restaurant on Sullivan Street, that they had once termed, "their place." After the second glass of Chianti, Sam found her eyes and apologized for his disappearance act. Perhaps she'd give him another chance.

"Any explanation?" she asked him.

"My son saw us together one night. I was kissing you under a streetlamp. It was kind of shocking for him."

"I thought you were divorced, Sam."

"My divorce wasn't final while we were dating."

"Oh," Laurie said.

"I felt guilty after my son saw us like that, being so intimate, you know?" He reached out and took her hand. "I was very conflicted. I'm sorry."

"And now?" she asked.

He didn't remove his hand from hers. "I'm an angry son of a bitch, Laurie. I'm furious that my wife divorced me for no apparent reason except what she termed, 'irreconcilable differences.'"

"Are you still in love with her?"

"Of course." *Should he have added that,* he wondered?

Laurie removed her hand. He assumed he shouldn't have added that.

"Look, I was married for nineteen years. We had two children together. I didn't think I was the controlling bore she said I was, but I guess I wasn't introspective enough. So, it took me nineteen years to realize that that's what she thought of me … call me dense."

"Where does that leave us?"

He found her hand again and held it. "I don't know, Laurie. Anger is a dominant emotion for me right now and it colors my feelings for you. Anger is the only thing I've been able to feel. I can't get past it to get anywhere else."

"What are you saying?"

"That I need time."

"All right," she said, trying not to show her disappointment, he was sure.

Time could be forever, he thought, as he stared into her eyes and smiled.

Chapter Twenty-Seven

Laurie was not prepared to find Nick spread out on the couch buried under a blanket with circles under his eyes the size of quarters. Jenna was in the kitchen, tearfully chopping onions for a tuna salad. Laurie could hear the knife against the cutting board.

"Was there a death in the family?" Laurie asked as she tossed her jacket on a chair. "You look like hell, Nick."

"Sam Hollander?" Nick asked as he leaned up on his elbow.

Sam approached Nick and shook his hand. Jenna came out from the kitchen and gave Nick a concerned once over.

"My wife, Jenna," Nick said.

Laurie noticed the frown around her sister's mouth, though she attempted a smile. It was clear that the chaos in Nick's life was escalating.

"Onions," Jenna said out of nowhere. "Makes me tear up."

"Oh, me too," Sam said as he watched her disappear back into the kitchen.

Laurie pushed Nick's legs out of the way and sat beside him on the couch.

"What gives?" she asked him.

She looked at his haggard expression; he probably hadn't slept in days. She heard Sam ask if he had a headache because he had a damp cloth across his forehead.

"Yeah, I've been getting headaches lately. Never had them before, must be stress." Nick studied Sam's face. "So, the miracle man," he said.

"Well, I don't know about that but perhaps I can help," Sam uttered. "Have you read my books? There are similarities in my books to your experiences."

"Yeah, but I read your books after I had my experience in Fox Hollow."

Sam sat back. "You're not alone in this. I have several patients with confused memories."

"I've had trouble sleeping, but last night I just fell into a deep sleep, almost like someone had knocked me out."

"More nightmares, Nick?" Laurie asked.

"What kind of nightmares do you have?" Sam asked him.

"Last night was different, not like the ones I was having in the early part of the summer. The one I had last night was altogether different."

"How so?" Sam asked.

"I was in the ground, covered in dirt, it felt like I was being buried alive, like I was in a grave, covered by a net of some kind."

"Do you know who put you in the grave?" Sam asked.

"No, I don't remember, but it terrified me to be lying there. Something was holding me tight, like I was a mummy, wrapped like a mummy, and I knew I had to get out of the wrapping, that's the only way I was going to survive, I had to rip this thing off me."

Sam leaned in closer to Nick. It looked as if he might remove the damp cloth from Nick's forehead, but he didn't.

"I finally made it out of the grave, but someone grabbed me." Nick's breath had intensified.

"Do you remember anything else, Nick?" Sam asked.

"The thing that grabbed me was an alien."

"An alien? What did he look like?" Sam studied Nick's face as he questioned him.

"Transparent," Nick said and brought his hands to his forehead, as if he had a sharp pain. "Ah, yes, but tall … with blue eyes. I could see them in the dark."

"Sure it was an alien? They aren't usually described that way."

"I think he was an alien."

"Can we take a ride out to Fox Hollow Road tomorrow?" Sam asked.

"I'm counting on it," Nick said, his energy level noticeably increasing.

"You should probably take it easy today though," Sam said.

Nick removed the wet cloth and sat up. "Elizabeth Tennyson did not turn out to be the Betty Logan I remember, though she did look somewhat familiar," he said to Laurie.

"You went to see Betty Logan?" she asked.

"Yeah, I just thought I'd learn something."

"Did you?" Laurie studied him.

"No," he said softly. "Not anything that makes any sense."

"So, the people from your past don't appear to be who you remember them to be, is that correct?" Sam seemed to be studying Nick from a new perspective as he leaned back.

"Yes. How is that possible?"

"It isn't possible," Sam said quietly. "It isn't possible at all, but I've had memory lapses myself, must be because I'm getting older." Sam attempted a chuckle.

Laurie wished she knew what Sam was thinking, but Nick's thoughts were clear. Sam's poor attempt at humor had put him off. It was as if Sam was diminishing Nick's experiences.

"I know it sounds completely surreal but I'm telling you the truth. God knows, I'd prefer age related memory lapses to my present reality." Nick glared at Sam.

"I never said you were having age related memory lapses. Look, Nick, my job is to analyze what I find, without judgment," Sam said.

"More analysis?" Nick clenched his teeth and continued to glare at him. "I've had enough of analysis. I thought you were a psychic of sorts."

Sam smiled. "I'm a doctor of sorts. Look, you may be suppressing memories in order to protect yourself from something. That might cause you to misinterpret the truth," Sam said. "And by the way, I'm not psychic. I just believe in things most people don't.

"You mean like bullshit," Nick said.

Sam didn't seem in the least perplexed by Nick's remark. "You could be conveniently forgetting some very important information. But there is a reason for your memory loss. We don't know what the reason is yet. Maybe you're not supposed to remember, and this is all very intentional. Physical trauma can certainly cause memory loss." Sam smiled at him. "Have you fallen recently?"

Laurie was confused. She had expected Sam to just delve right into the alien stuff, tell Nick about Pharaoh's Star, but Sam did nothing of the kind. She wondered if he actually thought that Nick was a madman. He was acting too much like Jenna.

"Physical trauma? Look, I haven't fallen and I'm not conveniently forgetting anything. Won't hypnosis prove that?" Nick asked, clearly disappointed in Sam.

Sam remained calm, even though he must be able to feel that Nick was about to explode.

"Hypnosis will relax you enough to give us the truth as you experience it," Sam said.

Nick got up off the couch and walked over to the large picture window. "The truth as I experience it is absurd," he said.

"The truth is often absurd," Sam said. "It's always been that way. The truth that man couldn't fly was proven false with the Wright Brothers. The belief in ten Gods was eventually transformed into a belief in one. I imagine our belief in God will eventually transform into a knowledge we don't have today. So, which is it really? Remember, that once upon a time man didn't wear suits, cell phones did not exist, computers were unimaginable, and women couldn't vote. Today's truth is tomorrow's absurdity, Nick."

Chapter Twenty-Eight

Nick drove the Cherokee out toward Fox Hollow, slowly turning in where the Pine Trees stood tall and shielded the road sign from view. He stopped the jeep just after they turned onto the road. He showed Sam the sign. *Robert Nichols*, it read. Clear and sharp, *Robert Nichols.*

"What do you make of that, Sam?" Nick asked and watched as Sam lowered his head and looked up toward the top of the trees, "when I first drove in here that sign read Fox Hollow."

"It was dark, wasn't it?" Sam asked.

"Well, yeah, it was dark," Nick answered, "but I know what I read. The light from the moon illuminated it. Are you going to believe anything I'm telling you?"

"What year were those boys abducted?" Sam asked,

avoiding Nick's comment.

"1967," Nick said as he drove toward the open field.

"And in 1967 the road was called Fox Hollow?"

"Yes." Nick stopped the Cherokee at the edge of an open expanse of wildflowers and overgrown grass. The Maple trees looked on with a musical sway, as if they were about to flirtatiously bend their limbs to curtsy.

Sam had decided that Nick definitely had the behavior of an abductee, but Sam was troubled by it because someone else's memories were also in his head. He knew by Nick's dream that he was picking up on somebody else's experiences. Maybe the aliens had experimented with his memory and in the process, they had fused his mind with someone else's. Sam's patients often told him that the aliens did some kind of probe into violence, they believed that violence wasn't in our genes, but in our memory, and often compared the minds of two different people, a violent one and a non-violent one. Sam was beginning to believe that Nick had been used for years in alien science and it had really fucked with his head. Sam wondered if hypnosis could help him, Nick deserved his life back.

"This road seems very familiar to me, though it changes every time I'm on it," Nick said as he got out of the car, "I can't explain it, but it's as if I'm seeing it from a different perspective each time."

"But it's always familiar?" Sam asked.

"Yes, always."

It had rained all night and the sky was a spectral gray. The fog was slow to lift, and it lay over the meadow with a fugacious impermanence. There was a chill in the air and Laurie shuddered. She pulled the hood of her sweatshirt up over her head. The grass was wet, and they could hear their footsteps as they walked, crunching, and sloshing through the damp earth.

"You saw the boy in this field?" Sam looked around him.

"Yes," Nick said.

"Let's stop here then."

Sam laid an old brown blanket on the ground. "This is a perfect spot to clear our heads. Be very quiet and sit very still, like this. It's possible he'll appear again if he knows we want him to."

Sam sat cross-legged on the blanket and put his hands on his thighs. He turned his palms up.

Laurie sat beside Sam and copied his position. "We're meditating?" she asked.

"In a sense," Sam whispered low. "Close your eyes and do nothing. Just listen."

"What are we listening for?" Laurie whispered back.

"The wind. If you listen to the sound of it, it will lull your thoughts."

"I doubt if I can put my thoughts into lull mode, Sam, I've got too much on my mind," Nick said as he sat down next to them and put his palms up in the same position.

"Don't work at it, don't edit yourself, and don't dismiss what comes up. Acknowledge everything. Try and detach," Sam said softly. "Thoughts are okay, let them be there, and don't try and control them. Besides, you could use a little relaxation."

"Okay." Nick shrugged. "I'll try."

Sam heard the resignation in Nick's voice. "Meditating will ground us," he said gently. "It might open your mind to something important."

"Okay." Nick closed his eyes.

The three of them sat in the meadow with their knees almost touching. Laurie and Nick mimicked the low guttural sound that Sam forced out from his diaphragm.

"Listen to the wind," Sam said again. "Listen, very carefully. Keep your eyes closed. Try to clear your mind of everything but the sound and the movement of the wind."

"Crocket?" Nick yelled as he jumped up and circled the field."

"Nick?" Sam called.

"Crocket?" Nick yelled again.

Sam ran to up to him.

"Crocket?" Nick was screaming out the name.

"Are you calling a dog?" Sam asked, catching up with him.

"Yes, Crocket."

"Why did you open your eyes, Nick?" Sam grabbed his arm and turned him around.

"I heard a dog."

"What dog?" Sam looked out over the meadow. "You heard a dog?"

"Yes," Nick said. "Crocket."

"That's his name?" Sam asked.

"Yes," he said.

"Did you hear a dog?" Sam looked at Laurie as she approached them.

"No," she said. "Did you?"

"I don't think so." Sam's eyes returned to Nick's.

"You've got to be kidding?" Nick said. "You didn't see it? He's a big, old brown mutt."

"You called the dog, Crocket, Nick?" Sam studied his face. It was good that he was recalling his early life, then maybe, the other memories were leaving his mind.

"Yeah, must have heard someone call him that."

"But you don't remember exactly how you knew his name?"

"I often say things that just come out of my mouth ... I have no idea what they mean," he said.

"Did you ever have a dog, Nick?" Sam asked him. "Think, did you ever have a dog?"

"Yes, once I had a dog, but I don't remember what I called him."

"You don't remember your dog's name?" Sam asked. Confusion wasn't necessarily a bad thing.

"No, I can't remember. Maybe it was Crocket."

Sam put his arm around Nick's shoulder. "It's good Nick. It's all good that you remember."

Nick shook his head, he seemed thoroughly confused and looked at Sam helplessly.

"Who would do this to me?"

"We'll get to the bottom of all of it," Sam said.

"Through hypnosis?"

"I hope so."

"Let's go up to this guy Quinn's farmhouse," Sam said.

"What for?" Nick asked.

"Well, let's start with a big old brown mutt," Sam answered.

Chapter Twenty-Nine

Quinn was clearly not pleased to see Nick's Cherokee come to a stop in his driveway. Nick could see the grimace on the old man's face as he stood up on his porch.

"Good morning, Mr. Quinn," Nick said as he got out of the car.

Quinn stared at them. Nick noticed he seemed startled by Sam's presence.

"How can I help you now, Mr. Dowling?" Quinn asked.

"You remember my sister-in-law, Laurie? And this is Sam Hollander, a friend." Nick smiled graciously.

Sam reached out his hand. Nick noticed that Quinn hesitated.

Sam looked at Quinn's face, as though searching for something. He took a few steps back. "Do I know you?"

Sam asked.

Quinn shook his head, "No," he said. "I don't think so."

"You look like someone else, I guess." Sam studied him closely, and it made Quinn increasingly nervous.

"What can I do for you?" Quinn repeated.

"Do you have a dog, Mr. Quinn?" Nick grinned, as if assuming the obvious.

Quinn looked back at all three of them carefully. His jaw was set firm as he glared at them. He put his hands across his chest.

"No."

"Ever see an old brown mutt on your property?" Sam looked around before returning his eyes to Quinn.

"Not on my property," Quinn told him adamantly.

"Are you sure?" Nick asked. He had noticed a twitch in the old man's eyebrow.

"Not on my property," Quinn insisted. "But the country is full of old brown mutts. Might a wandered."

Sam reached for Laurie's hand. "We'll ask your neighbors. Must be theirs. He could be lost," Sam said politely. "We just wanted to make sure he had a home."

"Sorry to disturb you," Laurie quickly piped in as Sam led her back to the jeep.

"I thought you wanted information," Nick said as he started up the car and drove back down the road. "You sure didn't spend much time with Quinn."

"Didn't need to. I interviewed your Mr. Quinn a number of years ago. Yet he pretended he didn't know me. He knows me." Sam laughed. "Strange coincidence."

"What?" Laurie said, as she turned all the way around to find Sam's eyes in the back seat. "You interviewed *him*?"

"Yes," Sam said. "I never forget a face. I've got a file back at the office on this guy."

"You're kidding?" Laurie gave him a quizzical smile.

"I was up here because there was a claim about a space craft."

Quinn had showed up out of the blue; it had been quite a surprise for Sam.

"I can't believe this." Nick caught Sam's gaze through the rear mirror.

"Several people were said to have seen crafts that summer," Sam told them.

"What the hell did you interview him about?" Nick asked. "Don't tell me he saw a flying saucer?"

"Well, if I have it correctly, Quinn said that aliens had threatened him. I think he even called it blackmail at some point. He'd been a sheriff out here. He talked about seeing a spaceship. He told me that he had killed one of the aliens."

"What? Quinn?" Nick said. "That's incredible. Are you sure?"

"He couldn't produce an alien body or wouldn't produce it so I couldn't take him seriously. He said he buried it around here though."

"Who would have ever imagined that that old man would have spoken to you about aliens?" Laurie said softly.

"I can't recall all the details," Sam said. "But I'll get to those files first thing on Monday, right after we get back to the city. I might find something useful in them."

"So then you think there's a connection between the kidnapping or murder of the two boys and Quinn seeing a space ship?" Nick asked.

Sam nodded his head slowly. "Could be. I don't remember everything he told me. I interview so many people. But I do remember that his story was pretty spectacular at the time. I couldn't stop talking about it because it was so bizarre."

"This all has to connect somehow," Nick said. "The missing boys, my missing life, space abductions. Don't you think that it's all connected, Sam?"

"I sure do," Sam said.

Sam felt sorry for Nick. He wished he could give him all the answers. He wondered what the aliens wanted with him in the first place, but then again, their abductions were random. They experimented, assuming, he supposed, that it was for the good of mankind to fuck with a person's head.

As Nick drove the jeep down Mountain Road the fog was so thick it appeared like a heavy grey stage curtain, and though it was mysteriously engaging, it also obstructed their sightline. Nick turned on his lights.

"Shit!" Nick suddenly called out.

"What is it, Nick?" Laurie turned to him.

Sam sat forward and leaned into the front seat. "Something wrong, Nick?" he asked.

"There's a boy," Nick whispered.

Sam looked straight ahead, into the mist.

"Through the fog ... a boy. Can you see him?" Nick leaned close over the steering wheel.

Laurie strained forward and peered through the glass.

Nick slowly brought the Cherokee to a halt. He and Sam sat very still.

"The curtain of time has parted for me. He's real and he's not," Nick said.

"Who is he?" Sam asked.

"He's me and I'm with my dog, Crochet. My feet barely touch the ground — the big, old dog is lumbering beside me, looking this way and that. God, how I loved that dog."

"What else, Nick?"

"It's moving but it isn't."

"I don't see anything," Laurie said.

"Through the fog there's a form ... a boy, a dog," Nick uttered.

Nick put his foot on the gas, and slowly they drove into the vapor ... passing through the transitory, beguiling mist ... disintegrating outline after outline.

"It's gone," Nick said, as the car picked up speed and the road curved out before them. "But you saw it, didn't you?" he asked, turning to Sam.

"Was it really there Sam?" Laurie asked.

"Something is always there," Sam whispered. "If you stop to look."

Chapter Thirty

It turned out to be a pleasant evening. The absurd and the ridiculous had a night off.

"Run into any flying saucers out at the meadow?" Jenna had asked when the three returned.

They'd all responded the same. "No, no, nothing unusual," they'd said.

Good. Jenna was relieved not to have to listen to any more nonsense about aliens and spaceships.

Much to her surprise, as the evening wore on, she enjoyed her sister's company and even Sam Hollander's company. She actually found the infamous "alien buster" amusing. Jenna noticed how affectionate Sam was with Laurie, and as far as she could tell, he was a perfect gentleman. She appreciated his concern as he took off his sweater and put it around Laurie's shoulder before the fire kicked up and warmed them. He helped Jenna clear the table, something not even Laurie offered to do. Sam also insisted on helping Jenna with the dishes.

"Oh, no, please Sam. Don't bother. We have a dishwasher," Jenna insisted, but he followed her into the kitchen anyway.

"You'll never get all those dishes on the first load. I'll help, really," Sam said.

Jenna threw him a towel, "Tell you what, I'll wash, you dry?"

"Sure."

Sam became more and more appealing as Jenna got to know him. She still felt a pang of disappointment though, despite his charm, he was far too eccentric. How she would love it if this truly likeable man turned out to be Mr. Right for Laurie, Jenna only wanted the best for her sister, and Sam appeared supportive and caring, so unlike the egoists that Laurie usually introduced her to ... so maybe, there was a future here ... just maybe eccentricity was more of a plus than a minus.

"You don't approve of me, do you?" Sam asked as he leaned against the counter. He had only dried one pot and there he was, already attacking her with his fantasy life.

Jenna sighed but continued running a brillo pad around a casserole dish. She really didn't want to get into this; she wanted to keep liking him.

"You're very direct, aren't you?" she asked, turning her head sharply to find his expression. He wore a grin, obviously making light of what she knew to be a serious issue. Her husband needed help, but not *his* help.

"I'm surprised you agreed to Nick's hypnosis session on Tuesday. I didn't think you trusted me." Sam reached for the dish and took it out of Jenna's hand.

"Look," she said, as she turned to face him again, feeling somewhat uncomfortable, "I don't trust you and I don't believe in aliens. Is that surprising? I have a PhD in psychology, not in paranormal studies."

Sam laughed so hard that Jenna thought he might drop the dish.

"Wow, that was meant to be an attack below the belt, wasn't it?"

"Just a fact."

"Look, Jenna, I also have a PhD in psychology: Teachers College. You can check me out. You'll discover that I was a conventional psychotherapist for years. I'm a licensed hypnotherapist now, as well. You can verify it with the American Psychological Association if you'd like."

Jenna stepped back from the sink and stared at him. "Don't you write books about all this stuff?"

"Yes, I do. People need to know about this stuff, as you call it."

"How did you go from being completely legitimate to..." she darted her eyes back and forth, as if looking for the right words, but came up, however unfortunately, with only one, 'this bullshit'?"

Sam did not seem fazed by her comment. He picked up another dish and began to dry it.

"I became disenchanted with psychotherapy. I was treating too many typical neurotics, mostly narcissists, consistently boring and predictable people. You never cure them, you know. They just go on and on and on."

"Well, people in pain do go on and on, I guess, hoping we'll help them." She didn't like that he condescended to his patients, judged them so harshly.

"I didn't mean to be insensitive. I guess I'm pretty

much jaded. I actually started out being a strict Freudian," Sam said. "But then, I started looking into Jung's theories. Freud is actually very one dimensional, don't you think, in practice, I mean?"

Jenna avoided an answer. *Freud, one dimensional? Really*, she thought.

Sam continued talking as he opened a cabinet to put a glass away.

"Though I do give a lot of credence to the Oedipal and Electra complex, I find it limiting, Jung is much broader, certainly he was in touch with a spiritual understanding of our human maladies, wouldn't you agree?"

Jenna started to say something, but then, changed her mind. She thought Jung's theories were interesting, but she didn't think that symbols, or personality types, had any place in conventional therapy. Sam paused for only a moment before pushing the start button on his monologue again. She knew they'd have the argument of the century if she allowed herself to express her feelings about Jung.

"About six years ago, I started seeing patients who say they'd been abducted by aliens or have had dreams that would imply that they had. I was very skeptical, at first, of course. Now, I'm not. I know that their experiences are real. There are just too many similarities between the abductees, too many coincidences. I've been fascinated with the subject ever since."

"Couldn't it be the 'collective consciousnesses' of these alien abductees, and not some coincidence of similar experiences in space?" she asked, trying to keep the edge out of her voice. "Couldn't it just be too much Hollywood? Too much ET?"

Sam laughed. "Ouch!"

"But you don't see patients anymore?"

"I still council people who've been abducted. I administer hypnosis as a form of therapy. It's really the only way to get at the visions these people have had. I began seeing only abductees about five years ago, raised all sorts of money from private citizens to council a lot of these patients without charge. A lot of so called "legitimate people" are paying me quite well to be sort of a space detective."

He leaned his elbow on the counter and looked at her. She knew by his expression that it was clear what she thought of him — charlatan, bullshit artist, fake. It was also clear that he wished it were otherwise.

"You must have been really bored with psychiatry, Mr. Hollander," Jenna said softly, looking for a way to hurt him. *How dare an intelligent person resort to this,* she thought as she looked at his perfectly normal smile.

"For Nick's sake, you and I need to form a truce." Sam suddenly turned serious. He put his hands around his chest and leaned back. The dishtowel was slung over his shoulder. "I'm not here to hurt anyone, Jenna," he said, but I believe your husband has had an experience with aliens. It would be helpful if you believed him."

"Let's just say this," Jenna looked him squarely in the eyes, "I intend to get to the bottom of my husband's amnesia and find the truth, whatever it is. Hypnosis should be helpful."

"So you think he has amnesia?"

"He must have some form of it."

"Well, I concur."

"Well, we're in agreement then?"

"It would seem." Sam tapped his fingers on the counter before speaking. "Jenna, if the truth you find is not as you would have it be," he asked. "What then?"

"I can't argue with the truth, Sam," she said softly

"Whatever it is."

Sam held out his hand. Jenna shook it slowly, looking into his eyes and finally, despite herself, released a smile.

Sam hadn't packed pajamas; they were an oddity to him. He sat on the edge of the bed in his jockey shorts thinking about Nick. He could have anyone's memory, that of a mass murderer for all Sam knew.

The moon threw light in Laurie's eyes and made them look like a river lit by stars.

"You make a fine cup of tea, Sam."

She leaned up on the pillows and stretched. It would be the first time that they'd share a bed and wouldn't be sweating and sliding over each other like hungry adolescents.

"What are you thinking?" she asked him.

Sam took her hand. "Life is much more complex than we're aware," he said.

"Is Nick telling the truth?" she asked.

Sam nodded. "I think so."

"Jenna told you that he cries in his nightmares?" Sam asked, turning to her fully now, his knee against her hip.

"Yeah."

"Umm," Sam said, running his hands over the sheet that shielded her stomach.

"Best not do that." She yawned. "We're not capable of quiet sex."

"Perhaps we should learn?" He began to play with her breasts with the tips of his fingers.

Laurie slid farther under the sheets and frowned at him, "Not here, Sam."

"Okay. I can be strong." He laughed softly, as he lay down beside her.

"Let's talk about other things, nonsexual things."

"Many abductees have memory confusion. It's very consistent," Sam said. "Non-sexual enough?"

"Yes, I've heard they do."

"There are so many similar consistencies between abductees," he said quietly.

"The boy through the mist," she turned to him, "do you think he was really there?"

"I believe he was there."

They lay in bed for a while on their backs, starring out of the large glass window into darkness before falling asleep.

Chapter Thirty-One

Sam and Laurie left New Kingston that Monday afternoon. He quickly dropped Laurie off and went directly to his office. He was anxious to find the file on Andrew Quinn.

Sam had promised Nick that he'd stay off the subject of UFOs in front of Jenna, so he kept his mouth shut every time he recalled something else about his visit with Quinn. He certainly did not want to add any more stress to their family dilemma by dominating the evening with his space abduction tales, though most of the time, people couldn't get enough of them. Sam was invited everywhere in Manhattan for just that reason, for amusement, he supposed. People practically tore the fabric from his clothes just begging for another case history of an alien sighting. He found it ironic that he had often talked about

Andrew Quinn, the country cop that had once claimed to have killed an alien. People always loved that story. How odd that country cop would be the very same Andrew Quinn that now lives in Nick Dowling's bewitching Fox Hollow. Perhaps Quinn had purchased Nick's old house to prevent anyone from digging up his land and finding one too many skeletons.

Quinn's was a dormant file, a real cold case because Quinn refused to offer any proof to his claim. So be it. No one who spotted aliens was ever taken seriously. So the Country Cop tale eventually became no more than good parlor fodder for all those parties Sam found himself at. It certainly was an interesting coincidence running into Andrew Quinn again.

He wondered how Nick would feel, abducted as a man. It was possible that the aliens would abduct him for a second time, maybe they still had use for him. Sam had an uneasy feeling about it. If Nick had some sort of tracking device on him it was a sure thing they were coming back.

Sam wondered if Nick had ever seen those Substance cities on Pharaoh's Star that replicated the earth. Sam was beginning to feel that Nick's abduction wasn't for an hour or a day, it was for a long time, maybe as long as a decade. Maybe Nick didn't remember anything because there was nothing in his head. Sam knew it would cause Nick a great deal of despair to discover he'd spent so much time in space, that he was used to satisfy the curiosity of space creatures, that he was robbed of his memories. Without memories, he was practically dead.

Sam pulled out Quinn's file. He found it in a box he had labeled 1989, Highmount Experience. It seems that in 1989, several people had reported seeing alien spaceships in the sky over the Catskill Mountains. They were referring to the space cabins. Sam knew it was a good thing to see them, but it never went anywhere at all significant. UFOs were fiction to the majority. What ignorance, Sam sighed. A majority of fools.

He was still practicing psychotherapy at the time of the Highmount Experience, but he was hungry to find people who claimed to have been abducted. Perhaps if enough people talked about aliens then knowledge would be created, knowledge that would allow entry into the evidence of impossibility.

God was a big part of this. Even the Pharaoh's had an overzealous desire to find God, according to Sam's patients; not that Sam didn't recognize the correlation between God and the Pharaohs; he felt that faith in any deity was an absurdity if one did not believe in other possibilities — in alien creatures as invisible as the Almighty, but twenty-first century man didn't act or think rationally. They had too few philosophers, and the few they had were not listened to with the same amount of interest that movie stars and hedge fund investors were listened to. Majority rules with us, Sam often mused.

"Are we in sync with their faith, their bible?" He had asked his patients. "Or does their faith appear outside of language, unable to be contained or defined by it?"

Each of his patients had said the same thing. "Faith, to them, is knowledge. Whereas, faith, to us, is the lack of it." They'd come out of hypnosis not even remembering what they'd said.

They knew it under hypnosis, but not when they were supposed to be rational?

What arrogance to believe that we are the final masterpiece, Sam often thought. "Once upon a time, apes stood on the earth with no vision of ethereal perfection, no vision at all of man. How those apes must feel now to see heaven materialize on earth, to see that God has blessed us with beautiful women, sports cars, and jet planes. As it stands now, we're the Apes of tomorrow.

Maybe, that's all this desire to understand the universe was for Sam, a journey to prove the existence of a spiritual other world. Why can't society today accept that other worlds had to be outside of their perception of time and space? And, if this other world existed at all, then wouldn't we assume it was definitely 'somewhere?' Aliens, Gods, angels, all connected through fiction, — through a creativity so much more profound than the limits of our body of knowledge. Sam remembered what his father used to tell him; truth is not tangible. Truth is instinctual. Truth is in the heart of every human being, but for the most part, it is misconstrued ... and suppressed.

Eventually, Sam Hollander became somewhat of an expert himself on uncovering alien abduction experiences in clinically normal people, and every person with unexplainable dreams, or disturbing experiences of time out of place, chose hypnotherapy to discover a root cause for their confusion with Doctor Sam Hollander.

The incidence at Highmount was all over the papers in the fall of 1989, and Sam was eager to find out exactly what these people had seen, knowing that alternate realities had split the universe just enough to allow exposure. So, he spent two weeks at some drafty motel on Route 28 interviewing fifteen people who had reported seeing a craft, in six different locations. All of their stories were consistent. They had each seen a large, triangular aircraft that emitted a very low noise, like a drill, when it moved. When it was stationary, it was completely silent. All fifteen people interviewed said the craft appeared to hover very low to the ground, and then, it disappeared.

Some said it had moved very quickly, almost too quickly for the human eye to see.

After two or three days of the Highmount interviews, Andrew Quinn had approached Sam at his motel. Sam had made a note in a diary entry that evening that it had been a brutal night and the winds were howling like they were going to take the roof right off his room. Quinn had on a sheriff's uniform so Sam thought he might be looking for someone. But Andrew Quinn was specifically looking for Sam Hollander and he had an astonishing tale to tell.

It was clear to Sam, that in this millennium, space aliens could not appear, except in imagination or dreams, perhaps. Society's reaction to aliens was dangerous; they would surely be killed, become a taxidermy exhibit, and thrown into a museum, or written out of history with a weather balloon theory. Quinn was a perfect example of fear and its dangers.

Sam remembered the way Quinn had sat in the chair opposite his bed, had sat with his hands across his chest, taking in deep breaths as he spoke.

"Did you see the spacecraft, Sheriff?" Sam asked.

"I saw something once, just like what those people are talking about."

"Once?"

"Twenty some years ago."

Sam reached for his tape recorder and took the chair opposite Quinn's.

"Do you mind?" Sam asked.

"Who hears that?" Quinn sat forward.

"No one. I just transcribe it later." Sam tried to appear calm. A man in a uniform would usually reject seeing spacecraft.

"I've been a sheriff here since 1959," he began. "In

1967, two boys were kidnapped right out of their own backyard in New Kingston. You remember that story? It hit the city papers."

"No," he said. "I was only a kid myself then."

"Look, I never told a soul what I'm about to tell you. It's just that I've got nothing to lose with you, right? You won't print nothing unless I allow it, right?"

"That's right. Nothing gets printed."

"You believe in these things. No one else does. Hell, I never did."

"Yes, I do believe in these things," Sam said.

"I just need to tell someone about it, about what I saw. It made me crazy, had a bit of a breakdown over it."

"So this isn't related to the craft recently seen here in Highmount?"

"I didn't see a spaceship last week, but I sure as hell saw a spaceship twenty years ago."

"Please continue," Sam said gently.

"Those boys weren't murdered like everybody thinks they were. Well, at least not by human beings, they were taken by those people in the spaceships. They murdered them, must have, right?"

Sam pushed the tape recorder closer to him and sat forward. "How do you know that?"

"Those boys were always sleeping outside in the summertime, and they got 'em, those space men, they got 'em, don't you think?'"

"Spacemen?" Sam asked curiously, always playing the skeptic, knowing he had to. "Did you see the space men take the boys, Sheriff?" Sam asked.

Quinn nodded, "I was out on the mountain road that night and I saw something odd in the sky over by the Nichol's place. I went there to investigate it."

Quinn suddenly stopped talking and started taking

breaths like he was trying to keep himself from crying.

"Are you all right, Sheriff Quinn?"

Quinn went back to his story quickly, not stopping to acknowledge Sam's question. "I saw the two boys on the ground, out back, near this large ship." Quinn stopped talking and stared at Sam, waiting for his reaction.

"Go on," Sam said, gently coaxing him.

"It was incredible. What I saw ... it was incredible."

"Go on."

"I saw one boy being lifted right up inside this huge thing. I wasn't even thinking. I just reacted. I grabbed the other boy, Robbie Nichols, and I started running with him. He kept yelling at me to put him down. He kept screaming that he had to save his friend, the Dowling kid."

Sam watched as Quinn got up. He seemed very edgy and agitated now.

"What happened?" Sam asked him.

"I fell in the dark and the boy got away. I tried to hold onto him, but I couldn't. I screamed at him to run home but he ran back toward the ship. I got up and followed as fast as I could move. That's when I saw those creatures."

"Creatures?"

"Yes."

"Where was the boy?" Sam asked and noticed the cold sweat that had broken out on Quinn's face. "Where was Robert Nichols?"

"One of these shadowy looking men had him in his arms. Then he let go of him as I approached. The kid was slumped over, sort of like he'd been knocked out. I couldn't tell if he was still alive, but I told the alien not to hurt him. I went for my gun. Then one of the creatures put him under the ship, under a hatch of some kind. I watched as he was lifted up. For a moment, I couldn't move, I was frozen in fear. Then I snapped to. I grabbed one of those little men. It was an impulse."

"You say that Robbie was lifted?"

"Yeah, nothing seemed to be holding him, but he was being lifted into this ship by something. Then I saw this big mechanical thing. It came down and took him all the way inside."

"Then what?"

"I grabbed one of those suckers from behind and I shot him in the back of the head. He let out this odd sound. I remember that. It was awful."

"You killed it?"

"Yes."

"What did you do with the body?"

"Buried it," Quinn said.

"Where?"

"Can't say."

"Why not?"

"They returned that night; found me in my own damn bedroom and demanded the body back. They said I had to leave it exactly where I buried it and they'd come for it."

"And did you?"

"No, I didn't unbury it."

"Why not?" Sam asked him.

"Would you touch it again? I couldn't. I couldn't go near it. It was disgusting."

"And the boys?"

"They got them both, I guess. Took them away." Quinn was restless and started pacing. He was a great deal more restless than he had been only moments before.

"Why didn't you report this to the FBI?" Sam asked.

Quinn laughed and turned to him. "I told my buddies at the Sheriff's Department what I saw, and they locked me up in a loony bin. They called it stress over the disappearance of those boys."

"I understand," Sam said quietly.

"You don't doubt my sanity, do you? You got what I'm saying on record?" Quinn asked.

"Those creatures spoke to you directly? You had a conversation with them?" Sam asked, trying to stall his leaving. "Did you go inside their ship?"

"No."

"Did the aliens speak to you? Did they speak English?"

"Yes. Yes, they did. I knew what they were saying but their lips hardly moved. I heard their voices, but their lips were small, their voices were strange. Voices inside my head, that's what it sounded like." Quinn turned to the wall. "I had a breakdown after that."

"You're back on the force though, you're wearing a uniform."

"Damn right, they owe me. Damn right."

"Can I see where you buried the body, Sheriff Quinn?" Sam went on cautiously. It would be quite spectacular for him to be able to produce an alien body.

Quinn walked over to the small motel window and looked out. When he turned back to Sam his expression was ashen and grave. "I buried it right where I killed it, right there in the woods. That body is my only assurance against those little bastards. Without it, they might come back for me. I mean, what use would they have for me if I gave them back their goddamn body?" Quinn laughed nervously. "They keep coming back looking for it. I can hear them out there in the dark sometimes." He laughed. "They'll never get it ... and neither will you," he said.

"Could they have taken the body back without your knowing it?"

"They don't have that body, Mr. Hollander."

Sam's notes ended there. He had put the file away soon after his return to the city and told a lot of people about Andrew Quinn's claim. People were fascinated, but there was no body. This was not Roswell. He had asked Quinn if he'd agree to a hypnosis session in the hopes of recovering more information about a body that could never be found, but Quinn had refused.

"I've got nothing more to say about it," he told Sam upon leaving. "I won't take your calls no more. I've been sick about this for years. I needed to get it off my chest, that's all. You're the only person I know of won't think I'm crazy."

"But Sheriff Quinn, it's extremely important to have proof of aliens. Can you understand that, real proof?"

"What are you going to do with that tape," Quinn asked.

"File it. That's all I can do with it, Sheriff."

"I'll deny anything you print. I just needed to see it in your eyes. I needed you to acknowledge my sanity, that's all. That body is my only defense against them. They want it real badly and as long as I got it, I'm living another day."

"They're nonviolent," Sam said.

"What?"

"They won't hurt you; they just want the body. They don't want our government to get it. Remember Roswell? It will just be covered up. I'm not even sure what I would do with it."

"That's what you say."

And the door had closed loudly behind him.

Chapter Thirty-Two

Nick was eager to get his hypnotherapy session over with, maybe hypnotherapy would prove he wasn't insane. But dogs that appeared out of nowhere? Boys who disappeared and reappeared? Forty year old road signs that no longer existed? Certainly sounded like the visions of a madman.

He depended on Laurie now, and he confided in her. He looked to her for acceptance, and that was hurting Jenna. He could see that, but he couldn't prevent it. He needed to be believed. He needed Laurie. He had to put his trust in Sam. Sam, at least, accepted the fact that discoveries lie ahead, as they always have, and parallel universes may indeed, one day, be fact.

"Think of Hubbell," Nick had tried to reason with Jenna. "Before he discovered that the universe was expanding like an inflating balloon and Earth's home galaxy was not the entire universe, and way before Einstein added the dimension of time to the three dimensions of space, Galileo pointed a telescope to the sky and observed four moons orbiting Jupiter. Look at the evolution of our own knowledge! And don't forget Copernicus; he revealed that the earth was not the center of the universe to people who believed that if they walked far enough, they'd find the end of a flat world."

"That's astronomy," Jenna had said. "Not Science Fiction."

"The scientist, Stephen Hawking, doesn't deny divine possibilities to explain our universe," Nick said defiantly.

"I'm sure he's not referring to aliens to explain our universe," Jenna said.

"Look, does the genetic buck stop with humankind? *Do humans come from the ape, really, or did we choose the ape's evolution within which to house our souls?"*

Jenna made a face, as he suspected she would. She still hadn't gotten off his back about Sally Harnick. She was pleading with him to go back and speak with her so he could uncover his deep-rooted paranoia, or schizophrenia, whatever it was that was causing him to appear mad.

But Nick didn't want Jenna's explanations for his confusion, for the hole in his mind that his experience in Fox Hollow had created. He wanted Sam to pull the answers out of his psyche no-matter what might be uncovered.

"Amazing how much sun I get in here," Sam said as he led Nick inside and then lowered the blinds.

Nick sat on the small cot against the wall. "I assume I

am to lie down?"

Sam laughed, "C'mon, you've done this before?"

Nick lay back and closed his eyes. "Never."

"Won't the ladies be joining us?"

"They insisted on parking the car on the street. I got disgusted with them. You can't park in the Village; it's awful. Laurie kept insisting we'd find something at this hour if we circled the block enough times. I'm dizzy from it."

"You're all right with this?" Sam asked.

"There's something I need to tell you before Jenna gets here." Nick said, a bit nervously.

"Go on." Sam took the chair beside the bed.

"Prior to 1982, I have no memory, no memory at all."

"Your mind is a blank?"

"Yes. I woke up in a hotel in Chelsea in 1982. I'd checked myself in under the name Nick Dowling. There was a column in the register book for hometown, under it I had written Phoenicia. I've just been assuming all these years that I was raised there."

"Why do I get the feeling you've never mentioned this to Jenna?"

Nick relayed his violent dreams to Sam, the woman he saw at his feet covered in blood, the child bent and broken.

"That's why I never told her," Nick said. "I'm afraid I could be violent, afraid I might have done something horrible and I'm blocking it. Jesus, I may be wanted for murder somewhere."

Sam knew now that Nick had the memories of someone despicable. The aliens had certainly done a number on him. Why don't they care what they're doing, Sam wondered? Is it because they think of us as dead people?

"You think your amnesia is caused by acts of violence? You think you're capable of murder?" Sam asked him carefully.

"I don't know."

"I don't want to scare you or put anything in your head, but I definitely think you've been a victim of alien experimentation."

"What the hell did they do to me?"

"We might get some answers under hypnosis. Can you accept those answers?"

"I can," he said slowly. "I must."

"Do you have the exact date of the kidnapping?" Sam asked as he pulled a pad out from the table next to him.

"Yes, we called the local newspaper out there. It was August 7th, 1967."

"I don't expect you to remember where you were in August of 1967, Nick, but let's see if you can recall anything at all of that night under hypnosis."

"I can't get to any memory before 1982."

"As far as you know, your name has always been Nick Dowling?"

"Yes."

"There's my bell, I'll let them in."

Nick lay back on his hands and stared at the ceiling. He was anxious. But he trusted Sam and he had to go through with this. He wanted the truth, even though he sensed that however it got played out, it might be costing him his marriage.

As Sam led Jenna and Laurie into the room Nick opened his eyes and smiled at his wife. She appeared distraught.

"Where'd you wind up parking?" Nick asked, trying to

226

soften her.

"We finally found a meter," Jenna said as she looked around for a place to sit.

"I had lots of quarters," Laurie added.

"Well, let's get started," Jenna announced abruptly as she sat in a large chair near the wall and removed her jacket.

Nick hoped that whatever came out under hypnosis would not drive them further apart.

Jenna realized that once Sam took the chair in front of Nick she would not be able to see her husband's face. She immediately wanted to move, to grab the chair that faced the small bed, but Laurie quickly sat down in it and turned to nod at Jenna, to reassure her.

"Just so you know, "Sam began, as he got up and stood in the center of the room and turned toward the women, "hypnosis is suggestive. It is my intension not to lead Nick, nor to put anything in his mind at all. I will simply ask him questions. I'll ask him to recall certain memories. Now, does anyone have any issues before we begin?"

Sam held a small prism in his hand. Jenna wanted to laugh out loud and ask him if the *Amazing Kreskin* had mentored him, but she willed herself to be serious ... and respectful. The prism was pretty, she had never seen anything quite like it. It seemed to contain a million sparkling colors.

"Please inform the patient," Jenna said, "that people can lie under hypnosis. They are in a highly relaxed and suggestive state, but, still in control of what they're saying and doing. The truth is not sacrament in hypnosis. Just so you know."

"That is correct." Sam met her gaze. "Anything else?"

"No," Jenna said quietly. "Please proceed."

"Are you ready, Nick?" Sam asked. He moved the prism over Nick's body; it was nothing more than a relaxer, but it helped patients recall memories. It would expedite the process.

"Yep," Nick whispered.

"Are you comfortable Nick?" Sam asked

"Yes, very."

"Do you remember what you did yesterday, Nick?"

"Yes."

"I want you to tell me. What did you do?"

As Nick went through a series of mundane chores his voice drifted -- a walk down Broadway for steaks at the butcher's — an afternoon nap — calls to his office — Sam placed the prism before Nick's eyes.

"He's going into a deep trance now," Sam said, turning around to look at Jenna. "But he will remember everything he says."

"What's he doing with his mouth?" Laurie whispered.

Nick seemed to be pushing his tongue behind his lip, as if he had an itch inside his mouth that he was trying to scratch.

"What is it Nick?" Sam asked.

"Something in my lip, actually, it's behind my lip, inside my mouth. It's hard. It bothers me."

"Can you remove it?" Sam asked. Perhaps it was nothing more than plaque.

"I don't think so. It feels like a hard pimple."

"I want you to try and relax. I'm going to take you back in time a bit. Do you remember your wedding?"

"Yes," he nodded.

"Both of your weddings?" Sam asked. Jenna had told

him that Nick had been married before.

"No, just one," Nick answered.

"Which one?" Sam asked.

"My wedding to Jenna, of course."

"When did you marry Jenna, Nick?" Sam asked.

"1989, on Long Island," Nick told him.

"Nick, is your lip still bothering you?" Sam asked as he watched Nick move his mouth around, as if he were chewing something distasteful.

"Yes, something hard is behind my lip. I can't get it out."

"No need to concentrate on that now, Nick."

"Okay."

"I'd like you to let yourself go back to the night of August 7th, 1967."

"Okay."

"How old are you, Nick?"

Nick began to giggle.

"I'm ten."

"Do you know what time it is, Nick?" Sam asked.

"It's night."

"It's nine P.M., Nick. Where are you?"

"My backyard."

"Who is with you?"

"Carl and Pete. Me and Nicky."

"You and Nicky?"

"Yes."

"Then who are you?"

"Rob Nichols."

Jenna sat up straight in her chair. Laurie turned around, her eyes as round as gambling chips.

"I thought you were Nick, Nick Dowling," Sam said. *It's working*, he thought. *His memories are returning.*

Nick was giggling very hard.

"What's so funny, *Rob*?"

"We got em'."

"Got who?"

"There're so confused. They think they got Nicky, but they got me."

"And where are they taking you?"

"Pharaoh's Star."

Sam sat back; it was all falling into place. "What happened to Nicky?"

"They're confused. They get everything wrong."

"What do they get wrong?"

Nick was laughing almost uncontrollably. "They couldn't tell the difference between me and Nicky but they're the ones who look alike.

"So you played with their ignorance?"

"Yeah, they thought they had Nicky, but they had me."

"Did they ever get Nicky?"

"I don't know."

"Then Nicky is on Pharaoh's Star?"

"I don't think so."

Nick's childish giggles stopped abruptly. He called out for Nicky, screamed out his name, "No, no, please!" he cried. "Please, please don't hurt him, not again, please, please, don't hurt him anymore. I was supposed to watch him. I promised Mrs. Dowling. I promised."

"All right, Rob Let's move forward. Let's move forward now. It's 1977. How old are you now, in 1977?" Sam asked quickly.

Nick breathed deeply for several seconds before answering, "Twenty."

"Where do you live?"

"Substance City Y, Phoenicia."

"Where is that?"

"Pharaoh's Star."

Jenna stood up and went to her husband. Sam quickly reached out and held her back.

"What is your name?"

"Nick Dowling."

"I thought you were Rob, Rob Nichols?"

"No. I'm Nick."

"That's enough," Jenna said.

"Please, just a bit more," Sam looked up at Jenna and flinched at her expression.

"This session is over," she whispered fiercely.

"We're really getting at something," Sam said as he attempted to keep her from Nick.

"This session is over, I repeat." Jenna glared at Sam.

Sam sighed and covered Nick's eyes with his hand. He brought Nick out of the trance. Nick looked at Jenna, as if for a moment, he didn't know who she was. He sat up slowly and rubbed his eyes.

"I've seen enough," Jenna said. "And I've heard enough."

"He said his name was Rob Nichols, Sam." Laurie glanced at Sam, and then, back again at Nick. "Is that what this is all about? He switched his name at some point?"

"We'll talk about it," Sam said.

"He's confused," Jenna said. "You can't accept what he says right now. He's using this identity crisis to shield some awful memory. This is not about aliens," Jenna screamed out.

"Jenna." Sam looked at her and reached for her arm. "He's getting at the past as he finds it. Please try and understand."

"I'm trying to be patient, Nick," Jenna said softly, "Trying to keep it together but this is absurd." Jenna glared at Sam. "Do you think I'm an idiot?"

"You knew why we were here, Jenna. You knew he was going under hypnosis," Sam said and tried to reach out for her.

"Going under hypnosis to find the truth," Jenna said. "Not to keep up this absurd camouflage about aliens."

Nick reached inside his mouth and slowly moved his tongue around.

"What is it Nick?" Laurie asked. "Do you have a toothache?"

They watched as Nick put his hands in his mouth and applied a great deal of pressure to the back of his lip. Finally, he pulled something out from the inside of his mouth. It was a small, hard piece of metal, about a millimeter long.

"What the hell...?" he said as he held it up and stared at it. "What the hell is this?" He looked at Sam.

"Give me that," Sam said as he went for a plastic bag. He took the object and dropped it inside. He felt his hand shaking, they were coming back for Nick. They must be coming back for Nick. If they weren't they never would have implanted a tracking device. "Is it entirely out of your mouth, Nick?"

Nick shook his head in disbelief. "No, I don't think so. What the hell is it?"

"Sometimes they implant devices." Sam looked at him and felt completely helpless to deter whatever plans the aliens had.

"Oh, now I've heard everything. Are you going to tell me that the aliens have implanted a tracking device inside my husband's mouth?" Jenna asked, as she put her hands on her hips and gave Sam a hateful look.

"I don't know, Jenna. I have to get it analyzed," Sam said.

Analyzing little metal tracking devices implanted by aliens was the last straw for Jenna and she grabbled Laurie' hand. She insisted on leaving the "mental institution" after stopping, briefly, before Nick.

"Are you alright?" she asked.

"Yes," he whispered. His voice was raspy.

"He's fine, Jenna. I'll take good care of him," Sam said.

Jenna gave him a menacing stare. "Here are the keys to the jeep. It's right out front. Okay? I'll take a cab home."

Sam nodded, kissed Laurie on the cheek, and watched the two women leave.

Sam collapsed into a chair. He was still disturbed about the tracking device. "Nick, you remembered being Rob Nichols under hypnosis. Do you still remember being Rob Nichols?"

"Yes, yes, I do." Nick seemed completely bewildered. "I don't have all the details, it's still sketchy, but it's closer than ever. I just have to fill in the faces."

Sam smiled. "That's good, Nick ... It will all come back to you now. But I think you're memories have been infused with someone else's, after the abduction."

"Whose?"

"That's what I'd like to find out. You mentioned that people confused you with someone, called you by another name. You might have taken on his physical characteristics along with his memory."

"Harrison Hinckley," he said. "Pete mentioned it, also Elizabeth."

Sam got up and went to the computer. After a while he turned to Nick. "Harrison Hinckley was from a town in upstate New York. He killed himself after he killed his wife and child."

"That could be what my dream is all about. What was his wife's name?"

Sam read over the article again. "His wife was Natalie."

"Natalie Miller?"

"Right."

Nick rubbed his head. "Shit," he said.

"They never found his body."

"So what are you saying, that he could be alive? You think he's dangerous?"

"His memories could live inside your head, and he could be alive. It's possible."

"I guess anything is possible at this point. But you didn't answer my question, is he dangerous?"

"If he's aware that you're being mistaken for him, he could be."

"What the hell could he do, I mean, so what?"

"I'm not sure, Nick. It just makes me uneasy. He could take over your life."

Chapter Thirty-Three

Jenna didn't like the idea of lying to Nick, but she had to put an end to this charade. There was a three-day conference in Albany for psychotherapists that she attended every year. This year, however, she would let Nick assume that's where she was, but she would actually drive out to their house in New Kingston and do some sleuthing on her own — see if she could find out enough information to put the missing pieces of her husband's life together. She was afraid of what she might discover, but the only way to save Nick would be to reveal his real past, and whatever devastating ordeal had driven him to such extremes.

Lunch with Laurie had been excruciating. Laurie suspected that Nick was really Robert Nichols and not Nick Dowling. She insisted that aliens had messed with his memory, and that explained everything. Jenna tried to listen, as if Laurie were a patient with bizarre excuses for repeating endless patterns. At the end of their lunch together, Jenna could see the disappointment in Laurie's eyes as Jenna sat stone faced and refrained from commenting.

"What are you thinking Jenna? For God's sake, what do you think about all of this?" Laurie finally blurted out, in a completely exasperated and overemotional way, just like their mother.

Jenna was glad she had ordered wine with lunch. It had made the hour bearable and had relaxed her.

"Laurie, my dear sister," she said, "what I witnessed in your boyfriend's office was the biggest bunch of bullshit babble I have ever heard. It frightens me, how delusional you all are."

Laurie was clearly hurt and sat back in her chair. Jenna noticed that her eyes were watery. But, as usual, Laurie regained her strength and met her sister's expression head on.

"Nick was the one under hypnosis, Jenna, not Sam," she finally said, and tried to smile, but her lips turned down instead of up. "It was Nick who was babbling."

"Nick is looking for anyone dumb enough to buy into his illusions," Jenna snapped. She saw her sister's hurt expression and immediately felt that she was being hard and impenetrable.

"I'm sorry, Laurie, but this whole experience has been very stressful."

"I understand," Laurie said and reached for her sister's hand. "And if Nick does turn out to be Robert Nichols?"

"If he is in fact, Robert Nichols, I can only assume he was kidnapped and robbed of his identity by a human being, not a little green man. I will admit that it's possible that he was stolen from his own backyard, once upon a time. But then, why doesn't he remember that, Laurie?"

"Jenna, if a human being stole him why would he be calling himself Nick Dowling? It doesn't make sense. The kidnappers would have been apprehended for the kidnapping if they'd used the Dowling's name. I think the boys confused the aliens by exchanging their identities, and when they wiped out Nick's memory, they wiped out his real name with it."

"And so, because the aliens thought he was Nicky, he thought of himself as Nicky from that point on?" Jenna asked.

"Yes, Jenna, and he remembered under hypnosis that he actually was Robert Nichols."

"Look, I know you would rather believe in space creatures, Laurie, but I prefer to believe in something a bit more credible."

Laurie shook her head in disbelief. "Do you really think Nick would do something like that, pretend all of this?"

"Delusional people will do anything to be believed," Jenna said as she reached in her purse for her lipstick, a hint to Laurie that lunch was over, most assuredly over.

Laurie shook her head. "I would have expected more from you, Jenna."

"Like what?"

"Like trust."

As Laurie paid the bill, Jenna quickly walked outside. She needed the air, needed to escape Laurie's insane explanations. She wished she could rattle some good sense into her sister. She felt the usual disappointment; the familiar sense of failure between them to come to an understanding. As they stood there on Spring Street, looking uncomfortably agitated, Laurie spontaneously reached out and hugged her tightly.

"I know we're coming at this from two different places, Jenna, but I do support you and love you. I hope you know that."

Jenna kissed her sister's cheek. "He's very convincing, your Mr. Sam Hollander," she said, "as convincing as Nick."

"Do you like Sam?" Laurie asked.

Jenna slung her purse over her shoulder and winked at Laurie. "Sure, sis," she said, "but with reservations." She waved behind her as she walked away.

Jenna hailed a cab uptown and went straight to Sally Harnick's office. It was the first time she had ever barged in on Sally without calling first, but Nick's comedy hour with Sam had unnerved her. Nick had too many people buying into his delusions, and he was validating himself through Sam's acceptance and Laurie's insane giddiness over these absurd fantasies. It had become like group think. Jenna had no one but Sally for a reality check.

Neither Laurie, nor Nick, had discussed anything with her parents, at least, not yet. Ronnie only knew her father was having nightmares, but Ronnie never kept anything from her grandparents for very long. Jenna knew it would only be a matter of days before she'd get the inevitable call from her mother, "What's this I hear about Nick having nightmares?" and she would have to run down a litany of lies — stress — age — disturbing sense memories — whatever — anything but spacecraft abductions. That's all Doris Rubin would need. She'd insist on confronting her spirit guide and she'd demand that Nick call the best psychic on Park Avenue.

"Where did you find this jackass shrink?" Sally asked, falling back into her large leather chair.

"Laurie's boyfriend." Jenna smiled halfheartedly.

"You've got to get rid of him." Sally said quickly.

"How? He and Nick have bonded. He'll hate me if I bar Sam from his life. He won't permit it. Would you?"

"What are you going to do? You said you had a plan?"

"I'm going up to the house. Nick thinks I'm going to be in Albany next week, but I'm going to do some investigating."

"What are you looking for, Jenna?"

"What you told me to look for — something that may relate."

"Do you want me to come with you?"

Jenna could tell by Sally's expression that she was mentally scanning her next week's appointments.

"I hadn't planned to attend that conference, but I could take the time," Sally said.

"No. I wouldn't think of it. But I will be in touch."

Sally reached over the long, shiny Maple wood desk for Jenna's hand.

"It will be fine, Jenna. We'll get at the truth. You'll see."

Chapter Thirty-Four

Since Jenna wasn't exactly sure what she was looking for she thought it best to start with the kidnapping. She drove into the town library for back issues of area newspapers and discovered that Andrew Quinn had been a sheriff in New Kingston during the 1960s, 70s and 80s. She also read that he'd gone on Sabbatical following a nervous breakdown right after the kidnappings. Quinn had been one of the officers at the scene the night Robert Griffin Nichols and Nicolas Michael Dowling had disappeared. Jenna found this to be an unusual coincidence.

The search for the missing boys had lasted several months. Their bodies were never recovered, nor was any indication that they might still be alive. No clues were ever discovered at the scene that might have led to any helpful speculation. The only witnesses, Carlton Nicholas, the seven-year-old brother of Robert Nichols, and Peter Shelby, his eight-year-old friend, were fast asleep on the back porch and heard nothing. Robert Nichol's parents had said that they'd heard three pops in the night but didn't know for sure what the sounds were, only that it could have been gunshots. The next day the family dog was discovered shot dead by a presumed hunter. Sheriff Quinn concluded that the only blood at the scene belonged to the dog. There were no bullets found in the immediate area and no way to tell if the dog had been shot before the boys disappeared.

The two boys had gone out that evening to sleep under the stars; something they had often done over the summer months. Just days before their abduction, Nicky had talked about space people in the woods. No one took him seriously. He was, after all, autistic. When Carlton Nichols and Peter Shelby were questioned about space people they said they hadn't seen anything out of the ordinary.

An old man by the name of Jasper Reed had been under investigation for the possible murders of the boys, but there was no evidence at all tying him to the crime. However, his name always came up when the Nichols and Dowling boys were mentioned. Town opinion was split on what might have happened that night. A handful of people believed that Robbie Nichols had been kidnapped, and there were some that believed he was sold to a child pornography ring. People were certain that Nicky Dowling was murdered once it was discovered he was autistic, and therefore not a valuable commodity in the child for sale market. They speculated that Robbie would grow up, remember his roots, and return to allay his parent's grief. But as the years went by, Robert Nichols' return to New Kingston never came to pass. For years, coverage on the case was printed on the anniversary of the boy's disappearance. Most people concluded that Robbie's failure to return was proof that he had definitely been murdered that night in 1967, along with Nicky Dowling. The gossip was that the bodies of Robbie and Nicky were buried somewhere on the Nichols property or dumped in the back of a car and discarded in woods. People felt that Jasper Reed had gotten away with murder. No one believed that the boys were stolen by space creatures and went to live in some alternate state of reality on a spaceship called Pharaoh's Star.

Jenna might have accepted that her husband had been kidnapped and sold to a ring of pedophiles, but that's not the story of his youth she had gotten. According to Nick, he was raised by middle class parents, lived in a modest home, and worked his way through college. But, perhaps, that *was* a lie because the truth brought him too much shame to admit. But Robert Nichols had been ten years old at the time of the abduction. Wouldn't he have attempted to contact his biological parents at some point? He most certainly would have remembered them.

Jenna sat back from the microfiche and put her hands to her head. If Robert Nichols was indeed alive, he must have memories of his childhood, even if he was completely manipulated and controlled by his abductors. He would remember being snatched away from his real parents. And of course, he would not have been renamed Nick Dowling, unless he purposely chose the name for himself later on in life. He would certainly have remembered being Robbie Nichols, no-matter what kind of brain washing he'd been subjected to, and he probably would have been raised as far from New York as possible, especially if he was a stolen child, sold for a price.

Nick insisted that his childhood was uneventful. But, what if Nick witnessed the autistic boy's death and transferred his survivor guilt by taking on his friend's identity?

Yes, Jenna decided, *perhaps, ten- year- old Robbie Nichols saw some awful man kill Nicky and it caused a memory lapse, wiped out his life prior to that moment. Certainly, that was a possibility.*

But Jenna always came back to the same disturbing fact, why wouldn't Nick remember choosing to become Nick Dowling? Why wouldn't he have told her that his childhood had been wiped out by a violent crime?

The only thing Jenna knew for certain was that her husband was never a poor little autistic child kidnapped by aliens. But there was a real identity for Nick, somewhere. She just had to discover where to look. She had to find his real parents if they were still alive.

Whatever the scenario turned out to be, one thing for certain, Nick would not have been able to call himself Nick Dowling all his life. At some point in time, he became Nick Dowling, and Jenna had to find out when.

Jenna called Sally that evening and told her she believed that there was a slim chance that Nick could be the missing Nichols boy.

"How old did you say he was at the time of the kidnapping?" Sally asked.

"Ten years," Jenna told her. "I know, he'd remember."

"Of course, he'd remember."

"Well, he seems to be remembering something."

"No, no he's not really. He's searching for answers, or pretending to search for answers, but he's not remembering anything useful."

"So, you don't think he could be Robert Nichols?"

"Why does he call himself Nick Dowling?"

"Trauma," Jenna said quickly. "Maybe he saw the boy murdered. He took on his identity out of guilt because he couldn't help his friend."

"Jenna, your husband is almost fifty years old. The autistic boy was probably killed right away. How could Nick have gotten away with a false identity as a child? That's when he would have started the transfer. He had to have grown up with a different name."

"I guess." Jenna sighed.

"How old was Nick when you met him?"

"Twenty-eight." Jenna could almost hear Sally thinking, forming opinions. "Look, he could have gotten amnesia right before he and I met. Perhaps he was married to another woman as someone other than Nick Dowling because all of a sudden he doesn't remember being married to anyone else other than me."

"Jenna, he would have known if he was ever an amnesia victim. What did he say his name was when you met him? Did he ever allude to another name?"

"No. He has always been Nick Dowling to me."

"Any middle name?"

"No."

"Find out if this kid Nicky had a middle name."

"He did. It was Michael."

"So, what's Nick's middle name?"

"He doesn't have one."

"Don't most people have middle names?"

"Well, it isn't illegal not to have one."

There was a long pause before Sally spoke again. Jenna put her head back on a white, soft pillow and waited for her response.

"My bet is that your husband, whoever he may be, stole the identity of Nick Dowling."

"Basically, what you're saying is that Nick is lying?"

"You're ignoring the obvious."

"What do you mean?" Jenna asked.

"I don't believe he is Robbie Nichols. I think the boys are both dead, victims of a horrible sex crime. At some point in time your husband was caught in a lie and decided to become Nick Dowling."

"And the day I forced him to find the house he grew up in he became Rob Nichols."

"Yes, he did, because lo and behold, there are the real parents of little Nicky. Very strange. And so, all of a sudden, he becomes Robbie Nichols? C'mon. And let's not forget all the other people that don't know who the hell he is."

Jenna closed her eyes. She knew Sally was right. Whoever Nick was, he probably wasn't Robbie Nichols either.

"I guess I'm not thinking straight. A part of me wants to believe his lies. I mean, no one from Phoenicia knows him. It doesn't make any sense."

"He probably knows by now that he never should have returned to the Catskill Mountains. He took the chance of being remembered."

"But nobody remembers him, Sally."

"Jenna, look for something else, someone in the area who might have needed to change his identity for some reason, someone who would have heard about the murders, maybe even grew up hearing about them. I told you how I feel about this. If you ask me, your husband is from around there, he may even be from Phoenicia. He knew he could steal Nick Dowling's identity because it was a real identity; he'd have a birth certificate if he needed one. Maybe he had a subliminal memory of Nicky's name. It could have simply been an unconscious choice to have decided to call himself Nick Dowling, a name he haphazardly remembered from his childhood because of the publicity around the kidnappings."

"Sally, if he were from Phoenicia, why didn't Darla Paine recognize him, or Pete Shelby or Elizabeth Logan?"

"Because he's fifty years old, Jenna, not twenty. Would you recognize the person that sat next to you in a high school home room class, especially when they're not giving you their correct name?"

"Why didn't he steal Robbie's identity? Robbie wasn't autistic."

"He probably figured it wouldn't matter. Maybe Nick, or whomever he is, just took the identity of the boy that resembled him most."

"But why?"

"That's what we have to find out."

"What about his first wife?"

"You don't know what name he was married under, Jenna. So that could be difficult."

"But maybe he wasn't married before."

"Then why did he tell you he was? He's intent on forcing his delusions on you. He's demanding that you believe him." Sally sighed several seconds long. "Look, Jenna, by all means, find the ex-wife if you can, if there is one. It may be too early to form an opinion on this, but I think Nick is running from something in his past, and now he's feeling pressured. He's using a preposterous lie to convince you that he is someone other than who he is, perhaps, someone who might have done something terrible years ago. Maybe he denied being married to anyone else because he doesn't want you to find his ex-wife. So find her."

"He's not capable of something terrible, Sally."

"Jenna, sometimes, with men, you don't really know what you've got there."

"Cynic," Jenna whispered as she hung up the phone, but the thought was disturbing.

Chapter Thirty-Five

"Who's that?" Harrison asked.

"Why, I don't know," Gregory said as he looked out the window. "I never saw him before in my life."

"Get rid of him, I'll be back in the kitchen. "Watch what you say. I can hear you; you know?"

"Of course, of course."

Gregory stood at the door and peered at the serious stranger. "Can I help you?"

Sam produced a card from his wallet. "May I come in? I'd like to speak with you."

Gregory read the card and looked up at Sam with a perplexed grin. "You're a paranormal investigator?"

"Yes, I am, and I have reason to believe..."

Gregory cut him off. "I'm afraid I don't believe in that stuff."

"Gregory, there's a chance that your brother is going to contact you. There's a chance he's still alive."

"I don't understand, what's paranormal about that?" Gregory stared at him and said nothing more.

"Please, can we talk?" Sam said.

"Come in," Gregory said quietly.

Sam took a seat on the couch. "I know how this is going to sound a bit crazy. Believe me, I understand your skepticism."

"I imagine you're met with a lot of skepticism."

"Yes, I am."

"So my brother isn't dead, you say? Then where is he?"

"I believe he's been released."

"Released? Released from what?"

"From a spaceship called Pharaoh's Star."

Gregory quickly thought of his brother's confusion, his shock when he was told what year it was. "Pharaoh's Star?" He tried to laugh.

"Look, I need to make a switch, offer the aliens your brother instead of my friend. I am afraid they're coming back for my friend, and I need to prevent that."

Gregory thought that might be one way of getting rid of Harrison. He didn't want him there, that was for sure, but this Sam Hollander seemed a bit insane.

"So you want me to what?"

"Just call me if he shows up here and I'll do the rest. I think he'd come to you."

"So you want me to turn my brother over to a bunch of aliens?" Gregory laughed loudly.

"Your brother is a menace to society, he's a killer. You won't miss him, and neither will anyone else."

"You're trading my brother for your friend?"

"Their memories have been infused. Nick is being mistaken for Harrison."

Gregory knew that Harrison could hear the conversation, he became afraid and tried to laugh again. "I wouldn't turn my brother over to you, to... to...murder."

"I wouldn't murder him; I'd just give him to the aliens instead of my friend. I think it can be done. He'll be safe."

"That's preposterous. Absurd."

"The aliens won't murder him."

"Then what will they do with him?"

"I'm afraid I don't have all the answers but they're non-violent. They are not going to hurt him."

Gregory stood to his feet. "I'm going to have to ask you to leave. You're a crazy man."

"Look," Sam handed Gregory another one of his cards. "Your brother is a dangerous man. Call me, please. If he shows up here. You know he's a dangerous man. I can help you."

Sam walked quietly out the door while Gregory stood in the center of the room wondering if he'd just imagined the encounter he'd just had. Harrison came to him quickly.

"Give me his card."

Gregory looked at him a moment before he realized what Harrison wanted.

"C'mon, c'mon," Harrison uttered.

Gregory handed him Sam's card.

"The car keys."

"What are you going to do?"

"The keys to your car. Quick, hand them over. I'll be back in a few hours. I need to know who the hell that quack is and where the hell he lives."

Chapter Thirty-Six

It's easy to forget how beautiful the mountains are under the Florida sun, but the minute Cecile spotted them curving out in front of her, like nature's mighty shoulders, she welled up.

"It's good to be home," she said and reached for Griff's hand. As the van turned off the thruway Cecile wondered why she'd ever left the Catskill mountains.

But Florida was a good place to be, humid and hot. And she was in her seventies now, too old for long and brutal winters. She and Griff took walks every morning on the beach and felt lucky and privileged to be living under the Palm Trees. Sometimes, there was nothing better than feeling sand in the bottom of her sneakers, or the fierce Atlantic rushing out to splash at her knees. There was nothing sweeter than endless blue days with everything so bright with color. Florida was like a pastel quilt, all blues and magentas and greens.

Yes, Florida was a good state, but it didn't have the deep red and gold of autumn; it didn't have the stillness, or the twists and turns of a country road. Most importantly, it didn't have her son, Carlton Nichols.

He was a good boy, her son, Carlton. She always knew that he was going to grow up preferring boys over girls, but so be it; though she missed having grandchildren. Griff had a problem with it though. It was years before he came around to an acceptance of Carlton's sexuality with a befuddled avoidance of the subject.

Cecile smiled to herself remembering how much Griff had adored both of his sons, always working fewer hours to be with them. Their children were such good boys. They'd fix the broken wings on birds, and Carlton took home any stray animal he found. Robbie had been so introspective and sensitive, befriending the children his classmate's made fun of, especially that little autistic boy, Nicky Dowling.

Cecile was proud that Carlton grew up to become a writer, like his father, though Griff was a journalist and had written for The Times Herald Record his entire career. Carlton wrote books. He wrote those wonderful mystery stories that always got solved in the end. Carlton liked closure. That's why he always accepted his brother's death. Both he and Griff put a stone marker out in the meadow in Robbie's memory. For years they'd go out there and talk to him, as if he were really in the earth, really able to hear and understand that they'd come to terms with his demise, and they were there to comfort his spirit, as well as their own.

Cecile never went to the field and sat beside Robbie's stone marker because she knew he wasn't dead. Yes, her son, Robbie, was walking the earth, needing her to find him. She never stopped believing that.

Of course, she didn't talk about it much. She used to, in the beginning, but then, Griff got so angry with her. Cecile knew he needed to let go and lay their son's death to rest; so, Cecile stopped insisting that Robbie was still alive, for Griff's sake.

She and Carlton never talked about it either, not since he was a boy. He was so young, but he had loved his older, protective brother more than anyone on earth, even more than his parents, more than their beloved dog, Crockett, more than anything.

Children do not process death very well. Perhaps, no one does, but children, especially, are confused by it. Sometimes the pain of loss never heals. Sometimes, the pain even dictates the choices made later on in life. Cecile often felt that her Carlton was so torn apart by Robbie's absence that he chose a partner so solid and overbearing that they would never disappear.

Carlton had lived with the same man for years. His partner, Steve, worked in the city as an attorney and he came up on weekends to stay in the house that he and Carlton had bought, and had lovingly restored. Cecile met Steve for the first time right after she and Griff sold their house to Andrew Quinn. She was impressed at the wonderful renovations that Carlton and Steve had made on their new house. It looked like a showplace, a farmhouse that should be on the cover of a magazine. It certainly rivaled anything she'd ever seen in House Beautiful. Of course, she attributed it all to Carlton. Carlton had always had her flair for decorating.

She often wondered what her shy and reclusive Robbie would have grown up to be like. Carlton had been so much more outgoing than Robbie. The brothers didn't resemble each other much, except around the eyes, those vivid blue eyes. Robbie had inherited her looks. She had been quite a looker when she was young, and once, some visiting photographer had asked her to model for a magazine. But she'd met Griff by then and wasn't much interested in a modeling career. Carlton took after Griff's side of the family. He was not very tall, but he was husky and his shoulders were broad. His hair was a beautiful shade of brown, thick like Griff's, and wavy. Robbie's hair had been so straight that she was always cutting it away from his eyes. Griff's mother used to call Robbie *little pompadour, little pompadour*, because he started Brill Creaming his hair into a pompadour in front. It used to make them all laugh because he'd smear so much of that gook in his hair that it threatened to crack right off his head.

Carlton slipped his arm through Cecile's and proudly showed her around the house. She commented on the beautiful periwinkle he had chosen for the living room, the antiques he had traveled three states over to find.

"Oh, you two have done such wonders." She squeezed Steve's arm affectionately, not wanting him to feel that she was overlooking his contribution.

Carlton's office was filled with flowers and photographs, mostly photographs of his childhood, but he had a lot of smiling pictures around of his later youth in high school and college, pictures of her and Griff. Of course, there were several of Carlton and Steve over the years. And he had a favorite photo of Robbie on the bookcase. It was the one he'd always cherished of his brother. Robbie had his arms around Crocket and a huge smile on his face. Cecile felt her heart skip as she looked at it. She knew Carlton was watching her as she smiled sadly and put it back on the shelf.

"This is a fine room, son," she said.

"Why do you need a television screen this big, Carlton?" Griff asked. Cecile turned and watched Carlton laugh.

"Why not, Dad, if you can afford it?"

"How's your book coming?" Griff put an arm around his son's shoulder. "How many people get knocked off in this one?"

"Oh, just a handful, Dad."

"Ever see old Andrew Quinn?" Griff asked as they walked back into the brightly lit parlor.

Cecile was surprised that Griff would ask about Andrew Quinn. They never spoke about him because Cecile had never forgiven him. He was a real sore spot, as far as she was concerned. It wasn't enough that he closed the case on her son's disappearance, but to add insult to injury, it was Quinn that had bought their house. He had actually given them the asking price, and rather than let the house sit on the market, they sold it to Andrew and moved to Florida the day following their closing. Carlton visited them twice a year in Florida, but they had not been back to the Catskills since.

Right after the dream, Cecile decided that she wanted to question Andrew Quinn about her son's disappearance. Yes, especially after the dream she'd had. She felt that Robbie was reaching out to her, now more than ever. Something had never been right about the way Quinn had handled the case, but she'd always been under such pressure from everybody else to just let it be. But now, she wanted to know more about what had really happened that August night in 1967, especially now, after the dream had brought it all up again.

Later that evening, after they had eaten and Griff had gone upstairs to retire early, Cecile and Carlton settled in the living room. At one point, after they had talked for a good hour, Cecile observed that Carlton suddenly became preoccupied and quiet. He seemed to be staring at nothing in particular and she knew his thoughts were on overload.

"What is it, Carlton?" she asked. "You look perplexed."

Carl sat forward and put his chin in his hands.

"Mom?"

"Yes?"

"You still believe Robbie is alive somewhere?"

Cecile sat up straight. After a moment of wondering why Carlton was broaching a subject he'd always avoided, she nodded her head. "You know I feel that way. Why?"

Carlton got up and walked to her. He sat on the couch beside her and took her hands.

"Look, I don't want you listening to rumor, but Pete Shelby ... remember him?"

Cecile nodded again and felt herself swallow.

"Well, he says that there's this guy around town calling himself Nick Dowling."

Cecile put her head back. Her eyes were pinched. "Is he Nick Dowling?" she asked slowly.

Carl responded quickly, "No, he couldn't be. He's not autistic like Nicky, but he has a memory of our old farmhouse, and he asked Quinn to let him in to see it. He's been acting strange."

"What do you mean?"

"Well, he keeps saying he's been on Robert Nichols Road before. He's even been saying that he's been in our old house before. Pete told me that he referred to our road as Fox Hollow. It hasn't been called that in years, Mom."

"What does Quinn say about this?"

"Nothing. I mean, Quinn doesn't react to anything."

"Where is this Nick Dowling?"

"I haven't seen him. Pete Shelby has, though. He says he wants me to meet him."

"Why?"

"Because he could be Robbie," Carlton said slowly as he looked into her eyes. He noticed the pain that came into them, and he watched his mother clutch her heart.

"Look, Mom. This could be a bunch of nonsense."

"Why is he calling himself Nick Dowling if he's our Robbie?"

"That's the thing, Mom, I don't know."

"Where is this man Dowling?"

"He's from the city. He has a house in New Kingston he uses weekends."

"Then he should be in town on Friday or Saturday?"

"Yes, I would suspect so."

"We're going up to our old place tomorrow morning. I want to speak to Andrew Quinn. Once we get in there, the moment you get a chance, I want you to take your father for a walk."

"Why?"

"Too many unanswered questions, Carlton. No bodies, barely any investigation, no clues, no evidence. I need to talk to Quinn, and you need to distract your father for a while, so I can."

"But it's been nearly forty years, Mom."

"And there's always been too many unanswered questions."

"That man, Jasper Reed, didn't he do it?"

Cecile shook her head adamantly. "He was a harmless old man that you kids used to tease. He was too frail, even for little boys. I knew Jasper Reed all my life. His wife died of cancer right after their twenty-fifth wedding anniversary. He deteriorated after that. He was no sex pervert. He was a sad, sorry old grieving man and nothing else."

Carlton put his arm around her. "This could be a hoax, Mom. Please, don't expect anything from this, okay?"

Cecile put her head on his shoulder. "I wouldn't dare to dream it could be so, son. I wouldn't dare."

Chapter Thirty-Seven

Jenna turned onto Robert Nichols Road and drove toward Quinn's farmhouse. She noticed how beautiful it was to see the old colonial suddenly appear in the distance, seemingly out of nowhere.

The house looked very white against the sky, but its dark green shutters in need of a paint job, seemed cracked and old.

Andrew Quinn wasn't outside. She was hoping he would be so she could talk to him out in the open. She hadn't called ahead. She knew that was rude, but she was too afraid he'd refuse to see her, and she didn't want to take that chance. She needed to speak with Quinn, and she didn't want to be told she couldn't.

She noticed his truck in the driveway and breathed a sigh of relief. At least, he was home. Good. She wasn't exactly sure how she'd broach the subject, but she had to get the information she'd come for. Jenna wasn't altogether certain that she accepted Sally's premise that Nick couldn't possibly be Robert Nichols. Maybe, he was. Couldn't he have suffered a trauma after the kidnapping? Couldn't that trauma explain his confusion now? Couldn't severe trauma cause lapses in memory? Perhaps, Andrew Quinn had something to tell her about that night that could prove helpful.

Jenna sat for a moment, still hoping he'd come outside, and they could have a friendly conversation in the sunlight. She didn't know how comfortable she felt being alone with him inside the house; he still gave her the creeps. After a minute or two, she realized that if she wanted the information she'd have to ring the doorbell.

It was obvious that Quinn was not pleased to see her. He stood in the doorway for several moments and searched her face, as if trying to recall who she was

"You people ever hear of a telephone?" he finally asked.

"I'm sorry, Mr. Quinn. I was hoping to just take a moment of your time. I have some questions. You might be able to help me."

"Questions? Questions about what?"

"The Nichols and Dowling kidnapping," she said quickly.

"Nichols and Dowling?" His expression looked hard as rock as he glared back at her.

"Yes, please, Mr. Quinn. It won't take long." She hadn't wanted to blurt it out like that, but she didn't know what else to say to Quinn.

"What could you possibly want to know about those

old kidnappings, Lady?"

"Please, it's really important," Jenna pleaded.

Quinn grumbled something that she couldn't quite understand and stepped back from the door.

"C'mon in then," he said reluctantly. "I've only got a minute or two to spare, though."

Jenna followed Quinn inside the house. He led her all the way back into the kitchen. He nodded with his head to an old Formica table. Jenna slid a shiny red chair out and sat. The sun was streaming in and made the room look messy and unclean.

"Well?" he asked as he leaned against the counter. "How can I help you, Mrs. Dowling?"

She decided to jump right into it. Wouldn't do any good to try and make small talk with Andrew Quinn, even if she did know what to say to him.

"You investigated the case, right?"

"Yep."

"Well, my husband, Nick Dowling, thinks he may be the missing Nichols boy. Could that be valid?"

"What?" Quinn asked and shifted his weight. Then he laughed. "He have all his marbles, your husband?"

"Look, he remembers being in this house -- on this road. You were Sheriff then, weren't you? You knew both boys?"

"Mrs. Dowling," Quinn began, "those boys were murdered. I tried to find the perpetrators and I tried to find the bodies. I couldn't, but those boys are gone. The bodies were probably moved off the land. The FBI said it was a dead end. I couldn't argue with the FBI, now could I?"

He was looking at her as if she were a two-year-old child.

Jenna played with a crumbled-up napkin that had

been left on the table, near a stack of magazines.

"There's something that bothers me about the case, Mr. Quinn."

"What's that?" he asked, as he pulled his mouth back and peered at her.

"What about the three pops the parents heard that night? Does that prove the boys were shot?"

"No," Quinn said. "It turned out to be nothing; except for the dog — the dog was shot. The Nichols had their music on inside the house that night. They couldn't have been sure of what they heard."

"Weren't there any traces of blood? It just seems so absurd that the parents heard shots — didn't they run out and call the boys in?"

"That's how they knew the boys were missing, Mrs. Dowling. That's when they called the police." Quinn glared at her. Jenna knew he was getting more and more annoyed at her questions, but she persisted.

"Mr. Quinn, you've seen my husband. Do you think he could be Robert Nichols? You knew those boys, knew the families. Do you think he could be Robert, if not Nicky?"

"Mrs. Dowling, it was almost forty years ago. I don't know what Robert Nichols would look like now and besides, if he were Robert Nichols, why the hell would it just suddenly come to him?"

Jenna looked at her hands and sat back. It was then she noticed a stack of newsletters spread out near the magazine pile. She was surprised to see they were on extraterrestrial sightings. She reached for one and picked it up.

"You're interested in this stuff?" she asked incredulously.

Quinn laughed uncomfortably. "No," he said slowly.

"Aren't these journals written by people who believe

they've had experiences with aliens?" she asked.

"I wouldn't know," he said. "I get that crap in the mail. I use it to stack things on."

Jenna thought that it was an odd coincidence, being that her husband believed himself to be an alien abduction victim. That was certainly one subject she wouldn't bring up with this redneck cop, though. He probably did use the junk mail to stack things on; he certainly didn't believe in extraterrestrials.

"Do you think it's possible that my husband could be Robert Nichols?" she asked again.

"Why doesn't he remember being Robert Nichols, Mrs. Dowling?"

Jenna put her head down and rested her forehead on her hand. She realized she might have to accept the fact that Nick's mental state was severely precarious ... either that, or he was lying.

"Mr. Quinn, do you remember any other crimes in this area?"

"No, there were no other kidnappings around here."

"How about rapes or murders?" she asked tentatively, hoping for a negative response.

Quinn shook his head. He must have been wondering why she was asking.

"Are you sure, Mr. Quinn?"

"Well, there was that Hinckley incidence, but it didn't take place here. In happened in New York City, but the boy was from our area."

"What happened?" Jenna asked.

"The kid killed his wife and child."

"Oh, my God," Jenna said.

"Yeah, it was a terrible crime, very violent," Quinn said as he took the kitchen chair at the opposite end of the table. "Harrison Hinckley was from Phoenicia."

"What was the wife's name?"

"Natalie Miller."

"Natalie Miller?" Jenna sat forward. She'd immediately made the connection to the murder the elder Dowling's had mentioned. "What happened?"

"Harrison Hinckley was a disturbed kid. He seemed to grow out of it when he became a teenager, but he was still pretty strange. He graduated Phoenicia Central in, oh, I don't know, in the mid 70's. He went to New York City and wound up working for some newspaper."

"Really? A newspaper you say?" Jenna asked, noticing the coincidence, that Harrison had a newspaper background, like Nick.

"He married his hometown girlfriend; Natalie Miller, very pretty but conceited, you know? Always flirting. I hear the two of them lived rather well, some fancy apartment in Manhattan. Three years into the marriage Harrison wound up killing his wife and son. It was a terrible thing, all over our papers, 'cause he was a local boy, you know? She cheated on him, I think, or maybe he just went nuts ... happens."

"Where is he? What happened to him?"

"Probably dead."

Jenna felt her heart beating quickly.

"Probably?"

Quinn looked confused, like he wasn't sure what she was getting at, or wanted to get at.

"They found his car by the 59th Street bridge and they speculated that he jumped off and killed himself. He is presumed dead."

"Was his body ever found, Mr. Quinn?"

"No, they never found a body."

"How do they know he's dead?"

"Mrs. Dowling, I don't know what you're insinuating

here but the man killed his wife and child, he shot them both several times after he bashed her head in with a board. Then he drove out to a bridge and threw himself in the river. He's dead. Harrison Hinckley is dead."

"Like Nicky Dowling and Robbie Nichols?"

Quinn glared at her. She was looking for answers that would explain her husband's behavior. He felt his stomach turn over. He could give her the answers, but she'd just think he was crazy too.

So Robbie Nichols was sent back from space and didn't know it. But he could know other things, couldn't he?

Quinn looked at Jenna. "Mrs. Dowling," Quinn began, and stood as he heard a car drive up. He walked over to the window and looked out. He turned back to Jenna and smiled as sympathetically as he could.

"I'm sorry, but your husband isn't Robert Nichols. Robert Nichols was murdered. The case is closed, was closed some time ago. Harrison Hinckley is dead, too. No one would have survived that jump. I'm not quite sure what you're suggesting here."

"But a body was never recovered, am I right? I assumed they combed the East River?"

"Look, I don't know what you're trying to get at, but like I said, the New York City Police Department concluded that Harrison Hinckley was dead."

"They assume he's dead."

"Yes, like Robert Nichols. You're going to have to look elsewhere to explain your husband's behavior, Mrs. Dowling. Maybe he needs a doctor."

"I am a doctor, Mr. Quinn."

Quinn looked at her and sighed again. "You've got to

look elsewhere, Mrs. Dowling. Those boys are all gone."

"Interesting coincidence," Jenna said as she stood and extended her hand. "I mean about none of their bodies being discovered.

"I guess."

"Well, I will be looking elsewhere."

Jenna noticed that an SUV had pulled up in Quinn's drive, right behind her old pick-up. Three people got out and started to walk toward Quinn's front door. They stopped as Jenna came down from the porch.

"Did we block you in?" the younger man asker her politely.

"I'm afraid so." She noticed that his eyes were a brilliant shade of blue.

"Honey, why don't you pull the car over there and let this lady out?" the woman said. Jenna noticed that she was very attractive for a woman her age and looked familiar.

She watched as the younger man backed his car up and pulled it over to the side. She noticed that his car was a Cherokee, and she smiled.

"Are you a friend of Mr. Quinn's?" the older man asked her.

Jenna shook her head, "No, I just know him. I'm a neighbor, actually. I have a house in New Kingston, not too far from here."

"Oh? Pretty area, isn't it?" The woman said politely.

"Yes," Jenna said. "It's very lovely."

"This used to be our house. We haven't been back in seven years." the woman said and extended her hand. "Cecile Nichols."

Jenna gasped. *Nichols? As in Rob Nichols? And didn't*

Nick tell her his mother's name had been Cecile? She knew she appeared as shocked as she felt. She was taken off guard and didn't know what to say.

"You can get out now," the younger man said as he walked toward her.

Jenna took the woman's hand and shook it, "Jenna Dowling," she said slowly. She noticed the expression that came over Cecile's face. She too, was shocked.

"My husband, Griffin and my son, Carlton," Cecile said. Jenna noticed that the younger man looked at her and nodded his head; the older man did the same.

Cecile finally let go of Jenna's hand. For one split second Jenna felt consumed with an overwhelming sense of sadness. It was almost as if it had come out of this woman's touch and had entered her heart. She faltered a bit. She wanted to say something, but her mind went blank. She looked up into Cecile Nichol's eyes. In them, she saw some hopeful, desperate expression and she stepped back.

"Nice to meet you," Jenna said, her voice shaking slightly. As she walked to her car she was aware that Cecile Nichols had not moved, and that all three of them just stood there, and watched, as she drove back down the drive.

Chapter Thirty-Eight

Quinn was looking at her in much the same way Griff looked at her when she expressed her disbelief about what had really happened to Robbie.

"You know we did everything we could, Cecile," Quinn was saying.

Cecile tapped her fingers around the rim of the cup. The coffee he had given her tasted like old, soiled underwear that had been carelessly boiled and strained.

"No, Andrew, I don't know that. You put the lid on the case so fast it blew up a wind."

She had gotten him angry, and she knew it. Quinn got up from the table and walked to the counter.

"I've always understood your anger and your despair, Cecile," Quinn said as he looked out the window. She knew he was looking for Griff and Carlton. He probably knew she'd drop the subject the minute they got back to the house. Unfortunately, for Quinn, he couldn't see them, so she had plenty of time. Carlton had dragged his father out for a walk across the land the minute they finished just one cup of coffee, as she had made him promise to do.

"The boys are dead and gone," Quinn said softly, as he turned back to look at her. "I'm sorry. You know I'm sorry. I've always been sorry."

"Sorry isn't enough, Andrew. No evidence was ever taken from the scene. Why not?"

"There wasn't any."

No footprints, nothing left behind, no witness?"

"We've been through all this, Cecile, nearly forty years ago."

"We heard what we think might have been shots that night."

"Someone shot your dog, remember?"

"That's one shot, Andrew. We think we heard two more shots. We ran in and took the younger boys inside but when we called for Robbie, he never answered."

"There was no blood but the dog's, Cecile."

"Are you sure, Andrew?" she yelled out as her fist hit the table. She could feel the tears welling up in her eyes.

"Cecile, we did everything we could. There was nothing left to do."

Cecile stood up and walked to the kitchen door. After a moment, she turned to him, "What do you make of this man claiming to be Nick Dowling?"

"Nothing."

"What do you mean, nothing?"

"He's a nut, Cecile. That's all he is."

"I want to meet him. I want to talk to him. Was that his wife I saw when we drove up?"

Quinn took a deep breath and nodded.

"What did she want, Andrew?"

"She thinks her husband could be your son," he said quietly.

"My God," Cecile said and slouched against the door.

"Are you all right, Cecile? You want some water?"

"What do *you* think, Andrew? Could he be Robbie?"

Quinn met her gaze across the room. "You know your son's kidnapping took its toll on me, you know that, don't you?"

Cecile said nothing. She remembered his breakdown. She'd always attributed it to the stress of having failed the families so badly.

"I got real sick," Quinn said and bit his lip. He looked away from her. "I think it was because I couldn't help your son. The other boy, well, you know, he had something wrong with him, but Robbie was such a fine boy."

Cecile stared at him in disbelief. She felt like she wanted to spit in his eyes.

"If I thought for a minute that I could bring him back, that he was still alive, why, I'd do anything, anything but give you false hope," he said.

"And that's what you think it is, then, false hope?" she asked quietly.

He walked to her and took her hand in his. He squeezed it firmly. "I've met this Nick Dowling and I think he's a quack. I don't want him breaking your heart, Cecile; I don't want him to do that."

Cecile patted his hand and quickly let go of it. She felt the same dissatisfaction she'd always felt after speaking with Quinn. She wondered what she was hoping to get out of questioning him again. But she felt that he was lying. She had always felt that he was lying.

"Thank you for your concern, Andrew. I'm going to

collect Griff and Carlton. Thank you for letting us pay a visit to our old house, but we've got some shopping to do."

"Anytime, Cecile."

"Do you mind if they come back on Saturday, the leaves are turning early this year and they love to take that walk up behind the house?"

"Sure, Cecile. You just tell them to come on over anytime they want."

"Why did you buy our property, Andrew?" she asked quickly, taking Quinn off guard.

"I liked it," he said.

"You know, Andrew," she began as she turned to face him, "I feel that my son is alive. That's all I have, a feeling, an instinct, some sort of strange telepathy. Silly old woman that I am, I've got to trust it. If I lose that feeling then I've lost faith in God, lost faith in everything that I need to believe in. I have to have faith in everything I know to be true in my heart whether I can prove it or not, see it with my own eyes or not. Do you understand?"

"Sometimes, believing in something isn't enough, don't make it come true," he called out to her as she quickly walked toward the front door and closed it behind her.

Chapter Thirty-Nine

Jenna headed directly over to the library. She had a disturbing feeling about Quinn's mention of Harrison Hinckley. She wanted to prove to herself that her husband was not in any way related to that monster, a man who had shot his wife and child to death, and then, according to record, had killed himself. But it was possible. Anything but alien abduction was possible. It was also disturbing that Harrison's wife had been named Natalie Miller. Why had Nick thought that Natalie Miller's house was his?

Her husband could have been related to the Nichols family. Cecile Nichols, in particular, had features very similar to Nick's, and the younger man had his eyes, not many people have eyes that might have come from the brush of Van Gogh's palette. But, it was probably coincidence, or colored contact lenses. Jenna didn't know what to believe at this point. Sally was so sure that Nick was not Robbie Nichols. Quinn seemed positive that both boys were dead. And, least she forget, then ten-year-old Robbie Nichols had never resurfaced. Why not, if he were, in fact, alive? Wouldn't he want to see his real parents again?

There was no evidence to explain why her husband took someone else's identity and couldn't remember the kidnapping. It just didn't make sense ... Unless it was all a lie, his childhood, even his damn name ... all lies. Jenna now knew that at some point, after buying their house in the Catskills, her husband became a desperate man; forcing an absurdity on the people he loved most in order to protect them from a horrible truth. But what was the truth?

Jenna also knew that she had to be open to the fact that her husband could be anyone, even Harrison Hinckley. But if he did turn out to be Robert Nichols, then there had to be a reason why he'd want to shake that identity at some point in his life and become Nick Dowling.

There were only a few articles in The Catskill News about Harrison Hinckley, but the coincidences were extraordinary. He had graduated high school the same year as Nick insisted he had. Harrison had moved to New York City, as Nick had done. The articles went on to say that Harrison Hinckley had been a track star in high school, was a bit of a ladies' man and had edited the school newspaper. He also played the lead in the senior class play and was a member of the Drama Club. Jenna almost held her breath as she read that he was working for a major New York Newspaper at the time of his wife and son's murder. But Harrison Hinckley was a journalist, not a circulation marketing manager. Harrison had landed a job covering school sports for The New York Post. Nick did not follow sports, and he said he'd only worked for the Post briefly, but he was a runner. He ran every damn morning in Central Park. Running was the only sport Nick had ever had the slightest interest in.

The Catskill News had printed only one photograph of Harrison Hinckley, taken at the time of his wedding. The photograph was not terribly clear. In the photograph, Harrison's hair appeared brown and not light, like Nick's. Harrison had a short-cropped beard and Nick had always been clean-shaven. Jenna knew she had to see more photographs, dig up more information on Harrison. Certainly, if Harrison were from the area, he would have grown up hearing about the kidnapping of Robbie Nichols and Nicky Dowling. He might very easily have stolen Nicky's name after he somehow survived a jump off the 59th street bridge.

The phone rang at nine that evening, and the answering machine light was twitching maniacally as Jenna rushed through the door. She had been out all day and had grabbed a quick bite to eat in town. She'd driven into Phoenicia and had discovered, through local town records, that both of Harrison Hinckley's parents were dead.

She also learned that Harrison Hinckley had a brother that was still living in the area but had not been home when Jenna called to ask if she could meet with him.

She had driven over to Phoenicia Central High School and had found a 1975 yearbook in the office. When no one was looking, she had carefully slipped the book inside her briefcase and walked out. She had never stolen anything in her entire life before that moment, but Jenna needed the book more than she gave a damn about being caught with a stolen yearbook.

Inside a restaurant, Jenna scanned through the cast of characters. They were all there, Elizabeth Logan, Darla Paine, Pete Shelby, Harrison Hinckley. The only missing person was Nick Dowling.

"Jesus, I've been trying you all day," Sally said as Jenna breathlessly picked the phone up.

Jenna flopped into a chair and quickly told Sally about her visit with Andrew Quinn and her brief encounter with the Nichol's.

"Look, I've been speaking with some colleagues of mine. They are all coming to the same conclusion," Sally said.

"Memory loss is possible." Jenna quickly responded, her body suddenly jolting upright. "I've been doing some reading on the subject, as well," she interjected as she heard Sally sigh.

"Yes, if Nick had been sufficiently traumatized he might have blocked out the actual kidnapping."

"So he could be Robert Nichols? There is a family resemblance. I'd so much rather believe that he's Robert Nichols and not Harrison Hinckley," Jenna stood up and went into the kitchen.

"Not so fast, Jenna. Who's Harrison Hinckley?"

Jenna reached into the refrigerator and pulled out a Dr. Pepper.

"Harrison Hinckley killed his wife and son in 1980, and then, supposedly jumped off a bridge. He was from Phoenicia."

"And his body was never found, right?"

"Right," Jenna said and took a swig from the bottle.

"You think they could be one and the same man, Nick

and Harrison?"

Jenna sighed and didn't answer.

"Well, that theory might make more sense than Nick's amnesia. Amnesia doesn't last for forty years. We know for a fact, he's not Nick Dowling."

Jenna went back to her chair and sunk into the cushions. "There is a slight resemblance between Harrison Hinckley and my husband," she said. "Also, his murdered wife was named Natalie Miller, who just happened to live in the house Nick led us to in Phoenicia."

"This hocus pocus is frightening," Sally said.

"Unfortunately, Nick resembles Cecile Nichols as well as Harrison Hinckley. The children looked a bit alike too, little Nicky and Robbie but one was definitely bigger."

"Well, any two people could resemble one another. It would seem not a one of us is in the least uncommon."

"Yes," Jenna said. "Nick led me to Natalie Miller's house in Phoenicia, let's not forget that. Why on earth would he lead me to Harrison's wife's house?"

"The coincidences are just too bizarre. I'm very concerned."

"I'm beginning to wonder if I really want the answers, Sally."

"Then you're stuck with a man who believes he was abducted by aliens."

"There are worse things to be stuck with."

"Maybe the real Robert Nichols was kidnapped, and the experience was so traumatic that he blocked the kidnapping, and the first ten years of his life. At some point, when he's much older, he gets into trouble, commits a crime, a murder or something, and he takes off to avoid capture. Perhaps, at that point, he unconsciously changes his name to Nick Dowling."

"So, he's either Harrison Hinckley, murderer, or

Robert Nichols, criminal and possible murderer?" Jenna asked despondently.

"I'm sorry, Jenna … but perhaps."

"Well, you've been saying all along that my husband is concealing something. That makes him a liar, doesn't it?"

"Yes, he's lying to protect you and himself from something. I'd say the truth."

"Should I hire a private investigator?"

"Well, perhaps a PI can find out if Harrison Hinckley is really dead, or if anyone fitting your husband's description is wanted for a crime."

"My husband's description, my God, my husband looks like everyman. No, I don't want the answers … I want my life back the way it was."

"Jenna," Sally said gently, "no one knows Nick. People he went to school with can't place him. He's trying to force an absurdity on his family. Unfortunately, he's got Laurie backing up his bull about alien abductions. We have to discover who he really is and what really happened to him. The truth is always better."

"Better? Perhaps, but not always easier to bear," Jenna said softly and closed her eyes.

Chapter Forty

Hours later, Jenna heard a car engine outside the door and jumped up. She quickly went to the window. It was Nick. She realized she was fully dressed. She didn't remember falling asleep. The sun was out. It was bright and cold in the house. She hadn't turned up the heat when she came in, and now, she was freezing. She wondered what the hell time it was. She didn't even remember saying goodnight to Sally. She must have passed out on the couch. She remembered her dreams though, so many dreams. They were catastrophic and absurd. She thought she was talking in her sleep. She woke up weeping, but she couldn't remember why. So much crap about aliens and spaceships.

Nick looked distraught and panicky as he ran up the walk and into her arms.

"Jesus," he said, after he hugged her, "Why haven't you called me? I've been worried sick."

"I'm sorry."

Nick rubbed his temple. "What are you doing here, Jenna, you're supposed to be at a conference."

"Well, I got sidetracked."

"I'm just happy to see you. When I called the hotel in Albany they said you'd never checked in."

"I should have called you. I'm sorry."

He held her out at arm's length. "Where were you yesterday?"

"It's all this talk, all this talk about spaceships. It's disturbing. I needed to escape."

"Maybe if you'd called me, Jenna, I wouldn't have been half out of my mind with worry."

"I knew you had a busy week; I didn't want to disturb you?"

"Why didn't you tell me you weren't going to the conference?" Nick asked.

"Jesus, Nick, I didn't know you needed a keeper."

"I was just worried. It was the hypnosis session, it disturbed you, didn't it?"

"Yes. I needed time alone." Jenna stared at him a moment longer. "What did you think of it?"

"I think it cleared up a lot."

"Funny, but I thought it just made things more confusing."

"Are you all right?"

"Yes, I'm fine."

"So why did you come up here for real?"

Jenna went to sit down. She reached out for Nick's hand, and he came and sat beside her. "I've been here since Tuesday. I've been gathering information."

"Information on what?"

Jenna wondered if she would be making a colossal mistake by bringing up Harrison Hinckley's name. Her husband was very vulnerable. But Nick was not a violent man, had never been a violent man; it was absurd to think there was a relationship between Nick and Harrison. Nick could never hurt a child. Jenna reached out for the yearbook. Nick stared at her curiously, and anxiously.

"What's that?" he asked.

"Phoenicia Central, class of 75'. Look familiar?"

Jenna watched as Nick took the book from her hand and opened it. She knew he was looking for the graduating class, looking for Nick Dowling, looking for himself.

"You're not in there, Nick," Jenna said softly. "There is no one by the name of Nick Dowling in that book."

Nick sat back on the sofa and closed his eyes. "I must be Robert Nichols then, Jenna."

"Robert Nichols isn't in the yearbook either, Nick."

Nick turned to her. She noticed the strain on his face.

"I have something to tell you. I should have told you years ago," he began. "I'm so sorry I never did but I was afraid."

"Told me what, Nick?"

"In 1982 I woke up in a Chelsea hotel room and I had no idea who I was."

She caught her breath. "This is getting too absurd," she cried out.

Nick continued quietly, despite Jenna's reaction. "Listen to me, Jenna. I had checked myself in as Nick Dowling and next to my name I had indicated that I was from Phoenicia."

"You kept this from me, something as serious as this?" Jenna's anger rose to the surface, and she tried to contain it. She knew that the answers could be sitting inside the book he held on to his lap, and she suddenly didn't want to know the truth. She had to get away from him; she stood up.

"I was afraid," he said.

"Of what?" she asked.

"That my memories were blocked because I'd done something I couldn't deal with."

Jenna felt her knees weaken. She needed support and held on to the back of the couch.

"Look on page fifteen, Nick," Jenna said, her voice shaking as she spoke. She watched as her husband found the page. Jenna noticed that nothing in his expression changed as he looked at the photographs of graduating seniors.

She pointed to Harrison Hinckley's picture as she sat down again and put her hand on his knee. Nick turned and looked at her quizzically.

"You think that's me?" he asked. "You and everybody else. Good ole Harrison."

"Who does he look like, Nick?"

Nick looked at the photograph closely.

"He's not me, if that's what you're getting at."

"Are you sure, Nick?" Jenna asked gently.

"Of course, I'm sure. That's not me. His hair is brown. We don't even have the same hair color. Look, Jenna, his features are completely different than mine. I know I resemble the guy but that's not me."

Jenna abruptly got to her feet, as if she didn't want to hear what it was he had to say. "My best friend had very dark hair in high school and over the years it kept getting lighter. And you do something to your hair, Nick. Are you really blond?"

"Jesus, Jenna, look at my body hair!"

"Hair color changes."

"This is absurd. I am not your best friend from High School, and I am not the teenager in that photograph," Nick said loudly. "Let me explain. Sam told me I was abducted. They did something to my memory, somehow it possibly got fused with Harrison's."

"Harrison was abducted as well?" She raised her brow and looked at him skeptically.

"Look, when they sent me back to Earth this man Harrison's memories were in my brain, the teenager in that yearbook murdered his wife a few years later and I've got his goddamn memories. Sam told me what happened. That explains my violent dreams."

Jenna felt her heart pound in her chest, but she had to say it. She had to tell him, to force him to face reality. It appeared he was becoming more and more delusional.

"Harrison Hinckley is most likely dead. He jumped off a bridge, Nick."

"He's not dead. He lives inside my head, Jenna."

"Inside your head, Nick?"

"Yes." His skin was so pale that he looked drained of blood.

"He supposedly jumped off the 59th Street Bridge," she said. "But maybe..."

Quick tears come to the corner of Nick's eyes, and she wished she could recant; she also wished the answers she was finding were less severe.

"So, you would rather believe that I am a murderer than that I am a victim of some unknown, unexplainable phenomenon?"

"But you said that your memories were suppressed because of something you couldn't accept, something you might have done. Oh, Nick, if you did this horrible thing we'll face the consequences together."

Nick jumped to his feet and paced back and forth. Suddenly, he stopped and rubbed his forehead. "No," he said. "Jenna, Sam told me I had another man's memories, this man, this Harrison Hinckley's memories. But I am not Harrison Hinckley."

"Nick...." She began, as she rose to her feet as well and went to his side. "I don't know what to think. There are so many similarities between you and Harrison. And nothing else in your life makes sense. There was no abduction. There are no aliens."

Nick turned on his heels and walked out the door. It slammed behind him. Jenna couldn't move. She heard him start the car.

"Nick," she called loudly, but she still couldn't get her legs to move, "Nick! Please, honey, let's talk about this. We'll get help for you. We'll get the best lawyer."

By the time Jenna was able to get out the front door the Cherokee was moving fast and through the dirt kicked up from its wheels she caught the fleeting image of its midnight blue body disappearing into the day.

Chapter Forty-One

Jenna quickly got out the phone number for Gregory Hinckley and dialed before she changed her mind. She knew Nick was angry with her, but she needed answers and explanations, no matter how horrible the truth would turn out to be. She needed all the missing pieces accounted for, even if Nick refused to own up to his own legitimacy.

Gregory Hinckley agreed to see Jenna and to show her whatever pictures of Harrison he had. He reluctantly, but pleasantly, invited her to his home in Olive, a town not far from Phoenicia.

As Jenna pulled into Gregory's driveway, she admired the quaint, old farmhouse he lived in. It was landscaped with gardens that gave the house a happy feeling, lavender, pink and yellow flowers that seemed eager to welcome her. She noticed his sharp red sports car in the drive and pulled beside it.

"Thank you for letting me come over," she said quickly as he opened the door.

She was shocked to discover how blond Gregory was, as blond as Nick, but unlike Nick, Gregory was slight of frame, had much less hair and wore a small gold hoop in his ear.

"You didn't know? We were twins."

"Oh, no, no, I didn't."

"Yes, we're twins but Harrison was taller, and he had darker hair."

"Oh," she said. "Nice car you have."

"Thank you," he said. "I love the Mazda Miata. They handle so well."

"My husband likes them, too." Jenna smiled politely. "It's an MX-5?" she asked.

"Yes." He paused and looked at his feet. When he finally raised his head he saw the discomfort in his expression. "I don't get the chance to talk about Harrison much anymore."

"Yes, I'm sure it must be uncomfortable," she said.

Gregory motioned her in. As Jenna stepped into the open foyer she couldn't help but let out an expressive sigh.

"What a wonderful house you have," she said as she looked around. "It's beautiful."

The house was filled with lovely antique furniture and oil paintings that she quickly surmised were worth a fortune.

"I'm glad you like it. I'm an interior designer, so compliments are always welcomed." He smiled slowly. "I work mostly in the city, but this is my beloved retreat."

Jenna took a seat in a chair that seemed woven in silk,

a lovely amber colored couch. She noticed that Gregory had brought out one small photo album and had placed it on the coffee table.

"Harrison was a very nice man, but he always had emotional problems."

Gregory looked nervously around, and Jenna could tell he was quite anxious.

"I guess he was always very troubled," Gregory said and took a seat on the couch beside her. "May I get you some coffee?"

"Oh, no," Jenna said. "Please, I don't want to put you to any trouble."

"No trouble. Why don't you look through the photo album and I'll put on a pot."

He leapt to his feet and nearly ran to the kitchen. She reached out carefully for the album and opened it. It was old and a few pictures fell out from the sides.

"How long have you owned this wonderful house?" she called out.

"Twenty-five years now," he yelled back.

"Then Harrison has been here?"

"Oh yes, he was here with Natalie right after I bought the house."

"I love old houses," Jenna called to him. "Nick does too, my husband."

"So, you think your husband may be Harrison? You think my brother is still alive?"

"I don't know. I'm not sure," she said as she nervously glanced at the photos and found nothing recognizable in the old black and white prints. She breathed a sigh of relief.

"My brothers and I didn't have a very nice childhood," she heard Gregory say. "What about your Nick?"

"Boring," he tells me. "Typical" Jenna said as she

stared at some color photos of a little tow-headed boy that could have been Nick, or any other man she knew past forty.

"Well, my brothers and I were the children of alcoholics. I guess that sums it up."

"Both your parents?" Jenna asked.

"I guess that being so well off financially made our father terribly bored, but Mother could still drink him under the table. She was bored too."

Gregory made a sound with his breath she couldn't really decipher.

"Harrison hated our father; He was the oldest and felt very protective of the rest of us."

"Who is this lovely woman, the one with the big hat?"

"Well, if she's lovely, she must be our Aunt Carol. She was a journalist. She was like visiting Royalty when we were kids. Harrison adored her. I guess you could say she influenced his life; she's the reason he became a writer instead of an actor, I think."

"There aren't many photographs here. Don't you have any of Harrison when he was older, wedding pictures perhaps?" Jenna asked as she looked around the room. She was hoping to find something framed — something that was most definitively Harrison, and not her husband.

"I'm afraid not," Gregory said. "Harrison took all the photos and I never found them in his apartment, never knew what he did with them."

"Is this your mother?" Jenna asked, as she stared at a photograph of a young woman with three small boys by her side. "Looks like you're at a picnic."

Jenna heard him laugh. "Yes, must be Mother, the opposite of lovely, wouldn't you say?"

"There are three boys in the photograph," Jenna said.

"Yes, our other brother, Randy. He's severely retarded.

He's in a home in Westchester. He's been there since our parents died. I don't see him much, I'm afraid."

"I'm sorry." Jenna continued to stare at the photograph. "What was your mother like?"

"Oh, our mother was a bitch on wheels. Harrison married a woman just like her."

"Men often marry their mothers."

Gregory rubbed his hands together as he walked back into the room. "The coffee is on."

"Why do you think that Harrison killed an innocent child, his only son?" she asked.

"I don't know," Gregory said. "I can't answer that. Harrison was very problematic as a kid. He took medication most of his life, so he could function."

"Oh? Do you know what he took?"

"No, I don't remember."

"Sometimes drugs can really damage the mind."

"My brother believed that his son was retarded — or would become retarded like our brother, Randy. There was no indication of that, but Harrison became obsessive about it. We all tried to reassure him otherwise; that the boy was just hyperactive and would grow out of it. His obsession with his son's mental state became paranoid. I believe he eventually had a terrible breakdown over it. His wife's infidelity didn't help matters either, and, in my opinion, Harrison was never diagnosed properly. There were always clear and obvious signs that he needed more help than he got."

"Was he ever hospitalized?"

"There was a hospital in New York City, a Warren Ardsley Wright Institute on East seventieth street?"

Jenna realized he was asking her if she knew it. Of course, she knew it, she herself had worked there right out of college. The institute saw young patients who were diagnosed with clinical depression.

"I know of it," she said. "Was he in therapy there?"

"Yes, but I don't believe he stayed in therapy for very long."

"I see," she said.

"Mostly he acted very normal, but I knew he wasn't in his right mind, he couldn't have been, not when he committed the murders."

"Did Harrison have any identifying marks on his body?"

"No, but my brother was left-handed, if that helps."

"Oh, really?" Jenna said quickly, "Anything else?"

"He got a tattoo right before he...killed himself."

"A tattoo?" Jenna breathed a sigh of relief. Nick hated tattoos.

"Oh, you haven't seen these," Gregory suddenly jumped up and opened a drawer in a beautiful old cherry desk. He handed her another small book of photographs. "These are pictures of Harrison in high school. He was on the track team."

Jenna opened the book and stared at a handsome young man. He was tall and slender, like Nick, but his hair was definitely brown and he wore it down to his shoulders. "Did he always have brown hair?" she asked.

"Oh, he was a blond baby, we all were. But he had streaks of grey hair by the time he married. From around the age of ten or so he had brown hair."

Jenna didn't like what she was thinking, her husband's vanity about his hair, always lightening it from what? But then again, he didn't have a tattoo, and he wasn't left-handed. "Do you think he really jumped off that bridge?"

Gregory raised his eyes, as if he was used to giving that question a lot of thought.

"Yes, I do. I don't think he wanted to go to prison. I also think he was devastated by what he'd done. I think he was tormented and terribly frightened. He couldn't have lived with something so heinous. My brother was never a violent person, but his wife cheated on him, not that that excused his actions, of course. She wanted a divorce and I imagine he went into a jealous rage. I don't know why he killed the baby. He seemed to have loved the child so much, but, oh God, who knows? I think he would have jumped off that bridge. Yes, I do believe that he did. How could he have lived with himself?"

"Can you think of anything at all, Gregory, anything that is specific to your brother?"

"Harrison had bad headaches, like our father."

"Migraines?"

"I think so."

"Anything else?"

"He was a wonderful actor. We all thought he should go into the theatre, but he loved journalism. He continued to do amateur theatre right up until he disappeared."

"Really?" Jenna asked, thinking that Nick couldn't possibly be Harrison Hinckley; he didn't have any acting ability that she knew of. But those headaches he'd recently complained about disturbed her.

"What kind of tattoo did he get?" she asked as she thought about the scar on Nick's wrist, an accident he'd had as a child with a tin can.

"It was a bracelet, a link bracelet with his wife's initials."

Jenna felt a sense of relief. "My husband hates tattoos," she said.

Gregory bit his bottom lip for a moment and then he stood up and faced her. She noticed how carefully dressed he was, how perfectly content he appeared in this lovely, quaint little house.

"Gregory, do you remember that case, the one about the missing two boys in New Kingston?"

"Oh, God, you mean the kidnapping that happened back in the 60s?"

Jenna nodded and watched the expression that came over Gregory's face.

"Oh, Harrison never got over it. He knew the boys."

"He knew them?"

"Nicky Dowling and he were in this special camp for several years. It was for children with issues. They met there. He met Robbie through Nicky. I'm so grateful Harrison wasn't murdered that night, as well."

Jenna rose to her feet. "Harrison was there that night?" she knew she was visibly upset, and she took several deep breaths. She heard her sister's voice in the back of her head ... *breathe, Jenna ... deeply, from the diaphragm.*

"He hid in the woods. He'd snuck out that night and had gotten himself all the way to New Kingston on his bike. Nicky swore there were space creatures on the other boy's land and Harrison wanted to see them."

"Did the police question Harrison about the other boys?" Jenna asked.

"Oh, no. He got out of there as quickly as he could and rode home. He made me swear not to open my mouth. He was afraid our father would kill him for sneaking out. So, actually, no one ever knew that Harrison was there that night but me."

"Could he have seen the murder of those two boys?"

"Well, he might have."

"Was he ever inside Rob Nichols house?"

"Oh, yes, he loved it. He thought Robbie had the perfect family. He was envious, I think."

"My God," Jenna fell back into the cushions. She was too confused to think straight. *Harrison was there? Harrison knew both boys?"*

"Is that important, Mrs. Dowling?"

"If he saw the boys murdered then it was traumatic for him."

"He never said he saw the boys murdered."

Jenna suddenly felt too anxious to sit. She stood to her feet and paced a bit.

"Well, my husband isn't your brother. I thought he might be, but my husband doesn't get headaches, only recently, not a long-term thing with him," Jenna said as she heard the coffee perking from the kitchen.

Gregory nodded his head up and down, as if in sympathy … or relief.

"Among other things, there are important differences that don't match up. They do look a bit alike, but you don't seem to have any photos of Harrison past his wedding. It's hard to tell."

"It's all right," Gregory said and put his hand on her sleeve, "Wherever Harrison is, I hope he's not suffering anymore."

Jenna reached into her purse and pulled out her wallet. Reluctantly, she opened it to a photograph of Nick. It had been taken right after Ronnie's birth and Nick was holding the baby in his arms. His blond hair was falling to the tip of his eyes, and his face was in a wide grin. She watched as Gregory took the wallet from her and stared at the photograph of her husband. She heard him gasp loudly and put his hand to his heart. After a bit, he shook his head.

"They look so alike," Gregory said. He stared at her for a long time. "That's not Harrison," he finally said.

"I'm sorry." Jenna looked at him. "I didn't mean to give

you false hope."

"Sometimes it's best to let sleeping dogs lie," he reassuringly told her as he squeezed her arm. "Now, let me get that coffee."

Harrison quietly emerged from a back bedroom after Jenna left. He had heard practically everything they'd said. He'd become angry and anxious listening to them. Gregory was clearly a detriment to his plans, he talked too much. Well, what did he expect from his little gay brother? His brother certainly had not been happy to see him when he'd knocked on the door, but Gregory let him in. At the very least, he had let him in.

He could see Gregory at the sink, washing dishes. Behind his back Harrison hid the gun he'd found in the end table next to Gregory's bed. He'd been so surprised to find it, shocked that a fairy would know what the hell to do with a gun. But it was loaded and ready to go, couldn't trust living alone in the country, he surmised, even pussies like Gregory needed to know how to shoot.

"Oh, that you?" Gregory asked, not turning fully to face him.

"Yeah," Harrison said.

"He does look quite a bit like you," Gregory called out, surprised me a bit." He turned back to the sink.

"Nice coincidence," Harrison said as he walked quietly toward Gregory.

"How was I? Were you listening?" Gregory asked nonchalantly, over his shoulder.

"You talk too much," Harrison said, raising the gun and aiming it at Gregory's head.

Gregory didn't turn around, never saw the gun that went off. He grunted once and slumped to the floor.

Harrison watched the blood as it ran over checkered squares and dulled the bright new shine on the floor.

He bent down and listened to the sounds that came from Gregory's mouth and cringed. He sat for several minutes staring at his dying brother. He got out an old tablecloth and covered the body. Finally, he got up and headed into the bathroom where he washed himself in the shower. It was all starting to make sense, his memory loss after being fished out of the East River, but who had fished him out of the river? He couldn't remember. He didn't want to think about that. It terrified him. But, there was a guy calling himself Nicky Dowling. Harrison knew he wasn't Nicky; he had known Nicky too well. He couldn't explain it, but he sometimes felt he'd been merged with this guy, whoever he was. Well, the devil was his friend. It was perfect, oh, so perfect, he was going to be free of it all. All he needed was this Dowling guy's jeep. He went into the den and found a phone book. In it, he found a listing for a Nick Dowling in New Kingston.

"Perfect," he said.

He tossed the phone book aside and walked upstairs to Gregory's bedroom. He sat before the mirror.

"This isn't going to be easy," he said as he reached for Gregory's electric shaver.

By the time he finished he had given himself a receding hairline and had bleached what hair he had left, a light blond. He found the pair to Gregory's earring and stuck the end in his ear until he had made a hole.

"Shit," he cried out in pain.

After he cleaned the blood off his neck, he found a pair of white pressed slacks and a yellow polo shirt. In Gregory's shoe bag he found expensive loafers. He rummaged through Gregory's jewelry box and found two rings that fit him, and a gold necklace that he clasped around his neck.

Of course, he found pancake makeup in Gregory's medicine chest and covered the tattoo on his wrist. He'd gotten that tattoo days before he murdered his wife. Her initials, as if he could keep her, like a token reminder of how she'd wrecked his life.

Harrison stared back from his image in the mirror. "Can't tell us apart," he said.

On his way out the door, he grabbed the keys to the Miata.

Chapter Forty-Two

Nick wasn't sure where he was going; he just kept driving. His wife couldn't possibly think he was Harrison Hinckley. He couldn't even shoot a rabbit, for Christ's sake! How could he be capable of killing a baby? But the pieces seemed to be coming together and he didn't like the way they were fitting.

Nick knew he was driving pretty fast, too fast for the high curvy turns, so he slowed down, even though he wanted speed. He wanted recklessness. He couldn't get over what Jenna had come up with. She would rather believe he was a monster than a victim. She was a psychotherapist, for God's sake. Jenna must have the insight to know that he isn't capable of murder, despite those damn dreams he had, nothing but dreams.

He found himself on Robert Nichols Road. He slowed

down and drove up to the edge of the wide, open meadow. He got out of the car and walked out toward an old piece of stone in the distance. It was chilly but the air felt good. All around him he could see the tips of mountains. The colors were deep. It was turning out to be a beautiful autumn, the prettiest one he remembered. He took up some small rocks and started pitching them, hitting the large grey stone until they split. He threw the rocks as hard as he could, so hard that they even chipped the marker. It was shaped like a palette in the ground, damp and grey, like a tombstone. Nick picked up sticks and dirt, more rocks and pieces of wood, anything he could find, and he threw them like weapons against the cold damp stone.

"God damn it, Jenna," he repeated. "I couldn't possibly be Harrison Hinckley, I couldn't be!"

It took a moment before he realized that he was being watched by two strangers. One looked older but he was very spry and walked quickly. The younger man looked angry, as if Nick had done something wrong and he was about to be punched. Nick heard one of them say, "What the hell is he doing?"

He tried to smile as they approached. He figured that they must be friends of Quinn's. Either that, or they were trespassers like he was. Damn, but he wasn't in the mood to defend his fucking behavior.

"What are you doing?" the younger one said apprehensively. He looked familiar.

"Hi there," Nick said. "Just pitching rocks."

"Out for a walk, young man?" the gray-haired man asked.

Nick noticed that he had a nice face.

"You fixing to knock that piece of stone out of the ground?" he added.

Nick laughed uncomfortably, "It's a good place to let off a little steam."

"Guess so." The older one scowled at him.

"Yeah, I like this meadow." Nick did his best to seem friendly. "It's peaceful."

"Should put you in a more peaceful frame of mind then," the older man said, and pointed with his chin. "If you take the path behind the house you'll have yourself a beautiful walk. That should temper your mood. We just came down from there. Colors are magnificent. The leaves are turning early."

"That would be nice to see," Nick said and forced a smile. He was embarrassed that he had been caught having a tantrum. "How long a walk is it?"

"Three miles," the younger man said.

"Sounds nice. Think Mr. Quinn would mind?" Nick asked. He suddenly felt like a boy, even his voice changed.

The younger man laughed. "Well, you never know with Quinn, but I'll tell him I told you that it was all right. We're old acquaintances."

"That's nice of you but I can't take that walk right now, maybe later today, though. I have to get home," Nick said.

"What's your name?" the younger man asked. "I'll tell Quinn to let you up there anytime."

"Thanks," Nick said.

"The colors are the most vibrant I remember seeing this time of year. You don't know what you're missing." The older man gave Nick a smile as he pointed off to a dirt path. "That path will take you past a waterfall. You'll come to a fork in the road and if you turn right, you'll hit a valley. It's quite lovely."

"I wouldn't advise walking that road, Dad, not in less you're in great shape. If you turn left, it's a lot easier," the younger one interrupted.

"Young man here looks to be in fine shape," The older man said.

"Well, I'm used to long distance runs. I'm sure I can make it," Nick piped in, wondering why it felt familiar ... competing, feeling as if he could do anything the old man thought he could do.

"Come back and take the path then," the younger man said, "it's really great, but watch the mud, it gets slippery."

"Thanks," Nick smiled. "I will," he said.

"I wish you wouldn't pitch stones at this marker." The older man looked stern, parental.

"I'm sorry sir. I had no right to do that. I'll apologize to Mr. Quinn."

"No need."

"Really, I feel a lot better." Nick smiled. There was something pleasant about these people, something he liked.

"Well, bye now," they called in unison as they walked past him.

Nick noticed that they stopped at the stone marker, like it actually was a grave. He watched for a moment as the younger man pulled a small blanket from his backpack and spread it on the ground.

Nick went back to his car. The strangers had altered his mood and he felt rejuvenated and hopeful. He decided to go home and talk to Jenna, try and get her to understand things from his perspective. He wasn't Harrison Hinckley, he was just carrying around Harrison's memories in ways he didn't yet understand, but they'd get to the bottom of it. As long as she agreed to trust him, it would all come clear.

He was surprised not to see Jenna's old pickup truck parked in the drive. He wondered where she could have possibly gone. Despite himself, he felt his anger return. The first thing he did, after he tossed his car keys on a side table, was to pick up his cell phone and call Sam.

"She thinks I'm a monster," Nick said into the phone. "She thinks I'm Harrison Hinckley, Sam."

"I'm sorry, Nick," Sam said softly, "she has to explain it however she can."

"Why can't she accept that somebody fucked with my head?"

"Harrison is still alive."

"If I could find him I could prove I'm not him, couldn't I?"

"I don't think you'll ever find him, no one will. He's a fugitive, he can't be found. Unless he took refuge with his brother, that's our only hope."

"Sam, how do I prove that I lived in space for ten years? How do I find my parents?"

"I don't know if you ever will prove it, or if you'll ever find your parents. Look, let's schedule a hypnosis session for this week. How's Wednesday morning? Can we do that?"

"Life on Pharaoh's Star? Is that what you want to know about?"

"If you were there I want to know all about it."

"Maybe I'm just insane," Nick said.

"Let's see how much more you remember under hypnosis."

"Whatever you say."

Nick went out onto the deck and threw a cushion on a wooden chaise. The sun had come out and the heat felt good on his body. He lay back and closed his eyes. He fell asleep trying to recall his mother's face. Soon he was lost in the images of his dreams.

He was in a room. His friend was there, his friend ...

looked so much like Sam ... maybe it was Sam ... and they brought in the wet man and laid him down. He was tall, tall, and handsome. He looked dead, but maybe not. He was drenched and his clothes stuck to him. A long needle was run between the two. Sam was visibly upset. "What are you doing to him?" he shouted.

The space man nodded his head. "Are they so different?" He seemed perplexed.

"God, yes," Sam cried out.

But the space man did not respond as he punctured the wet man's head with a new device, slender and small like a tiny pitchfork.

Nick put his tongue to the place where the small piece of metal had been found in his mouth and fell into an even deeper sleep.

Chapter Forty-Three

Laurie was immediately sorry she had picked up the phone, it was her mother.

"Darling, what's this I hear about Nick?"

Laurie put her feet up on the couch. She really didn't want to be the one to bring her mother up to date on Nick.

"Just a little sleeping disorder, Mom." She crushed the shell off a pistachio and rested the phone in the crook of her shoulder.

"Ronnie mentioned nightmares?"

Laurie wondered just how far she should go with this.

"Nothing serious, Mom."

"So, what kind of nightmares, darling?"

"Oh, just, you know, typical nightmares."

"What are they about?" Doris asked.

"Oh, just run of the mill nightmares." Laurie shifted her position on the couch. "Hey, I just read this great article in Cosmopolitan, Getting Noticed After Forty."

"You're changing the subject, dear."

Laurie knew it would only be a matter of moments before Doris had the whole story, down to the alien device pulled from Nick's lip.

"Now, don't be upset, Mom. You know Nick's job is very intense."

"His job is giving him nightmares?"

"Well, maybe."

"So, what is he dreaming about?"

"Monsters, nothing to worry about, just monsters."

"Monsters, what kind of monsters? That horrible boss he has — the one with those strange shark eyes he mentioned?"

"Real monsters, Mother."

"What? Like Bin Laden?"

"No, space creature monsters, little gray buggy looking men."

Laurie heard the gasp in her mother's throat.

"You're making a joke of this?"

"No, Mom. I thought you were."

"I dreamed the other night that Nick was flying."

"You're kidding?"

"No, I'm not. Tell me everything."

Laurie didn't know where to begin, but once she got started it seemed she couldn't stop talking. Her detail-by-detail account lasted over an hour. She began reluctantly, leaving out certain things, but then, eventually, she circled back and recounted while Doris waited patiently for all the information. Finally, Laurie ended her tale in an elevated mood of excitement.

"Sam had the metal device analyzed and one-third of

it is an unknown substance. The rest is silicon and carbon, I think."

"That thing he pulled from Nick's mouth? My God. I've read a lot about alien abductions. I can't believe this. You didn't tell me sooner?"

"You know Jenna, Mom. She didn't want you to worry."

"She didn't want me involved. Isn't that what you mean? She knows I would believe he was abducted."

"No, she doesn't want Ronnie to know anything. I mean, his whole life doesn't make sense. What would his daughter think of that?"

"So, Jenna comes to this conclusion? She thinks he's some maniac that killed his wife, murdered his baby?"

"She doesn't know what to think, Mom."

"Where is she?"

"She's at the house upstate."

"She needs her mother. She's not thinking clearly."

"She's fine, Mom."

"Jeffrey?" Doris called up the stairs. "Pack a suitcase; we're going upstate to visit the children!"

Chapter Forty-Four

Jenna stared at her mother. Her parents had shown up unexpectedly but now that they were there she was relieved to see them. Even though she'd been lectured to for over an hour while her father just sat shaking his head, nodding and smiling at Doris like she really was a rational human being.

Once again, Jenna was incensed with Laurie for spilling the beans, every detail, every word, and every insane thought in Nick's head was now ample fuel for her mother's obsession with the paranormal.

"You don't really believe he is this man, this monster? Oh, Jenna, really!" Doris exclaimed with a shocked, flabbergasted and over emotional clutch of her breast.

"No, Mother, I've spoken to Harrison Hinckley's brother, and I don't believe Nick is Harrison Hinckley,

Harrison Hinckley was left-handed. Nick is definitely right-handed."

"I thought he was amber dexterous, wasn't Nick always amber dexterous?" Jeffrey asked.

"Well, yes, but he uses his right hand, not his left. He always uses his right hand," Jenna said.

"You're showing him no trust, no trust at all."

"He needs the truth, Mother! He needs to own up to the truth, whatever it is. We'll stand by him."

"No, no, he needs you, not your interpretations, your judgment, your arrogance. Please!" Doris screamed.

Jenna sat back in the couch and held a pillow to her breast. Despite her best efforts, she couldn't help it, and she began to cry. After a moment, Jeffrey sat beside his daughter. She felt his arm around her shoulder.

"Daddy, you don't believe this nonsense about space aliens, do you?"

"No, I don't believe in space aliens, Jenna, but your mother does make sense, on a certain level."

"How can I believe in lies?" Jenna asked tearfully. "How can you?"

"I don't believe in lies, and I don't accept everything I'm told. Your mother knows how I feel about UFOs," he said. "But I don't want to judge. Would you like anyone to tell you that you are insane for being Jewish?"

"Being Jewish has nothing to do with believing in little space people, Daddy," Jenna exclaimed loudly.

Jeffrey cupped her face in his hands.

"Jenna, I don't understand what Nick is going through, but I've known the man twenty years. He is listening to the troubled waters of his soul. He'll figure it out."

"And in the troubled waters of his soul he doesn't find God, he finds aliens?" Jenna asked sadly.

"We hope he finds truth. In the final analysis, that's what God is. And the truth God finds for Nick is not mine, or yours, but his alone. Give him the chance to discover who he is. I can't be angry at a man who is obviously struggling with a crisis of some kind," Jeffrey said, and glanced apprehensively at Doris.

"And when you discover he's telling a real story and he is perfectly sane, then what?" Doris said quickly. "You haven't read one book on the subject. You don't know anything about these things, Jeffrey."

"No, darling, I don't know anything at all about space aliens. I only know Nick. And I don't believe he's capable of violence. But perhaps ... I should move in with you for a while, dear?" Jeffrey held his daughter's hand. "Just to make sure everything is okay?"

Jenna hugged her father close. "You think he might be shielding some horrible secret, Daddy?"

"Truth is here," he said and put her hand on his heart. "I don't want him to hurt you, for that, I'll kill him. But I can't be angry at a man that may be.... disturbed."

"You think he's disturbed then?" Jenna wiped her eyes.

"I don't know what to believe, but I do think he'll snap out of it, and if he doesn't, well then, we'll take the necessary steps." Jeffrey said and looked out the window, away from his daughter's troubled expression.

Chapter Forty-Five

Nick had awoken from his nap feeling restless, too restless to sit and wait for Jenna to return. He knew he couldn't go back over to Quinn's, but he needed to do something, so he drove into town and slid into a parking space on Main Street, right in front of *Kicking Stones*, an antique store Jenna was always browsing through. He laughed to himself and wondered if he'd ever feel that loose again, loose enough to kick stones down a dirt path with a friend.

He noticed an old wooden statue of an owl in the window and got out of his car. He thought the owl was beautiful. While he was wondering whether or not to price it, he happened to catch sight of the younger man he'd met in the meadow earlier that day. He was walking Nick's way.

"Hi."

The man stopped in front of the store and smiled at Nick.

"Oh, hi."

Nick turned his attention back to the wooden owl.

"That's nice," the man said. "I should buy that for my father. He loves owls."

"Really?" Nick seemed shocked for a moment. "Me too, got a thing for owls." He laughed.

"We met in the field, over by Quinn's."

"Yes," Nick said, "I remember." Nick held out his hand. "Nick Dowling." He smiled politely. "You have a house here?"

Carl didn't say anything for a moment. He just stood there and stared at Nick.

"Are you all right?" Nick asked.

Carl nodded, "Yes, I have a house here...." He shook Nick's hand. "Carl Nichols," he said. "I live on Little Red Kill Road."

"You're Carl Nichols?" Nick stepped back and looked into his eyes.

"Yeah," Carl answered. He stared back at Nick, confrontationally.

"Oh," Nick said. He felt a bit stupid and lowered his eyes.

"Look," Carl began, "There was a kidnapping around here nearly forty years ago ... do you know anything about that?"

"Yes, I know about it."

"One of the boys kidnapped was named Nicky Dowling. The other boy was my brother, Robbie."

Nick squared his jaw and looked at his feet.

"I'm sorry," Nick said.

Nick didn't know if he should blurt out the truth or

fall on his knees and weep. His mind stood still. It wasn't letting him do anything other than stare at nothing.

"I heard about you from Pete Shelby," Carl continued and watched as Nick raised his face and found Carl's frown.

Could this be my brother, Nick wondered? *Could this be my brother?* He didn't know what to say.

"He says our old farmhouse is familiar to you?" Carl went on.

Nick felt a gulp in his throat and an odd hollowed out feeling in his chest.

"Yes, it is familiar to me," he said.

"Why?" Carl asked with the same confrontational stare.

Nick tried to think of something to tell him, that would make sense, but suddenly, two people were standing behind Carl Nichols and he turned his attention on them.

"You ready to head home, Carlton?" Cecile asked as she stood beside him. She paid little attention to the man who stood in front of her son. "I spent all my money down the street in that sweet little shop on the river."

"I know you." Griff smiled, "The angry man in the field."

Nick laughed softly. The woman was staring at him now, but not confrontationally like Carl; she seemed more in shock. She looked familiar. She was pretty, like the woman in his vision. Her face was sad, so sad it seemed to take hold of his soul, like something unfathomably tender.

"Mom, this is Nick Dowling," Carl whispered his name.

Griff stepped back and Cecile stepped forward. She looked into his eyes.

"Nick Dowling?" she whispered.

"Yes," he answered slowly.

Cecile turned away from him quickly. He could hear her breath. No one spoke for several seconds. Nick felt that he was being ripped apart. Cecile must have felt it, too.

"Excuse me, I'm not feeling well," Cecile said and reached for her husband's arm. "Carlton, is the car open?" she asked and looked behind her, up toward the parking lot.

"Yes, I'll be right there, Mom."

Griff held out his hand and shook Nick's. "Good to see you in better spirits, Mr. Dowling," he said softly.

Griff turned quickly and walked back to Walnut Street with his wife. Nick noticed the man was holding the woman tightly, as though she might fall. After watching them for a moment, Nick turned back and faced Carl Nichols.

"I don't mean to cause any pain," he said quietly.

"Then don't," Carl said as he walked away.

They didn't speak on the way home. Carl drove slowly. He was too distracted to drive fast. His mother sat beside him quietly looking out of the window. He raised his eyes to the rear mirror and watched his father do the same, stare at nothing in particular — their jaws set — their thoughts as inaccessible as a lottery win.

Carl pulled into the drive and carefully stopped his car behind Steve's new Mercedes.

The investigation into Nick Dowling's past had come back empty. "There's nothing on this guy," Steve had said.

Of course, the name was common, and several Nick Dowlings had been found across the country, but none of them seemed to have any connection at all to the man under investigation.

"Interesting thing is, I can't get a birth certificate in this area for any other Nick Dowling, except for the Nick Dowling that was kidnapped with your brother," Steve told him.

He and Steve concluded that this present Nick Dowling had changed his identity. "Probably running from corporate theft, something like that," Steve had said. "I'll keep looking."

"Why is he messing with us?" Carl questioned, and Steve shrugged his shoulders. "Macabre sense of humor?

After he turned off the engine, Carl felt his mother's hand on his arm. His father started out of the car but sat back down when Cecile began to speak.

"Carlton, I want you to find a phone number for Nick Dowling, and then, I want you to see if they're available this evening," she said as she turned to him with a slow smile, the one he knew well, the one that insisted on no rebuttals.

"For what, Mom?" He felt his father's confusion from the back seat. Perhaps, it was anger. He couldn't tell. His father had not been at all happy to have just met the whacko Pete Shelby thinks is the murdered son of Cecile and Griff Nichols.

"We're inviting the Dowling's to dinner, Carlton. I've bought enough food to feed an army."

Carl heard the rear door slam behind him and knew that his father was about to blow smoke.

"Yes," he said quietly, "if you think we should."

"Yes," she said. "Did you notice his eyes?"

Carl nodded. He felt his stomach tighten. "Yes, Mom, I noticed."

"Like yours, bluer than cobalt glass."

Chapter Forty-Six

Nick was surprised to see Doris and Jeffrey's gray Buick when he drove up the drive. *Shit, what are they doing here*? he said to himself.

He noticed the new pick-up and was relieved that Jenna had returned. He thought she might have gone back to the city, totally disgusted with him. He was happy to see she hadn't abandoned him, though he was still insisting that his bizarre tales were the truth. *What the hell was he supposed to do, admit to being Harrison Hinckley just to appease her anxiety? Jenna couldn't take the truth*, he thought sadly.

He was furious at having to defend himself. But then again, how could he blame her, how could he expect her to legitimately explain his life to anyone — their daughter, or her parents, even good old Sally.

Oh, this is my husband, Mr. X, and he was raised in space. Hasn't he adjusted well?

Nick tried putting himself in another frame of mind for his in-laws and wondered if he'd have to reveal how many freckles he has on his body to prove he wasn't Harrison Hinckley; he wondered if that would make Jenna happy.

Jenna was just accepting Carl's invitation to dinner when she'd heard Nick's car. She was excited to tell him they'd been invited to the Nichol's. She was hoping that being with the Nichol's family would put an end to his delusions.

Nick seemed glued to the floor. "That's wonderful," he said, breaking out into a smile.

"I accepted, that's all right, isn't it?"

He nodded enthusiastically. "Yes, of course."

"When I told Carlton Nichols that my parents were here they invited them too."

"That's fantastic."

Nick kissed her cheek and drew her into his arms.

Doris rubbed his shoulders and massaged his temples as they sat around the living room staring out over the mountains. Jeffrey was attentive and had just finished telling him about a friend of his who had experienced visions during the war that he swore had saved his life.

"That's quite a story," Nick responded and winked at Jenna who had her feet comfortably placed in her father's lap.

"So, these people we're seeing tonight, you think they're your real parents?" Doris asked in a whisper, as if it were a secret she'd sworn to protect.

"Yes," Nick said quietly.

"Where are you going to say you've been all this time, Nick?" Jenna asked. He could tell she was trying to be helpful.

"I don't know. I think I'm going to have to follow my instincts and tell them the truth," he told her.

"And if they don't believe you?" she asked, sitting upright, looking at him earnestly. "I mean, the truth is a bit bizarre, don't you think?"

"It won't matter," he said, "as long as I can prove I'm Robert Nichols."

Jenna glanced at her father. Jeffrey nodded several times and tried to smile. Doris spread her fingers across Nick's back and rubbed deeply.

"Stress," she uttered. "I feel it in your muscles. Let go, darling. There are several things we can do for stress." She gave her daughter a wide grin. "I suggest you find a few."

It was the first time they had made love in weeks. Jenna followed Nick into the shower, and as he started to move his soapy hands around her body, she played with him under the warm soft spray of the water. After they made love, they dried each other off and she watched him dress. They said very little. He sat there and looked back at her, in his pressed jeans and light blue shirt.

"You're so handsome." She kissed his forehead.

"Not so bad yourself," he said.

"I have an urge," she said, and went into the bathroom for that super gel he wore in his hair when he wanted to look younger. Nick watched as she rubbed the gel in her hands and slicked back his hair, making a little pompadour in front with her fingers. He turned and looked into the mirror and laughed.

"I used to wear a pompadour when I was young," he said. "I do remember that."

"Really?"

"I seem to."

"I dreamed of you like this … with a pompadour. Though all little boys wore them once, didn't they?" She giggled and kissed his cheek. "Anyway, I like it on you. Wear it for me tonight, Nick."

"Of course," he said and reached around to hold her close.

Chapter Forty-Seven

"You'll never change, will you, Sam?" Elijah said.

"Go away, Elijah."

"Not this time brother. I have to talk some sense into you."

Oh, he was so pompous. Always wore a suit of seersucker and his black hair was a sea of dark waves. Handsome like some Ancient God, some 1940s Hollywood star. They couldn't possibly be twins, Sam's features were so irregular, his cheekbones too high. His legs, too thin.

"I have a duty," Sam said, thinking of ways to get rid of him, never should have given him a key. What was he thinking?

"I have to find Harrison. I must find Harrison. Not sure where to begin. I think finding him is the only way to save Nick's marriage, not to mention his future."

Elijah laughed. "To what end do you have a duty to find a dead man?"

"I'll offer him up to the aliens and bargain with them for Nick's life."

"And you know where to find these aliens, they speak your language?"

Sam shook his head. He knew it was a hopeless quest. No one spoke to aliens. "I will do it telepathically. They might know what I want. They might."

Elijah reached out and took Sam by the shoulders, they were the same height, tall lean men with hard muscles and penetrating eyes.

"If you don't put an end to it, Sam, I will. No one believes in aliens, brother."

"You are ignorant," Sam said.

Sam stepped away and turned his back. He hated these confrontations with Elijah, they made him feel like a madman.

Nick stopped the Cherokee abruptly and ran out. There was an ambulance in Carl Nichol's driveway. Nick could see the stretcher coming through the front door. Cecile Nichols was on it. Griff Nichols was following behind, trying to hold her hand. He could see Carl and another man he didn't know at the doorway, both their faces in a tight grimace.

"What happened?" Nick yelled.

Carl Nichols left the doorway quickly and came to his side.

"We don't know. My mother collapsed," Carl said. "She was standing by the stove, and she just fell over."

"Give us some room here," one of the men carrying the stretcher said abruptly.

Cecile reached out her hand to Nick. "Griff, look, look," she said softly.

"What is it, dear?" he asked as he bent down near her face.

Nick reached out and took Cecile's hand as Carl gently touched her head.

"Little pompadour, little pompadour," Cecile whispered.

"Mom," Nick said softly.

"Don't you remember, Griff, our son wore that silly pompadour?"

"Yes, yes, of course," Griff said.

"Son," she called to Nick breathlessly. "I knew I'd see you again. I always knew it. I love you so."

The doors closed as Nick stood there forlornly clutching his wife's hand. The siren wailed off in the distance until it was no longer heard.

"I'm sorry," Nick heard his wife say to Carl Nichols. "I'm sure she'll be fine."

"Yes, yes, I hope so," he said and glanced quickly at Nick.

Steve came down from the front door. "Let's get going to the hospital," he said to Carl.

Nick watched as Carl and Steve got into a dark green Cherokee. Griff had gone ahead in the ambulance. Nick watched as Carl Nichols turned to stare at him. His face was a stern mask. For an instant, Nick wanted to jump in the back seat, and when the car stopped in front of him, he thought he might get an offer to do so.

But Carl Nichols leaned out of the window. "Don't

upset her," he said, "we'd prefer you don't visit."

"How will I know how she is?" he asked.

"We'll call you," Carl said and drove off quickly.

Nick turned to his wife. "She knows I'm her son," he said with a catch to his voice.

Doris and Jeffrey Rubin walked swiftly up the drive and looked apprehensively at the tears in Nick's eyes.

"God, what happened?" they asked. "Did she have a heart attack?"

But Nick didn't answer them. "She knows I'm her son," is all he said.

Carl Nichols kept his promise and called Nick that evening.

"A mild stroke," he told him, "She has to take it easy."

Carl said nothing more than that and coughed uncomfortably in the silence between them. Obviously, Carl wanted to get off the phone before Nick could ask when he might visit Cecile, but it seemed apparent to Nick that Carl and Griff Nichols wanted nothing more to do with him.

He was deeply depressed after hearing about Cecile's stroke. Jenna was sensitive to what had happened and dropped all that crap about Harrison Hinckley. Doris Rubin pointedly stayed away from any subject on the paranormal, knowing it would upset her daughter. Jeffrey remained in an unusually mellow mood, more so than Nick would have expected, considering that his son-in-law is insisting that he was abducted by aliens and raised in space. But nothing lifted Nick's mood, he was too worried about Cecile.

In an attempt to raise his spirits, they talked mostly about Laurie's play, her blossoming romance with Sam, and Ronnie's apparent success at Yale. Jenna did bring up, however briefly, getting scientific proof of Nick's biological link to the Nichols and he was prepared to do that. But, despite the fact that he had looked into Cecile Nichol's face and heard her call him, "son," he felt like there was a hand around his throat and he might lose his breath at any minute and never see her again.

"What's the matter, Nick?" Sam asked carefully, as he watched him sit on the edge of the bed a few days following Cecile's stroke. Nick's despair had been immediately apparent. Of course, Sam had his own problems, he had not been able to locate Harrison. He'd gone back to Gregory's house, but no one answered the door. If Harrison was there he was well hidden. Sam had roamed the streets night after night to no avail, and Gregory Hinckley didn't answer his phone, probably recognized Sam's extension. Sam hopped that Harrison had just expired somewhere and he'd hear about it on the evening news.

Nick relayed his meeting with the Nichols, and how Cecile had had a mild stroke, but she had recognized him as her son. Sam was happy. At least it was going to work out for Nick. He'd have his memories, his family.

"It's odd, but Jenna had me slick my hair into this pompadour and she noticed it right away. It was like a sign to her that I really was her son."

Sam pulled a chair over close to Nick. "I need to give you back everything you lost," he said.

Nick picked up his head sharply, "that would be nice."

"I need you to remember something, Nick. I want us to go back to the night of the abduction in today's session. You're almost there. You've almost got it all back."

"Okay."

"Something is disturbing me about Quinn, and if I'm right ... well, you need to remember it."

"I want to, Sam. I want my damn life back."

"I don't want to put any words in your mouth. Your memories must be fully yours. I'm going to put you in a state of deep meditation. I want you to tell me everything you know, and exactly what happened the night you were kidnapped by the Pharaohs."

Nick lied back on the small cot and put his feet up, "What's bothering you about Quinn, Sam?"

"I've got a theory, that's all it is." Sam stood up.

Nick thought Sam appeared nervous and edgy. "You all right?" he asked. "You seem a bit wired."

"I'm fine. Let's get to it, okay?"

Nick closed his eyes. After a while, Sam asked him to open them. He listened to the sound of Sam's voice, soft and melodic, almost like a prayer. Nick looked into a small prism that Sam held before his eyes. The prism gave off flashes of white light. Soon, the light was all Nick saw. He felt consumed by the brightness of it. He closed his eyes, and when he opened them again, the light had dimmed. Through a long tunnel with quavering sides, he saw a boy. The boy had blond straw hair and his movements were quick and sharp.

"Who is the boy you see?" Sam asked.

"Nicky."

"Where are you?"

"In the field," Nick said as he walked through the tunnel and stood beside the boy.

"Where in the field?"

"Out by a large piece of stone."

"What are you doing there?"

"They asked us to come."

"Who asked you to come?"

"The Pharaoh's."

"Why?"

"To show us the ship."

"Why?"

"To take Nicky away."

"What's the matter, Nick?"

Nick started to breathe quickly. He was clearly frightened by something.

"It's him."

"Who?"

"Quinn."

"What does Quinn want?"

"He must have followed us. Maybe he saw the ship in the sky."

"Does Quinn touch Nicky?"

"Yes." Nick sighed. "He touches him. He touches him everywhere," Nick said sadly.

"What are you doing now? Your legs are moving."

"Running away. I lost Nicky in the dark. I don't know where he is."

"Why are you crying?"

"I can't help him. I'm scared."

"Who has Nicky?"

"Quinn has Nicky. He's hitting him on the head. The Pharaohs are there. They don't know what to do. Oh, no."

"What?"

"Quinn's got me."

"Where's he taking you?"

"To the ship."

"Quinn saw the ship? He's there with the Pharaohs?"

"Yeah, yeah; he wants to shoot them. He keeps mumbling that he's going to kill them."

"You're still moving your legs."

323

"I got away, got away from Quinn."

"Where are you now?"

"Oh, they think I'm Nicky. We told them I was Nicky."

"Why?"

"I couldn't let them take Nicky without me. I had to watch him. I promised to watch him. We wanted them to take both of us."

"Where are the Pharaohs?"

"They're taking me somewhere, somewhere far."

Sam sat back in the chair. He wanted to go on, take Nick through the ship, through all the years on Pharaoh's Star, but instead, he brought Nick out of the trance, brought him back to a safe place.

"It's okay, Nick. You're all right, now."

"Oh, my God."

"Did Quinn kill Nicky?" Sam asked, as Nick sat up. He was in a cold sweat.

"Yeah, Quinn shot him. Oh God, it was because Nicky kicked him and he was so crazy that night, so out of control. He just shot him."

Nick cried and put his head in his hands, "Oh, my God, he shot him in the head, that bastard; he didn't even blink, he just shot him in the head."

Chapter Forty-Eight

Harrison drove the Miata toward the Margaretville Sheriff's Office. Carefully, he pulled in the drive. He had found a colorful scarf on the seat, and he tied it around his neck. He emerged from the car with a tilt to his head, and a smile, a bit of tongue, a bit of teeth.

The first man at the desk eyed him oddly. "Can I help you?" he asked.

"Oh, I hope so," Harrison said and sat in a chair. He kept his legs together and pursed his lips.

The Officer looked about to laugh but moved his chair back instead. "Please, what seems to be the problem?"

"Ever hear about Harrison Hinckley?"

The officer thought for a moment and then shook his head.

"Well," Harrison began. He spoke softly, not forgetting

his brother's soft lisp. He told the young officer all about Harrison Hinckley, how he'd killed his wife and child and jumped from a bridge.

"We all thought he was dead," Harrison said and leaned in close. "He's not."

The officer was listening intently. After a moment he called an older officer over.

"Ever hear of Harrison Hinckley?" the younger officer asked.

"Sure," the officer said. He pulled over a chair. "Sergeant O'Leary," he said to Harrison.

"He' s here," Harrison said, shaking the officer's hand. "I saw Harrison Hinckley. I saw him in Margaretville."

"Really?" Officer O'Leary reached for a pad and took a pencil out of his breast pocket.

"He's my brother, I'd know him anywhere. I believe he's using the name Nick Dowling as an alias."

Officer O'Leary wrote down the name. "Nick as in Nickolas?"

Harrison nodded.

"We'll look into this," he said.

"Oh, please don't tell him I told you, he's very dangerous."

"Of course not," the younger officer said. "But we may need you to make an identification."

Harrison hung his head. "Of course," he said and averted his eyes.

Jenna leaned back into the soft buttercup yellow chair and stared at Sally.

"I hope I look as good as you do when I'm sixty-eight." Jenna didn't want to talk about anything important. Mundane chatter has a purpose – it distracts.

"You'll look better." Sally laughed, "Develop a taste for wine and take a multivitamin daily."

Jenna leaned her head back into the soft crinkle of leather. It felt rich and generously comfortable.

"I'm so relieved that Nick didn't turn out to be Harrison Hinckley," she said.

"So, Doris was furious that you spoke to the man's brother?"

"Yes, she thinks I should have just gone on faith."

"Look, mild mannered married men murder women. That's a fact."

"If Nick knew I needed proof, he'd be very hurt, you know."

Sally smiled gently. "So don't tell him you spoke to Gregory Hinckley. He never needs to know."

"That detective I hired hasn't found a thing."

Sally raised her eyes, "He hasn't found a history on Nick?"

"No, but he says that's not unusual, especially if there's been a name change."

"So, we're essentially back to where we started?"

Jenna felt weary but not altogether defeated. "I'm really beginning to believe that Nick is Robert Nichols. For one, Cecile Nichols seems to think so. She called the house and wants to see Nick this weekend. She's delaying her trip back to Florida for more tests, but I think also, to spend time with Nick."

"She's out of the hospital?"

"Yes, and she wants to see him."

"Jenna, if we accept he's Robert, then we have to wade through his science fiction bunk. He isn't telling the Nichols about his childhood in space, is he?"

"He hasn't told them anything yet. I don't think Griffin or Carl Nichols believe that Nick is a long, lost member of their family, but Cecile certainly does."

Sally walked out from behind the desk and looked out over Central Park. Jenna watched as her friend turned to her and sucked her breath in. Jenna knew she had something unpleasant to say.

"I think it's time we talk about having Nick undergo some serious testing, Jenna. This could be physiological. He could have something wrong with his brain. That would explain his visions. I'm going to suggest he sign into the Eddington Psychiatric Center for a few days."

Jenna sat forward in her chair and gaped at Sally as if she'd lost her mind.

"You can't be serious?" she said, on the verge of tears.

"Jenna, he wants us to believe he spent over ten years of his life in space. Of course, I don't think he is Robert Nichols, and you shouldn't either. I think that poor woman needs to believe he's her son, but he isn't. He's a man who needs clinical help. He's not in his right mind. Something medical is causing his psychotic delusions, or he's lying, and that makes him dangerous."

Jenna looked at her helplessly; she didn't know what to say.

"I'm sorry, Jenna," Sally turned back to the street below. "Give it some thought," she said quietly, "just give it some thought."

Chapter Forty-Nine

It had been a long week for Nick. He couldn't get the images out of his mind, Quinn in the woods hitting Nicky on the head, grabbing at his crotch, and slamming him with the back of his hand. Nick saw himself hiding in the trees, afraid to help, crying so badly that he could barely breathe — trying so hard not to make a sound. Then the Pharaohs came and took him away, called him Nicky. He kept trying to tell them he wasn't Nicky, he was Rob, but they didn't listen. They were gentle though. He remembered that.

Nick wanted to go straight to the police. He wanted Quinn's head in a noose, but he knew they'd never believe him. No wonder Quinn bought that damn house; Nicky's body really was buried there, and Quinn didn't want it found. Of course not, the boy was shot with Quinn's gun.

Poor old Jasper Reed might have had a hunting rifle in his living room, but Nick doubted that he'd had a pistol. They could probably still prove that the gun that killed Nicky was the same gun used by the local Sheriffs. Quinn would have been under investigation for sure. But still, how could Nick be absolutely certain that Nicky's body was out there? He saw the whole thing under hypnosis, but now, it all seemed like a dream again. How could he really prove he was Robert Nichols –– and if he did prove it — and Robbie Nichols was the only one that could have seen the murder, the only other person there that night, then where the hell did he go afterwards, Pharaoh's Star? Hardly!

Nick hadn't told Jenna anything about his latest hypnotherapy session. He wanted to be absolutely sure there really was a body buried in the woods. He put in a lot of overtime at work and when he finally did get home in the evenings, Jenna wasn't there. He felt that she was going out of her way to avoid him. He thought they'd gotten close again, but she was distracted and tired when she finally did get home, going right for the eleven o'clock news, insisting that she was too exhausted for conversation.

Carl had called to tell him that Cecile's stroke had been mild. She was back at his farmhouse and had asked if Nick would visit with her. Nick called her immediately and she made him promise that he'd come to see her, and he eagerly assured her that he would be there on Saturday evening. He and Sam had planned to take that Friday off so they could get out to the field at dusk. Nick wondered if he could pinpoint exactly where Quinn had buried Nicky. If he was going to implement Quinn, he needed to come up with a body.

"Do you think Quinn can see us from the farmhouse?" Sam asked as they entered the woods.

"Only from the upstairs windows, I think."

"Well, let's hope he's not up there peering at us," Sam whispered as they slipped into Quinn's field.

They walked down through the trees until they could see the stone marker. The dusky sunlight threw a golden glow in front of them and left a warm hazy corridor of light that filtered down to the ground below.

"I don't have a clue as to where he might have buried Nicky," Nick said. He sat on an old piece of wood and looked around. "How the hell are we going to find Nicky's body, look at all this land?"

"You're trying too hard, Nick," Sam said as he spread an old musty blanket on the ground. "Why don't you lie on the blanket and try to clear your head? Perhaps, you'll remember under hypnosis."

"Perhaps I didn't see him bury the body?"

"And perhaps you did."

"Sure," Nick said. He watched as Sam leaned their two shovels against a tree. The blanket felt soft on the earth. Nick could feel the dampness on his skin, even under his jacket. Above them, geese flew past in the sky, and they watched the perfect formation of their flight.

"I want you to tell me everything you can remember about Pharaoh's Star, Nick," Sam said quietly. "The more you can recall about it, the better off you'll be. You need to remember everything."

"I thought this was about finding the body, Sam."

"Well, it is, but your experience on Pharaoh's Star is important. It's my job to help you uncover your abduction experience."

"I don't remember Pharaoh's Star, not really."

"Yes, yes, you do," Sam said as he pulled the prism from his backpack.

"You're going to hypnotize me?" Nick laughed. "So you can learn about Pharaoh's Star?"

"I don't really need to know about Pharaoh's Star, but you do. And then, we'll go back to the night of the abduction and see if you remember anything at all about where Quinn might have buried Nicky Dowling's body."

"You think we can really find Nicky?" Nick asked and looked around at endless acreage.

"Yes," Sam said, "I do."

"Okay, then, take me to Pharaoh's Star."

Nick listened to the sound of Sam's voice. He could see the lights from the prism flash before his eyes.

"Relax," Sam said.

Nick tried to clear his mind, to concentrate only on the prism. He felt as if he lay there for a long time listening to Sam, to the geese in the distance, to the breeze that caused the trees to dance as gracefully as the birds that flew. He drifted, drifted until it felt as if he, too, were flying. Then, so briefly, he saw the boy's face. Soon after, he felt like he was floating, past the moon, the stars, past the universe.

"Where are you Nick?" Sam finally asked.

"Pharaoh's Star," he said. "Must be. The ship is covered in a shield, like a bubble of crinkly wrapping paper."

"Where is Pharaoh's Star?" Sam put the prism away and sat more comfortably at Nick's side.

"In space," he whispered.

"Who lives there?"

"Pharaohs... and some of us."

"Where do the Pharaohs come from?"

"Earth."

"That's true, they come from Earth." Sam looked up. The night was almost too still.

"Yes, they are us, what we become ... some of us, anyway."

"When do we go there?"

"It's almost Biblical; I know that Pharaoh's Star is in the future, but it feels so much like the past," Nick said.

Sam looked up toward the sky. He'd heard a sound, like a blender. It was low but seemed to be coming closer.

"You look nervous," Nick said. "Is something wrong?"

"Well, a bit wrong." Sam looked toward the sky again. I wonder if they can capture us.

"Capture us?"

"I want to restore your full memory," Sam said.

"Well, not sure if you want to hear this, but I do remember Harrison's experiences, clear as my own now. He screwed the hell out of Elizabeth Logan. I picked that all up from his memories ... and Darla Paine. Wow! He wanted to screw her badly because Pete kept bragging about their sex life. But he sure had the hots for Elizabeth, but she was so demanding, made him mad as hell. I have his memories pretty clearly in my head. Maybe we shouldn't erase them, they're pretty hot." He laughed softly.

"What about Harrison's wife?"

Nick rubbed his forehead. "She lived in that house, the house I thought I had grown up in. That's why I went there. I knew it so well. I went there to see Natalie because it's where Harrison would have gone. His memories are clear but not coherent, more like flashes."

"Do you remember Natalie's murder?"

"No, not really. I just remember Harrison's obsession with her. She was very difficult, but I don't have any memory of violence. They wiped it out of me, must have, except in my dreams."

Sam noticed that the sky had darkened, and the sunlight was nearly gone. He felt something in the air, but he didn't know what it was.

"Where did you live on Pharaoh's Star?"

"There was a box, a white box. Mostly I was there, like a damn corpse."

"And when you weren't there?"

"They took us to Substation Six. There were roads there, cars, houses, but no one seemed to be in them."

"Weren't there any other humans like yourself?"

"Yes, minions are the ones in the coffins, like us. The Pharaoh's tried to keep us separate."

"Coffins?"

"In a substance city called Station Y, Phoenicia. There was a freezer there. We were kept there, sometimes."

"Station Y, Phoenicia, is a freezer?"

"Partly, yes. They kept us in the boxes there. It was cold but it didn't kill us."

"Do you ever feel they're coming for you again, Nick?"

"Yes. I dream that sometimes, that they get me, and I'm never returned."

"How advanced are they, do you know?

"Well, there are the Arbors."

"Arbors?"

"Robots. They have very human like robots. They refer to them as 'Arbors'."

"Are there more Arbors on Pharaoh's Star, Nick?" Sam asked. "Or more Pharaoh's?"

"There are still more Pharaohs. The Arbors are like their slaves."

"How well do you remember them? What are their emotions like?"

"The robots have none. The Pharaoh's mostly have just one, or maybe they just show one."

"One emotion?" Sam asked. Sam knew that Nick was remembering his observations of Pharaoh's Star. Sam was pleased. This was very good.

"It's a reasoning ... an acceptance. They feel differently. It is mostly without sentiment."

"You're doing well, Nick."

"The aliens don't talk to God. They talk to each other. I remember that. They say God is everywhere in time, to far back to find. They are very spiritual."

"What do you think the Pharaohs want?"

"Pharaoh's Star is not natural, not a natural environment. But, one day, it will be all there is."

"You know that now?"

"Yes. The planet Earth dies. They want to be there for us then, that is if they can't save the planet. We will need them if they can't save our planet."

Sam nodded his head. Nick's knowledge was all there.

"What do Pharaohs eat?" Sam asked. He wondered how they would get food on a spaceship.

"Fruits and vegetables. There is no meat. There is no killing of any kind. I like meat now, though. It took a while. There is abundant food on Pharaoh's Star."

"So they took you from your backyard in 1967 and you lived on their planet in a box they called the freezer? Did you run and play, do everything you can do here?"

"I never heard other children but Substation Six was like earth."

"They must have been there though, children I mean."

Nick turned to Sam very suddenly, "can they abduct me again? Why would they want to? I'm safe, right?"

Sam laughed uncomfortably. "They might abduct you again, for a purpose. But the Pharaohs would never intentionally hurt you."

"Somehow that doesn't make me feel any better."

"No, I don't guess it would."

"They don't understand our behavior any more than we understand theirs. They say we are innately violent. When they left Earth, they evolved differently. They became one, a unity … .no opposites. If we do not change, we will not be accepted on Pharaoh's Star. We'll disintegrate."

"When did you return from Pharaoh's Star, Nick?"

"1982."

"Alone?"

"Yes."

Sam began to feel as if they were being watched, observed.

"I don't want to ever go back there," Nick said.

"Do you know why they brought you back?"

"No."

"You would have died there if they'd kept you. You'll die if they take you back. Not immediately, but soon enough, unless they keep you as they must have kept Harrison, as alive as a dead man can be."

"I don't understand. They have Harrison?"

"I think they abducted him and you were both used in their memory experiments. I think they dumped Harrison back to Earth, not sure when though. You were a mistake, Nick. Your whole abduction was a mistake. There's no mystery to it at all."

"It doesn't make sense to me."

"Where is Nicky?"

"He lives in time. That's what I saw in the field. Everything he said to me was said that night. *Come with me Robbie, missed you, it's so big, so big, so big.*"

Sam looked behind him. He thought he'd heard a rustle in the leaves.

"Yes, Nick, you are able to see through time. It has something to do with being on the ship and living way in the future. I want you to go back to the night of August 7th, 1967. You can see the past."

"All right."

"It is a little after nine P.M. You see Quinn hurting Nicky. You watch him shoot Nicky. But don't be afraid because I'm here with you, okay?"

Sam watched as Nick nodded his head.

"Do you know where Quinn put Nicky's body?"

Nick sat up quickly. "No," he said, "I don't but....."

Sam was alarmed and got up on his knees. Nick had gotten to his feet. "Lie down, Nick. We have to find Nicky's body."

"Don't you see the dog?"

Sam looked around him. The sound was stronger. Bright white lights shone down and enveloped them. Sam looked up. Suddenly, he saw it, the underbelly of the ship, the lights, the soft low whir of its engine. It took up all the sky in his sightline.

"God damn it, they're coming for you, Nick."

"The dog knows where Nicky's body is, Sam," Nick said, ignoring the lights that now seemed to hover directly over them. "I wouldn't know where to find it. Quinn buried Nicky after the Pharaoh's had taken me. He shot the dog after he buried Nicky. The dog went after him."

"Don't let them do this, please, don't let them do this." Sam called out and put his hands over his ears.

"Come quickly," Nick said and started running. "The dog is scratching up there, up there near that old piece of stone. Get the shovels! I think Crocket is showing us where Nicky is."

"Nick, the ship is over us. Nick!" Sam called. "Run!"

"Damn it, get over here. I know where Nicky is. Crocket is leading me."

Sam moved away and grabbed for the shovels. He wasn't sure if Nick was aware of the danger. Sam hurried up to Nick, glancing quickly back over his shoulder. The ship hovered low to the ground.

"Shit, the dirt looks fresh, Nick," Sam said as he shone the flashlight on the ground. "It's recently been disturbed."

The two men quickly began to dig away at the dirt. It did not take long before they hit something. Every now and then Sam glanced back at the ship over him. It remained low, camouflaged by the dark night.

"It's a shallow grave. It must have just been dug," Nick said as he got on his knees and stared into the hole.

"Shit, what is it?" Sam asked and shone the flashlight down.

There was a bag, tied at the end.

"My God," Nick uttered and jumped back. Inside the open bag a skeleton and a perfectly preserved body stared blankly at nothing.

"Jesus!" Nick said and stood up quickly.

"Two dead people, Nick," Sam said. He was shivering, it was the most macabre thing he'd ever seen. "There are two dead people here. One of them must be Nicky but who is the other one?"

"Robbie and Nicky?" Nick said slowly. "Then who am I?"

"One must be an alien." Sam looked at Nick, "You were definitely Rob Nichols and Quinn did not kill Rob Nichols. And this body does not look like you. It's a man."

Nick looked in the hole. "The preserved one must be a Pharaoh. Why didn't his body decompose?"

"Look at both skulls," Sam said, "they've got holes in them."

"The bastard was telling the truth. Quinn did shoot an alien. He was telling the truth," Nick cried out. He killed a Pharaoh and maybe they don't decompose.

"He probably keeps checking to make sure they were still here." Sam said. "That's why the dirt is fresh. He thinks that's his ticket. He thinks the aliens won't kill him as long as he's got proof of their existence. The asshole doesn't accept that they're non-violent. And he sure as hell doesn't want Nicky's body found, either. But all they want is what belongs to them, this man, whoever he is, was not alive at this time in history and therefore his essence, his physical self, survived ... though his mind is dead. They can't let this man be found by the wrong people and handed over to science. They know it isn't something our civilization is ready to accept, and they would clearly prove he is not one of us."

"What should we do?" Nick asked.

"Nick, the Pharaohs are here. Look at the sky. Look how close the ship is. They know we have the alien's body."

Nick looked up and saw the lights over him. He heard the sound. He felt them near.

"Help me bury the boy, Nick." Sam picked up a shovel.

"What are we going to do?"

"Leave the alien body where they can see it. That's what they want. They want the alien body."

Nick and Sam quickly took the alien body out of the bag and put the skeleton of the boy back in the ground and buried it in the hole. They made the spot look as undisturbed as possible. They didn't want Quinn to know they'd found the grave, not yet, not until Nick could prove he really was Robbie Nichols. Then he could tell the authorities that Quinn was Nicky's killer. Gently, they took the body of the alien and lay it in the field, right at the edge of the trees, and quickly left the woods.

Quinn stepped away from the window. The darkness arrived without being noticed, just leaving its shadows behind. But the dusk had given him ample light. He descended the stairs and went to his gun case.

"Little bastards. God damn little bastards."

He took out the Merkel SR1 and put his head to the muzzle.

"All a man has is his reputation. That's all a man has." He set the stock on his shoulder as he reached out and caressed the barrel.

Quinn got out his rod tips, and gun oil, and all the neatly stacked brushes he saved for cleaning his prized possessions.

"Fine as ever," he said as he reached for his bullets. "Fine as ever."

Chapter Fifty

Right after Nick left for the country, Sally's phone number bounced off Jenna's caller ID with annoying precision. Jenna's first reaction was to ignore the call.

"Let the damn answering machine take a message," Jenna said aloud.

She had been so perturbed by Sally's suggestion that Nick undergo some psychological testing that she was dangerously distracted all week. Just that morning she had carelessly walked out in front of a taxi, and the day before, she had missed her subway stop. She knew on some level that Sally was right, but she wasn't ready to let that in. Her quest to discover her husband's true identity had left her in an exhausted state. She refused to accept that Nick was a madman. Still, even having a midlife breakdown could not explain why his past didn't exist.

When she was being rational, Jenna assumed that Nick was an amnesia victim who had decided to start a new life. He might even have children he didn't want her to know about. He must be lying to her. What could he possibly be thinking, to insist on an alien abduction, knowing that she would never accept something so preposterous?

"Jenna?" Sally's voice rang out from the machine. "Are you there?"

Jenna grabbed the phone, a last-minute impulse. She stood there with the damn thing in her hand, as if she'd forgotten what to do with it.

"Yes, Sally?" Jenna sat back in a chair — right on top of the last-minute jacket Nick had tossed there — deciding quickly that it was too light for early autumn in the Catskills.

"Are you all right?"

Jenna put the jacket on her lap and ran her hand across the fabric. She looked distractedly at a lone, light hair that had fallen on the camel-colored collar.

"I'm fine, just tired."

"I've been watching a lot of television lately. Some of it is newsworthy ... worth mentioning."

"Yes?" Jenna wanted to hang up, throw years of friendship out the window and pretend she'd never heard of Sally Harnick. Yes, hang up before Sally mentioned something awful about Nick— his buried past as a murderer — and of course, Sally would pressure Jenna into going to the police. She'd insist Jenna turn Nick in to the authorities.

"They did a report on the Hinckley case the other night. It was on 48 Hours. There's speculation that Harrison Hinckley is still alive, but nothing conclusive."

Jenna felt herself breathing from somewhere she

hadn't located in years, that deep place in her stomach that Laurie had always referred to as "her center."

"Are you serious?"

"People say he's been spotted over the years. He seems to be a bit like Elvis, every few years there's a sighting."

"Sally, Nick is not left-handed. I told you what Gregory said, his brother was left-handed."

"But he's amber dexterous; didn't you tell me that once?"

"My husband doesn't get migraines or tattoos, two more characteristics attributed to Harrison."

"I'm not convinced."

"How did they end the show, do they conclude that he's alive?"

"Someone that knew Harrison Hinckley said he had spotted him in St. Thomas, in 1990, but nothing ever came of it except some little blurb in the paper," Sally told her.

Jenna stood quickly. Nick's jacket fell to the floor, and she bent to pick it up She noticed that her hand was shaking. Again, she laughed nervously. "Nick and I went to St. Thomas in 1990, I think, or was it 1991?"

"The police are pretty sure he jumped off the bridge and drowned."

Jenna sat down again. She'd tossed Nick's jacket back on the chair. She sat across the room and stared at it — the familiar metal snaps, the scent of Nick — the soft corduroy feel of the deep beige material.

"It was '91, I think." She smiled.

"Jenna, Nick could have had his looks altered. He might only marginally resemble Harrison at this point."

"Nick doesn't have any scars, Sally," Jenna said quickly. She felt, at that moment, that Sally was confusing her, controlling her conclusions too much, even being uncharacteristically absurd.

"There is no logical explanation for my husband's behavior in anything we're coming up with. I think you're watching too much television."

"Well, then, it must be space creatures." Sally laughed. "Mustn't it?"

"Perhaps it is," Jenna said defensively.

"Look, I know how painful this is," Sally said softly.

She wanted to lash out at Sally. She was sick of her over enthusiastic interest in Nick's life.

"Look, Jenna, I don't mean to upset you, I really don't, but I've concluded that Nick doesn't come from some little Catskill town at all. I think he somehow wandered up there and took some random name. I think he's a tortured man. We must get him into therapy — maybe even get his DNA tested. There are a lot of men wanted in this country that have never surfaced. I'm sorry, Jenna, but your Nick is likely one of them."

"I still don't think he's capable of anything you're accusing him of."

"I know how difficult this must be, Jenna. But whoever he is, he's tortured by his past. He's done something he had to run away from, and now, he's crying out for help. These people always want to be caught, to be saved. He's actually set up a mystery for you to solve."

Jenna felt at that moment that nothing made sense, nothing at all, except, perhaps, all the years of her marriage to Nick.

"You know something, Sally? I don't know any wife and child murderers. I only know Nick. That's it. I have to accept that the truth will surface — eventually."

"The truth could be dangerous for you. I'm worried."

"Don't be. I'll be fine. My husband loves me. When the

truth is finally revealed it will be an epiphany, a new beginning … and I'll be there to help him through it. Now let's lay all our 'Nick is a monster theories' to rest," Jenna said, keeping her voice steady. "I'll keep you posted," she whispered wearily as she hung up the phone.

Chapter Fifty-One

Nick felt the crisp, cool morning air on his skin and slowly opened his eyes. The sky was like a fancy oil paint blue — maybe a peacock azure or a deep, sea breeze topaz. The lazy white clouds floated past his window and the light from the sun filled his room. He stretched out his arms and let out a loud, long yawn.

He rolled his body to the side of the bed and put his feet over the edge. It was a good morning for a run, a perfect morning to jog up a country road. He threw on an old pair of sweatpants and reached for a gray and white pullover, the one he always wore when the air was cool. He laced his running sneakers and opened his bedroom door.

"Sam," he called, "I'm going for a run, want to join me?"

The house was still and quiet, but from the sliding glass doors to the deck Nick could see Sam sitting quietly in a chair, his head in his hands.

"Sam, what is it?" Nick asked as he walked outside and sat on the railing.

"Just feeling uneasy," Sam said as he looked toward the sky.

"What about?" Nick asked quietly.

"Don't know," Sam said as he shrugged his shoulders.

"You still believe they're coming for me?"

"I feel uneasy. "

"It's catching."

"I wonder if I'll ever be able to prove that hundreds of people have visited spaceships. It's making me mad; you know. I doubt it all a good deal of the time."

"What can I do about Nicky's body, Sam?" Nick asked. "Quinn covered the murder up. He could have easily done that; he was in charge of the investigation. I can't prove it though, not unless I admit to being an eyewitness."

"Sure, then where were you for the ten years following the murder?"

"Pharaoh's Star, of course." Nick smiled.

"Ha!"

"Guess not."

"Why do you think Quinn killed the boy?"

"Well, Jenna would probably say he was projecting self-hatred. I wonder if he ever killed anyone else. He was a bully. He tried molesting me, but Crocket would never let him near me. Big bastard was afraid of dogs. So many things are coming back. Quinn shot Crocket without flinching, shot Nicky without flinching."

Sam turned to him. "I'm not quite sure what to do now."

"Well, I guess we're going to have to figure out how to

implement Quinn. Maybe, there were other boys molested by Quinn and they'll come forward. I don't know if a bullet found in the skeleton's skull is going to prove it came from Quinn's gun, but it might."

"Yeah, it might."

"Do you think the Pharaoh's have that alien body?" Nick asked. "God it was weird, it looked dead but then again it didn't."

"The aliens have it by now," Sam said. "Stupid bastard really thought he was getting something over on the Pharaohs." Sam chuckled. "I wonder if Quinn will notice that the plastic bag is lighter."

"At least all my confusion is cleared up."

"What do you mean?"

"They hooked me up to Harrison Hinckley and I got his memories. I got his bad childhood, his fantasies, and his passions. But I'm not him, I'm me."

Sam stared at Nick for several seconds. "Harrison is out there," he said slowly.

"What?"

"They dumped Harrison off the ship, probably not too long ago."

"Why?"

"They were through with him," Sam said. "But I think he must have memory issues if he's alive. He probably has all your childhood memories."

"Well, at least I'll be able to prove to Jenna that I'm not Harrison Hinckley. I'll have a DNA test."

"Then all we'll have to do is think of some way to make your missing past make sense."

"She has to believe me, Sam."

Sam looked out over the mountains. "The Pharaohs might come for you. You should know that. We didn't get all of the tracker out of your body."

"I won't let them have me."

"Unfortunately, there is no defense against an alien abduction."

"Well, I don't want to go to Pharaoh's Star, Sam. I like it here," Nick said.

"They don't care, they're aliens. They don't understand your emotional attachment to this planet, to your wife, or your daughter. To them you're all dead."

"I'll carry a gun."

Sam noticed how hard Nick's expression became.

"You can't use violence with the Pharaohs, only reason. And reason will or will not work."

Nick saw a car turn up the driveway and leaned off the deck. "Then we'll find a way to make them understand."

"It looks like Jenna," Sam said.

"Jenna?"

"Yeah." Sam waved toward the car.

"What is she going to accuse me of now?"

"I thought you'd like to see me." Jenna hugged her husband. "The police called me. I drove up as quickly as I could."

Nick hugged her back tightly. "The police?"

"It's my fault," Jenna said. "I went to see Harrison's brother. He told me you weren't Harrison and then apparently he went to the police and told them you were. I think he's trying to protect his brother."

"I'm not Harrison. If they do any DNA testing it will be proven that I'm not." Nick smiled at her.

"I don't know why Gregory did that though. Why wouldn't he have told me that you were Harrison if he believed you were? He's lying to the police, I know it."

Nick put his arms around her. "I love you Jenna, there's nothing to forgive."

"I'm so tired of doubting you, Nick, so tired of it." Jenna took his hands and held them tightly.

"I understand how you feel." Nick kissed the top of her head.

"I guess the police will come here if they think you're Harrison."

"Let them come then. Maybe you need to hear it from them that I'm not Harrison."

"I've started to re-think everything. I know you're not capable of murder."

"That's great, Jenna, that's really great," Nick said.

"48 Hours did a retrospective of the Hinckley crime. You know, no one can prove whether he's alive or dead."

Nick looked quickly at Sam, who was now sitting on the edge of his seat. "You're kidding?" Nick said.

"Yes, they have nothing conclusive."

"Interesting," Nick said.

"Yep," Jenna said.

"Jenna, what's your point?" Nick asked.

"Well, there's this swindler from the Catskills. He's presumed missing. They say he staged his death, but he's not really dead."

Nick felt the anger again and wondered what bullshit Jenna and Sally could have possibly come up with now.

Jenna looked into Nick's eyes and waited for a response. Nick stared back at her with a blank stare.

"He was your age," she said casually.

"Yes?" Nick said.

"There was a serial rapist in the area as well. They never caught him." Jenna looked nervously at Nick and picked her nails. "I've been reading up on this all night."

Nick got up and went to Sam's chair. Sam looked up at

him curiously and tried to maintain his smile. Jenna continued, as if she were lecturing to a class of investigators.

"There are so many men out there who have actually gotten away with horrible things. One man murdered several women and he's still at large. Then, there was that child killer. He wasn't caught for years. He lived a completely normal life not twenty miles from us."

Jenna stopped speaking and stared at her husband for several moments, "Don't you see what I'm saying, Nick? I went to the America's Most Wanted site — it's all there."

Nick carefully shook his head and stared at her in disbelief. Jenna continued as she stood up and began to pace the room.

"You know, these television shows, Nick ... they're on night after night, and they're all about men getting away with horrible crimes."

"I don't get it. Am I supposed to be the rapist, the swindler, the child molester or that guy that just killed a lot of women?" Nick asked carefully.

"No, of course not, you're not any of those people. I guess I'm not being clear. I'm just saying that you might have done something that you did get away with, and well, let's just let sleeping dogs lie."

"I see," Nick said sadly.

"Nick, you've blocked what you've done. Leave it there. Leave it alone and lets go on from this point. There's no reason to unscramble your past. I know you, Nick. If you did something to hurt anyone you would have blocked it out. Of course, you would have. I would have. Sam would have. You would have been far too ashamed to admit it to me. But I'm with you."

"I'm not blocking anything out anymore, Jenna."

Sam stood up and grabbed Nick's arm. "Nick, give some thought to what she's saying."

"What are you talking about, Sam?"

Sam took Nick aside. "Excuse us," he said.

"Look, Nick. Save your marriage," Sam whispered. "Jenna needs to get beyond the abduction theory. This could be your ticket. Play it out. Pretend to go along with what she's telling you. Damn it, Nick, do it. Give all this other shit up. You won't ever have an explanation for your missing years."

"What are you two whispering about?" Jenna asked sharply.

"God damn it Nick," Sam said quietly. "Tell her there's nothing to remember. Tell her you're over it, that whatever you did is history and you're willing to forget about it. God, man; she is."

"I haven't done anything, and I won't pretend I have," Nick shouted and turned back to Jenna. "I am the victim here, Jenna, no one else," he said.

"Nick, I'm just saying that bad things happen to good people." Jenna appealed to him. "That's all. Let's put it all to rest, spaceships, aliens, murders, all of it."

Nick sat back down and looked from Sam to Jenna. "No, I finally have the truth," he said solemnly, and let his eyes rest on his wife. "Please don't force a solution on me, Jenna. I am not a monster. I am sorry the truth is unsettling for you, but I never killed anyone, and I can prove it. I was abducted and I can prove that too." He looked at Sam.

Sam stepped forward and went to him. "For God sakes, Nick."

"I'm not saying you're a murderer, Nick. I'm saying you're concealing something you're ashamed of," Jenna cried out in frustration. "It could be anything."

"No, I am not concealing anything," Nick yelled. "Look, I'll bet that you won't find Robbie Nichols on Quinn's land because Robbie Nichols is standing right in front of you and I'm going to be able to prove that. You will find a bag of bones up on Fox Hollow, the bones of the real Nicky Dowling. That's the truth," he said as he collapsed back into the sofa. "The real Goddamn truth. The bad thing happened to me and to Nicky, not to anyone else."

"What bones are you talking about?" Jenna asked. "I don't follow you," she turned and looked at Sam, he hung his head.

"Sam and I had a hypnosis session," Nick said sternly."

Jenna glared at Sam. "This was supposed to be a personal visit, Sam."

Sam looked back at her quietly and waited for Nick to speak.

"Jenna, I remembered what happened the night of the kidnapping."

"What?"

"Andrew Quinn killed Nicky Dowling."

"What?"

"I remember everything."

"What? My God, Nick. You can't be serious."

"I am serious," Nick said quickly, "Look, just give me this. Let me ask the Nichols' if they'll agree to a paternity test. If it turns out that I'm not Robert Nichols, I'll do whatever you want. I'll go to any doctor you suggest, and I'll make every effort to uncover the truth, or I'll lay it all to rest and never mention it again. But for now, I want to see Cecile. I believe she's my mother." Nick stared at her; his eyes searched her face. "Please, Jenna, just go the distance with me on this?"

Over Nick's shoulder Jenna glanced at Sam, then she met Nick's gaze. "And after that, if you turn out not to be related to the Nichols, you'll give up all this bunk about spaceships and little space creatures?"

"I swear, Jenna." Nick took her cheek in his hands. "And if Cecile turns out to be my mother, will you, at least, admit to the possibility that I'm telling the truth, about my abduction?"

"Yes," she said, after a long pause. She closed her eyes and squeezed his hand. "Yes," she repeated.

Nick brought her face close to his and gently kissed her.

Chapter Fifty-Two

Sam stood in the shiny brass elevator. He could see his reflection in the dusty brass. He might have laughed out loud if he wasn't feeling so badly; he looked like an alien, he was so bedraggled.

As he opened the door to his apartment he could see the night sky through his windows. The round wicker chair looked inviting.

"Am I out of my mind?" he whispered. "Are there really aliens?"

Sam fell back into the chair. There were no stars, never was in the city. He put his hands behind his head and thought about his parents and his brother.

"Do you really believe in this stuff?" they asked him, over and over again. They treated him like he was an invalid with delusions about his injury.

"You're ignorant," he told them.

His brother always got angry. Good old Elijah. Good old Elijah who thought that Sam was a con artist, not a serious investigator but a con artist.

Sam sat forward. How many times had his brother insisted that it was all in his head? How many times had he tried to force him into believing that he was still a child with an active imagination?"

"It isn't in my head," Sam insisted until he got tired of proving himself, defending himself. "Oh, go think what you want, just leave me alone and stop trying to convince me I'm crazy."

His brother got on his nerves. It had become a competition between them. One of them was insane and one of them wasn't.

"Well, I don't believe in alien creatures, brother, must rub you the wrong way," Elijah told him with a smirk.

Sam felt exhausted and he was worried about Nick. That tracking device usually meant they were coming back to re-claim him, even though they hadn't wanted him in the first place but they probably thought he was useful in some way. Sam felt so certain about it and prayed he was wrong. But perhaps Nick held some sort of answers for them.

He knew what Elijah would say, "Can't let that happen." He'd laugh. "Tracking device? Really, Sam, you are a bit much."

He didn't need his brother's trust, but he would have welcomed it. But he'd been coming up against Elijah all his life.

"Everywhere you go you want agreement. Get it from your crazy patients. I can't give you agreement, brother. I think you're a selfish, self-centered asshole who just happens to be out of his goddamn mind. I can't believe we're twins. We're nothing alike." And then Elijah would look away in disgust.

"Are my patients out of their goddamn minds as well, Elijah?"

Ah, that would send Elijah to the computer where he'd berate Sam terribly. "The famous, Dr. Hollander and his insane non-fiction crap about his insane space abduction patients. I'm glad it's made you a good living, Sam, but it's all a bunch of shit. Why would your patients come up with it? How do your patients know all about spaceships? You've got a webpage, brother. Right there. Your patients are nuts and so are you."

Elijah would bring up the URL. "You don't think your patients haven't been able to find you in internet limbo, bimbo land? Read your bio right here on your webpage? Good picture, Sam."

And Elijah would read as Sam listened. He couldn't convince him; he would never be able to convince him.

"Brother Elijah Hollander who does something with his life, though Sam isn't sure what it is because he's too self-centered to care what anybody else does."

"You're some corporate asshole who makes money. How's that?" Sam said aloud.

His brother had no soul. Sam looked up at the sky. He wished it were different. They were always fighting.

"The alien's experiment with our memories. I'm not sure why." He wanted Elijah to know that, not that it would ever matter to him, but it mattered to Sam to know that.

"Poor Sam," Elijah would say.

"They take your memory," Sam said. "And they jumble it all up."

"Were we from the same womb? The same parents?" God, Elijah was a bastard. "Oh, shit, Sam. There are no aliens. There is no such thing as an alien abduction."

"All we see is all we know?" Sam tried to get him to think about it, but Elijah didn't think, he just reacted.

Nick stared out the car window. He couldn't wait to see Cecile. He felt nostalgic. What a good feeling. Nostalgia took hold of his memories and allowed him ample space enough for Captain Crunch, Winky Dink, and wooden yo-yos. He remembered it all.

Nick had a brother, a family. He wanted to get to know who his brother was. He vaguely remembered being someone's hero; being followed everywhere, even out under the stars to sleep.

He remembered flying airplanes with his father. He could see himself running out in the field, *higher dad, higher!* He could see himself caught in his father's smile. He remembered. He remembered so clearly ... now would they?

Finally, Carl's old Victorian farmhouse appeared before him, framed as it was by old barns, surrounded by cow pastures and mountains. Nick felt his heart pounding in his chest as Cecile opened the door and stood on the porch, smiling that same smile he had seen in his vision.

Nick stepped quickly from the car and began to walk toward her. Cecile held her arms out to him; her smile had almost turned to laugher. Nick walked faster now toward the steps, three steps up the porch and he would soon be in her arms.

He took all three steps at once. Suddenly, he spun around. POP! The shot rang out. POP! Falling so fast — falling over ... spinning up ... now flying into her arms. No! Flying past the moon —the stars — flying —flying — flying ... into the arms like wings, the eyes like dark lakes...the probing, probing questions in his ears … why, why, why … they ask … seeking the answers he could not bring.

He brought his hands to his face and stared at the blood.

Nick slowly opened his eyes. His shoulder felt as if it had been pummeled by a steel girder and then flattened by a Mack truck's wheel. He looked around the room. Looked like a hospital, smelled like one too.

"Son?"

Cecile sat by his side, her hand in his. He smiled broadly, and the pain subsided, forced from his body by the rush of his emotions.

"Mom," he said.

She wiped the tears from his face. "Are you all right?" she asked.

"What happened?" he asked.

"Andrew Quinn shot you."

Nick tried to sit up.

"Relax," she whispered as she propped the pillow behind his head.

"He shot me?"

"Yes, then he shot himself. Right there where he was standing, not more than fifteen feet from our door."

"He's dead?"

"He left a note confessing to the murder of Nicky Dowling. He also confessed to the murder of an alien."

"Did they find an alien body?"

She widened her eyes. "No, of course not. They found the bones of a little boy, that's all."

"Yes, Nicky Dowling."

"I'm sure they'll identify him soon."

"I think they forgot the pain pills," Nick said, as he grimaced.

"You want the nurse, son?"

"Not yet."

Cecile held his hand more tightly. She couldn't stop the tears.

"Rob," she said. "What a fine man you are."

"I remember that night so clearly now, do you?"

"Oh, yes. I've never forgotten it."

"I told you I had to sleep out under the stars to protect Nicky from the space people, but it was Quinn he needed protection from."

"Why did Andrew kill that poor little boy?" Cecile asked slowly.

He avoided answering her question. "He really did kill an alien. They must have come for the body by now, that's why no one found it."

"Yes, son, I'm sure they did."

"Nicky kicked Quinn, that's why he killed him, he got angry."

"What? Why?"

"He was molesting him. Quinn never left Nicky alone. I tried to protect him, I couldn't."

Cecile stiffened. "My God." She turned to him. "Why didn't you tell us?"

"Shame — hard to admit something like that going on."

"Did he come after you?"

"Crocket always scared him off."

"Do you think he hurt Carlton?" She asked tentatively.

"Ask him, Mom."

Cecile looked into his eyes. "Where did you go, Robbie?" she asked.

"I went to a ship called Pharaoh's Star."

She looked at him carefully. "When did you come back?"

"I came back in 1982. I didn't remember anything until now, until coming up here to the Catskills; then it all started to unravel."

"Were you alone on that ship?"

"No, I don't think so."

"You were there for ten years."

"Yes."

"You were the only human?"

"They're all human, Mom, but human the way we'll all become, centuries from now. I didn't really mix with the Pharaohs, not that I remember. They brought me into the Substance Cities with other abducted children, to observe us."

Cecile touched his cheek. "I think we should keep this to ourselves."

"What will you tell Dad?"

"Let's get that paternity test done and then worry about it."

"Yes. I can't wait for that, for proof."

"I'm grateful to have you back, that's all I care about."

"Where's Jenna?" he asked, suddenly aware she wasn't with him.

"I asked for time alone with you. She's right outside. I like her, son."

"I'm glad," he said.

"I told her you were mine, my Robbie."

"Did she believe you?"

"I think so."

Nick smiled. He would have taken a hundred more bullets just to sit by his mother's side, and to hear that his wife believed him.

Chapter Fifty-Three

Jenna turned into their driveway. Nick was frantically trying to reach Sam on his cell phone. "Damn it," he said. "Can't get to him."

"Honey, why don't you relax?"

"This doesn't make any sense; his phone keeps ringing and no one picks up."

"What's so urgent?" she asked.

"Just want to tell him what happened, that I was shot. That you believe me now." He smiled at her. "That my mother believes me."

"Look, he forgot to turn on his answering machine, that's all." Jenna reached out and stroked his arm. "Thank God you're all right," she whispered. "That sick son of a bitch."

Sam stepped away from the window. Did the Pharaohs know where Harrison was? he wondered.

His brother entered the room. "I thought I'd find you here, starting out into nothing."

"It's nothing until it isn't anymore, isn't it?"

Elijah laughed. "I respect your passion." Elijah stood beside him as they stared at the sky, the same sky, and saw two different things. "Odd thing being a twin, I can hear everything you don't say."

"You don't understand, Elijah, there are beings out there that could save our planet."

"The sky holds nothing but stars and planets without human life. You know that, don't you? Only human life there is, is here on Earth, not out there."

"I have to help Nick. That tracking device he found in his mouth disturbs me."

"Ah, yes, tracking device."

"I need to get up to the country, make sure he's okay."

Elijah smiled. "Well, since we have a dinner date later, I'll wait for you. I always do. Will you be back by dinner?"

"Of course."

"Then I'll be here, reading up on UFOs." He smiled as Sam grabbed his car keys.

That morning, they had painted an old table and chairs what they called "country white." It was a hot day. They took a nap after breakfast. When they awoke they decided that they would barbeque steaks for dinner with sliced up tomatoes and grilled corn.

He reached out and took her in his arms and slowly slipped off her blouse, and then, her jeans. Soon he was moving inside of her, kissing the strands of her hair that fell on her forehead and the tips of her eyes.

"Are you back with me now, Jenna?" he asked.

"Forgive me," she whispered. "Robbie."

"We have no butter for the corn," Jenna said. "I've been so preoccupied, didn't think to get it. We could use a quart of milk, too."

Nick stepped out onto the deck. "Did you hear anyone walking around?"

"What?" Jenna called from the kitchen.

"Looks like a car down there by the road."

"You think it's the police? They haven't questioned you yet, have they?"

"Well, for all I know they're watching the house."

"I wouldn't worry about it, it's clear you're not Harrison. I don't know what got into Gregory, but you'll be able to prove you're not Harrison."

"That I will."

"Are you up for a drive into town, honey?"

"Sure," Nick said as he walked back into the kitchen.

"We could use some milk and butter," she said again. "You sure you're okay to drive into town? I've got so much to do."

"Not to worry, it was only a flesh wound. I won't be long. I'll take it slow." Nick grabbed his sweatshirt from the closet and left the house.

As he got to the end of the long drive he had an uneasy feeling, not sure he could explain it. He drove down the road and thought he saw Sam's car pass him on the way. He wanted to stop but the car had been going quickly. *Jenna will amuse him until I get back*, he thought. He watched as the car pulled in their drive. He drove on and picked up speed.

"If they come for me I'll outrun them," he said and laughed out loud. "No one is going to take me anywhere I don't want to go."

From out of nowhere a thick fog enveloped Nick's car. His foot was on the gas, but the speedometer was at zero. He couldn't see out the windshield. He kept his foot down hard on the gas, but he wasn't sure the car was moving. Soon he'd pass Fox Hollow, if he could only get the damn car to move, he'd turn up there and wait out the fog.

"Jesus, what is that, what the hell is over me?"

He looked up but he didn't recognize what he was looking into.

"I'll get out of here," Nick said and slammed his foot down harder on the gas.

Harrison drove toward Nick Dowling's house, or whoever the hell this guy was that was calling himself Nick. He planned to kill the guy, steal his jeep. But, suddenly, Nick's jeep was coming right at him. He was positive it was Nick's jeep because he could see the guy behind the wheel. He was looking up at the sky instead of at the road. The car appeared to be moving, but not moving at the same time. How was that possible? Harrison wondered. He saw the guy calling himself Nick Dowling clear as day inside the car. He looked frantic. Then a thick fog appeared from a perfectly clear sky and covered the jeep entirely. In just moments, the fog cleared, and the jeep appeared to be empty.

Harrison stopped his car. Had he really seen what he thought he'd seen? Harrison rubbed his eyes. By the time he opened them, the jeep stood alone on the side of the road.

Harrison looked all over, but the man inside the jeep had disappeared. There was no one in sight. He got out of his sports car and walked over to the jeep. It was empty, though the key was inside. Harrison quickly got back into the Miata and drove it as far back into the woods as he could. When he was sure it couldn't be seen from the road he ran back to Nick's jeep.

Things couldn't get any better than this for Harrison Hinckley.

Just one more thing to take care of, Harrison thought as he raced toward the city. Can't have that crazy man telling people that he was alive.

"Good to find you home, Medicine Man," Harrison said, after Elijah opened the door.

Elijah stared at the man before him, he was too effeminate to fear, though he looked oddly fierce.

"Medicine Man? Now, that's funny," Elijah said, deciding to play along. It was what Sam would have wanted him to do. He clearly must be one of Sam's friends ... or patients. Elijah peered at him more closely.

"May I come in?" Harrison smiled.

Elijah opened the door wider and stepped aside.

Harrison looked around before removing the gun from his pocket.

"I guess there's money in voodoo," Harrison said.

Elijah felt his knees buckle as Harrison pointed the gun at him.

"Don't do this, good sir," Elijah said. "I really don't know you at all."

Harrison pulled the trigger and watched the body slump, falling backward. He'd shot him once between the eyes. It was very quick, very painless, and very clean.

He found an old trunk in Sam's bedroom. He shoved the body inside, which was not an easy thing to do, but finally, it was done. He dragged the trunk downstairs without being noticed, not on a Friday night, not with so many people leaving the city, moving in and moving out.

He drove back to his brother's house in Olive. He'd pulled the back seats down and had managed to slide the trunk in easily. When he got to Gregory's he treated himself to some left over filet he'd found in Gregory's refrigerator. After he helped himself to a beer, he covered Gregory's body up in a blanket and slid him beside the trunk in the back seat of Nick Dowling's jeep. He pulled into a gas station and filled a plastic container with gas. Then he headed west on Route 28. After he made the turn onto Fox Hollow, he pulled up to the meadow, but didn't stop. He drove right through, straight toward the stone marker and the trees.

From where he was sitting the sky was somber and nearly black. He popped on his headlights nice and low and shone the lights straight back into the woods. That gave him the illumination he needed.

He dragged his brother's body out of the jeep, and into the front seat, driver's side. He popped the earring out of Gregory's ear.

"There you go, Gregory, enjoy the ride. Nice to have shared your DNA."

He propped the body up and placed his brother's hands on the steering wheel. It was disgusting to touch a dead body, but he knew he had to.

The hard part was getting the Medicine Man out of the trunk, but he dragged the bastard as best he could and put him in the passenger side. Then, he got the plastic container of gasoline from the back seat and covered the car with it. He threw several lit matches at the car and observed, with a certain amount of fascination, as the jeep went up in flames.

He watched it burn, saw one of the bodies turn black and disappear. When he was able to tear himself away from the threat of an explosion, he ran back into the woods where he'd hidden the Miata.

Chapter Fifty-Four

"Oh, I hate funerals." Harrison sighed. He leaned forward toward his image in the glass and applied just a bit more mascara. He thought he looked quite good without much hair. He tilted his head. The small gold earring in his ear was also quite appealing.

Harrison stood up and brushed off his suit with his fingers. It was a very fine suit and it fit him so well. He wondered when he'd be able to wear it again.

He walked into the living room and looked around. It was such a soothing room. This should have been his house. After all, Gregory had bought it with inheritance money. So, this probably should have been his suit too. He'd been gypped out of his inheritance because of that whore he'd married, never had an opportunity to split the estate with Gregory. Well, in a matter of time, he'd sell the house, and all the wonderful antiques. He'd move, maybe to London or Paris, especially before one of Gregory's queer friends caught him gawking at a woman. Oh, God, but he'd missed acting. This character was going to be so much fun to play. He looked out the window, up toward the sky, and winked.

The funeral of Harrison Hinckley, alias Nick Dowling, was a somber affair, as Harrison suspected it would be. Jenna was weeping. She was surrounded by women who were weeping too. As a matter of fact, the whole room was weeping.

"I wondered why he hadn't come home. I thought he stopped somewhere. I should have known he was in trouble," she sobbed and clung to the arm of some older woman she called Sally.

"The car went off the road and crashed. Car went up like an inferno," the sheriff told them as he shook his head from side to side.

Harrison walked to Jenna and extended his hand. He realized immediately that she was staring at his arm. He glanced down quickly. The makeup had worn off. He pulled his hand away to hide the tattoo on his wrist. She probably hadn't noticed. He'd have to be more careful.

"I'm so sorry about your husband," he said."

"Thank-you, Gregory."

"Horrible."

"Yes."

"And his friend." Harrison said. "Both so young to die."

Jenna looked at him in an odd way. "Yes, Sam's brother. It was very sad."

Sam's brother? Harrison was sure he hadn't heard right. "A fire is such a terrible way to go, but maybe the crash killed them first," he said.

He didn't like the way she was looking at him.

"I hope so."   She walked away suddenly and whispered to the older woman, who looked a bit too concerned. A tall man brushed by him. He held a pretty woman's hand. My god, the Medicine man? He felt that at any moment he would have a stroke. He walked back inside and searched for a chair. He watched the man he thought he'd killed stare back at him. He could see the woman's diamond from where he sat. Must be engaged, he thought. He laughed it off. So, the Medicine man had a twin? He rose to his feet.

He was intercepted at the door. He stared back into the man's dark eyes.

"What was my brother doing in your car?" Sam asked

Harrison looked at him oddly. "That wasn't my car," he said. "I believe it belonged to the dead man, Nick Dowling."

Sam held in his temper. "You're doomed, Harrison," he said. "You're going to get what's coming to you."

Harrison shook off the threat and gave Sam his condolences. He hurried past him and quickly drove back to his big old rambling farmhouse in the quaint little town of Olive in his red Miata, with the top down, despite the cool air. Medicine man couldn't threaten him. No one could. Harrison had said his goodbyes. Now, it was time to move on. He wondered what kind of music Gregory liked in his old age. Growing up, they'd both been into good rock & roll, not the shit they played today. He switched on a station. No static. Good song, too. He was sure Gregory would approve.

"How divine," he shouted.

The wind felt soft against his scalp. The chill was a welcomed affront, and he flipped his scarf behind him.

"Ain't nothing like the real thing baby," he sang along with the music as loud as he could get it out, with a slight high-pitched lisp. "Ain't nothing like the real thing."

Harrison decided not to let it bother him. Paranoia could be his downfall. Harrison Hinckley, the notorious killer of his wife and child, had been Nick Dowling all along. That's all these grieving fools needed to know.

Harrison laughed out loud. Should he tell them that their precious Nick Dowling had floated up to the sky? Why, Harrison had seen it with his own two eyes. The devil must have power. It did his bidding, moved mountains for Harrison to walk between, parted oceans for Harrison to disappear within.

"How divine," he shouted.

The wind felt soft against his scalp. The chill was a welcomed affront, and he flipped his scarf behind him.

"Ain't nothing like the real thing baby," he sang along with the music as loud as he could get it out, with a slight high-pitched lisp. "Ain't nothing like the real thing."

The sound was startling. Nick brought his hands to his head.

"You all right, mister?"

He opened his eyes and looked out. A man in uniform looked back.

"Sorry 'bout the headlights, they hurt your eyes?"

The sheriff had a flashlight in his hand, and he held it now inside the car, into the man's face.

"You knock that thing against my car? the man asked. "Scared the shit out of me."

"Had to wake you up," the Sheriff said. " You're on private property."

Nick rubbed his head and looked around. "Jesus," he

said, "how long have I been here?"

"Don't know. I just saw your car from the road. You left the lights on, looked surreal."

"Where am I?"

"You're in Fox Hollow."

"I must have fallen asleep at the wheel. I had one hell of a dream. It's fading now, though."

"Lucky you didn't hit a tree."

"The moon was so full. I pulled over to see it."

"You did, uh? Quite a romantic."

Nick laughed. "Yeah."

"Well, maybe you better be moving on now, fellow. Like I said, you're on a private road."

"What's that sound?" the man asked as he looked up toward the sky.

"Little plane flying overhead, loud, uh? Could be a spaceship."

"Yeah, sure," Nick said.

"We get them out here."

"You're kidding?"

"No, really."

"I think it's got me."

"What?" the sheriff asked.

"The spaceship."

The sheriff laughed.

"You look familiar."

The Sheriff gave him an odd look.

"You mean I look like a dead man, is that what you're saying?"

"You all right to drive?" the sheriff asked him.

"I feel kind of woozy."

"You live far?"

"No."

"Well, that's good."

Nick put his hand on the steering wheel and turned on the ignition.

"Well, you take it easy now. Can you see your way out?"

"Yes, thanks, sheriff, I will. I'll take it easy."

Nick turned his car around slowly and drove into the darkness. The starlit sky above him blinked, with lights, like eyes, intently indifferent to his promise to return with a stick of butter and a quart of milk. Nick drove on to what he thought was Margaretville, until his memory faded, and the dark sky was upon him, and the silence of Pharaoh's Star consumed him.

The End

Books by Olivia Hardy Ray

Fox Hollow
Pharaoh's Star
Nobody's Road
Annabel Horton, Lost Witch of Salem
Annabel Horton and the Black Witch of Pau

Books by Vera Jane Cook

The Darlings
A Saffron Sun
The Fourniers: When Hannah Played Ragtime, Book 1
The Fourniers: Glamor Girl, Book 2
The Fourniers: The Memory of Music
Pleasant Day
Marybeth, Hollister & Jane
Lies a River Deep
Where the Wildflowers Grow
The Story of Sassy Sweetwater
Dancing Backward in Paradise